DONICK WALSH

AND THE RESET-BUTTON

NATHANIEL SHEA

This book is dedicated with deepest gratitude
to those who taught me to sing, to act, to dance, to live.

Dennon & Sayhber Rawles
John Loprieno
Joey Letteri
Eric Augustiny
Kathy Lewis
Bonnie Graeve
and
June Mohler

Thinking of you all with love.

"I am done with my graceless heart,
So tonight I'm gonna cut it out and then re-start."
— Florence + the Machine

"I close my eyes and I can see
A world that's waiting up for me
That I call my own.
Through the dark, through the door,
Through where no one's been before,
But it feels like home."
— *The Greatest Showman*

"Clear the slate and start over.
Try to quiet the noises in your head."
— *Dear Evan Hansen*

DONICK

*"But there's nowhere to hide from these bones, from my mind,
It's broken inside, I'm a man and a child.
I'm at home with the ghost who got left in the cold,
Who knocks at my peace with no keys to my soul."*

I AM AN ASSHOLE.

Is that how I should start?

Thing is, I don't treat people very well. If my high school took a census asking if Donick Walsh is kind, or nice, you'd hear a resounding no—probably from space. I've bullied a ton of kids over the years. Out of everything, *that* is what I'm most ashamed of. Kind and nice have never been me.

But I hate being an asshole. I hate being a bully.

I want to change; and the beautiful thing about change is, afterward, you're all different. That's what I want: to be different. I want to hit the reset-button on my life. But how?

Maybe I should start in another place.

Maybe I should start with football.

Passion can be a good thing. You *should* feel passion about what's important to you. Football was my life, but unlike the other guys on the team, I never had an ounce of passion for it. I was good—excellent even—but I didn't care.

Teammates, coaches, my dad…they all say it's a real tragedy that I'll never play again. At the end of the final game of the season last year, I ripped up my shoulder pretty bad. Crushed it, more like. Well, a 250 pound kid from the opposite team crushed it. That tends to happen when something big falls on you.

"If you continue playing with your shoulder in that condition," the doctors told me, "even after surgery and physical therapy, you'll damage it permanently. How would you feel if you could never use your right arm again?"

Pop actually cried. The look on his face had me wanting to laugh and rage at the same time. The news stirred nothing in *me*, yet *he* cried? Were those tears for his son: in terrible pain, unable to raise his arm higher than his chest? Or did he cry because I could no longer call myself QB? "College ball at UCLA! Drafted into the NFL!" I had been hearing that crap since I was ten. He actually told the doctors I didn't have *time* for an injury.

"What about Nicky's senior year?" he asked. "Colleges'll be looking at him!"

Now, a year later, it's unbelievable that he's still pressuring me to play. The warnings mean nothing to him.

"No problem, Pop!" I want to scream. "I'll play for three minutes and never use my arm again. It wouldn't be any big loss, right? Get it through that thick skull! Your Nicky and football are breaking up, and Nicky doesn't give a shit. I don't ever have to run those fields again, or throw that ball, or lug around all that frigging padding, and I'm glad, glad, *glad*! The reset-button has been hit for me, old man!"

Only, now I have to figure out what to do…what to be…and who I am…

I guess starting there doesn't feel right either.

I think I need to start with my first kiss.

I was eleven, and he—yes, *he*—was twelve.

Mikey. My best friend. My best friend—*then*.

What to say about Mikey? Michael. Michael Penrose.

I think—even now, after years apart—Mikey is the best friend I've ever had. He knew everything there was to know about me, and I knew everything there was to know about him. Including the fact that he's gay. Even before *he* knew it, I suspect. He wore glasses then—thick Buddy Holly things—and looked like a nerd. I didn't care. He was smart, and funny, and made me laugh. We liked all the same dorky stuff. Horror movies, anime, *Star Wars*, *Buffy the Vampire Slayer*. When we spent the night at each other's houses, we stayed up late to watch *Rick and Morty* and *Robot Chicken*. He was there when my dad put me into football for the first time. When my team of scrawny ten and eleven year olds had games, Mikey would come and cheer me on. At school we were never apart; we didn't really have any other friends. I never felt I needed anyone but him. He was my best friend, and as much as an eleven year old can recognize that he loves his best friend, I guess I loved Mikey.

For a while, I had been noticing Mikey getting hair under his arms. We would lie on our backs on the floor in the living-room at my house, staring at the TV. That fuzz peeking out of his sleeves as he cradled his head with his hands troubled me and I couldn't figure out why. I was jealous, I think, that Mikey was older (even if only by three months). It made me feel like I had been left behind. It also tickled something in my brain that made me feel possessive of him, and sometimes angry with him.

It was so…masculine, I guess. When I thought of Mikey, it didn't fit. I mean, we were just kids.

I also didn't understand why I had begun to wonder what would happen if he ever started liking some boy somewhere—in *that* way—and what would happen to me when he did. This made me wonder if Mikey ever imagined kissing boys. When I thought that, I wondered what it would be like to kiss a girl. Then, after thinking *that*, I only wondered what it would be like to kiss Mikey.

After school one day, watching sidewalk-cracks passing under our shoes on the way to my house, I asked, "Do you ever think about…you know…what it would be like to, um, kiss someone?"

His reply? "My mom kisses me all the time, Donny. Get real."

Typical Mikey.

"You know what I mean." I hoped he wouldn't notice my burning face. "Well? Do you?"

"Do *you*?"

I bit my lip. "Sometimes."

"Have you ever?"

"Kissed anyone?"

"Yeah. And not your dad."

"I don't kiss my dad!"

"You don't kiss him goodnight or anything?"

"No! You kiss your dad?"

"Well, my dad kisses me. He's mushy like that. Musicians, you know."

"You know what *my* dad is like. An angry dog or something. Besides, he's almost old enough to be my grandpa. Men weren't like that with their kids when he was young."

"Maybe he *would've* been mushy if your mom hadn't died." Then Mikey went off on a tangent to himself. "Is it insensitive to say it like that? 'If your mom hadn't died'? Should I have said, 'if your mom hadn't passed away'? 'If she was still alive'?"

"Doesn't matter," I said, because it didn't. Not anymore. "I don't remember much about her anyway."

"Well, answer the question." Mikey sounded more than a little embarrassed. But curious—like me. "Have you kissed anyone?"

"No," I told him. Then I got nervous. "What about you?"

"Who is there to kiss?" He paused, pushing his glasses up the bridge of his nose. "Do you ever think about kissing someone at school? Like, someone we know?"

Sometimes, I thought, *I wonder what it would be like to kiss* you.

I answered with a shrug.

It's funny thinking back on this now—we seem so innocent. If we had been a little older, we might have been asking each other about sex.

Once we reached my house, we did the usual: grabbed soda and chips and dumped ourselves on the carpet in front of the television.

After a few minutes, I had to bring the subject up again.

"Do you think you'll be bad at it?"

"Bad at what?"

"Kissing."

"Ask me if I think I'll be *good* at it."

"If you've *never* kissed anyone before, what's the difference?"

"If I say I think I'll be *good* at it, it'll be like putting hope into the universe."

"You might curse yourself instead."

Though he played off what he said next in his usual joking way, he didn't look at me. "I guess we can always, like, kiss each other and find out."

My skin seemed to freeze and boil all at once. His cheeks were pink. But I laughed it off. "Yeah right, dude! I would get your test run so you can pass off your quote-unquote *first kiss skills* on someone else."

"Don't *you* want to know?" His voice had become serious.

What did he mean? Did I want to know if I would be good or bad at kissing? If *he* would be good or bad at it? Or did I want to know what it would be like to kiss *him*. Yes. I wanted to know all three things.

It was the first time I had any idea that the thing I suspected about Mikey could also be true about myself.

"If *you* want to know so bad," I answered, sarcasm covering how nervous, scared, excited I felt, "why don't you kiss *me* then? I'll tell you if you suck."

He didn't say anything else. He only looked at me. His glasses made his eyes look enormous, like ponds of water. His lips were pink and dry, the bottom very full. We seemed suddenly devouring each other's faces with our eyes—we might have been searching for seriousness, or…I don't even know. He scooted closer to me. We leaned toward each other. I could feel his exhalations against my mouth, could smell the Doritos on his breath. His gaze fell to my lips when I licked them. His chin lifted, I tilted my head, wondering, wondering, wondering, if he would turn it into a joke just before our lips met. I heard him swallow.

I couldn't stand it anymore. I would burst out laughing if that last inch of space wasn't closed. So I closed it myself.

I kissed him.

I wish I could remember what it felt like—did my stomach flutter, my heart throb? While that kiss lasted, it must have been sweet and earnest, even in its awkwardness. I only remember what happened in the middle of it.

My dad came into the room.

What happened then I *don't* want to remember. It hurts too much. Everything I became from then on stemmed from that explosion of macho-dad bullshit.

I suffered through hours of his ranting and railing. He called me a pansy, a little faggot. His anger and disgust terrified me so much, made me feel so ashamed, I allowed myself to be convinced it was all Mikey's fault. I allowed my best friend to take the blame. Pop pushed the idea into my head so well, I grew to believe it myself—at least to all outward appearances. Thank God Mikey never heard all the things my dad said about him, or me, after ordering him from the house, screaming at him never to come near me again. Pop's parting shot was bad enough.

"Donick Walsh doesn't make friends with faggots!"

MY TAP SHOES and jazz sneakers are in my locker. It's after school, Tuesday, and most students are filtering off campus. I've held back, risking being late for auditions, to make sure I can get my dance shoes into my bag with no one seeing.

Oh, yeah, I guess there's one more thing I should explain before really launching into this.

One of my football coaches told me when I was thirteen

that the best thing I could do to make myself a better player, to move better on the field, was to enroll in dance classes. The look on my face when he brought up the subject must have been priceless. What in hell would "man's-man" Roland Walsh have to say about his only son wearing tights and cavorting with a bunch of girls and sissies? And how would that make *me* feel—to cavort with girls and sissies? I couldn't even guess, but I knew it would be a non-issue anyway.

However, shockingly, Pop thought it an excellent idea! A sacrifice, he said, made in favor of the game! UCLA! The NFL! Let Donick Walsh dance!

Except, once enrolled, first in simple beginner's ballet, it felt like therapy. It was the complete opposite of football. The positions, the steps, the music, were calming and un-chaotic. The instructors were kind. Their endurance and strength amazed me. Best of all, I knew none of my fellow dance students from school. I didn't have to be Roland Walsh's son at Saraswood Dance Center. I loved *that* more than anything.

But what a quandary. The thought of anyone learning I spent two afternoons a week in a dance studio embarrassed the hell out of me. Yet I didn't want to be anywhere else. Quickly, ballet wasn't enough. I added jazz and tap to my schedule. I took workshops on turns, partnership, and lifts. I got strong. I felt the difference on the field and in practice. By the time I entered high school, I knew if given a choice—football or dance—dance would win. When I danced, I liked who I became. The football player in me had to save face, had to be an asshole. The dancer in me was Donick without his mask, without the shadow of his old man forcing him into a shape that didn't fit. Still, if anyone found out and tried to laugh at me, I would have kicked their asses.

I did once. In eighth grade, I socked a sixth grader right in his mouth. His sister took classes at my studio, and when he saw me there, he tried making fun of me. He stood a foot shorter than me and wore glasses, which I then stepped on. I got suspended for three days. Pop never said a word about it.

I remember this as I glance around like some lame spy, hoping nobody will see the shoes in the half second they'll be between the locker and my bag. At least I'm already dressed in something I can move in. My football practice shorts are nothing out of the ordinary—this is Southern California, even if it is late February—but I'm wearing a really tight t-shirt, something my dance instructors insist on so they can "see the lines". A baggy sweatshirt covers it though. The less attention I'm about to get, the better.

No such luck. I'm reaching for the jazz sneakers first, when I'm goosed in one side, and shouted at in the opposite ear, making me almost jump out of my skin.

Leave it to my two best buds, Josue Jimenez and Ryan Pollard, to find me out.

"Why you dressed like that?" Ryan asks, leaning against the lockers.

He's a big guy—stocky and thick, with a beefy gut, and arms and legs like a four year old drew them. He's a senior, like me, and also an asshole. The only difference is sometimes I think he enjoys it. Ever since my shoulder surgery, I'm having a hard time standing him. So I guess *best bud* is becoming a figure of speech.

"I can't dress comfortable?" I ask, flustered, quickly stuffing the shoes into my bag.

"You were in jeans earlier," he says. "You look like you're going to football or something."

I'm tired of this. I've been hearing comments about football since summer.

"Yeah," Josue pipes in, "then his arm will fall off or some shit."

Josue is my age, but because he repeated a grade in elementary school, he's still only a junior. He's tall, not very muscular, but quick on the field. He became my replacement as quarterback. Ryan worried I would be angry when I found out, but I was happy for Josue. No one seems able to grasp how little I care that football and I have had a parting of ways.

Oh, and Josue is as asshole too, only I *know* he likes it.

He peers into my locker. "What the hell do you have in there, *güey*? Tap dancing shoes?" He sounds incredulous.

"Dude." Ryan speaks as though Josue is a complete moron. "Nick has been dancing since he was, like, twelve."

Josue gives me a funny look. "Isn't that kinda faggy?"

"Whatever that means…" I mumble.

"If it makes you a better athlete," Ryan says, "then you do what you gotta. What you bring 'em to school for?"

They were going to find out eventually, so I just say it.

"I'm going to audition for the Senior Showcase Revue."

Ryan's jaw drops.

"The Senior Revue?" Josue repeats. "Why would you do that? You wanna spend the next two months with the loser drama kids?"

I've prepared myself for this. I'll tell the truth, and paint it in a lie. I can't let them know I feel anything other than irritation over what my guidance councilor told me last week. Because, honestly, I'm looking forward to a new experience! I'm nervous enough to vomit, actually, but it'll be *good* nervous vomit…if that's a thing.

"I can't play football anymore, Jo," I begin, calling him by this somewhat mean-spirited nick-name that always makes us laugh. Who likes being called a *ho*? Assholery has crept into every part of us and I feel suddenly exhausted with my life.

"Doesn't mean you go all gay on us, Nicco." Josue means this as a joke. He and Ryan exchange very douche-like reactions. My stomach rolls even more. What reaction will they have if I were to tell them that my seeming straightness is going the way of my football career?

"Don't be a nimrod," I say. "I'm short a semester of PE credit. Mrs. Moes said I could either take freshman PE—and, um, no—or I could participate in the Senior Revue to make up for no football. She knows I dance, so it'll count toward the missing credit. But I have to audition. I probably won't get in and then it'll be PE with a bunch of fourteen year olds anyway. But I gotta go. I'll be late."

"We'll walk over with you," Ryan says.

How 'bout don't! I want to say. I hope they won't stick around the performing-arts building and watch. I would rather be dead.

I sling my bag over my good shoulder—still thinking its unbelievable that I now have a *bad* shoulder—close my locker, then walk, with the two assholes in tow, toward the hardest thing I'll ever have to do.

Ryan starts badgering me about cell-phones. My dad works for several cell-phone manufacturing companies as an independent contractor—something like a field-tester—troubleshooting new products and various services offered by different wireless providers. He could have anywhere from five to ten different phones in his desk-drawer at any one time, all working through this provider or that, as he tests them out. Sometimes he even has me help, giving me some smartphone to play with, wanting to know what I think of its capabilities. Ryan wants the new Android and he's been pestering me for a couple weeks to get my dad to hook him up. I don't care enough to remember. I certainly don't want to focus on it today. My nerves are making me wish I could think of any reason to bypass the theatre, get in my car, and go home.

I would like to say to my buddies, "PE is a much better idea! Bring on the freshmen!" I would like it if these buddies then told me not to worry, I'll be great, doing this audition is going to be good for me. But the truth is, I wouldn't get the support I need. They would say, "Yeah, blow that shit off. Let's go find Scott Blair and smoke weed in his car."

That's no reset-button. That's just more of the same passionless life. Or the wrong kind of passion. So I keep my lip zipped.

Josue and Ryan go on bantering back and forth as we cross the campus, walking along the parking-lot toward the PA building. They're talking about prom or something and how Josue needs to get some senior girl to take him so he can go.

For a week I've been looking…well, not *forward* to this audition, but viewing it from a distance as a sort of starting-line. It'll be a new and entirely different experience, and I have this idea that I can use it as this reset-button I so badly need. But leave it to fate, or karma, or whatever, to throw the shadow of my asshole-life over me just in sight of that starting-line.

A girl is crossing the student-lot to our left. She's very small, and not only does she have an extremely full backpack slung like a turtle's shell over her shoulders, textbooks bog down her arms. They have to weigh more than she does. She walks awkwardly, but she looks pleasant enough and, well, she has beautiful hair. Then, and I don't know how, she stumbles. She doesn't fall completely, but her stack of books and binders avalanche from her arms, splaying open in all directions on the asphalt. Her pencil case bursts, shooting pens, pencils, erasers every which way.

My friends begin guffawing, slapping each other's shoulders, pointing.

"Way to walk!" Ryan snorts.

Josue, through his laughter, calls out, "They teach motor-skills in, like, first grade, *perra*! You miss that day?"

They sound like hyenas. "Probably a dumbass freshman!" they say. "She looks like a fifth grader!"

I wanna pop each of them right in the chin.

Was I really awful like this? Was I rude and cruel?

Yes, I was. But I won't do this anymore.

Yet…I don't help her.

I watch her scramble onto her knees, scooping things out of the dust and engine-oil. She hears every word, the resentful glare she throws in our direction aimed not just at Ryan and Josue, high-fiving each other, but also at me. Because not long ago, no more than a few months really, I was laughing with them. Though I don't know her, she knows me. My asshole-reputation is clear as day on her face.

I don't help her. I don't confront my friends and tell them they're jerks. I go on my way, convincing myself it's my nerves that keep me from being better than yesterday.

Yet I know—and not very deep down—it's simple cowardice. It isn't even too late. I could still help the poor girl gather her stuff. But I don't.

A second later all thoughts fade when I see the milling students outside the arts building. Even the hum of Josue's and Ryan's pointless chatter dims in the face of my fear.

"Look at all the freaks," Josue sneers.

We've stopped about ten feet away. Some of the gathered students are familiar by sight, but it's totally *not* my crowd. I can feel the stirrings of something old in me recoiling, as though their taint will leave a mark.

"You sure you want to do this, bro?" Ryan asks. "That's some serious, like, social death over there."

Before I can answer, Josue's voice rises in a shout that pulls the attention of most everyone with ears.

"Check it out!" he cries. "It's the Three Muskequeers! What up, fags!"

Ryan cackles, "A dyke can't be fag!" He and Josue fist bump, knocking their shoulders into me. It makes my bad shoulder give out a stab of pain.

This is the part I forgot was coming—though how that's possible I can't even say. This is the *worst* part. Never mind the fear I'm going to make a complete ass of myself— despite hours and hours of dance classes these last six years. Never mind the gathered students now watching us. Never mind my regret at not helping that girl, or my growing repugnance toward these "friends" of mine. All of that is enough to ruin anyone's day. The clincher is *this moment*. The clincher is turning to see the three people getting out of a little red Hyundai that's just pulled in. (A half-dozen or so rainbow bumper-stickers are stuck all over the back bumper.) One girl, two guys, each out and proud, caring little for what the world thinks of them.

They look at us with disgust, and neither Ryan nor Josue can see that they couldn't give two shits what either one of them has said. This is a trio of absolute comfort in the skins they were made in, and I'm torn apart with jealousy, and the old desire to spit out hate. I know who they are. How could I not? Everyone does. They aren't the only gay kids at Kliewer High School, but they're the ones who practically run the GSA, making themselves into some kind of beacon for every gay kid on campus.

The Three Muskequeers—a name they gave themselves. Calista Martinez, with her short bowl of a hair cut, might pass for Peppermint Patty from the old Charlie Brown cartoons. Beside her is Brent Nanahara, Japanese and tiny, more than making up for Calista's lack of femininity in his skinny jeans and brightly colored tees that hug his thin arms and slight chest. I've never seen anyone take such care with his hair, for Brent's is like black oil, glossy and perfectly pomped above his forehead, always with one bright streak forking back through it like a bolt of yellow, or green, or purple lightning. He may even be wearing blue eye-liner today. And the third Muskequeer? The one that makes all this the hardest? Mikey Penrose.

My Mikey.

In my nervousness I had forgotten that *Mikey* is a drama kid. That's not so shocking, I guess. I've spent a lot of years not thinking about Mikey at all. *Forcing* myself to not think about him. Of all the abuse I've hurled at other kids, all the bullying I've done to anyone who seemed different or weak, I always made sure to keep Mikey below my notice, unless I needed to show off in front of my friends. I've ignored him, yes, and the crowd I run with has more than made up for it.

Maybe that's the worst kind of bullying, especially after such deep friendship—to give someone nothing; no acknowledgment, no validation, no recognition that another human being sees you.

What an asshole I've been. So many years of it. How will that reset-button ever erase all my mistakes?

MICHAEL

WE CALLED OURSELVES the Three Muskequeers—
my two best friends and me. We were theatre kids, so of
course we *would* do something like that. It started out as a
joke, but then it stuck.

For our tenth grade talent show, Calista, Brent, and I
brainstormed for weeks over some sort of act for us to
do. A Shakespeare scene? Out of the question (yawn).
Singing some (tired) showtune? Never. Love Brent to the
moon and back, but he couldn't sing to save his life. He
was more the pratfall type.

That's when it hit me. Vaudeville! A perfect combination
of comedy for Brent, mixed with song and dance for Calista
and me. Well, sort of dance for me. I'm not saying I had
two left feet, but I didn't have much training either. We
researched old sketches and reworked bits to play with three
people. Calista then found old Musketeer outfits in the
theatre's costume-storage. We then decided to bill ourselves
as The Three Muskequeers. I'm surprised we were allowed
to. Calista and I sang a lot, Brent sang a little (mostly off

key), and all of us told jokes and acted goofy, getting big laughs from the crowd. We won second place! And because we were a hit, that name—The Three Muskequeers—stuck. When people called us that, it wasn't malicious, for the most part. Even our teachers sometimes used the name. Now and then, though, it *was* hurled as an insult; coming from douche-bags like the trio standing on the curb.

When Calista pulled her Hyundai into the Kliewer High parking-lot, it was hard to miss them standing near the PA building. Of course, I could never miss Donny. I tried with everything inside me to hate him, but I mostly felt hurt, even after all the years that had passed.

Calista groaned. "Alert. Ugly dicklings all in a row."

Brent prodded his hair in the visor-mirror. "Who cares? That tall skinny kid has been calling me a sissy since I was eight years old. My *obaa-chan* has been telling me I need a haircut since I was six. I never listen to her and I'm not gonna listen to him."

Calista shut off the car. Craning her head, she met my eyes, checking my emotional weather. I could give her a perfect poker face. I had pressed down everything concerning my old not-friend long ago.

"We're here early anyway," she said. "We could go get something to eat before the singing auditions."

"We just came from Starbucks." Brent's voice fell into a plaintive register. It made him sound gayer than ever, honestly, but he was okay with it, and so were we. The three jerk-offs on the curb...not so much. "If you were hungry you should've got a sandwich or something. I wanna go see boys in tights!"

I gave Calista a smile, hoping it looked carefree. "I'm

good with watching the dancers," I said. "I've been looking forward to being a senior in the Revue since freshman year. I'm not missing anything. This is our show."

The Senior Showcase Revue! Once a year the theatre department, dance department, choir department, and orchestra joined together to put on a revue. It aimed to feature the seniors in singing, dancing, and acting roles, though underclassmen auditioned to fill out the ensemble. I had done the show as a freshman, a sophomore, and a junior. This year, as a senior, I would be featured and have a solo of my own. The show itself was an original creation overseen by Mrs. Peebles, the theatre teacher, in collaboration with the directors of the other departments. It always featured songs from musicals, films, and occasionally pop music if something fit into the show's theme. Being a senior showcase, twelfth graders from outside the performing-arts department often came out. A traditional musical came early in the school year, along with a couple of smaller events, but the entire arts department looked forward to *this* particular show. As soon as the current year's revue finished, underclassmen already began talking about their hopes for next year's.

So what the hell were Donick Walsh and his mouth-breathers doing outside the PA building? This was *my* turf!

"Can we go?" Brent had already pushed open his door, slipping out.

"Boys in tights, here we come, I guess," said Calista, grimacing. "But let me remind you about the *eww!*"

Brent popped the passenger seat forward so I could squeeze out, dragging my backpack after me. "I'm totally bigger than you," I said. "Why do I always get crammed in the back?"

Already I could hear the sound of laughter from the curb. Staring straight ahead—the usual way to ignore an asshole—we began to cross the lot.

"Check it out!" called the tall skinny kid, hawking out laughter. "It's the Three Muskequeers! What up, fags?"

"A dyke can't be fag!" countered the tank of a guy standing on Donny's right.

Donny, it surprised me to note, wasn't smiling. He looked pissy, his eyes ticking over the three of us, settling on me for a second before looking away. That was weird. For years, he *only* ignored me when he was alone. If his prick pals were with him, he always joined them in bagging on me. So why act differently this time? Best guess? He must have reached a new hatred-level.

"Such manly displays of maturity," Calista called back to them. "Your parents are doing excellent jobs."

The stocky kid spat out, "Suck it, muff-diver!"

"Wash it, Pollard!" And Calista flipped him the bird.

The skinny kid pointed at Brent. "What the hell is that? You carrying a purse, homo? Gotta have a place for your tampons?"

Brent *was* actually carrying something that looked like a purse. He used it as a book-bag, though it was far too small to actually hold any books. He hoisted it up on his shoulder and said, "No, it's for carrying douche-bags. Hop on in!"

"We'll fuck you up, faggot!" the big one shouted, and almost began lumbering into the parking-lot.

Unable to help myself, I looked squarely into Donny's face and said, "Grow up. We're not *eleven* anymore."

Donny's cheeks colored. He suddenly looked so angry I

thought he might bash my face into the trunk of Calista's car.

"Shut the fuck up, *pendejo*," the skinny kid shouted. He started to say something else, but Donny's voice sliced through the noise on both sides.

"Just…*everyone* shut up!"

He paused for a moment as if surprised at himself, then marched away.

Skinny called after him, "What's your problem, *güey*?" but he got no response. Stocky shouted, "You gonna let a couple of queers talk to us like that?" Still no response. Donny just stalked in the direction of the milling students. The remaining assholes stood for a moment longer, exchanging puzzled looks. We kept walking, leaving them behind.

"Buddha take the wheel," Brent muttered. "If I wanted to talk to some suppositories, I would carry on conversations with my *obaa-chan*'s bathroom cabinet."

Calista said, "That's really gross."

"Wasn't that a bizarre sitch though? Or *queer*, if you will?" Brent laughed at his own joke—an old one.

"Get some new material, babe," Calista said.

"Since when has Nick Walsh missed an opportunity to belittle…well, any of us?"

"Can I just say," I put in, "that I've seen Donick Walsh with Jason and Freddy there since freshmen year, and I still don't know their names."

"It's hard to remember what's forgettable," Calista said. Then she slowed. "Whoa, whoa, *whoa*! Did I just see Nick go into the theatre?"

"Liar," I said, but when I looked toward the lobby-doors I could see the milling students whispering to themselves, glancing over their shoulders. I could just make Donny out as he disappeared inside.

Calista blinked. "True story."

"He probably came to wail on the boy dancers," said Brent. "You know, put them in their place. Teach them to be dude-bros."

Slipping inside, we crept into the house, settling in the back row. Other students had trickled in, wanting to watch the dance auditions—one or two, like we Muskequeers, wanting to see what Donick Walsh could possibly be doing at Senior Revue tryouts. About thirty kids crowded the stage, the girls in cut-off sweats with leotards and tights underneath, the handful of boys dressed as though they were going to the gym—dressed just like Donny. Though most of the dancers went on warming up and stretching, more than a few turned shocked eyes in Donny's direction.

He looked uncertain, nervous. He paused at the table set below the edge of the stage where Mrs. Peebles and Chalice, the dance teacher, were conferring together. They smiled at him and Chalice shook his hand. Mrs. P., fairly young for a teacher, was tall and angular. Chalice—that's all anyone ever called her: Chalice—was small and wiry, in her fifties, and nothing but sinewy muscle and strength. Quiet had fallen and I could hear Mrs. P. speaking.

"Mrs. Moes told me you'd be coming." She handed Donny a sheet of paper. "I'm so glad you made it. We're going to start with the tap combination. You tap, yes?"

I thought my brain would fall out when Donny answered, "I do, yeah."

We Muskequeers exchanged incredulous glances.

"This is like a twilighty zone place," Brent whispered.

"This could be so embarrassing," Calista whispered back.

I couldn't take my eyes from my old not-friend. If ever a person looked exactly like a perfect picture of one-of-these-things-is-not-like-the-others, Donny was it. His timidity filled the air like a smell. He tried his best to look unconcerned with what anyone thought, but he failed.

"Dancers!" Chalice called, her voice echoing through the house. She always had a ton of presence for someone so small. "Get your tap shoes on if you have them. Warm up your ankles. We'll be starting in about three minutes. Those of you who don't tap, the jazz combo will come right after."

"You don't have to fill that out right this second, Nick," Mrs. P. said. "Just bring it to me before you leave."

We watched Donny attempt to stuff the audition-form into the bag slung over his shoulder. Even from as far away as I sat, his hands clearly trembled. He climbed the steps at the side of the stage, passing through the assembled dancers until he reached the stage-right wings, piled with bags and cast-off shoes. The dancers watched him from the corners of their eyes, the seven or eight boys looking especially uncomfortable. They knew Donick Walsh, and all were puzzled as to why someone who had tormented and bullied them had suddenly appeared in their safe-space. I could relate. The theatre was *mine*; *he* belonged on a football-field.

He actually fumbled a pair of tap shoes from inside his bag—a pair of very worn, broken-in tap shoes. Brent had it right. This was a twilighty zone place, for sure. Donny toed off his sneakers, then removed his socks. He padded barefoot to one side of the stage, tap shoes dangling from his fingers. He sat himself as far from anyone as he could and began stretching.

"Limber!" Brent hissed. Donny had thrown his legs out

to the sides, impossibly wide. "Look at the muscles in his thighs!"

"How 'bout no," Calista muttered.

I seconded that. Still, I had to admit, Donny looked as though he knew what he was doing. Not just anyone could point their toes like that. He looked more at home, in fact, than some of the girls—at home in terms of his stretches, that was. I could still sense his fear like a current. But asshole or no, he looked good. I hated myself for admitting it.

As the dancers began to slip into their shoes, Donny did the same, getting on his feet. Other kids were tapping away, the theatre becoming raucous with thirty pairs of tap shoes all doing different steps. Donny kept his gaze averted from everyone, not moving his feet. Instead, he kneaded the muscle in one shoulder, rotating his arm, grimacing a little.

Chalice climbed onto the stage. The tapping died away. She started talking, all business, asking the dancers to form lines.

Sitting in the back of the house with my friends, one or two heads scattered about in the seats in front of us, I wondered if Donny could see us beyond the light shining in his eyes. I wondered if he knew that we—that I—watched, and if it made his nerves worse. I *wanted* to hope it would, that he would feel like more of a fool than he was going to make of himself, but I couldn't. Standing on that stage—whether acting, singing, dancing—seemed to reveal parts of a person's soul. Anyone could sink their fingers into it in that moment of exposure and crush it. I could never want that for anyone, even if, at the back of my brain, I wished I could—at least where *he* was concerned.

"All right, guys and gals," Chalice said. "I want to do a

warm up first and test you on some basic steps. I really want a tap number in the show this year. If you can make it through a few of these steps, there's a good chance I'll use you in it."

My limited dance training made a lot of what she next said Greek to me. She gave vocal instructions, demonstrated once, then let the dancers do their thing. The theatre filled with the sound of thirty pairs of feet, including Donny's. At once, his body took up the rhythm. He looked so natural that Calista leaned into me.

"You *had* to know about this."

"I didn't," I whispered.

Chalice's instructions went on, the steps growing more complicated, but again, the swing in Donny's arms, the ease of his feet, astounded me. ("Lordy, look at his calves!" Brent hissed in my ear.) Not all the tappers were finding the progression of steps as easy as at first, yet Donny looked unruffled. When Chalice moved on finally to time-steps, she started the dancers, calling out "Now double!" after a few seconds, then "Triple!", and lastly "Quadruple!" As the step progressed in difficulty, more and more dancers stopped, at the limit of their skill, breathing hard, but smiling. There were two dancers, however, that did not stop until Chalice told them too—Donny and one other girl.

"I'm impressed," Chalice said, wearing the same surprised expression as many of the dancers.

Donny's cheeks glowed pink, either from exertion or embarrassment, I couldn't tell. He pulled off his sweater, knotting it around his waist. Sweat had already darkened the shirt beneath. Some of the other boys were similarly dressed, and I had to admit Donny, just then, looked more like a dancer than he did a football player.

"All right," Chalice continued, "onto the combination. Let's move quickly. We'll have a water break shortly. Here we go."

"That was crazy," Calista said. "Get a load of how tight his shirt is."

"Get a load of those shoulders," Brent muttered. "And his arms. And, damn, those legs."

"Get a load of the irony," I said.

Brent seemed fixated on Donny. Had all the years of abuse and bullying suddenly cleared away? Had my old not-friend become my current best friend's new crush or something?

The song Chalice chose for the combination was "Always Look on the Bright Side of Life" from *SPAMalot*. She said something about using it in the show. Brent remained wide-eyed and staring as she taught the dancers the steps. Once or twice, he breathed out, "I should've been a dancer."

Calista's eyes rolled. "Spare me your legs in tights, babe."

I couldn't stop watching. Everything I knew about Donny since the ending of our friendship warred with the guy on that stage. Who the hell was that? Six years of being ignored, or bullied and teased, separated the dancer under the lights from myself. Why did he have to be here? Anger spiked through me. Six years of resentment—and hurt—threatened to solidify into downright loathing.

Chalice clapped her hands twenty minutes later, the panting tappers pausing. Clearly Donny's nerves had gone from jagged spikes to smoothness, his fear ebbed away. He had discovered himself in his element. Seeing his flushed cheeks and the soft smile playing on his lips, I felt overwhelmed. How could one asshole, an asshole who had been my friend in another life, make me want to run out of *my* theatre, run from *my* auditions, and never come back? There was no chance he wouldn't be cast in the Revue. Aside from being a senior, he was *good. Better* than good! We would be in a show together, having to be around each other for the first time, after six years of awfulness. How could I feel at ease and comfortable if I had to keep my guard up, prepared for when he might decide to start calling me a faggot again, or threatening to kick my ass? There could be nothing worse than being humiliated in front of a group of people I cared about and whose respect I valued.

"All right, guys and gals!" Chalice called. "Five minutes! Grab some water, go over the steps on your own. We'll break into groups and you'll do the combination for Mrs. Peebles and myself."

The tappers immediately dissolved into chaos. Wonder of wonders, passing dancers were smiling at Donny, telling him (I was sure) how amazing he was and how they had no idea he danced. He looked modestly uncomfortable as he smiled back. Then, as he began to practice the steps on his own, one of the boys stepped close to him. It was Liam Hidalgo, a tenth grader who sometimes hung out with us in the drama-room at lunch. They spoke for a second or two, then Donny actually began going over the steps with Liam. Donny was all affability, and with a boy dancer wearing rainbow sweat-guards! They laughed together, and once Donny even touched Liam's arm.

"Did they pump a bunch of peyote through the air conditioner today?" I cried. "I'm going outside. I need to get my music."

"I'll come," Calista said, beginning to get up.

Brent said, "Are you sure you're a 'mo, Michael? Some

of these boys aren't wearing dance belts. This is better than anything the three of us could talk about."

"What a pal," Calista muttered.

"No, stay," I said to her. "Enjoy the, I dunno, possible camel toe?"

"It's a horror movie when you start saying things."

"I'm going to my locker." Then I added, mostly to myself, "It's kinda gross in here."

Calista gave me a concerned glance. She didn't know the whole story of my friendship with Donick Walsh, but she knew there was history. And because the complete history mortified and hurt my feelings, I preferred to keep her as unenlightened as possible. She didn't need to know just how troubled his presence made me. I tried to reassure her with a smile that felt tight as a guitar-string.

Outside, a handful of dancers waited for the jazz portion of the audition. Thankfully Donny's jerkass buddies were no longer hovering. I meandered my way through the campus toward my locker.

For the first time in…yes, *years*, crap I would rather continue to bury and ignore, began to surface in my memory.

It's not fair, you ass! I shouted at Donny in my brain. *You kissed me! I barely understood what being gay meant.* You *kissed* me, *and made me feel like a piece of trash for six years! And counting!*

That part ripped me up inside the most. He had been my best friend, and then, having kissed me, used the kiss and our friendship as a weapon to draw blood. Literally.

Then there was his dad. "Faggot! Queer!" Those words hurled at a child from an adult's mouth, a parent's mouth, are unforgettable. Donny's dad had always struck me as imposing, a pot boiling on a stove. He wasn't a big man, Donny already as tall, even at eleven. Yet Mr. Walsh was broad and bearded and spoke in a rough, rasping tone with a hint of the South in it. As a dad, he was older than the fathers of any kids I knew. Sometimes other students thought he was Donny's grandfather. I had sensed his disapproval of his son hanging out with me for years before the day Donny kissed me. I didn't know why he seemed to dislike me so much, why he gave me dark, distrustful looks. I suppose, in his mind, he felt justified at coming home early and finding his son and his son's best friend sitting close together on the living-room floor, ignoring the TV in favor of each other's lips.

"What the fuck is this? What's this faggot stuff going on in my house? Nicky! Is that what's happening here? Are you queer? A faggot? Get your fairy friend the hell out of my house! Get your stuff!" he shouted, turning on me. "I don't want some faggot hanging around my boy! I catch you in my house again, or anywhere near my son… Get the fuck out!"

I could hardly think from fear. I half expected he might take a swing at me before I could reach the door. I can't recollect much after that: Donny shouting at his father, hearing my friend begin to cry, Mr. Walsh berating him for it, even through the door he had slammed at my back after giving me a shove through it.

I hated to think what sort of night Donny went through. The next day at school when I sought him out, he would only say, "Leave me alone, Mikey," and turned away. I still couldn't grasp that we had done anything wrong, and for several days I dogged his steps, trying to get him to talk to me. He was my best friend. We had never spent so much time apart. We had never fought in all the years knowing each other. There were things I wanted to talk to him about, and everything nerdy reminded me of him. If I needed him so much, it was impossible, I thought, that he wasn't needing me. But my presence seemed to make him miserable, seemed to slowly make him angry.

Catching him by his locker at lunch a full week after the incident at his house, I tried to force him to explain why he didn't want to be my friend anymore. Somewhere in the scuffle that followed, in the mask of hatred I saw cross his features, my own best friend called me a faggot, shoving me face-first into the lockers. He did it hard enough that I stumbled, knocking my forehead into a lock, raising an enormous goose-egg and gashing my right eyebrow, sheeting blood into my eye.

The school reported the incident to my parents, of course. Donny was suspended for two days. I had to walk around for two weeks with half my face colored various shades of purple, three stitches in my eyebrow like spider-legs at the top of my vision. I hadn't told my parents about the incident at Donny's house, feeling far too ashamed. All I could say to my mom and dad now was that Donny and I had had an argument, that I had been bugging him and made him mad. I said that I hated him, that I never wanted to see him again and wished he would die.

"Boys do this sort of thing, Ninja," Dad said. He always called me Ninja because of my obsession with anime. "In a while, you guys'll patch things up and go right back to being best pals."

I knew it was impossible, and said so.

"Don't be so dramatic," Mom said. "Friends fight. Yes,

this was a little extreme, but friends are friends. When two people connect, and connect as strongly as you and Donick, the bond isn't severed so easily."

"I would say it's impossible, Ninja," Dad added.

But they didn't know. They *couldn't* know that seeing so much hatred in a person's face, even the face of a former best friend, can incite answering hatred with shameful ease.

After that, Donny never spoke to me if he could help it. We passed like ships in middle school corridors, in high school hallways, unless he could insult me in some way. The friends he made as football took over his life were disgusting jocks who picked on anyone that crossed their paths. They were the worst human beings, and over the years I watched my old friend Donny change into just another asshole.

DONICK

"If the music's pumping, it will give you new life."

IT'S SURPRISING HOW I'm able to *almost* relax as I learn the tap combo. The hard part had been walking through the other dancers when I first entered. Judgmental eyes surround me. Here are boys I've been cruel to. Reminders of my asshole-ness are everywhere, including a girl named Jackie Skarupa.

I know her because Josue seems to have a fixation with giving her a hard time. She's overweight and very freckled. Even now she looks unfortunate in her leotard and tights. If I'm honest, she gives the impression of being kind of slow. It doesn't help that she has to take classes for kids with learning disabilities. Crowning it all is her lazy eye. None of these things detract from how nice she is though. Her sweetness is on her sleeve. But the way she retreats into herself at the sight of me drives home my mistakes. A guilty sensation fills my throat like a fist.

At the start of the previous year, under Josue's goading, I passed her one morning, reached out, and knocked a paper coffee cup from her hands. The plastic cap popped off, hot coffee spraying all over her. It wasn't hot enough

32

to burn, thank God. But I don't think I would have cared if it *had* burned her. She came to school every morning carrying a Starbucks cup, and humiliating her was easy. When I laughed in her wounded, crestfallen face and actually said, "Can't you even figure out how to hold a cup, or are you too retarded?" I stabbed humiliation into her with the precision of a hammer to the head of a nail.

Her girlfriends had given me kill-stares; but they hadn't reported me. No campus supervisor saw it, no administrator pulled me from class. Bullies target those who won't say anything. What's the point in messing with someone who will fight back? The perfect target is a person who believes they *deserve* the cruelty.

Yet the things I've done to people—Jackie just one in a line—go beyond cruelty. I deserve *two* bad shoulders *and* shattered kneecaps. Even then, I don't think the karmic balance will ever wash.

And hey, if it's not enough to see the resentful expressions on the faces of the kids circling me, I have barely put on my tap shoes when I spot The Three Muskequeers in the theatre. They've planted themselves like a tribunal in the back row. I fight the desire to run, feeling like a complete wuss. But I have to do this or I won't graduate.

Once we finish the tap routine, I suspect I've done well. Maybe even better than that. When I squint into the house, Mikey's friends are still there, but Mikey is gone. If I had stunk up the place, he would have stuck around to make the most of it, right? His absence is a relief though. I would prefer he *not* see me looking like a clown.

And the other dancers are warming up to me! I don't want this to be important, but it is. Their compliments almost make me happy. I never cared how football games went. Winning or losing, praise from coaches and players and parents…it never made me feel much of anything. Acceptance here, though, approval here…I want it badly! If I can show these people that I'm not really the person they think, then there's hope for me. Jackie ignores me, but I'm not surprised. She should. Still, now I can think to the rhythm of our steps: *Reset-button, reset-button, reset-button!*

Chalice tells us to change into jazz shoes. More students have come in—there are fifty of us packed onto the stage. Friends greet each other, but the puzzled looks aimed at me never stop. There are a lot more girls, and one or two more guys.

"Thanks again for your help," a voice says at my shoulder. It's the boy I showed the steps to. He told me his name is Liam Hidalgo ("Like the horse!"). "You don't mind if I stick close, do you?"

I shake my head.

"I have a feeling this jazz combo is gonna have me crazy lost. I've only been dancing since last year. I wouldn't have come, but Chalice told me it would be a good challenge. Growth only comes from leaving one's comfort zone, she always says."

"Ain't it the truth," I say. Then I brush his elbow. "You did fine with the tap. I'm sure the jazz combo will be fine too."

I'm hyper-aware suddenly that I've touched him. Donick Walsh, pre-injury, would never have touched another boy in that friendly way. What would people think? Allowing myself to be even a little unreserved, however, is a feeling I like. It reminds me of being eleven or twelve, before my existence went off track. I want to bring my walls down.

That's terrifying, because I'm not sure what I've hidden behind them.

And this Liam kid? It's obvious he's gay. How could anyone miss it with those rainbow wristbands he's wearing? He's small and sort of mouse-like. He told me he's a sophomore but he looks like a freshman. I danced only to be better at football, but Liam dances for the sheer fun of it. The part of it I found fun I hid behind one of those walls—until today. The point is, Liam is the perfect target for idiots like Josue and Ryan. He's the perfect target for me. I can even picture myself calling him names, or throwing an apple or something at him across the quad during lunch. Maybe even going so far as to harass him on Facebook—which I ditched after my stint in the hospital. Social media is much too toxic.

Still, I'm a hypocrite. I *am* this kid. I'm here, just like he is, all for my love of dance—not just because I need the PE credit, I see that now. The difference between us is his sexuality doesn't shame him, and I've been running, terrified, since discovering I'm gay the afternoon of my first kiss.

As a few girls I know approach to exclaim over my being there, I at last calm down enough to think: *I'm starting over. I have to do these hard things.*

The jazz combination is in the style of Bob Fosse. The theatre is warm and we're all sweating. Chalice is using a song called "Money Makes the World Go Around". She moves me and three or four of the girls to the front row so the other less experienced dancers can watch us. It's a vote of confidence that has me feeling elated. And completely mortified. When we're supposed to practice for a few minutes on our own, it isn't just Liam who comes to me for help—it's, like, *nine* of them!

Let me pause here and go off on a tangent. Let's talk about what being gay means for me.

As FAR AS homophobic assholes go, you won't find a bigger one than my dad. I learned that to my own destruction at age eleven. In a quest for his approval, I turned my back on my own best friend. I even gave that friend stitches in return for the realization that he gave me. Namely, that I, just like him, am into guys.

Oh sure, denial is an amazing gift to someone in the beginning stages of becoming an asshole. Any bad behavior can be justified when it's done for the sake of protecting a lie. People say the most powerful emotion is love. They're wrong. The most powerful emotion is fear. Lies are all about fear, and while love hides a multitude of *other's* sins, fear hides a multitude of one's own. After all, fear is powerful enough to justify the denial of love, even when it's real and honest.

How can I ever let Pop know that his son isn't the manly, straight chip off the old block he wants? After the way he treated Mikey that long ago day, what can *I* expect? Pop can be scary! He's never hit me, but there are scars on my brain and heart that are worse than physical bruises. The kinds of scars he gives served to help turn me into an asshole, just like him. All that denial and fear has only made me hateful to everyone around me, even to myself.

I've had exactly three girlfriends. They *all* deserved better than me, because I had nothing to give them. Certainly not genuine interest. I was a jock known all across campus for being a great quarterback and a terrible human being. Even those three girlfriends grew to dislike me. I didn't want to spend much time with them. I didn't like kissing them, and I *never* wanted to go further than that. They weren't exactly nice girls themselves, but even watching the way I harassed any kid who was even a little awkward, or introverted, or overweight, or too this or that, eventually wore thin for them. And surprise surprise! None of my friends are any good at keeping girlfriends either. At least my disinterest has gone unnoticed so far.

If I look at porn, it's always straight porn, in case Pop checks my browser history. He doesn't need to know who it is I'm actually watching. My laptop wallpaper might be a picture of Henry Cavill dressed as Superman, but guys are into superheroes, right? Again, my dad doesn't need to know that I think Henry Cavill is über sexy, does he? There might be a folder on my computer (titled: Research Project—Eng 11) filled with pictures of Hugh Jackman as Wolverine and Jason Momoa as Aquaman. I suppose the clues are everywhere for him to find. If he really examined my life, his head might get forced out of his ass for once. (I mean, come on, the *dancing*! Even now that football and I have divorced, I've never stopped attending classes, and thank God he hasn't stopped paying for them!)

I've also been thinking that this is all really sad for me. I've been barricading myself behind denial and fear, when the real me, the me that realized he wanted to kiss his best friend, has no idea what it means to be gay. I've never had a crush on another boy because I saw it as impossible that that could be who I am. But brave people like Liam and Mikey and his Muskequeers…I could learn so much from them.

To acknowledge that openly is the scariest thing of all. My dad will hate me. My buddies will hate me. The people I should have befriended and learned from would never want me around. They're scared of me.

However, Liam is right. Growth only comes from leaving one's comfort zone, and that's just what I intend to do. I may spend the rest of my senior year a social outcast, but I can at least take comfort in knowing that who I was, who I am, and who I want to be, are not as out of my control as I think.

ANY DANCERS STICKING around for the singing auditions," Chalice says once we're finished, "hang out in the house for a bit. We're waiting on Mr. Hardy. Dancers, the cast-list will be posted after school on Thursday. First rehearsal next Monday at three!"

I'm going for my bag, when I suddenly have a bunch of smiling girls in my face.

"Oh my God! Nick! I never knew you were a dancer!"

"You're so good! Do you do ballet too?"

"What studio do you dance at?"

One of these girls *isn't* Jackie. She won't look in my direction as she and her friends leave the stage.

Liam, as we change our shoes, thanks me again. "You don't even need to check the cast-list," he says, walking with me to the stairs. "Just show up at the first rehearsal."

"You think? There were a lot of great dancers."

"Not me. I screwed up too many times. Chalice was right about it being a challenge. You made it look *way* too easy."

"You did fine, man. You gave it your best. I bet you get in."

"Only because they need guys. But I'll take what I can get. I started dancing too late to make a career of it, but that doesn't mean I won't try." He laughs. "Just what you need, right? A couple months of listening to me ask for help."

"If we both get in," I say, "then I don't mind. I like teaching."

"You've taught before?"

"Kid classes at my studio on weekends. At least when I didn't have games. I do it regularly now."

Chalice is in the middle of a chattering group of dancers. She looks ridiculously small in their midst, but her muscled shoulders and arms make her seem like a tank. I've only just met her and I already think she's amazing. I wish I had danced at school all these years. She's another person I could have learned a ton from. I pause at the bottom of the steps to thank her and she touches my wrist.

"Can you hang back a minute?" she asks.

My nerves firing again, I nod.

"What I tell you?" Liam whispers. "Has to be a good sign."

"Or a bad one. She's gonna tell me I stunk."

Liam snorts. "Yeah, right."

My cheeks are warm. In a low voice, I tell him, "This was really hard for me."

He shrugs. "But you did it. And I gotta say," he adds, lowering his voice and stepping nearer, "I was kind of afraid of you. But you're way nicer than everyone says."

I can't quite meet his eyes. There's sadness in my voice, sadness I can't control, as I say, "Believe every word."

He frowns, but I tell him goodbye and move toward Chalice.

"Come over here away from the hubbub," she says, leading me to a quiet corner at the back of the house. She then gives my hand a shake. "Really excellent job. It depresses me that I'm only just finding out about you. At least I'll have the chance to work on a show with you before you graduate."

"Work on a show?"

She grins. "Yes, work on a show. You're in, of course. I

never have enough guys, let alone guys with the training you've shown this afternoon. Congratulations."

I feel almost bashful as I struggle not to fight smiling. My skin shivers a little, and not just from sweat. "Thanks. Oh man, I've been so freaked. I talked myself out of coming, like, eight times today."

"I'm happy you didn't listen to that brain of yours. It's your own worst enemy."

"This brain of mine *does* get me into trouble."

She crosses her arms and regards me. "So, Nick, listen," she says. "I'm telling you already that we're casting you because I want you for one of my dance captains."

If it's possible, I'm even *more* floored.

"Don't look so shocked." Her smile falters. "Or maybe you really are surprised. Your audition was excellent. I choose three or four dancers to be captains because the Senior Revue is such an enormous job. Think of me wrangling forty dancers! And that's *just* dancers, not counting twenty-or-so singers that will require movement for their numbers. I need a few students who learn quickly and know what they're doing to keep the dancers on track. As a choreographer I'm about thirty percent preparation and seventy percent fly by the seat of my pants. Too much overthinking kills my vision. This means I teach, then forget. I need dancers like you to learn what I give and go over it with everyone when they inevitably forget it all. Please say you'll do it."

There's a funny something—pride maybe—rising like a bubble in my chest. I'm still totally surprised, but I stammer out, "Of course, I'm just…I wasn't expecting…any of this, I guess. I feel like I don't know what I'm doing here."

Chalice pats my arm. Then she says the best thing in the

world. It's as though something whispered it in her ear just so she could repeat it to me.

"You're finding yourself, Nick. That's what you're doing here."

I almost shiver again. I'm suddenly afraid, but I don't know of what.

"Meanwhile, Mrs. Peebles wants to see you before you head out. Congratulations again, and thank you." I think Chalice might have hugged me if I wasn't covered in sweat.

I look around for Mrs. Peebles, remembering I never gave her my audition form. She's standing at the edge of the stage turning over the pages of a stack of sheet music, marking things on a legal pad with a pencil she keeps sticking behind her ear.

"Chalice said you wanted to see me? I forgot—"

"Oh, Nick! Yes! So glad you're still here. I need your audition form. It has all your info on it. We need it for the cast-list. Welcome to the Senior Showcase Revue. I'm so glad to have you on board."

"I'm happy to be on board. I think."

"Think?"

"I've never really done anything like this. I'm kinda nervous."

"You'll be great." She waves her hand as though there are bigger and better things to concern myself with. I feel instant liking for her.

She's young for a teacher, not even thirty, I think. There's a frazzled quality to her, her dark hair knotted behind her head, wisps flying about her neck and ears, that pencil jutting precariously. I sense why the kids in her department love her so much. She's young and full of energy, fitting in with the manic quality of her drama students, but with the knowledge to earn their respect. By the time our conversation is over, she certainly has mine. I'm glad to know her, and just like with Chalice, I'm sorrowful that here, at the end of my high school career, this is the first time she'll be teaching me.

"How's your shoulder?" she asks.

"Good. As good as it'll ever be again, anyway."

"Dancing doesn't trouble it?"

"As long as I'm careful. Getting back into class at the same time I did my physical therapy helped. Dance isn't just about the legs and feet. Male dancers need to be strong all over."

"I've never seen a scrawny male ballet dancer, this is true," she replies. "Your councilor told me that your doctors specifically said no more football for you. Which I'm really sorry about, of course."

I make a face. "No great loss."

"No?"

"I was never really into it."

"Never showed."

"You learn to phone it in."

"Think of those Broadway actors performing the same role for months and months, sometimes years, every single day. If anyone thinks they feel it every performance, they're insane."

"They must feel it the majority of the time though?"

"Of course. Or else why do it?"

"I've had some time to ask myself that same question. Why was I doing it, when I felt nothing?"

"And?"

I shrug. "My dad pretty much forced me. He wanted me to play for UCLA. Now all that's gone. I don't know what I'm supposed to do."

Mrs. Peebles smiles. "It looks like you're supposed to dance, Nick."

"As a career?" I scoff. "Right."

"Why not? You have talent. Just because football is a closed door, doesn't mean *all* doors are closed. Sometimes things seem like they're a certain way, but when you examine them, they're something completely different. You could be a dance teacher, or a choreographer."

"Yeah, my dad would *love* that."

"Your dad doesn't have to be comfortable living *your* life. *You* do. Maybe a power bigger than all of us has intervened on your behalf."

"Well, that power sure likes to place great big mountains in my way. Just my luck, my doctors will probably tell me no mountain climbing."

"The doctors are okay with you dancing? There isn't any danger you'll re-injure yourself?"

"I can do everything most people do. Just nothing that will over-stress. Light pushups, but no more weight training."

"Well, don't take this wrong—I mean, I'm really sorry about your injury, and I wish it hadn't happened—but if it means I get to have you in the show, and also part of our theatre family, forgive me for being a little bit grateful."

"No offense taken. I'm glad to be here. Really. This was just…a very scary experience."

"But you did it. Do you know how many people wouldn't allow themselves to have an experience like this just *because* it's scary? And look what's happened. You're not only in the show, but Chalice picked you for a dance captain. You've accepted, right?"

"Yeah."

"Good!" She gives my healthy shoulder a squeeze.

And I realize something. Instead of coming right out and asking me how I'm doing, Mrs. Peebles has lured me, with surprising ease, into opening up to her. The instant liking I've felt for her turns into an appreciation I've never before felt for a teacher. Sometimes strangers have the ability to make you trust them, and Mrs. Peebles is one of those people. More and more kids have been filling the theatre but her focus has stayed on me. How rare it is for anyone, adult or no, to make you feel like like you have their complete attention. Like you are more important, at that moment, than anything else.

Dropping my eyes—this admission is difficult and makes me feel like I'm lowering another wall—I say, "I know all these kids don't like me. I'm afraid when they find out I'm a dance captain it'll make it worse."

"Do you think they should like you, Nick?" Her expression is unreadable, but there's genuine interest in her gaze.

Suddenly I want to cry. "No. I...I've been horrible to most of them. For a long, long time."

"You were very kind to Liam, I noticed."

"He asked me for help."

"And you gave it to him. He's one more person in your corner than you had when you walked in."

"That's true."

"Which brings me to something that needs to be said. I don't tolerate bullying in my department. I know you need this show to graduate, and I'm very happy you're here. But any bullshit will not be tolerated. For a lot of my kids, this is their haven, where they go for acceptance—"

"And they've never had that from me," I finish for her.

"Just making sure we're on the same page. I hope I have your understanding about why I need to say this. I get no pleasure from it. You've had a reputation as an extremely gifted football player. You've also had a very different kind of reputation that's preceded you. I need you to know, any nonsense, and you'll be out. We clear?"

I nod, shamed. It isn't Mrs. Peebles's fault. This is my own fallout. "Crystal," I say.

"Your reputation as a gifted football player is pretty much moot now, right?"

"Dead as dinosaurs."

"Let's let your other reputation die too." Then, what she next says raises goosebumps along my arms. "Think of this as an opportunity to hit a reset-button."

I can't swallow because that fist is back in my throat. I only nod.

"Now," she says in a brighter voice. "I have one other thing I want to ask you." She could ask me to jump off a cliff, I think. She's suddenly one of my favorite people. "Do you sing?"

I blink at her vacantly. "Huh?"

DONICK

"Being used to trouble, I anticipate it,
But all the same I hate it. Wouldn't you?"

I WONDER THE WHOLE drive home what I've gotten myself into. Then, making me grip the steering-wheel like a vise, I wonder what the crap I'm going to tell Pop? What excuse will I give for coming home late? What will I say I'm doing every afternoon for the next couple months? He doesn't know about my PE credits, or the conversation I had with my councilor. With a choice between seeing his son dancing in a musical or not graduating from high school, a dropout would be a-okay with him.

It's not just Pop I'm thinking about. I'm also thinking about Mikey.

For the last six years he's been twelve years old in my mind. Today I realized I don't know him anymore. At some point those Buddy Holly glasses came off. (Contact lenses?) He got taller than me, and I'm no slouch. He lost that geeky awkwardness and became…well, I really can't think of any way to describe him other than to say: *handsome*. His friends dress like stereotypes—Calista in her boy clothes; Brent with his perfect hair, tight pants, and too-small shirts. But Mikey just looks like…a guy. A *very attractive* guy. All that dark hair curling over his forehead… Did I *ever* notice, even when we were kids, that his eyes were that shade of green?

Because Mrs. Peebles took pity on me and said I could wait to sing with Mr. Hardy after all the other singers had auditioned and cleared out, I was able to watch the tryouts.

And wow! How did I never know Mikey could *sing* like that? When it comes to any sort of talent I might have, he makes me feel like a rusty hinge. Nothing but confidence, he stood under the lights, giving his name and song as though he were at a professional audition. I didn't know the song—something about dreams—but he said it came from the movie *The Greatest Showman*. He started, and I felt the air suck from my lungs, from the whole theatre. When he finished, deafening applause sounded as the kids on deck hooted and called his name. What a revelation to find out that, in the school's performing-arts world, Mikey is popular.

I literally prayed to God that Mikey wouldn't be around when my turn came. So what if Mrs. Peebles said I need only sing a few scales; I couldn't make a sound if Mikey stood watching, *listening*.

After a long succession of singers, nobody remained in the house but the teachers. Despite my relief, I'm sure I looked like a scared cat. Sitting at the piano where it had been pushed from the wings onto the apron, Mr. Hardy waved me forward.

He's a big, smiling man, with a round belly and a reddish-brown beard. "Mr. Walsh!" he said. "I've never had the pleasure, though I've seen your feats on the football-field time and again. I hear you wowed everyone earlier.

Going to sing for us now?"

The rest of me felt frozen, but my face might have been sunburned. "I'll try," I squeaked. "I don't really know any songs."

"No matter. I'll lead you through some scales. Simple and easy. Just *do-re-mi* and so on. Start here." He hit a note. I found it easily and sang it back. "Good. Open you mouth a little wider. Drop your jaw. Yes. Now, follow me up the scale."

I could hear the faltering of my voice, my palms going clammy. Could I possibly hit those higher notes? Mr. Hardy stopped me, then started again; this time he took the scale down. I felt more comfortable in that range, yet Mr. Hardy's expression remained neutral.

"Very nice," he finished. "Mrs. Peebles, we have another singer for the show. Our friend Nick has a nice strong baritone, maybe a second tenor. I could have used you in my choir, Mr. Walsh. Where have you been?"

I laughed, self-conscious. "I keep hearing that."

Then, out of nowhere, Mikey stepped out of the shadows in the wings. Every muscle in my body tensed. He stared at me with an expression of…dislike? Hatred? I couldn't meet his eyes. Where had he come from?

Embarrassment came to heighten my old way of viewing him. I suddenly resented the hell out of his being there. I wanted to tell him I thought he had a beautiful voice, but instead I acted like I always have. I pretended he wasn't there. I even went so far as to cut in front of him when we approached the stairs at the same time. I hoped his eyes on my back would see only a careless, pride-filled strut, when what I really felt was disgust—not for him, but for myself. Why must old habits die so hard?

When I get home, all the lights are off inside the house. There's no answer when I call out for Pop. It would be a relief if he wasn't home from work yet. I could take a minute to compose myself. But I hear the murmur of the television. Dropping my bag, I pass the kitchen where the smell of cooking lingers. The flickering of the TV throws shadows on the walls.

My dad sprawls in an armchair, still dressed in his work-slacks and polo-shirt, the collar buttons unfastened. His shoes are off, short legs stretched out, head thrown back with his mouth gaping around a snore. Wedged in his crotch is a Corona bottle, his glasses still sitting on his nose.

He looks mostly the same as he did six years ago, when he caught Mikey and I kissing right here in the living-room. Same beard, same broad forehead, same stocky build, only now he has less hair and a little more gut. I stare at him for a second or two, thinking a hundred things at once. I suppose the hair on his head and jaw *is* actually quite a bit grayer, the lines in his face deeper.

Lord, what will I say?

He senses me and sort of gasps himself awake. He almost overturns his beer.

"Nicky." Sleep fills his voice. "How long you been there?"

"Just got in." I'm glad the room is dark so he can't see my face.

"Where you been? I expected you home hours ago. Finished up early today. Wanted to go to Dorah Fine's Cafe but I nuked something. Got too hungry."

"Sorry. I got tied up."

"Doing what?" In the pale TV light I see his skepticism. This is a look I know all too well. My father trusts nothing

I say, and always I've been truthful to him—except about that day with Mikey. Maybe it's because of that day he distrusts every word I say. Considering the life I've led up to now, isn't he right?

"Working on a project," I say. "I'm behind on credits because of last year. I have to do some extra stuff to make up for it. For graduation."

"What kinda project?"

I shrug, a gesture that says *nothing important*. But I do say, "Woodshop. The teacher has some things to build for an event in the theatre or something. I dunno."

"Huh. How you gonna do any heavy lifting with your shoulder all busted?" When he says this, that southern lilt in his voice seems very apparent.

"No heavy lifting. Just hammering nails, running drills. That kinda thing."

"'Cause if you're gonna be working your shoulder in any way that might hurt it more, you'd be better off doing that on the field. I'm not sure those doctors know what they're talking about."

I can't keep my face from showing how tired I am of this argument. "I know, Pop, but really, it's nothing. Just helping out. I have a lot of credit to make up. Makes for a busy year, which sucks because most seniors have shorter days."

"Not you, huh?"

I shrug again, acting like the TV distracts me so I don't have to meet his probing eyes. "There are some other guys helping out. How was work?" I ask right away, wanting this uncomfortable part of the conversation over, though there is no comfortable conversation between my father and me, ever.

"Had to drive out to the middle of nowhere and test out cell reception on a handful of new phones. Not much to do, really, but a lot of driving to get it done. Don't know why I ain't retired yet."

"Least you got home early."

"I was hoping for pastrami and got stuck with microwavable garbage."

And the guilt trip. Right on cue.

"Sorry 'bout that, Pop."

"I got a few long days coming up so you'll have to fend for yourself. Next week we can go out some night and eat, maybe catch a game on one of the TVs near the bar."

"Actually, Pop," I say, trying to sound nonchalant, "this extra credit I'm trying to make up is part of a really big project. It's gonna pretty much be most days after school. I won't have a lot of time between that, classes, homework. I'm making up English 11 too, remember? Two English classes at once. Lucky me."

"You were in hospital, for Chrissake. Couldn't they give the injured QB a pass or something? You could barely hold a pen for months, let alone be in school."

I laugh falsely. "Too bad it doesn't work that way. But it has to get done. So I'll do it."

"Rest when you're pushing daisies, I guess. But I don't know why you're still dancing, Nicky. Football's a dead dream now, ain't it? What's the point?"

I don't like when he brings up dance. It's just a matter of time before he stops wanting to pay for the classes. If I told him that without them I would feel as though I *want* to push daisies, he would look at me like I came from Saturn.

"Helps my shoulder," I say. "It's gotten a lot stronger

from doing my exercises at the *barre*. It doesn't hurt nearly as much now. I've got almost full range of motion again."

He sighs and gives his head a shake, sucking at his Corona, the mouth of the bottle leaving a wet sheen on his lips. That head shake is his well-known gesture for not understanding the reasons why I do anything.

"More power to you, I guess," he mumbles, eyes flitting back to the TV. "There's more garbage to microwave in the freezer. Go eat some dinner. Then you can sit with me and we'll put on ESPN."

Doesn't that *sound like the best night of my life*, I think with a shudder. "I've got a butt-load of homework to do," I say. "You'll have to veg on the couch without me. Sorry."

I spend the rest of the night in my room ignoring the episodes of *Bob's Burgers* I let play on my laptop. My brain is going over and over everything that's happened today. I wish I *had* said something to Mikey about his singing. Maybe the fact he came near enough for me to see that scar in his eyebrow—the scar *I* gave him—had me feeling like I couldn't talk to him.

Or maybe I'm just an asshole.

Right before falling asleep, I lay in the dark and mutter to myself, "This has been the strangest day I've ever had."

MICHAEL

"It's not about aptitude, it's the way you're viewed."

"**T**HIS HAS BEEN the strangest day I've ever had."

That was all I could say when my mom knocked on my bedroom door, asking about auditions.

My laptop sat open on my desk, homework plastering the screen, even while I eyed the Crunchyroll shortcut on my internet browser. Mindlessly watching violent anime sounded like the perfect fix for an overwhelmed brain. *Attack on Titan*, maybe, or *One Punch Man*. Something to blank out my thoughts—because I couldn't get Donick Walsh out of them.

When had he learned to dance like that? And how in hell had he wound up auditioning for the Senior Revue? Calista and Brent were no help. Witnessing Donny's moves had them seeing him in a new light (especially Brent). New sides to familiar jerks could clear away old grievances, I guessed. But *I* wasn't moved. Once an asshole, always an asshole, in my book. How else to explain the way he had ignored me when he left the theatre?

He had come onto my turf and made himself look *good*! It wasn't fair!

"He is *not* good-looking," I groused to myself. "Talented, yes—I guess. A jerkoff, yes. Good-looking? Never."

"Talking to yourself?" Mom asked, tapping at my door. "Not a good sign. Straight-jacket territory."

"Just thinking out loud."

She leaned against the jamb, looking expectant. "Well?"

"Well?"

"How did the audition go? This *is* straight-jacket territory."

"Oh. Yeah. It's just…I dunno. This has been the strangest day I've ever had."

She crossed to sit on the edge of the bed. I swiveled in the desk-chair, turning back and forth a little with my toes on the casters.

"Your song didn't go well?" she asked.

I wrinkled my nose. "You smell like goats. Did you work on some goats today?"

"No. Four dogs, a Siamese cat, and someone's pet tarantula." I made a horrified face. As a veterinarian, Mom sometimes worked on the weirdest animals—if a great big spider counted as an animal and not an aberration. "Don't change the subject. *Was* it your audition? You and your dad practiced that song a ton."

"That went fine. *Better* than fine, actually."

"Good. Think you got in?"

"That's not even a question."

"Careful. Your head's inflating."

"I didn't mean *that*. It's the Senior Revue. I could suck and they would still feature me *because* I'm a senior. But I don't—"

"—suck?" she finished for me. "Hmm…how *do* you find hats that fit?"

"I just borrow yours and dad's."

"Clever boy. Strange day, you said." Her face brightened. "Mail! There was mail!"

I shook my head. "No college letters yet. I think it might still be too early. Though that does have me antsy."

"Don't think about it. You'll be busy with the show soon. That'll help."

The sound of doors opening and closing came from downstairs. Dad's voice bellowed, "Where are my roses?" His pet name for all of us. Our last name: Penrose. Therefore, we were his roses. Before we could call back, the high-pitched squeals of my five year old twin brother and sister almost shattered glass as they ran to meet him. Topher and Cady, the embodiment of noise pollution… but also, my heart living outside my body.

"All roses accounted for except Georgie!" Mom shouted. "She went to a friend's!"

"Will we need to pick her up?" We heard Dad's footfalls on the stairs, the twins scampering in his wake. "It's pretty late."

"Haven't heard from her," Mom replied. "Did your sister text you, Michael?"

I shook my head.

Dad, briefcase in hand, appeared in the doorway. He wore a green polo-shirt tucked into his jeans. A hideous look, I thought. Not to mention it drew attention to his serious dad-bod. But he often said he was lucky his job didn't require him to wear a suit and tie. He taught orchestra at a local private school—grades K-12, so his classes consisted of all ages. I had been to his concerts and thought it pretty cool to see kids my age playing in a band side-by-side with third and fourth graders.

Topher and Cady darted around his legs to come into the room.

"Michael's bed is not a trampoline, guys!" Dad said. Then to us, "Hello, my dears! Happy days all around?"

"For the most part," Mom replied. She turned her face up so Dad could kiss her. "Some of us had the strangest day ever. Christopher, Catherine! Your father told you to stop! I gave a tarantula in pre-molt a check up this morning though. It was not happy to be out of its burrow."

Dad came and brushed his lips against my temple. A far as dads go, mine had never had issue with showing his children affection—I loved that about him. "Ninja had a strange day? Couldn't be any stranger that examining a tarantula. What happened? Bad audition?"

"That went fine," I said. "Everything else was just…one of those days."

I found I didn't want to tell them. Mom, maybe, but not Dad. Dad was a listener, not a talker. If I needed feedback, I went to Mom, and this sort of felt like Mom-territory. Especially considering my past with Donny.

"We've all had those," Dad said. Then to Mom, "Love, I'm going to give Georgie a call. I'll pick her up and grab pizza for dinner." The twins immediately began chanting, "Pizza! Pizza! Pizza!" in time with their bounces. "Ninja, tell me about the audition when I get back. All right, you two, off the bed! Come with me!"

He left the room, taking the sound machines with him.

"Pizza," Mom sighed. "It's better than having to cook, I guess. I'm exhausted. I forgot my gloves and got clawed." She looked at a series of scratches on the back of her hand.

"Vicious giant awful spider?"

"Yes. Loves catnip and meows. So, about this strange day…"

I looked away. "It was just the auditions."

"You said yours went well."

"It did. It's just, I guess…"

"Spit it out."

"So, you remember Donny Walsh?"

"He hasn't been giving you trouble, has he?"

I scoffed. "He hasn't acknowledged my existence in years."

Aside from calling me names when he passed me in the halls, or laughing when his friends tried to trip me. But all that stuff seemed to happen in front of an audience. When alone, he acted like today—as though he didn't see me. Then, suddenly, I realized Donny had been ignoring me completely since last spring, whether with his friends or not. We had shared one class last semester and he had been mostly quiet and sort of withdrawn, a big difference from his usual self. Because I tried my best to pretend he wasn't there either, I hadn't noticed. Until just now.

"What's Donick have to do with anything?" Mom asked.

"He auditioned today."

"To do what?" Her tone grew interested. "Build sets? Hang lights?"

"For the dance call."

Mom stared. "You're joking."

"I wish."

She laughed again. "Strangest day for sure! Well? How was it? Poor guy, he probably embarrassed himself. Being gifted as an athlete doesn't necessarily make you gifted anywhere else."

"Yes, he was awful," I spat.

"Really?"

"Don't sound so pitying. He was awful all the way to Broadway."

"He was *good* then?"

"Very good."

"Isn't that interesting? Good for him!"

I touched my eyebrow. "See this? Remember who gave it to me. You might show a little less sympathy for someone who scarred your child."

"You two were just boys. We thought you'd make up in a few days. All these years of animosity have always shocked me. I don't understand it."

"Someone scarred your son—scarred him *forever*—out of pure hate, I might add, and you're Dismissive-Mom?"

"Please, you can barely see it anymore. Besides, sometimes people don't hurt others out of *hate*, Michael."

"Disfigurement and blood are, what? Acts of love?"

"Of course not! Those are just the unfortunate byproducts of the thing. Anything can be an act of love, or friendship, Michael, even if it turns ugly. And don't forget who his father is. That's all Donick's got. Dysfunction doesn't come from nowhere. Also, losing his mother to cancer like that, when he was so little? I've tried to understand him over the years, even when he's picked on you so much. But I don't think *you've* tried to understand him. You're still so angry."

"He's been nothing but a psycho!"

"Maybe he doesn't know any other way to be. If that's the case, think of him in this new situation. If he's as good as you say, he'll be in the show."

"Oh, he'll be cast," I said, resentful. "There's no way either Mrs. P. or Chalice would let him get away. He ended up singing too."

"The plot thickens."

"And he didn't sound completely horrible."

"Don't you wonder *why* he was there today?"

"I don't care," I snapped, but my whirling thoughts proved that was untrue.

"What about football? It's February, the season's over… Maybe he wanted something else to do with the new semester?"

I opened my mouth to say something, then shut it again, frowning. "He didn't play football this year," I said. "I just realized."

"He wants to try something new then?"

"Not *so* new. Anyone who can dance like that has been training for years."

"Well, how's he look? I haven't seen him since you boys were kids. He must be all grown up."

"He looks like a seventeen year old. What do you want?"

"Details, smartass."

I made a show of looking long-suffering. "He still has blonde hair."

"Is he tall?" Something in her tone, something in her face, made me feel as though we were gossiping about a passing crush—interesting mother/son chats that had been happening since I first came out to my parents in freshman year.

"I guess. I'm taller than he is now."

"All that football, he must look like a bulldozer."

"You want to know how muscular he is?" I gave her some serious side-eye.

"Yes!"

"All kinds of gross."

"I'm not hearing details."

"Fine, yes, he's muscular. But not bulky like that fat jerk of a friend of his."

"Mean. And?"

"And…his legs are like tree-trunks. Brent wouldn't shut up about them. Like, serious dancer-legs."

"And?"

"And…he's hot, all right? That what you want? Donny Walsh is tall and muscular and blonde and very cute. And it's *so* not fair!"

She grinned. "Why not fair?"

"Because jerks shouldn't get to be gorgeous, that's why!"

"Ooh, *gorgeous*!"

"Now you're Evil-Overlord-Mom."

Dad poked in his head again, stuffing his wallet into his back pocket. "You're talking about me? Gorgeous is right here!"

"No, Hon, the evil-overlord part was about you. The gorgeous part was about Donick Walsh who was, apparently, at dance auditions, and proved he has more talent than what he shows on the football-field."

I wanted to face-plant my head onto the glass top of the desk. Mom could have at least waited to tell Dad everything *after* we had finished talking. *And* I wasn't in the room.

"Donny Walsh, eh?" said Dad. "That's a name I haven't heard in years. You two friends again?"

"Hell no!" I cried.

"Fiery Ninja." Dad then looked at Mom. "I'm off to get Georgia Rose. The twins are already buckled in the van. Be back in a bit." He kissed the air at her, then vanished. The sound of Mom's minivan starting in the garage drifted to us through the floor a minute later.

Mom said, "What were we talking about? Oh! Yes! Gorgeous Donick Walsh! Have you *always* thought he was gorgeous?"

"Gross! When we were actually friends—you know, when dinosaurs roamed the earth—I didn't even know I was gay."

"Oh, Sweetheart, I did! I wondered about *him* too!"

"Donny?" I said, appalled. I thought about him kissing me that day in his living-room. Then I remembered the bloody gash above my eye and the awful things he had said to me…the hate he had regularly given for years after that. "Mother, you have terrible gaydar."

"I was right about *you*."

"Donny's über straight. Like, über straight homophobic, blow up Brokeback Mountain, picket to cancel *Drag Race*, straight. He's had girlfriends and stuff."

"If all that's true, he's going to have a rude awakening when it comes to being around all those theatre people. And the dancers? Yowza!"

"Ain't that the truth," I said, laughing. "It's gonna be great. I wish I could be a fly on the wall at dance rehearsals. He's gonna get himself kicked out. He even looks at anyone sideways and he'll be gone. I bet if Mrs. P. knew what he did to me, she wouldn't cast him at all."

"Don't think like that, Baby. You don't want to be *that* person."

"Sometimes I do."

She fell quiet for a second or two. At last, she said,

"Well, your birthday is in less than three weeks. What about your party?"

Damn! I hadn't thought of that. My face fell. "I was going to invite the whole cast, wasn't I?"

"You pretty much know everyone. That's your guest-list right there."

"How can I invite the whole cast now? I don't want Donny here. Nobody else will, either."

"Could you only invite some of them?" She asked this in typical Mom-fashion—an innocently posed question, laced with suggestion.

I made another face. "I guess not. There'll be, like, fifty people in the cast. Someone will feel left out or offended. I don't have an issue with anyone. Except *him!*"

"Do you even expect that Donick would come?"

"No."

"Then it's not a problem, right?"

"Probably not."

"Ooh! My baby is almost eighteen!"

"Mom, don't squeal like that!"

"What? It's a big deal!"

"Big enough for the parents to be out of the house the night of the party?"

"Nice try. Mom and Dad will spend most of the evening upstairs minding their own business—"

"—except when Dad sits at the piano and plays all night."

"Don't act like you hate it. A house full of musical theatre fans? Your dad willing to play for anyone who wants to sing will be the biggest win for your party. Besides, if you insist on a sleepover—a *coed* sleepover— a lack of chaperonage would be detrimental to the peace of mind of your parents."

"It's not the coeds you need to worry about, Mother-Dear. You should worry if there *aren't* girls here."

"Sassy-pants."

"Almost legal adult sassy-pants. Possibly *mobile* sassy-pants?" I pressed with every ounce of charm, and hope, I could muster.

"No driving until after graduation, sir. And the topic wears thin. Now, I'm going to wash the smell of shedding tarantula off my skin." She went to the door, but paused there. "Give some thought to exactly what you want to do about your birthday. You wanted to give an invite to everyone at the first rehearsal. If you don't want Donick Walsh to come, you'll have to figure something else out."

I drummed my fingers on the desk once she had gone. She was most likely right and Donny wouldn't come, even given an invite. But what if, for some perverse reason, he did show up? What would that do to the party-morale? It was hard enough thinking about tolerating his presence at rehearsals for the next few months, but having him in the same room with me, *at my house*? No, thank you!

Besides, even if he was invading my turf, I at least had the comfort of knowing my turf was also full of my friends. *He* was the odd man out.

DONICK

"It's hard to dance with the devil on your back,
So shake him off."

I WAKE UP THURSDAY morning—the day the cast-list will be posted—feeling nervous. I'm full of fear Mrs. Peebles and Chalice reconsidered and won't have me in the show. I'm also terrified of the reactions of the theatre- and dance-students when they see my name listed, not only as a dancer (and dance captain!), but as a singer too.

Wednesday was bizarre. Neither Josue nor Ryan asked me how my audition went—typical. Then I felt all day like randos stared at me. Nobody said a word, but I'm sure everyone at the tryouts began running their mouths right away. I made their lives hell, so they can't have much good to say. And worse? I need something from them now—acceptance.

I did run into Chalice, Mrs. Peebles, and Mr. Hardy at different points. They each stopped me just to say hello.

"You excited for rehearsals to start?" Mrs. Peebles had asked as I walked with her a little way toward her classroom.

"I don't know if excited is the word," I said. "I'm feeling *something*. Terror, maybe. I'm dreading the cast-list."

She laughed. "You already know you're in the show."

"Seeing my name will make it real. *Everyone* is going to know."

"It'll surprise you how supportive your fellow cast-mates will be."

"I guess we'll see. Thank you, by the way, for what you said at auditions."

"I only want us on the same page."

"I deserve what you said. You were also right about the other stuff. About making a clean start. I won't have any friends in the show, and I don't know how I'll change that, but I *am* going to try. I will be drama free, I promise."

"This show will be good for you. Music and performance, they speak to people, and not just the audience. You say something with the way you dance, Nick. We all saw a hidden part of you yesterday. And that sounded different out loud than in my head."

I paused a little way from her door. Several of her students waited outside—among them The Three Muskequeers. Calista looked at her phone, but Brent eyed me. I supposed my insults over the years about his hair and clothing hadn't stopped him from finding some new appreciation for me. Mikey, however, pointedly looked anywhere else. I wondered what he had told his friends about me. Guilt squirmed through my belly like a knot of eels.

Mrs. Peebles caught the turn of my eyes. She looked amused. "You *can* come inside, you know."

I tried to laugh. "No, I don't think I can."

"Change your mind one day. Everyone is welcome. Before and after school. At lunch. You'll find friends in there."

I glanced at Mikey again and thought sadly, *Not him. Never him again.*

The stares I received Wednesday have morphed into tentative smiles and hellos today. Confused, I hardly know what to say in response. Ryan, Josue, and some of our other buddies dart me funny looks, as though wondering who I am. Their friend Nick Walsh can't possibly have losers greeting him. Nick Walsh would sneer at these social outcasts, tell them to piss off. For the first time, my so-called friends are noticing I haven't been doing things like that for a while now.

Sitting at our usual table in the quad at lunch, surrounded by football players and chattering groupie-chicks that make me wonder how I ever thought I could fool myself into thinking I had interest in them, I spot Liam Hidalgo. He's walking in the direction of Mrs. Peebles's classroom.

I watch him, unable to keep from smiling. He's a person who knows nothing about self-consciousness or depression. He waves to someone in one place, stops for a second to talk to someone else, not knowing the chew-toys surrounding me would begin saying horrible things, or throwing food, if they noticed him. They would want to know what his name is so they can harass him online. I wish, suddenly, I could be more like Liam.

An idea strikes and I summon courage I never knew I had until Tuesday's audition. I get to my feet and hurry over to him. (*This will get easier*, I tell myself, *the more I do it*.) I admit, there's an ugly, sinking emotion in me, like the residue of old poison, because I wonder what people will think. I shouldn't care, but I do. I want to cut that ugly feeling out of me. Liam doesn't deserve it.

Surprise paints his face, a quick look of fear passing behind his eyes as he glances at the table where my friends have turned to watch.

"Oh, hi." His voice shakes a little. "What—what's up, Nick?"

The stares of my buddies stab my back like knives, but I give Liam a smile anyway. "The cast-list. It's supposed to be up today. Wanna walk by the theatre with me later? We can check it together."

He blinks in surprise. "Yeah, I guess."

His hesitance makes me doubt this great idea of mine. "No big if you don't want to. I guess I just don't want to go over there by myself."

"No, let's do it. I don't want to look by myself either. Getting in is a long-shot. But, yes, let's check together. I'm in the library last period so—"

"I'll meet you there," I say.

"Good deal. Thanks, Nick."

"For what?"

"For talking to me. You don't have to. I mean, I know who your friends are." He darts his eyes over my shoulder again. "They aren't exactly—"

"Nice?"

"I was going to say likable in any way, shape, or form, but that works too."

I glance over at them myself. "I know. I was like them for a long time."

"Was?"

I feel my face get hot. "I'm…trying something…new."

"New is good." Liam then looks puzzled. "So, why are you still hanging out with them? Seems like a case of *old is bad*."

"Great question. Without them, I guess I wouldn't have any friends at all. Totally my fault. But it is what it is."

"Doesn't have to be. New is good. Remember that. I'll

see you after school." He walks away, giving me one last smile over his shoulder.

Could I have a crush on a boy like that? I think, then feel nervous. I've never allowed myself to have a thought like that before. But, as Liam said, new is good, and thinking like that is definitely new territory. This makes me feel happy somehow.

The expressions on the faces of my friends, however, instantly deflates me.

"What're you talking to that swish for?" Ryan asks, shooting Liam's back a disgusted look.

Then most of the guys are talking about Liam, and it's not good talk. Josue actually talks about threatening to beat him up, just to put a scare in him. And I say nothing. I sit, the world's biggest asshole-coward, and let these jerks trash him. Doing nothing but the wrong thing for so long makes it seem impossible to do the right thing, even on a small scale. I sit there, feeling sick inside, thinking, old is *definitely* bad and wondering if change is even possible.

After school, I don't know where Ryan is, but I can't shake Josue. Scott Blair, a stoner douche-canoe who hangs with us sometimes, is hovering, making me wish he and Josue would go find Ryan and leave me alone. Scott won't stop trying to get us to go smoke weed in the back of his mom's Oldsmobile. Josue doesn't want to be alone with Scott, because when Scott gets high, he also gets weirdly philosophical and that sort of thing is way over Josue's head. I've smoked weed once or twice, and honestly, it's not pleasant for me. It makes me feel like I want to start blabbing all my secrets, and that's not something I can afford to do.

I try to walk fast toward the library, but Josue and Scott

won't be shaken. I have anxiety about Liam seeing me with them, and about them seeing me with Liam. I'll examine that conundrum when I'm alone and can drown in self-pity.

When I'm in sight of the library, I can't see Liam anywhere. I wouldn't blame him for ditching me, but I *am* disappointed. I had looked forward to hanging with him, even for just a few minutes. My friends take so much out of me. All the energy of pretending I'm not withdrawing from them is draining. Liam makes me feel the exact opposite. He's calm and genuine. But I know nothing about him other than he loves to dance. And of course, his last name is the name of a horse.

I guess I'm walking toward the theatre alone—even with the pair of nimrods tailing me.

Scott is talking about a bong or something, and Josue is saying the three of us should go to Del Taco after hanging out in Scott's car. Grotesque idea! I'm more preoccupied with the looks I'm about to get as I approach the theatre and the cast-list on the doors.

There's a small crowd gathered, making my heart beat double-time. There are smiles and laughter and hugging. I see dancers from the auditions, and some of the singers, but thankfully, not one of the Muskequeers.

"Stay here," I say.

"Where are *you* going, *güey*?" Josue eyes the milling students with loathing. I wonder if these theatre kids realize their energy and flamboyance make them prime bully-targets. It shouldn't be so, but it is.

Still, I've spent years doing the bullying to hide the fact that I'm just like them. When comparing Mikey and his people with me and mine, who are the happy ones?

"I have to check the cast-list," I say.

"What's a cast-list?" Scott mutters.

"What the shit are you talking about, Nicco?" Josue asks.

I give him an impatient look. "You realize the pre-conversation to *this* conversation happened only, like, two days ago."

"Huh?"

"Auditions?"

Josue goes on looking derpy.

"Dude," I say, "you need to stop hanging out with this jerk." I mime sucking on a joint.

Scott says, "Screw off, Nick!"

"No problem," I say and begin walking away.

"Hey, *güey!*" Josue calls after me. "What in serious hell is going on with you?"

I clench my teeth and keep walking. My friends seem to care as much about what's going on with me and my life as I'm beginning to care about them and theirs.

I slip through the milling students and climb the steps, shaking—maybe even more than at the auditions. There isn't exactly silence, but the chatter falters a bit. Eyes turn to me. When I catch a glance, I try to smile, but it seems to make their reactions to my presence worse.

A pocket of space opens before the paper taped to the glass. The students to either side of me clear off as though I'm a leper.

I look toward the bottom of the list. There I am in bold letters: **WALSH, DONICK—CHORUS/DANCER (dance captain)**. It wasn't a dream, then. I'm really doing this. Dance captain…right there for everyone to see.

At my shoulder, startling me, comes Liam's voice. "Oh

God, did I make it?"

"You *are* here," I say. "What happened? I went by the library."

"Am I on the list or no? Check for me, will you?"

I look, afraid for him—and a little for me. I'm going to need him. I'll have at least one friend if he's around. A grin breaks out on my face. There he is: **HIDALGO, LIAM—DANCER.**

"You made it!" I say, louder than I intend. Heads swivel.

"Really?" He all but shrieks, pushing past me to check for himself. "Sweet Jesus, I've been a wreck all day! What about you? Did you—" he pauses, peering at the list. "Dance captain?" he cries, incredulous. "No way! You're a rock star!"

"I knew already. They told me Tuesday."

"And you didn't say anything?" He gives me a playful push. "What's the matter with you?"

"A lot of things. I didn't want to jinx it. This has been scary."

Liam shows no compunction about having this conversation in the middle of an audience, but I'm suddenly aware of all the listening ears.

Another voice speaks up. "Dance captain? Wow!" It's Mikey's friend, Brent. He's dressed louder than ever in a yellow paisley-print shirt with shiny white buttons. His eyes look strange because he's wearing light-colored contacts. The strap of his purse-thing bisects his narrow chest. He smiles at me as though I've never made fun of him for his hair. There's a bright pink streak running through it today.

"Hey," I say, awkward, worried that Mikey isn't far behind.

"It's deserved. You were brill."

"Thanks." My reply is almost a mumble and my ears

feel like a pair of volcanoes.

"You made it too, Li?" Brent asks. "Good. Now you can chill." He smirks at me. "This big girl has practically been crawling up walls for the last two days."

"He's not the only one," I say. "But, yeah, he was, uh, *brill* too."

"Hear that, Li? Like Gaga telling you you can sing."

Liam says, "You take a lot of energy, Brent. You know that?"

"I've been told." Brent looks over the list again.

"So," I stammer, trying to think of something to say. "How 'bout you? Did you make it in?"

Brent shrugs. "I'm not really about being on stage. I'm gonna stage manage. Mostly I'm here to build sets."

"You *designed* the set," Liam says.

"You did?" The surprise in my tone is almost embarrassing.

Brent nods. "It's my senior-project. I'm the only senior in set design class, so I got to do a scenic design with Mrs. P.'s help. Your set will be a Brent Nanahara exclusive—thank you, thank you very much."

"Very cool," I tell him, and mean it. I hadn't expected someone like him to be into something like carpentry.

Liam asks, "Do you guys know each other?"

"We've interacted." Brent meets my eyes, smiling, albeit peculiarly. "Officially," he goes on, holding out his hand, "I'm Brent."

"Nick, officially." We shake.

"You really did a great job on Tuesday. I don't think anyone on the whole planet expected *that*. We're gonna have a bangin' show."

"My first!" Liam chirps.

I smile at him. "Mine too."

Brent pouts his lips. "Aw! Show virgins!"

I snort and feel the burning in my ears spread to my neck.

Brent suddenly waves his hand in the air and calls across the gathered heads, "Calista, Michael!"

My eyes dart around. Calista and Mikey are standing together, muttering back and forth. Their eyes land on me, expressions dark.

"My sign to vacate, I guess," I murmur. "See you guys later."

Brent continues to wave and his friends reluctantly start up the steps. I keep my gaze averted and ignore them—ignore Mikey. Again. It isn't until I'm walking along the parking-lot that I realize Liam has followed.

"Sorry I didn't meet you," he says. "I saw through the window you were with your friends. I didn't want to interrupt." I know what he means: he didn't want to attract their notice.

"No harm done." Then, feeling out of my element, I ask awkwardly, "You need a ride home or something?"

"Naw. I'm gonna hang out for a while."

He stutters a little when he speaks, his manner shrinking in on itself. I look around and spot Josue and Scott standing a little way off. They're whispering to each other and watching me.

I say, low and quiet, "I wish I could say don't let them bother you, but I know they do. They bother me too. I'd like to tell them to take a hike."

"Then why don't you?"

"It's not that easy."

"Yes it is."

I look at him, but he just shrugs.

"Have a good weekend if I don't see you tomorrow, Nick. First rehearsal on Monday!" He turns and walks back to the theatre.

My car is just beyond Josue and Scott and I have no choice but to pass them. It's then that Josue grins, elbows Scott in the ribs and points. Stepping off the curb nearby is that same small girl from Tuesday, with the same overstuffed backpack, and the same enormous pile of textbooks and binders in her arms.

"Check it out!" Josue exclaims. "Dumb bitch ate it the other day and spilled all her shit on the ground. Frigging classic, dude! I bet she does it again."

I feel dirty. The girl has heard. She jerks her chin away so we won't see her face. So we won't see her hurt expression. She's half expecting, I think, that we might follow her and give her a shove.

Josue is turning his grin in my direction again, when I find my feet changing directions. I beeline for the girl. Her steps falter, expression anxious.

"Hi," I say to her, hoping my smile doesn't look terrifying. It feels terrifying on my face.

"Hi?" she says, like a question.

"Hi," I say again. "Can I give you a hand?"

Surprise falls over her like a blanket, distrust too, but she does try to smile. "Um, that's okay. I'm just walking to the corner. That's where my mom picks me up." She has the barest hint of a lisp.

"At least let me carry some of those books to the corner for you. It's like you're carrying the Matterhorn or something."

She just blinks at me.

"You know, the mountain in Switzerland. Or at Disneyland," I add, feeling stupid. "Seriously, let me help. It's the least I can do."

She glances toward Josue and Scott.

"Don't worry about them. They're jerks. I don't think they know any better."

She looks at me again, still distrustful.

"Here." I hold out my hands, pulling most of the books from her arms. Her expression remains puzzled, but she lets me do it. I gesture with my chin. "That corner at the stoplight?"

"Yeah. Thank you."

I smile again, this time with more feeling. We begin heading in the direction of the streetlight at the edge of the campus.

I say, "I don't know how you carry all this every day. It weighs a ton."

"I'm stretching myself pretty thin."

"These are all eleventh grade books."

"Yeah."

"You're a junior?" I ask in surprise.

She giggles. "Yeah."

"I was banking on freshman."

"I'm short, I know." She giggles again.

"That explains so many books. Junior year is crazy. These are all AP classes."

"I'm stretched *really* thin."

I chuckle with her. After a moment of silence I ask her what her name is.

"Gabby Rosen."

"I'm Nick—"

"—Walsh. Yeah, I know."

"You do?"

"Everyone knows you, practically."

"That old reputation of mine," I murmur.

"Well," she says, "I'm glad you're actually nice."

I stare hard at the American flag on the cover of the book at the top of the pile. The weight of the stack is making my shoulder ache. I say, "What happened the other day? When you dropped everything?"

"Oh my gosh!" Her cheeks go crimson. "So embarrassing!"

"My stupid asshat—I don't even know—*friends* isn't the word anymore—I can't stand them. Those morons should have helped you. They shouldn't have made fun like they did."

"They are kinda mean."

"You don't know the half of it. Anyway, I just wanted to tell you that I'm sorry."

"You don't have to be sorry. You didn't do anything."

"That's what I'm sorry for. I *should* have done something. Helped you pick up your stuff. Told them to shove it, at least. They're so rude."

"Totes rude."

"Anyway, I hope you won't think too badly of me. Wrong place at the wrong time."

We're almost at the corner now. She pauses, brushing a tendril of her pretty hair behind her ear as the breeze tries to catch it. She smiles, her eyes large and sparkling. It still surprises me that she's a junior. She looks like she should just be starting middle school. She barely reaches my chest.

"You're really kind," she tells me. "I wasn't expecting that."

"It's this thing I'm trying." I'm smiling at her, but it feels crooked and self-conscious. "What happened Tuesday bothered me. I saw an opportunity to make it right."

She gives another of her little giggles. "Like that old TV show, *My Name is Earl*. My dad watches it."

"Never seen it."

"It's about this guy who goes around trying to make up for being bad."

And I blank out for a moment.

"Nick?" she presses.

I come back to myself with a shake of my head. "Sorry," I say. "I was just…I dunno, lost for a second."

"There's my mom." She takes the stack of books back into her arms. I tell her I would be happy to help her to the car, but she shakes her head and says she's got it. "Thanks again, Nick."

I call after her. "If you ever see me around school, Gabby, don't be afraid to say hi, even if I'm with those jerks. Yeah?"

She smiles again, then unloads her books into the backseat of the car. Soon she's inside and the car zips away.

I walk slowly toward my own car, deep in thought.

It's about this guy who goes around, Gabby Rosen had said, *trying to make up for being bad.*

I think suddenly of that movie, *Clueless*. It's a favorite of mine, though nobody knows that. I watch it pretty regularly when I'm holed up alone in my bedroom. Young Paul Rudd was hot, what can I say? Alicia Silverstone's character has a moment where she considers giving herself a makeover, only she thinks, *I'll makeover my soul.*

The fragments of my personality, pulled every which

way for years, suddenly begin to see the shape they're supposed to be in.

"*I* need to makeover my soul…" I murmur. But in order to really do that, I have some serious mistakes that need fixing.

I feel lighter, all at once, than I have in years. There might actually be a spring in my step. *Thank you, Gabby Rosen!* I think.

Josue and Scott are still lingering. "Dude," Josue begins, but before he can say anything more to me, Scott elbows him.

"Fag attack! Watch your ass!"

Josue looks, as do I, and it's Mikey and Brent walking through the lot near us. They don't look over, but they have to have heard.

Josue calls, "I wondered why it suddenly smelled so penisy!"

Without turning, Mikey calls back, "Must be you. What else would a dick smell like?"

It's so unexpected to hear Mikey talk like that, and his retort is so perfect, I burst out laughing. Josue, shocked at Mikey, at me, only sputters, looking outraged.

Mikey darts an unreadable look in my direction, then he and Brent turn away, wandering onto the sidewalk in front of campus.

Josue hawks up phlegm and spits at his feet.

Scott says, "That fairy burned you good, bruh."

"Little bitch!" Josue mutters, glowering. "I'll fuck him up!"

"Yeah, sure you will," I say, still smirking. As I walk away myself, I begin to grin and think, *Truth hurts, doesn't it, Jo?*

MICHAEL

"I don't need more reminders of all that's been broken."

"HERE WE ARE," Calista said on Sunday afternoon, walking into my bedroom with Brent on her heels. We were going to have a last hangout before rehearsals swallowed us. "Safely arrived at Otaku Hall. Oh, cute, babe! You're wearing your glasses today!" Then she nearly did a double-take glancing above my bed. "Good grief! A new wall-scroll?"

Brent grinned at me. "You know you're gay, right?"

"What's gay about two male ice skaters wrapped in each other's arms?" Calista snorted. "What a logo. *Yuri!!! on Ice.* Complete with 26,000 exclamation points."

"Neither of you have watched it," I said. "I want to show you the first couple episodes."

"The day just got gayer."

"Said the big butch lezbo," Brent quipped.

They threw themselves on the bed and I took the desk-chair.

"What's this juicy thing you wanted to tell us?" Brent asked.

My cheeks warmed. Adjusting my glasses, I tugged open the desk-drawer.

"Friday during lunch," I began, "we were hanging out in Mrs. P.'s room, right? Remember when I left to go to my locker? Well, there was something inside."

"Some bastard didn't shove anything gross in there, did they?" Calista asked.

"I dunno," I answered. "What counts as gross?"

"Remember in tenth grade when some asshat shoved in a bunch of pages torn out of a gay-porn mag?"

I reached into the drawer. "Judge for yourself."

I handed over a piece of paper folded in fourths to make a sort of greeting card. Drawn in red marker on the front was a lopsided heart.

"Ooh! A love note?" Calista's eyes brightened.

"Open it and see."

She and Brent peered into the card. I had looked at it so many times I had the message memorized, but Calista still read it out loud.

"'It's clichéd and old-fashioned, I know, but Michael Penrose has a secret admirer. I hope he doesn't mind if I admire him from afar because I think he's sort of wonderful.'" She looked at me, eyes serious. "What do you think?" she asked, as Brent took the card to look it over again. "Someone's messing with you?"

"Dunno. I didn't even know how to react when I found it. I thought it was a joke. But now…I dunno."

"I'd kill for someone to admire *me* from afar," Brent said. "Everyone just admires me to my face."

"Be serious. Do you think it's a joke?"

Brent shrugged. "It's kinda, like, elaborate for a joke. What if some asshole like those douches from outside the theatre tried this and got caught. It might look a *little* weird."

"Do you *want* it to be for real?" Calista asked.

I blushed again. "Maybe. I mean, it could be a psycho. Or someone completely disgusting."

"You make it sound as though a psycho is more desirable than someone completely disgusting."

"Like someone without a penis!" said Brent. "Totally disgusting!"

Calista rubbed at her eyes. "So much gay."

"It has to be a *guy*, though, right?" I said. "I mean, everyone knows about me. And say it is serious. Say some guy somewhere is…um…into me."

"Don't say it like it's impossible, babe. Of the three of us, you've had the most action."

"Well, Brent…he's had a lot of…crushes."

"Hookups, you mean. But *you've* dated. Like, for real. Brent and I can't say that."

"I've had exactly two boyfriends, neither lasting longer than three months. I'm sort of nil in the action department. Nothing aside from making out ever happened. And where are those boyfriends now? Both of them left school."

"Maybe you should've done more than make out," Brent said. Calista smacked his shoulder. "Do you ever hear from Dillon?" Brent then asked.

"He never kept in touch," I said. "And Joel is at that art school now. From what I hear, he's dating, like, the whole tenor section of his choir. So, no, I don't hear from either of them. Besides, who'd want to? They were lame. Either too gay, or not gay enough."

"What does that mean?" said Calista.

"It means I don't want some guy who's afraid to own up to who he is. Dillon always made a big deal of questioning whether or not he really was into guys. And Joel? Come on. The walking pride-parade? He never saw anything of value in himself that wasn't connected to his orientation. Where's the normal guy who sits right in the middle? Besides, Joel was short and Dillon was even shorter. Not into it."

"Jeez, babe, I don't know whether to say you're superficial, or not. Look, it was one card. Unless you're getting stuff like that every day, it's a non-issue. A secret admirer doesn't necessarily mean that person has a crush on you."

This notion disappointed me.

"I mean, *I* admire you," she went on. "But if you think I might be crushing on you, Michael, the whole foundation of our friendship is in jeopardy."

Brent snorted.

Calista added, "Maybe it's some girl somewhere who appreciates your friendship. Or a guy. I'm just saying. You probably know the person and this is their good deed for the week."

I dropped the card back into the darkness of the drawer. "I don't know what to think," I said. "I've never had anyone do something like this before."

"Let's talk about your birthday party instead," said Brent. "It'll put off the animated ice-skating. Eighteen! You need to start thinking of hotties we can invite. Maybe some hunk from the GSA will come and we can get you some action. Otherwise, it'll just be your dad at the piano. Snore."

"Speaking of party invites." Calista looked closely at me. "Are you still going to invite the *whole* Revue cast?"

"That's another thing," I said. "I talked to my parents and they think I should go ahead with the original plan, but I'm not so sure."

"Why?" Brent asked. "What?"

Calista said, "This is about Nick Walsh."

"Ooh! Eye-candy! He *needs* to be there!"

I sighed. "If I invite the whole cast, that's a possibility. I can't just invite some of them to avoid *him*."

Brent's brow furrowed. "What's the big? You used to be friends a long time ago, right?"

"It's complicated," said Calista. "Even I know that. But you've never told all the deets."

I bit my lip for a second or two. "All right," I then said. "Here's what happened." And I told it, beginning to end, leaving nothing out—not the kiss, not Mr. Walsh's gross tirade, not my head bashed into a locker. Neither of my friends had heard the whole story. When I finished, two pairs of eyes, round as quarters, stared at me.

"No wonder you hate him so much," Calista said.

"I don't hate him! I just…can't stand him. He's an asshole. And he's been an asshole to each of you at one time or another, don't forget."

"I don't hold onto crap like that," said Brent. "What am I gonna do with it? Besides, with shoulders like that, not to mention those legs…damn!"

"Gag," I said. "Donick Walsh is a homophobe."

"If he's a homophobe then someone needs to tell him how that works, because he was pretty chummy with Liam Hidalgo."

Calista said, "They were looking at the cast-list together."

I thought of Liam and felt a spark of irritation. Then guilt. I couldn't expect Liam to dislike Donny just because I did. Liam was a nice kid, reminding me a lot of Brent—only with the flamboyance dialed down.

"All I know is," Brent went on, "that when I talked to him outside the theatre, he seemed different. Not so fucktarded."

"He probably knows he has to be on best behavior," I said, "or Mrs. P. will kick him out of the show. I don't even know why he's doing the show anyway. Who cares if he can dance? The theatre is not his place."

Calista frowned. "He *has* to do the show, babe."

"*Has* to? Why?" Suddenly I felt very interested.

"Because of what happened in football."

"I don't follow football. And I sure as hell don't keep tabs on *that* jerk."

"Nick's shoulder is basically shot. Ruined." Calista exchanged a look with Brent, reluctantly adding, "It's kinda sad, actually."

"Totes," said Brent. "He can't play anymore. He has to do the Revue because there's been some, like, screw up with his credits. I heard Mrs. P. talking about it. Without football, he won't graduate unless he does the show. It's some arrangement through the dance department."

I started to speak, then fell quiet. That's why he hadn't played football this year. Even I wasn't blind to his potential to go to an amazing university on his football skill, let alone a future beyond that. At last, I asked, "How did he hurt it?"

"I don't know all the details," said Calista, "but it sounds pretty bad. He was in the hospital last year and missed, like, a ton of school. I remember hearing something about it."

After another pause, I said, "I really want to say he deserves it."

"But you won't," Calista said pointedly. "Because that would make *you* an asshole."

"I won't. That sucks. It does. That explains why he's been so…not himself this year. Kind of quiet, I guess. Withdrawn."

"But you don't keep tabs on him or anything."

"We had Spanish together last semester," I said, feeling defensive. "His avoidance of me seems particularly pointed. He can't even get up the energy to give me dirty looks anymore."

"It's gotta be lonely, you know? He has this path to success marked out for him, treats most everyone like a jerkhole in the process, then he loses it all. It makes me wonder how many people actually visited him in the hospital, or asked him how he's doing."

I gave a bitter laugh. "We're actually talking about Donick Walsh like he's not an ass."

"He's *totally* an ass. And maybe he'll be on best behavior so he gets his credits from the show, and then he'll regress right back. But maybe not. He has no choice but to get to know a lot of kids he's spent his whole life treating like garbage."

"Theatre changes people," Brent put in.

"Not him," I said. "He's always been an ass, and he'll always stay an ass. Despite whatever happened to him."

"Except, from what you told us, he *wasn't* always an ass."

"Don't split hairs, B."

"I think," said Calista, "you have to invite him to your party. Like it or not, he's part of the cast. He's never done anything like this before and he's out of his element. Yes, he did a shitty, mean thing to you—to a lot of us. But there are two kinds of theatre people. There are the shit-talking, fame-hungry, backstabbing diva bitches, and the do-anything-for-you, welcoming to all, make-you-a-part-of-their-family types. Which are you gonna be?"

I groaned. "Fine. Everyone gets an invite. Including Donny, or Nick, or whatever he calls himself now. But I don't have to be his friend."

"None of us want to be his friend, but we can at least make sure we keep as much tension out of the show as possible. Obviously your history with him is a little more intense than anyone else's. After all," she added, beginning to grin, "he was your first kiss."

"You suck."

"I can't believe you never told me."

"It's ancient history."

Brent *tsk*ed. "Please, Michael, if that history was so ancient, we wouldn't be talking about it now."

"Well, I don't want to talk about it anymore. Let's watch TV."

"First, pizza!" he said. "Calista, order!"

She tugged out her phone. "Boys."

DONICK

"So where's the challenge if you never try?"

I CAN'T BUILD UPWARD with my foundation full of cracks. Gabby Rosen made me realize that. Those cracks are the student body of Kliewer High. I damaged that foundation, therefore, I'm the only one who can patch it. That can only be done one person at a time. Some of these kids have been at my mercy for years. An apology won't erase that. But I have to try. Whether they forgive me or not is none of my business. I can only own my mistakes.

Of course, I already know who will be the hardest person to make amends to: Mikey. To him, I'll have to be honest about what a hypocrite I've been.

And because of Mikey, I do something that has me in a cold panic all weekend.

Friday morning, I spot my buds in the quad, bundled in sweatshirts, yet still wearing their flimsy gym-shorts. They snicker and snort, all while Josue carefully folds a sheet of paper.

Starting my morning in their company is the last thing I want. Just the sight of them dampens the bright mood I've been in since yesterday. Besides, the library is calling.

I want to get warm there and wait for first period with my nose stuck in *The Awakening*, which won't read itself and might be detrimental to an upcoming vocabulary project in English 11. I *need* to pass that course this time around.

Ryan spots me, however, and waves me over.

"Jo has a great idea!" he snorts.

Josue grins. "I'm gonna get that *pinché joto* that mouthed off to me yesterday."

My gut sinks. "Michael Penrose?"

"Yeah. Michael fucking Penrose!"

"What? Because he called you a dick?"

"I'm not letting him get away with it."

"Wish I'd been there," Ryan puts in. "I would have shoved my foot up his ass."

Josue cackles. "He'd've liked that!"

"He was right though," I say. "You *were* being a dick. You're both being dicks right now."

Ryan squints at me. "What's your problem?"

I want to say, "*You guys* are my problem!" but I only ask Josue what he's planning.

"Why?" he snaps. "Gonna run and tell the little poodle-walker?"

"I don't talk to that dipshit," is my response. I even manage a passable scowl as though the very idea is gross.

And I don't want to call Mikey that, but it slips out, courtesy of these stellar human beings. Not to mention my old habits. Can't let anyone know I've been thinking about Mikey *a lot* these last few days.

"You're eighteen years old, Jo," I add. "You're gonna graduate next year. *This* is what you're doing?"

"Check out Saint Nicco," Josue mutters. On the front

of the make-shift card he begins outlining a sloppy heart with a red Sharpie.

"Get outta here if you're not gonna, like, take that stick outta your ass," Ryan says to me. Then he slaps Josue's shoulder. "Dude, it's perfect! It totally looks like a love note or some shit. You should just write, like, *ass pirate* inside!"

"Naw, *güey*. I should write something that he'll think is serious." Josue cackles again. "*Love, your secret admirer*, you know? He'll shit himself!"

I reach out and snatch the paper from where he uses *American Voices* as a desk. His face flares with fury. "Don't be a prick!" he snaps.

"Think about this, dumbass," I snap back. "I have to spend the next few months in rehearsals with Michael Penrose and all his friends. Crap like this starts happening, who do you think will get blamed? I can't have my credits jeopardized by getting kicked out of the Revue. I won't graduate if that happens." I flap the card in the air. "*This* is the dumbest shit ever. *You're* acting like a prick."

I start to walk away, pushing the folded paper into the pocket of my hoodie.

"Screw you, Nicco!" Josue shouts. I hear him get to his feet. "You break your shoulder *and* your personality? I'll fuck you up, *puto*!"

I turn suddenly to face him, taller and brawnier than he could ever hope to be. "You can try," I say.

Ryan pushes between us, laughing awkwardly. "Come on, this is whack. Jo, sit down. Nick, I don't know what's going on with you, but you need to, like, build a bridge. You're no fun anymore."

"None of us have been any fun, ever. It's time to grow

up. Leave Michael Penrose alone. Both of you. I mean it."

I walk away, leaving my "friends" to stew. I think avoidance of each other is on its way to being a permanent fixture. My friendships with them have always been a dead-end, I see that now. Who I am, the *real* me, is not someone they would want to pal around with. It will royally suck to be treated like some sort of Ralph Wiggum for the remainder of my last year of high school, but peace of mind is much more important.

I sit at an empty library table, feeling too keyed up to concentrate on my reading. I tug out the folded card, its lopsided heart vibrant against the white paper. I imagine myself finding something like it in *my* locker, full of promise, only to see jaunty rainbow letters calling me QUEER, or permanent-marker telling me to SUCK A DICK. I picture Mikey finding it. The hurt he would feel makes me queasy.

I think of all those theatre kids who like him; how he has a witty comeback for assholes like Josue; how he doesn't care what people think of him. He likes all that dorky stuff that has always appealed to me too, but which I pretend not to like anymore. Not to mention that heart-stopping singing-voice.

Suddenly, I realize Mikey *does* have a secret admirer… and it's me!

Jesus, but sometimes I miss my friend!

So I decide to do something stupid. I'm going to push this card through the slats of Mikey's locker myself. Only I'm going to write something genuine inside. Someone out there thinks he's wonderful, only he never needs to know it's me. I'll let this card tell him, since *I* could never work up the nerve. Maybe, somehow, it might help make up for the past. After all, he was my first kiss. I don't really remember it, but it's the only kiss I've experienced so far that mattered.

Still, I have to be careful. It can't say anything overly mushy, or…well, *gay*. I want it neutral, yet heartfelt, a testament to the friendship I miss and should never have thrown away. It has to be something that anyone might write. I jot an idea or two in my notebook. When I know what I want to say I carefully pen it in a strange slanting script, finishing just as the bell rings.

Right before lunch, I leave class with a bathroom-pass, the folded paper in my pocket. I know where Mikey's locker is because it's in the same hall as mine. I make sure the area is clear, then, with my breath locked in my lungs, I pass his locker, pause, and slip the card inside. For a tense instant, I think the paper will be too thick to fit through the slat, but at last it shoots home. I almost run like hell, thinking, *Holy crap! What did I just do?*

I then spend the weekend worrying the idea like a dog with a bone. I'm positive that, somehow, everyone will know what I've done when I walk into school on Monday.

IF I THOUGHT entering the theatre for the auditions was difficult, it's nothing compared to the fright and anxiety I feel walking in for the first rehearsal.

I had hoped to see Liam Hidalgo at some point on Monday. It would make it much easier if I could walk in with him and not feel completely friendless. But he and I don't cross paths. I resign myself to making my entrance all by my lonesome. Then I think about arriving late to avoid having to sit by myself, but a good impression is better, so I go right to the theatre once school ends.

The teachers are already inside, greeting students and talking together. On the stage is a broad ring of chairs—about fifty in all. Here is Liam, at last, but he's sitting with a couple of his pals (one of whom is Jackie Skarupa), so I know I can't rely on him as a buttress. Mrs. Peebles smiles at me, Mr. Hardy shakes my hand, Chalice pats my arm. I know the teachers are on my side, at least. Still, my stomach knots.

I give Liam a little wave. Jackie glances at me, then looks miserable and says something close to Liam's ear. *Not* too *obvious*, I think, but I can't allow it to bother me. I sit in an empty chair and wait awkwardly, my backpack in my lap, tugging out my iPhone and opening random apps for something to focus on. I hope I don't look as desperately out of my element as I feel. Random girls sit to either side of me, telling me again how they had no idea I could dance. I'm grateful not to look so lost anymore. Also, it's a comfort to realize not everyone is going to dislike me right off the bat. However, there are plenty who would rather sit on the floor than sit next to me.

I hear the sound of Mikey's and Brent's voices before I actually see them. Their friendliness to everyone makes me envious. I watch Mikey's face, feeling my cheeks get hot when his eyes skip to me, then skip away. For a moment, he looks very unhappy. If it wasn't simply my presence bending him out of shape, I might almost make myself panic and think he knows I sent him that secret admirer note. He and Brent plant themselves not far from me—out of my line of sight, thank goodness. I'm finding it difficult not to look at Mikey whenever he's present. It's like looking at an interesting stranger, made all the more interesting because he wasn't always a stranger.

Calista appears a moment later, wearing enormous glasses on her face, plopping down in the seat between her friends.

Mrs. Peebles steps into the circle after a minute and calls for attention. Voices die away. Every chair is full.

"Welcome to the Senior Showcase Revue, guys!" Immediate cheering. Mrs. Peebles speaks louder to take back attention and everyone quiets instantly. "For those new to our family, I'm Mrs. Peebles. Or just Mrs. P. I'm the drama teacher here at Kliewer High." Applause. And more applause when she then introduces Chalice, followed by Mr. Hardy.

Happiness glows from every face, and though I try to look excited, I feel weird joining the cheering.

Mrs. P. goes on, explaining that rehearsals are Monday through Thursday, with a few Saturdays. Thinking with some measure of panic that that's a lot of time I'll have to account for to Pop, I barely hear that Monday and Wednesday will be for singing, with Tuesday and Thursday for dance.

"Oh, and Spring Break will fall right in the middle of everything," Mrs. P. adds. "Don't worry, we won't be calling rehearsals during the week you guys are off. Otherwise, attendance is crucial. Sometimes emergencies happen and life gets in the way, but still…when you're here, there's more of a chance you'll be in the numbers we're working on. We often choose singing parts from who's at rehearsal. When you're present, you get featured. If you're consistently absent, parts get taken away. Just so we're all clear on how this works. We've got a monster of a show, but it always ends up a success."

Mrs. P. then says what seem to be magic words: the

revue's song-list and the theme for this year's show. A buzz ripples through the cast.

"Our theme," she says with a dramatic pause, "is 'Born to Make History'!" The buzzing turns into more cheers. "For those of you who've never done a Senior Revue, this means we explore various ideas based on that theme. We'll use music from shows and artists who are just that: history makers. We'll also explore ideas about our own personal histories. Some numbers are for fun and variety, but a lot were chosen with the theme in mind. We always try to be very uplifting as a send-off for our seniors. A special thank you to Michael Penrose. He helped with the set-list and suggested many songs that helped flesh things out."

Once again Michael shocks me, though I can't bring myself to glance over at him.

It's Chalice's turn to talk now. She wears a black leotard and black jazz pants, the overhead work-lights throwing her corded arms into sharp relief. I know what's coming: the dance captain announcement. My dread has me losing her train of speech. After a minute, it comes. My face gets hot. She's calling names, and suddenly, I'm being told to stand along with three other dancers. Now my face, my neck, my ears absolutely *burn*. I bet I look like a tomato. I get to my feet, sliding my backpack to the floor, sure I've stopped breathing. The other dance captains also stand, though they look way more at ease. Chalice begins clapping and the rest of the cast joins in. I try to smile…and fail, I'm pretty sure.

"These are the dancers to go to about choreography," Chalice says, "I teach it, then move on. Do *not* come to me. I won't have the answer you want." She smiles to show she isn't intending to be harsh.

There's another smattering of applause. I've never been more thankful for anything than I am to sit again and try to disappear.

"Come in jazz attire tomorrow, dancers," Chalice continues. "I won't be as strict with the dress-code as I am in class, but please wear jazz shoes or jazz sneakers unless I tell you I want something different. *Don't* be late! We warm up first and…well, I guess I can go ahead and announce it. This year, one of our biggest dance numbers is going to be Madonna's 'Vogue'." Gasps and murmurs follow this, the dancers smiling and grabbing at each other. "We'll start in on it tomorrow. It'll be one of the few times we'll use a track and not live music. Be on your A-game and ready to work."

Chalice gives way to Mr. Hardy. He speaks quickly, saying something about learning company numbers first, and that solos, duets, group songs will come later. Then he's talking about harmonies and how we should bring something to record our vocal parts during rehearsals. But I've zoned out again.

The entire experience has suddenly become very real. I'm overwhelmed by the information, by the gathered students, by the concept of *me* learning to do all these things.

I come back to the present when Mrs. P. again steps forward.

"I would like to introduce two more students who are going above and beyond," she says. "First, Brent Nanahara." Brent actually blows kisses to the kids who cheer for him. "Brent is our set designer and stage manager. We'll definitely need all spare hands. If you can volunteer any time, we would appreciate it. If Brent asks for help, please consider saying yes. He's designed a beautiful set and it won't build itself."

I have to chuckle. If I volunteer, I'll be removing the lie I told Pop.

"And next," Mrs. P. continues, "Calista Martinez, go ahead, stand!"

Calista rises and someone says, "Where'd you get those glasses?"

"Calista will be doing double duty, singing in the show, and taking charge of wardrobe. She'll actually build some costume pieces from scratch, but we also have a lot in our stores. Some things you'll all have to provide yourself, but we'll have a lot here for you."

Calista raises her voice and takes charge.

"I'm going to need to get everyone's measurements. There's a lot of you and only one of me, so please be patient. Today I want the seniors to stick around so I can get a head-start with them. I'll try to get to everyone else over the next couple weeks. And please! Once I start pulling pieces for you and you begin trying stuff on, I don't want any complaints about the look or style of your costumes. These *are* costumes, *not* street clothes. Meaning you aren't always going to feel comfortable. Just suck it up!"

She sits.

Calista is just…sassy and…well, cool. She seems like someone I might really like to be friends with. How could I have been so blind to how amazing people can be? But she won't want to be in the same room with me if she can avoid it.

Mrs. P. dismisses us a few minutes later, reminding everyone to check the contact-list to ensure all phone numbers and e-mails are accurate. The gathered students clap one last time when she lets us go. I'm relieved that this first meeting is over. I tell myself that every day will get easier, but for the very first day, I've had enough of new territory.

Mikey is suddenly standing and shouting, "Wait, wait!"

"Oh, yes, I forgot!" Mrs. P. says. "Guys, guys! One last announcement."

Everyone settles again. As Mikey talks, he seems to look at everyone—except me.

"For those who don't know me, I'm Michael Penrose. I wanted to let you all know my birthday is coming up in a couple weeks, my eighteenth!" Cheers erupt. "I'm having a party at my house a week from this coming Friday. I'm giving an invite to everyone. Please come! Think of this as less a birthday party and more of a cast bonding party. We can all hang out and get to know each other."

"Michael has a serious party house," Brent puts in.

"There's going to be lots of food and soda and stuff. There's a pool too, and a hot-tub, if you want to bring swimsuits. And it's a sleepover. There's tons of room and people can crash wherever."

Calista snorts, "And Michael's dad will be playing piano all night." There's laughter; several people are nodding and exchanging looks. I had forgotten Mikey's dad is a music teacher.

"So if anyone wants to being sheet music to contribute to the squareness," Mikey adds, "there'll be plenty of opportunities to sing or whatever. It wouldn't be a party at my place without that. I hope everyone will come. Help me turn eighteen, and let's become a family and stuff!"

He finishes with an appealing smile and sits again.

A few second later, the exodus officially begins, but not before a lengthy lingering of cast-members chattering and acting hyper. A lot of them are waiting to see the song-list for the show, which Mrs. P. is taping to one wall.

"Seniors!" Calista shouts. "Meet me in the back hallway! Be patient! I think there are fourteen of us!" She vanishes through a door in the wings, followed by a handful of students.

I'm feeling self-conscious again, and wish I could run away. Students pass back and forth, but mostly they ignore me. Liam waves goodbye, but doesn't come near. I take my backpack down the stairs and find a seat in the front row of the house, pulling out *The Awakening*, attempting to read for a few minutes. I figure I'll wait until most of the cast has left before I go find Calista.

Also, I want to think; putting Kate Chopin in my face makes it seem like I'm busy.

Mikey's birthday is coming, and he's having a party. I remember his house well—enormous and sprawling with a huge backyard. Brent is right, it really is a party house. Only, I've never been there for one. Apparently, from the vibes I got, many people have. I can imagine Ryan's and Josue's reactions if they found out I had been to a party with all these theatre kids.

Not that I would seriously consider going. I know better than to assume Mikey's invite includes me. I have no business being at the Penrose house. I betrayed my best friend. Seeing Mikey's parents again after all these years...I know I would never be welcome.

How I wish things weren't so complicated. Because I want to go. I want to be there with everyone, trying to build new friendships and have experiences that are the complete opposite of the BS going on with my usual crowd. But I won't ruin Mikey's birthday by forcing my presence on him, or anyone else.

A shadow falls over me. I glance up to find Brent. He's standing with his hands on his hips, silver studs winking from his white leather belt. He's also wearing white loafers with no socks and his pants rolled above his ankles. Even the streak running through his hair looks white today.

With a little stammer, I say, "Hey, Brent. What's up?"

"I need to ask a favor."

"Building sets?"

"I know you'll be wicked busy with the show—dancing and singing and all—but I was hoping if, when you have time, you'd volunteer. We've got a lot of stuff to build."

"Yes," I say without a pause.

He looks surprised. "Really?"

"Yeah. Just let me know. If I'm available, you got me."

He looks pleased. He's still wary of me, but that stiffness in him seems less. "Thanks," he says. "You've got your whole shoulder thing, I know, but we won't have you do any heavy lifting."

"I'm cool with whatever. It keeps me from lying to my dad." I don't know why I tell him that.

"Lying to your dad?"

"He doesn't know I'm doing the show. He wouldn't approve. If I tell him I'm helping out with woodshop, it won't exactly be lying, and I'll have no trouble being at rehearsal."

"Why doesn't your dad approve?"

There's something in Brent's voice when he asks this—a hint of…I don't know…*knowing*, I guess. I'm sure Mikey has already filled him in on the kind of man my father is.

I make a face. "He's a grouchy asshole. Doesn't like plays and stuff."

"He was okay with you dancing?"

"That was for football. All things serve the pig-skin."

"Gross."

"You're not wrong."

"Anyway, that was all I wanted. I'll let you get back to your book."

Brent turns away, but I call after him, almost without knowing I'm going to do it. "Will you sit with me a minute?" I say. "I just—I—*will* you sit?"

There's the tiniest pause. He gives a look around, hesitance all over him. Then, maybe because he's curious, he lowers himself into the seat beside mine. His back is stiff, and so is his voice when he says, "What's up?"

I start talking, fumbling for the right words. I try to meet his eyes, but it's difficult.

"I don't know exactly how to say this, so I guess I'm just gonna blurt it out. I know I haven't been…great to you over the years. I—I've said some pretty ugly things and called you a lot of bad names. I just need you to know I'm sorry for it. If I could take it all back, I would." I sigh, feeling like I can't catch my breath. "I know you won't ever be able to forget it. I haven't. I just—I *am* sorry. I don't want you to worry about me doing anything or saying anything like that to you ever again. If I can keep my jerky friends from bothering you, I will." I make a scoffing sound. "Best of luck to me with that."

He's watching me with no expression. He isn't wearing his eyeliner today or his colored contacts.

"You've been really cool to me shea last few days," I add, "talking to me when most people won't. Not that I blame anyone. I guess…well, any help I can be when it comes to your sets, please ask. I owe you big time."

He keeps on staring. I begin to think he's going to tell me to screw off. But he just shrugs. "It's cool," he says. "I don't hold onto crap like that."

I chuckle nervously. "You and I are…are cool, then?"

"Cool as a fridge."

"I'm glad. You're better than me. I don't think…well, I don't think I could even stand to be in the same room with somebody who treated me like that."

He chews the inside of his lip, glancing at the stage where a handful of seniors are talking amongst themselves, waiting to get in to see Calista. Mikey is there. Every once in a while his gaze shifts in our direction, like he's wondering what his best friend and his worst enemy could be talking about. I suddenly hope Brent won't tell Mikey what I've said to him. But I have no right to ask that.

"You have a lot of people to win over, Nick," Brent says.

"I know."

"People like you and your friends, the types who attack others for the things about themselves they can't change… that's the most lasting kind of damage there is. Look at me. Your friends see how I dress, my hair, the eyeliner, and they attack it. All that stuff is me. When someone hates me for it, it makes it really hard to *be* me. But I don't know how to be anyone else. When I get called a faggot, or any of the other things I hear almost on a daily basis from certain people on this campus, it can be a real head-trip. Those people don't approve of me. But, like, I have nothing else to give."

His words strike home on a very personal level.

"I know what you mean," I say.

We sit in silence for a moment longer. Then Brent gets to his feet.

"Well, I appreciate what you said. And I appreciate you being willing to help with the set. I gotta go ask a few more people to pitch in if they can."

"Call me anytime."

"Thanks," he says, and smiles at me. "See ya."

As he walks away, I release a pent up breath. That was so such harder than I expected. But Brent is one less enemy than I had before.

When I get in to have Calista take my measurements, she's all business and barely speaks to me. I think about trying to break the ice with another apology, but somehow it doesn't seem like the right time. I do tell her I like her glasses, and though she looks surprised, and says they're fake, it doesn't defrost her. Still, I know she's someone I want to be friends with. I only hope, like with all the people I owe apologies to, that I haven't burned my bridges permanently.

MICHAEL

"Soul is in the musical."

THOUGH MOST SENIORS went home for the day at lunch, we Muskequeers took a last period drama class with Mrs. Peebles. We should have been reading scenes, but with our first singing rehearsal tomorrow, we were too preoccupied to give much thought to modern playwrights.

"What songs are you the most excited about, Michael?" Liam asked.

"Well, I love 'History Maker'. That's going to be the finale."

"Is that from a musical or a movie?"

Calista rolled her eyes. "Here we go…"

"Zip it!" I said to her. Then to Liam, "It's a song from an anime. It's phenomenal, *and* sung in English. I recommended it sort of as a joke, but Mrs. P. dug it. Now it's the Revue's theme."

"I don't really watch that stuff," Liam said. "What else?"

Brent put in, "Well, I'm…*wicked* stoked about 'Popular'."

"Of course you are," I said, shaking my head and making a face. "It's overdone. *That* I did *not* recommend."

"I'm all over the inclusion of some Bowie," Calista said.

Brent asked, "Which song is that?"

"The masquerade scene from *Labyrinth*," Liam said. "I love that movie. You should totally sing it, Michael."

"Not my style. Besides, it could be a girl. Mrs. P. is always switching song genders around. We sort of make our own versions of stuff. My first Revue, we did 'All I Ask of You' from *Phantom*, and had two girls sing it to each other."

"It was pretty hot," Calista said. "That's when I started figuring stuff out."

Liam's face lit up. "I can hardly believe I'm in the show."

"First dance rehearsal for you today, babe. Excited?"

"Scared. I suck. I hope Chalice will go easy on the dancers who aren't like, um…you know, those other famous male dancers…"

Brent added, "Or like Nick Walsh?"

"Thank God he's in the show," Liam said. My insides fumed. "I'm gonna need so much help."

Brent grinned. "Look at your face, Li! You're blushing! You aren't crushing on Nick, are you?"

I glanced sharply at Liam. Sure enough, his flush deepened. He dropped his eyes and laughed awkwardly.

"Nothing like that. I mean, he's über hot! Don't you think he's über hot? But he's not my type. He's too…I dunno…dude-like."

Brent laughed. "Like Calista, only with a penis." That earned him a single finger salute.

"And too tall," Liam added. "I'd rather the guy I'm into be closer to my height. But still…Nick's really nice."

"Nice is different than good," I mumbled.

"It would be easy for anyone to crush on him, girl or guy."

"Except for the monster homophobe hiding somewhere in that dude-like, über hot, male Calista," I snapped. All three stared. "Ignore me. Let's get back to the music, yeah?"

The discussion continued: Songs from *Hairspray*, *Spring Awakening*, *The Music Man*, "Drive My Car" by the Beatles, "Cover Girl" by New Kids on the Block ("Not the RuPaul song?" Brent giggled.), "Girl For All Seasons" from *Grease 2*. My Muskequeers grimaced at that one.

"Hey," I said, "it's a very underrated film."

Liam was beginning to say, "What about that song from *Chicago*? The one nobody ever seems to like. Isn't that more of a solo dance sort of thing?" when my phone vibrated. A text from Mom. My heart started to race.

It said: *Something in the mail from CalArts!!!* Smiley face, thumbs up. *It's waiting on the kitchen counter when you get home.*

A very embarrassing squeal popped from my mouth. A good portion of the class darted looks my way.

"Can we deal with that sound you just made?" Calista asked.

Bouncing in my chair, I read them the text.

Calista grinned and rubbed her hand in my hair. It was a curly mess anyway so, oh well. "Are you excited?" she asked. "CalArts, babe!"

"I don't know if I got in," I said. "It might be a rejection."

"It might be an *acceptance*. You're totally in! Don't be nervous."

"I'm not. Okay, I *am* nervous! This is my first response."

"Out of how many again?" Brent asked.

"Five. I feel like I've been waiting forever."

"Which school do you want most?"

"CalArts would be fine. I mean, an art school. What could be better? But, I dunno. I want to aim for New York. It's a toss up between NYU and Juilliard."

Liam asked, "How do you feel your auditions went?"

"Great! But they don't accept very many new students each year."

"Competition is fierce," added Calista

"I've got fingers crossed for a clean sweep. It'd be a dream come true to be able to have my pick of all five. But after this waiting, I'd be happy with just *one*."

The bell rang soon after, and Liam all but ran from the room to head to rehearsal.

"Let's swing by the dance-studio on the way off campus," said Brent. "I wanna watch the warmup."

"Watch the boys in their jazz pants you mean," Calista muttered. "I need more lesbians in my life."

"So do I! I would never have to go to a mechanic, or hire a plumber."

"You're a jerk. Did you know?"

I told them to go on without me because I wanted to talk to Mrs. P. for a few minutes and tell her about my CalArts letter. My jumpy nerves needed one of her pep-talks. She had been the one who helped me decide on schools to apply to, and had coached me through my audition monologues. But being in a rush, needing to get to the dance rehearsal too, I ended up walking to the studio with her while we talked.

"Whether a school accepts you or not," she said, "has no real bearing on your talent. I auditioned at a lot of schools when I was your age and didn't get into any of the ones I wanted. I don't know anymore what my object was as an actress, but things fall out the way they need to. You get where you need to be that way. Maybe if I had gone to the Tisch School I would be in a touring cast somewhere, or working on a movie right this second. But my path led me to being a teacher. My work is infinitely more rewarding here."

"You mean you'd much rather be advising me on college stuff," I asked, grinning, "than rubbing elbows with Chris Hemsworth?"

"Make that Leonardo DiCaprio and we can reevaluate."

I snorted. "Leonardo DiCaprio?"

"Hey, *Titanic* was my day. Your generation has no appreciation for the young, hot Leo."

"No such thing."

We had reached the dance-studio. There I found my Muskequeers with a few other students leaning against the frame of the open doors, watching. About thirty dancers, mostly outfitted in form-fitting black, barefoot, ranged across the room in lines like an army of Bob Fosses. Already music throbbed from inside, loud 80's pop with a lot of percussion and staccato bass notes. Mrs. P. passed inside and I paused by my friends.

"You decided to come watch?" Brent asked.

"Hardly." I lowered my voice. "I can do without the sight of Donny—or Nick or whatever—learning how to vogue."

"Don't knock the voguing. It's the only gay dance-form we have."

"You mean aside from all the other forms of dance? Besides, I look like some sort of stalker showing up like this. We loath each other. This will be weird enough without my making guest-appearances at rehearsals I have no business coming to."

"You're overreacting. Nick is actually turning out to be all right."

"Have you seen my scar?" I spat.

"My dear friend," Brent replied, giving me serious side-eye and a weird smile, "I'm not the right boy for you to be asking."

Calista mumbled, "Gross. Gay guys are just all about penis."

Brent and I said in unison, "Duh!" Then we all three burst out laughing. Dancers near the door glanced our way. Mrs. P., close to the front, frowned.

My eyes skipped across the room, easily picking Donny out—so tall and blonde. He and the other dance captains were in the front row directly before the mirrors. Dammit! Donny looked good—again! How could someone who was such an asshole look so graceful? *It's not freaking fair!* I said to myself, something I had begun to say a lot when confronted with my old not-friend.

I felt my face grow warm. He had spied me in the mirror, his cheeks reddening. Thinking, *Bastard!* I began walking away. Calista and Brent followed.

"Seriously," Brent said. "When he apologized to me, he sounded sincere. I was impressed. I didn't *want* to be. And I didn't want to believe him. But I did."

"I didn't even give him the chance to say anything to me," Calista put in. Her disgusted tone softened. "But if I'm honest, he does seem a little different. I mean, think about the things he's been through lately. It's gotta *do* stuff. I'll admit Brent is more forgiving about things than

I would *ever* be, but it doesn't change the fact that Nick *did* make the effort. That does sort of count for something—and I say that with absolute grudginess."

"Good for him!" I almost shouted. "He apologized to Brent and now they can be BFF. You're beginning to think he's nice, even with grudginess. But I remember what it felt like having my eyebrow sewn back on."

MICHAEL

"The light is dimming, and the dream is too."

*C*ALISTA DROPPED ME off and I darted into the house, beelining for the kitchen, before she even drove away. The twins sat at the table gluing pieces of paper together. I heard Georgie call from upstairs, "Michael's home! *Mom*!" Then the sound of feet.

I eyed the envelope on the counter. My mom and sister appeared, Mom still in scrubs and Georgie with the left side of her hair done in a French-braid, the right bushed out across her shoulder.

"We should wait for Dad, right?" I said.

"Nope," Mom replied. "He said not to. Go ahead." She had her hands clasped under her chin, eyes full of expectation.

I couldn't keep the expression of panic from coming onto my face. "I'm scared."

"Wuss," Georgie murmured, and grabbed at the envelope.

"Don't you dare, Munch!" I said, snatching it up. I weighed it in my fingers, then looked at Mom again, my heart, which had raced with excitement before, now sinking a little. "It's kinda thin. Shouldn't it be thicker?

Or a bigger envelope? If it's an acceptance letter, I mean."

"Not necessarily. Come on, Sweetheart, rip that sucker open."

I tried to answer her grin with one of my own, but it felt like a scream stretching my mouth. I began thumbing the envelope's flap. I pretty much mangled the thing to shreds. I tugged out the sheet of paper and stared at it. I could feel my hands shaking.

There was no chance Mom couldn't clearly see the way my face fell. She put her arms around me. No small feat with how tall I had grown in the last year.

"A no, then?" she murmured.

I tried to smile. "A no."

"Oh, Baby, I'm sorry." She gave me a squeeze.

Georgie cried, "Well, they suck!"

I tried to make my smile bigger, but my heart had now all but halted dead in its tracks. I almost wished I could cry. I hugged Mom back.

"It's okay," I said, trying to sound light. "It is."

"You're waiting on four more, Michael. That could be four yeses. It'll make this one little no seem like nothing."

"Truthfully, I don't want to stay in California anyway. I want to go to New York. You know that. Fingers and toes crossed for NYC."

She smiled in that way mothers do, as though they're putting all their love and affection directly into their faces, sending it out through their eyes.

"That's the spirit. Though a parent doesn't like the idea of their child moving so far away. You might try a little false regret, maybe?"

Georgie said, "I have to finish my hair. Belle's coming

with her mom to pick me up in, like, ten minutes."

She started to leave, but I said, "You wanna watch something with me before bed tonight?"

She paused. "*Fruits Basket*?"

"Doable."

Then my little sister, all thirteen years of her, skipped back up the stairs in her usual whirlwind of energy. Lately, she seemed to be vying for loudest ball of noise on the planet—after Cady and Topher, of course. I still loved the crap out of her, even when she was being more than her fair share of an adolescent. Honestly, there wasn't much more I would rather do than hang out with my siblings. Georgie could be annoying, and the twins were always getting into my stuff, but I was still their big brother. Sometimes I felt like I loved them like a dad.

As I shoved the rejection letter into my backpack, I said to Mom, "An actor's life is all about getting told no, so this is good practice."

"You want a snack or something?" she asked. "Grilled cheese?"

I scoffed. "You probably had your hands up a camel's butt today. No thanks."

"It wasn't a camel. No rehearsal this afternoon?"

"I'm there tomorrow."

"How is Donick doing?"

I frowned. "I don't know. Why talk about him? Trying to cheer me up?"

"Just curious."

I started for the stairs but she stopped me, hugging me again.

"Mom, I'm fine. Really." My voice sounded hollow to

my own ears, even with the attempt at putting feeling behind it. Some actor. A rejection shouldn't shock me.

"Four more letters on their way," she repeated. "The law of averages…or something. Meanwhile, do you want to text your dad, or should I?"

"I can do it," I said, then headed to my room.

Once alone, I let my face fall into lines of disappointment, the desire to cry coming over me again. I told myself to get a grip, that it was just *one* of five schools. But the truth was, rejection was rejection, and no one liked it. CalArts hadn't set out to personally wound me, but my ego felt majorly bruised.

I pulled the letter from my bag and spread it open on the desk. *Thank you for your application… We regret to inform you… Many apply… Difficult decision…*

Now would be the perfect time to really throw myself into rehearsals for the Revue, but I already anticipated how much *that* was going to suck. All because of frigging Donny Walsh!

Disgusted, I tugged open the desk-drawer and tossed in the letter. Only to catch sight of the vibrant red heart on the front of the secret admirer note lying inside. Shoving the letter to the back, I took up the card and closed the drawer. I still wasn't convinced that finding this thing in my locker hadn't been a joke, yet the possibility of it being real came as a nice thought.

"And if it is real," I muttered to myself, finding a thumbtack and fixing the card to the wall above the desk, "if an actual, honest person put this in my locker, then at least someone somewhere thinks I'm amazing…even if one random college doesn't."

Looking at that crooked heart as it seemed to burst from the wall made me smile. For real this time.

DONICK

AT THE FIRST singing rehearsal, I feel like a turtle without a shell. Liam won't be here as a buffer and I'm totally on my own. It's not the music freaking me out. It's knowing that, at *these* rehearsals, I can't avoid Mikey.

To warm up our voices, Mr. Hardy organizes us into sections. He's decided to have me sing tenor after all, and I find myself side-by-side with four other guys, including Mikey. He won't acknowledge me, and I feel resentful. Though I can't bring myself to acknowledge him either. Then my ear tunes straight into his voice and that feeling of admiration takes over. I could listen to him sing for hours.

The first song we learn is called "History Maker". It's written as a waltz. Most of us are hearing it for the first time, so we crowd around the speakers plugged into an iPod and listen through before we attempt to sing along. Mr. Hardy says he's still working on transcribing the music, so we'll have to learn from the track. Singing in front of people embarrasses me. Still, I can't do anything but try. And I'm actually beginning to like this whole being-on-stage thing.

During a break, Brent calls my name. He's sitting in the front row of the house—with Calista and Mikey. Something freezes in my chest. Brent can't be ignorant of how his friends feel about me. Still, I go over. Calista watches me speculatively, though Mikey turns his gaze away. He had looked mildly happy while we were all singing—not that I stared at him or anything—but now he only looks annoyed.

"Some of us will be set-building on Saturday," Brent says. "You free?"

I nod, afraid to speak.

"It'll be something like noon to four-ish. Mrs. P. usually orders pizza."

"Sounds good," I say, finding my voice, relieved I can make it after teaching my morning kid-class at the dance-studio.

A terrible pause follows. I don't know what else to say. While wondering if I should just walk away, Brent asks, "How was dance? Have fun vogueing?" He frames his face with his hands.

Calista grabs his fingers. "Don't do that."

"It's gonna be a good number," I say. "Maybe the most creative choreography I've ever done. I'm not used to someone else's style. I've only ever danced at the studio." I feel like I'm babbling, so I finish with, "Chalice said everyone will be wearing Mardi Gras masks or something."

"That's the plan," Calista says. "I want everyone to make their own. You know, have, like, blank masks and everyone can glue feathers and stuff to them." I'm surprised she's speaking directly to me. Mikey, on the other hand, keeps his eyes averted. I can relate. Looking at him directly is not an option.

Again, I can't think of anything else to say. All three

of them make me nervous. They're surrounded by a wall I built for them brick by mean-spirited brick. Breaking through it seems impossible.

"How're you doing with the singing?" Calista asks. "It's not really your thing, right?"

I shake my head. "I think Mrs. P. must be crazy having me here."

Mikey turns and looks me dead in the face. The little comma-shaped scar under his eyebrow is crystal-clear. "You sound fine," he says. No smile touches his lips, there's little inflection in his voice, yet it shakes me. As quickly and unexpectedly as he spoke, he's on his feet and walking away. His pals are silent, watching him vanish into the lobby.

"Okaaaay," Calista murmurs. Brent says, "That was… abrupt."

We pause, made awkward again.

At last, half to myself, I say, "I deserve *insults* from him, not compliments."

"You're right," Calista says. "You do. But that's not our Michael."

I sense from her words, and the slight stress she puts on *our*, that she's making a point. Mikey—or Michael— is *theirs*. Their friend, their Muskequeer. He belongs to them. He's not my anything.

"I deserve the same from you," I say. "I appreciate that you'll talk to me at all. I can't change any of the things I've said to you over the years, except to tell you I wish I had been nicer. I wish I had been your friend instead of—"

"My enemy?"

I pause, then nod. "The both of you are, well…Mikey, um, Michael is lucky to have you."

Brent looks at Calista while she just stares at me. Finally, she gets to her feet.

"I have a couple costume pieces for you to try on. Since there's no rehearsal on Friday, stop in the costume-lab after school for a few minutes."

"Okay," I reply, taken aback.

Then, just as Mikey did, she walks away.

After a second, Brent says, "That's basically her way of saying she appreciates what you said. You won't win her over so quick, but the door is open."

"If I can only figure out how to win over Mikey."

Brent frowns. "Do you *want* to win him over?"

"I only meant..." I find myself suddenly blushing. "I mean, he and I—"

"Used to be friends. I know. He told us."

"Everything?" I ask, feeling like a smoking chunk of dry-ice has replaced my stomach. The last thing I need is for Brent and Calista to wonder about my sexuality because of one little nothing kiss Mikey and I shared in sixth grade. I may have no interest in kissing girls anymore, but I'm not ready to be the subject of gossip.

"Pretty much everything," Brent says. "Best friends, then you weren't. Violence, blood, scar tissue."

Brent doesn't mention the kiss, and I can already tell he's not the type to hold anything back. I can't quite feel relaxed though. "I owe Mikey big time," is all I say.

"Not sure that's how I would phrase it, but yeah, you do. And he goes by *Michael* now."

My face gets hot again. "Old habits..."

"Look, you've been on best behavior so far—which you should make a *new* habit, bee-tee-dubs. That'll go a step in the right direction. Maybe Michael eventually won't hate you."

"He hates me?"

"Now *I'm* phrasing it wrong. Not hate, but you screwed him up. I know that much."

"I hurt him a lot. Then kept doing it."

"Now *that* is well said."

"I don't think he'll ever forgive me. I mean, you know him better than I do. What do you think?"

"I think you don't know him at all."

That hurts. Still, if Brent *wanted* to shoot to kill, he doesn't particularly look it.

"But," he adds, "Michael actually spoke to you, and said something nice. Maybe it's not completely hopeless. This version of you you've got going on, this…I dunno…*nice* Nick, that's a habit to keep around. He may never want to be your friend again, but you can at least show him that you're trying."

I'M EXCITED TO have Liam with me again on Thursday. I don't have to feel so awkward and self-conscious. Liam is a friend I'm basically starting from scratch with.

But my growing comfort in rehearsal is shattered when Chalice announces a partnership section in the middle of the "Vogue" number, and pairs me up with Jackie. I struggle to say hello, even as I hope she won't cry. She looks like she might. Guilt stabs me so hard I think I might start crying too. Still, I remind myself that I *have* to go through these things. It's only fair.

Once we start dancing together, however, I'm pleasantly surprised. Jackie is good, and moves well; I feel like she makes me a better dancer—something that's really important in ballroom dance. No one enjoys watching two people dance together when it looks like they can't get in sync.

So I say to myself, or, well, to the Universe: *You're giving me a message here. I take it I somehow have to make things right with this girl.*

And I think I know just what to do.

EVERY FEW WEEKS, on a Friday at lunch, the school choir department puts on a mini-fundraiser and operates something like a karaoke-bar in the middle of the quad. It costs a buck to sing a song, and usually there ends up being a long line of kids wanting to stand on the little concrete platform in the quad's center and try their hand at pretending to be a pop-singer or a rapper. A lot of the time the singers aren't great. My buddies, loving the bully-fodder, look forward to these days so they can heckle if a campus supervisor isn't nearby. This particular Friday, instead of sitting and listening to Ryan and Josue be nasty, I barely stop at the table for five minutes before I'm getting up to leave.

"What's up?" Ryan says. "Can't take another Taylor Swift cover?"

"I've got some stuff to do."

"You're, like, hardly here anymore." His heavy features look puzzled, distrustful.

"What you gotta do that's more important than watching these losers?" Josue asks.

"Rehearsal stuff," I say, not wanting to explain.

Josue gives me a dark stare; Ryan looks irritated. I'm different now; they can sense it. Thankfully, the other mouth-breathers at the table are too wrapped up in watching some guy in a Hogwarts T-shirt begin singing "We Will Rock You" to care what's going on with me. This is something I've noticed over the last six months—my old crowd of football jocks have relegated me to a position of non-importance, now I can't play. The only two paying attention are Josue and Ryan, and I wish they would ignore me too.

"Let's, like, do something this weekend, dude," Ryan says, then calls to Scott, "Hey man, can you hang tomorrow?" Meaning 'something this weekend' includes getting stoned. *Yeah, pass!*

Before Scott can reply, Josue pipes up. "Yeah, let's get lit, *güey!*"

I try to look disappointed. "Can't. I'm helping build sets."

Their sour expressions sharpen. Ryan shrugs his heavy shoulders. "Whatever, dude."

"I'm just busy right now," I say. "I'm worried about graduation."

Josue snaps, "Having too much fun hanging with all the theatre fairies, you mean."

Fire throbs through me. I would like to hit him. "Don't be a jerk," I say.

"*You* don't be a little bitch, Nicco," he fires back. "You've always been the first person to razz on those queers."

"Yeah, and I was a jerk for it!" My anger spikes and I almost shout to be heard over the music. "Do you know how many people hate me now? Hate all of us?"

"Who cares?"

"I'm tired of making people feel like shit."

"Sounds like you're starting to think you're better than us, Nicco."

Then, knowing he'll take it as a dig about his being

held back, I say, "Only smarter."

"Fuck you!"

"Your asshole is showing, Jo. Better cover it before people see who you really are."

I take one last look at his purpling face (and Ryan glancing back and forth between us) before I snatch up my backpack and walk away.

Josue shouts something after me, but it's lost in the *stomp-stomp-clap* of the music. Some of our friends at the table have looked over but no one seems much fazed.

I make my solitary way toward the dance-studio, feeling self-consciousness replace my anger. I poke my head through the open doors. A lot of students are eating lunch inside, some from the show. Jackie sits with her back to the mirror, chatting animatedly with a group of her friends. I'm glad she doesn't notice me. I couldn't handle that scared look right now, made worse by her lazy eye. A circle of girls from the show eat their lunch and talk together just inside the door. Smiles and hellos bombard me as they ask what I'm doing there.

"I'm looking for Liam Hidalgo." (Lord, do I sound as timid as I feel?) "I thought he might be here."

A redheaded girl named Melody says, "Sometimes he's here, sometimes he's in the drama-room."

I was afraid of that…

They ask me if I want to sit with them (which makes me smile), but I ask for a raincheck.

Back across campus I go, detouring around the library to avoid the quad. A minute later I find myself outside the drama-room. Mikey—no, he's *Michael* now—is inside, I just know. Where else would he and his Muskequeers eat lunch? My palms feel like they're itchy and swollen. Going inside will be the worst.

But I do it.

After the sun-glare outside, I have to squint to see who fills the desks. Laughter and voices make a cacophony. Mrs. P., at her desk near the door, winks at me. Most of the other drama kids haven't noticed I'm there.

When I at last catch sight of Liam, I have to give an inward groan. He's sitting in a cluster of eight or nine students—including all three of the Muskequeers. He is, in fact, right beside Michael, and a dismaying squirm of jealousy twists through me. I'm unclear as to who this possessiveness is aimed at. Brent spies me first and waves. The streak in his hair looks a little washed out. Everyone around him glances over, including Michael, and most look uncomfortable. Liam, however, calls out, "Nick! What're you doing here? Come! Sit!"

I know the rest of them want nothing less, but I'll only be a second, so I cross to their group. When I'm feeling out of place and vulnerable, my thumbs always find their way into the straps of my backpack. It's a protective-thing. They creep there now.

Hoping I sound calm, I say, "Hey guys," careful of where my eyes fall. "Mind if I steal Liam for a second?"

Liam gets up, looking curious, and steps toward me.

Calista, wearing the enormous glasses she had on at the first rehearsal, says to me, "Fittings after school?"

I nod.

Michael keeps his head down, picking at a bag of Cool Ranch Doritos. The sight of them makes me think of the Doritos on his breath when I kissed him years ago, and

I'm thankful Liam is moving toward the door. I give an awkward wave to the rest of them, then trail after.

"What's up?" he asks, once we're outside. He's wearing a floppy beanie that hangs down his neck like one of the seven dwarfs. A wave of pale brown hair fluffs across his forehead and there are freckles over the bridge of his nose. He's really cute actually, but I don't think quite my type. He seems like a little brother. I realize I'm protective of him, which could explain that weird jealous feeling I got when I saw him next to Michael.

"I need some information," I say.

"Uh huh?"

"Let's sit on the stairs."

Once we're seated, facing each other, close enough that our knees almost touch (giving me another guilty stab of self-consciousness; I wonder what people will think if they see us like this), I take a breath, and start talking.

"You know how we got assigned our partners yesterday in rehearsal?"

"Yeah."

"Well, you're pretty good friends with the girl I'm dancing with, right?"

"Jackie? We hang out sometimes. Why?"

I swallow. I feel every word leaving my mouth as though it wants to fight to get back inside. "Well…last year…um…I did something to her that was…not so nice."

"The tea thing?"

Though Liam doesn't look judgmental, I'm ashamed none the less.

"I thought it was coffee," I murmur, and can't help adding, "I really suck."

"She's…pretty scared of you."

"I don't want her to be. That's the thing. What I did was a total dick-move, and, well, she's a really good dancer, and, not that it's because she's a good dancer, but I want to try and make it up to her. She's just…really sweet, and…" I sigh, having run out of words long before this. "I dunno. I hoped I could talk to her, try to make it better. If that's possible."

"Give it a shot."

"Here's where I want your help though."

"Okay…" He sounds uncertain now.

"She drinks, well, tea every morning when she gets to school, right?"

"Same drink from Starbucks every day."

"What exactly does she drink?"

BECAUSE OF THE courses I have to re-take, I'm in class until the final bell rings. But once I'm out, I pitstop at my locker to shove in my backpack, unsure how long Calista's costume-fitting will take. As I'm standing there, I see Michael and his friends. I can overhear Calista just beginning to say, "I don't know why we have to see some shitty horror movie when we could—" when Brent's voice exclaims, "Nick! Perfect timing!"

I paste on a tight smile, and take the few steps toward Michael's locker, lead in my heels.

"Yo," I say.

"We're going over to the theatre right now," Brent says. "Walk with us."

Calista's eyes dart to Michael, who goes into the usual thousand-yard-stare. I feel like I've forgotten how to stand—I'm all awkwardness and knees and elbows.

Calista says to me, "You'll be in and out fast. I'm sure you've got Friday plans."

"Not really," I say. "I don't see my buds very often outside of school anymore."

"Too bad," says Brent, though he doesn't look like he thinks it's too bad. I tell him it isn't.

"You guys know," I add. "The jerks you see at school are the jerks they are everywhere. It's exhausting."

Michael suddenly speaks, directing his words to his friends. "I need to find Mrs. P. I'll walk over to the theatre after." The sun strikes his retreating head, the light catching in his hair and turning it a shade of reddish brown that reminds me of the trunk of a redwood.

Calista and Brent exchange the same look they did after Michael's hasty retreat on Wednesday.

I say, "Guys, it's cool."

Brent begins to say, "Yeah, but he should just—"

"Don't say he should just get over it," Calista interrupts. "This isn't a get over it kind of thing."

"But—"

I interrupt him. "It's *not* a get over it kind of thing. And listen, you should probably not call me over when you guys are together. He's your friend—"

"*You're* our friend now too," Brent says.

Calista snorts. "The jury's still out on that one."

"I just mean," I say, "he doesn't want me around. I don't want to make him uncomfortable, or endanger your guys' friendship."

"That's not a problem," Calista says.

I ignore this. "But I do like talking to you. I even enjoy Calista's sass," I add, wondering if I can get away with this.

She snorts again. "Sass? What sass?"

"It's like a vampire not being able to see its own reflection," says Brent.

This leads us into *Buffy*-conversation, and as we walk to the theatre I laugh to myself, thinking that of course Michael got his friends into *Buffy the Vampire Slayer*. Calista says, "I'm not allowing *Buffy*-love to win you points with me." But something grudging begins to loosen in her tone. It makes me smile wider as we talk about our favorite seasons and which of the Big Bads we like best.

Once in the theatre, we walk backstage and into the costume-shop (or lab, as Calista calls it), our talk dying down. Nobody is here, and I can actually hear a trapped cricket strumming its legs somewhere.

"I have your stuff on a rack," Calista says. "We'll try and make this quick."

"I'm in no rush," I say.

The costume-lab is a square room with a big table in the center, stools placed around it. Bolts of fabric, trays of buttons, baskets of thread, pairs of scissors, cover the tabletop. Stacks of frail-looking patterns are everywhere, the floor littered with wisps of string and oddly-shaped bits of cloth. Through a door across the room is a larger space filled floor to ceiling with hanging costumes. From this room, Calista, with Brent's help, pulls out a wheeled rack.

"You can change in here," Brent says, grinning.

Calista, beginning to pull hangers, adds pointedly, "Or go back into the storage room if you're shy or whatever." I take the pieces she hands me. There's a billowy white thing like the kind of shirt a pirate would wear. "I know it looks stupid," she says, "but I want to try some different looks for you for the masquerade part of the show."

I'm not bothered about changing in front of them—they won't see anything—so I slip out of my sweatshirt, then tug off my T-shirt.

I think I become as red as a cherry when Brent suddenly exclaims, "Dear Lord! Look at that scar! Holy God, that's gnarly!"

He's looking at my injured shoulder, and the pink puckered scar from my surgery. He comes closer, Calista watching with curiosity.

"Are you, like, bionic inside now?" He laughs a little, lifting a hand like he might touch it. Then he grimaces and draws back. "Seriously gross. You can see where the stitches were."

"Staples, actually," I say. "And yes. Scrap metal in there." Their eyes are still on me, and because *now* I'm self-conscious about being half-naked in front of them, I crack a joke. "Think it's noticeable?"

Calista shrugs. "Just in a bathing suit. Thankfully boy-body is not my thing."

Brent grins at me. "It *is* mine! And damn, child!" I think my face might melt off my skull when he blatantly looks me over. I quickly drag the pirate-shirt over my head.

"It's a pretty ugly scar, right?" I say.

Brent shrugs. "Chicks dig scars. Or so I've heard."

I grin at him and actually say, "Apparently dudes dig scars too."

"Oh, they do," he says. "All kinds of scars. Or lack thereof."

Calista makes a disgusted noise. "Ignore him. This is what I call his penis-floorshow. I can't with you right now, Nanahara. I'm gagging."

"That's the whole idea."

"Enough! Out! Go bother Michael, if he can stand you."

Brent leaves the room and I slip off my jeans, tugging a pair of bizarre green slacks over my boxers. I begin to tuck the shirt in, but Calista stops me and orders me out of the pants ("I hate them!" she says) and tosses me a pair of old-fashioned breeches that fasten with tiny buttons below the knees.

"Now *those*, I like! We can show off your legs!" She's studying me avidly, even as I stand there feeling foolish in my socks and bare calves. "We'll have tights for you. You can wear them under your pants once you do the quick change into the 'Vogue' costume."

I'm in breeches and a pirate-shirt, and talking about wearing tights. Where am I, who am I, and what am I doing? Still, there's so much more satisfaction in this than there ever was suiting up in football gear. But if Pop was a fly on the wall…holy crap!

Next, Calista gives me an old-timey coat that flares like a skirt. It's made of some shiny purple stuff with gold buttons and braid. Seeing myself in the mirror on the back of the door, I'm reminded of a guy from the seventeenth century or something.

"Very nice," she says, and makes some notes on a clipboard.

With her eyes turned away, I study my reflection. Yes, I look absurd, but I have to admit, that makes me like it. There are so many new things and people coming into my life—I like it all. It's all different. It's all a welcome change.

"I'll find a waistcoat for you to wear under the coat, hopefully with velcro so you won't have to deal with a ton of buttons."

"Waistcoat?"

"A vest."

"You know a lot about this stuff."

"I have to. I want to be a costumer. Plus, I think fashion is, well, *fashion*-ating."

I snort, but say, "It's good to be passionate about something."

"You probably miss football, huh?" There's interest in her face, and it's no longer particularly grudging.

"Not really. I wasn't that into it. I played for my dad." I pluck at the coat's buttons. "I don't know what my passion is."

"Duh! When you dance, it sure looks like *that's* your passion."

I smile again. "Well, I do love it…in a way I *never* loved football. I never even *liked* football. But performing, and not just being in class or learning routines for my instructors…that's all new. So, I dunno."

We're quiet for a second or two. Then she tells me to take off the costume so she can give me a few pairs of black slacks to try. She can tell just by looking which pants fit and which don't. As I try them on, we talk. Something about her makes me unafraid to open up. Maybe it's that she knows the right questions to ask, or the perfect things to say, but I think I could tell her my life story with ease and never regret it.

"Are you going to Michael's party?" she asks.

I sputter a little. "I hadn't…I mean, I assumed I wasn't really invited."

"The whole cast is invited."

"I figured I was the unspoken exception. Besides, birthdays equal fun. My presence will be the exact opposite for Michael."

"You've been to his house before."

"Yeah. A long time ago."

"Then you know how big it is. There're plenty of rooms to put between the two of you."

"Still…"

"Having you there will probably make him uncomfortable. For, like, five minutes. Then he'll be in party-mode. We all will. Which is why I think you should go. Cast bonding, you know? Let these people get to know you. A lot of the cast is getting comfortable having you around. Liam Hidalgo and some of the other dancers actually like you a lot. Plus Brent seems to like you, too."

"No accounting for taste, right?" I say, half-serious.

"Bitch, please," she says, making a face. "You're a *Buffy* fan. There's *something* likable about you, after all."

"It's a start." I pause, then say, "That's Michael's fault, you know. Liking *Buffy*. He liked it because his parents used to watch it when he was really little."

"I know."

"He got me into it. That never changed. Now it's a guilty pleasure."

"Why guilty?"

I look anywhere but at her. "Because it reminds me of him. I tried hard not to think of him at all for all these years. But now, when I do, I feel guilty. It also reminds me of when he was my best friend. So…guilty pleasure."

"You really did a number on him, you know."

I nod.

"I mean, come on! You were his first kiss!"

My head snaps up. As our gazes meet, I feel my whole body get hot with mortification.

"He told you about that?" I squeak.

"He tells us everything. But to be fair, he only told us, like, last week. We had no idea before that."

I sink onto one of the stools. So Brent *did* know the other day. "Oh God," I sigh out.

"It's only the two of us who know. Michael wouldn't run around telling people. Mostly because it's kind of humiliating for him."

I can only repeat, "Oh God…"

"Think how damaging that was. I mean, yes, you were his first kiss. But for him, it counted. Know what I mean? For you, it was, I dunno, a game or something."

I suddenly can't swallow around an enormous lump in my throat. "It wasn't a game," I mutter.

"Then why do something like that? Because, for a homophobe—"

"I'm *not* a homophobe!" I say, with sudden fire. "My friends are homophobes! My *dad* is a homophobe. *I* am not."

"Could've fooled…well, everyone."

"It's the best way to hide."

I say it without knowing I'm going to. Once it's out there, I'm frightened of the relief I feel. Because speaking in riddles is the best way to lead to the admission I know is coming.

"Hide from what?"

I try to swallow again.

"Hide from knowing that kissing Michael…well, it mattered. I wanted to kiss him. Back then. And then everything was just…a mess. I lost control of what I was doing."

"You wanted—" she begins, and cuts herself off. She's silent for a heartbeat or two. I lift my eyes and see her studying me. She gives a chuff of laughter. "Holy shit. Holy *shit*! It's true what they say about homophobes, isn't it? They're hiding in plain sight."

"I told you, I'm not a homophobe."

"It would be pretty hypocritical if you were." There's amazement in her voice. "So that's it, huh? The enigma of Nick Walsh? Some things make more sense now. The dancing, the obvious click when it comes to being on stage, your friendship with Liam Hidalgo."

"Calista, please."

"What? Don't tell anyone? You think I would do that? I know what it's like."

"I'm not even comfortable with being—you know, like *that*. Yet, I mean. I don't know…"

She laughs. "You can't even say it."

"It's scary."

"Who else knows?"

"Me. And, I guess…you."

"*Just* me?" Her eyes are wide. She says again, "Holy shit!"

"Please keep it that way! I don't know what to do. I can't handle being viewed as a hypocrite right now. God, if my dad finds out… Please *do not* tell Brent. And *totally* not Michael. He's going to hate me so much…"

She's quiet again. When I sneak another look at her, her expression is funny. She's half-smiling, half-confused. "This is wild," she says. "I mean, seriously. You don't even— you're, what, seventeen? You don't know who you are."

"I guess I don't."

"Because, come on, Brent was born covered in rainbow afterbirth. People like Liam too."

"Gross."

"I may not have waved that rainbow flag until high school, but I always knew it was a matter of time. I think Michael was that way too. He and I are a lot alike in personality when it comes to things like that. As stuff comes along, we just sort of adapt to the changes and carry on."

"I've been fighting against those changes my whole life. It cannot leave this room!"

"You may have been a dick to me for a lot of years, but I would never out someone before they're ready."

After a second or two of feeling like I might have a bewilderment-coma, relief suddenly sets in. I've admitted it to someone. Secrets lose their potency when they're told, and having told Calista, I can feel a hollow place inside me that once carried something cancerous.

Tentative, she asks, "Have you ever, like, done anything with a guy?"

I look appalled. "No!" I pause. "Have you ever done anything with a *girl?*"

Calista blushes a little. "Not really. I don't look at girls here. If I had a girlfriend in high school I couldn't be a cliché in college and lead bitches on to think I'm experimenting."

"I'm serious."

"I told you, no. That doesn't mean I haven't had crushes. Have *you* ever had a crush on a guy?"

I shake my head. "I shut those thoughts down pretty hard."

"And you're sure you're not, you know, bi or something? Maybe just curious?"

"I've had three girlfriends," I say, "and Michael's is the only kiss I still think about. Even though I don't really remember much of it." I rub a hand over my forehead. "He was my best friend. I should've been there so this wouldn't be so hard now. Instead I alienated him and locked myself so deep in my own head, I…" I don't know how to finish that sentence.

She ducks her mouth into her hand. "Sorry," she says, then bursts out giggling. "Like, the shade of it all! Donick Walsh, former football jock, is gay!"

I hang my head, mortified. "That sounds so…"

"Naked?"

"Thank you, Dracula."

She grins. "I love that you get my *Buffy* references. Seriously Nick. You *have* to go to Michael's party. I'm not saying come charging out of the closet, I'm only saying come hang out and absorb the local color. It's a performing-arts crowd. That means it'll be a *gay* ol' time. Let yourself start getting warmed up."

I stare at her, hesitant, for half a minute. At last, I sigh and say, "I'll think about it."

"Good." She pauses, as though going back to her clipboard, then adds, "And thanks."

"For what?"

"For telling me. For trusting me. Your secret's safe."

I say, "Thank you," and we smile at each other for a moment. Then I sigh. "All these years," I add, "we could've been friends and I did nothing but be an asshole. I'm lucky if I have your friendship now."

"Yeah," she says with a long-suffering sort of sigh. "I guess you have it."

I grin. "Even if it's given grudgingly, I'll take it."

MICHAEL

A TYPICAL EARLY MORNING walking-to-first-period conversation with Brent would be as follows:

Brent: Boys are really ugly when they're, like, completely naked. Ever think about that?

Me: How many boys have you seen completely naked? Groping in the back of a dark car doesn't count.

Brent: Calista would tell me not to answer that question.

Me: Calista's not here. How many?

Brent: I have the interwebs, don't I?

Me: I'm not sure that counts.

Brent: Come on! Don't you think guys're sorta—

Me: No, and neither do you. We'd both still be batting for that other team if we did.

Brent: Have you ever, you know, like, seen it? Up close?

Me: You know I haven't. And we both know that I

know you *have*! So stop rubbing it in.

Brent loved nothing more than to make everyone uncomfortable with what he called "cock-talk", and Calista called his "penis-floorshow". He made dudes everywhere wish they were dead by asking if they were circumcised, then adding the info to some sort of mental-list.

I didn't say anything more though, because I opened my locker and froze. There, just like last time, lay a folded piece of paper. I would have been less afraid if it had been a rattlesnake. I plucked it out with shaking fingers. I found, I HOPE YOU HAD A NICE WEEKEND! ENJOY YOUR BIRTHDAY WEEK! printed inside.

"Oh-em-gee! Another one!" Brent's eyes got so big I thought those colored contacts of his might pop out. "Whoever it is knows your birthday's on Friday! This totally means it's not a joke! You have a *real* secret admirer! I'm über jealous!"

Happiness darted through me. Having a secret admirer was sorta great. Scary too.

"It could be anyone," I reminded him.

"Anyone who knows about your birthday. This narrows it in a serious way." He sucked in a breath—like some Hollywood starlet's over-acted gasp. "It *has* to be someone in the show!"

I scoffed at that. "No it doesn't."

"Someone in one of your classes? Ooh! What about Gil Hamilton?"

"Gil Hamilton?" I snorted. "Not a chance."

"You invited him to your party, right?"

"I invited everyone in the GSA"

"Think *he'll* come?"

"He said he would."

Gil Hamilton, a senior from the wrestling team, had shocked everyone by coming out after winter break in junior year. An unapologetic jock like him, able to be himself like that, sort of fascinated me. He and I talked every day in Government. He had deep red hair and freckles, and eyes greener than mine. Though I stood a head taller, something about Gil's compact stature appealed to me. Yes, I thought he might be flirting with me at times, but mostly, he was just really nice. I couldn't imagine much where he was concerned. Well, beyond picturing him in his wrestling singlet, that is; which I sometimes did. My friends pushed me toward him, but I never seemed to feel a spark.

"You haven't shown interest in anyone since Joel," Brent said. "And Joel was a jerk. Gil is sweet. And hot! Set yourself up for a birthday smooch!"

"Set yourself up for that birthday smooch in my place, why doncha?" I slipped the note into my backpack, shoving my literature textbook after it. Though, if Brent hadn't been there, I probably would have stood gazing at it for a full five minutes, making myself late to class.

"Gil's into you I bet," Brent went on. "It's got to be him leaving you these notes."

"Not convinced. Remember when I read *Simon vs. the Homo-Sapiens Agenda* and I was disappointed when I found out who had been e-mailing him? It wasn't logical. I couldn't trust *that* situation, and I can't trust mine. Gil doesn't make sense."

We started toward the English building, Brent moving the conversation to some Korean movie he had watched on Netflix the night before. I hardly heard him, my thoughts too busy with my new note. Between my two ex-boyfriends, Joel and Dillon, I really couldn't think of anyone who had ever thought much of me. Gil seemed to like talking to me, and yes, he was gay. But Gil Hamilton equaled good-looking athlete. Michael Penrose equaled nerdy musical-theatre kid. What could Gil, or anyone, really see in me? Besides, per Calista's suspicion, these notes might, after all, be a friend's way of showing they appreciated me. It could be some birthday-thing from one of my Muskequeers and they had a really good poker face.

"By the way," Brent said as we paused at the open door of my classroom. His was three doors down the hall. "I should warn you that Calista's been working on Nick Walsh, trying to convince him to come to your party."

My mouth dropped open. "Why?"

"And," Brent added, "when we were set-building on Saturday, I kinda pressed him too."

"You two are terrible friends. We talked about this."

"I think he's actually a good guy."

"I think your brain isn't the organ you're thinking with."

"He helped hugely on Saturday and we all had fun. Even Calista is starting to be okay with him. I mean, he's talented and he likes *Buffy*."

I stared. "He still watches *Buffy*?"

"He and Calista talked about it forever on Friday."

I felt a surge of anger. "Why don't you guys tell me this stuff?"

"Because we know how you feel about him."

"Yet you're pushing him to come to my house. That makes a lot of not-sense."

"He apologized—"

"To *you*, not me!" My voice had risen. I ducked my head when faces inside the room turned to stare. Even Mr. Mizrahi, Brent's English teacher, glanced at us as he breezed toward his classroom.

"Would it make it better if Nick *did* apologize?" Brent asked.

I didn't know what to say. I had never thought of Donny telling me he was sorry. How would I react?

Still, I barked, "No. It wouldn't. I can't forgive, and I can't forget." Then I turned away.

Behind me, Brent murmured, "That's really sad," but I didn't look back, fuming, as I made my way to my seat. I all but threw down my bag, falling into the chair, gritting my teeth.

What was it about bullies and assholes? Was it because they disliked so easily, so indiscriminately, that the bullied *craved* their approval? Any jerk could apologize for the horrible things he had done, and those he had harassed would fall all over themselves to overlook it. Was the need for the approval of the disapproving so great?

Well, Calista might be able to overlook the fact that Donick Walsh had called her a muff-diver for years and made fun of her boy-clothes; Brent could be okay with having heard *faggot* and *queer* come from Donny's lips on a daily basis; I could not. The scar beneath my eyebrow wouldn't let me.

Thankfully, I didn't run into either Brent or Calista until lunch. I was feeling so spiteful, I even entered Government fully intending not to say a word to Gil Hamilton. But approaching my seat, seeing Gil sitting in the desk behind it, hands in the pockets of his letterman jacket, earbuds in his ears, I softened. I didn't want to be a person who cut off his nose to spite his face—and Gil really was cute, sitting there bobbing his chin to his music. My nerves fired when he caught sight of me and grinned. He pulled one hand free of his jacket to tug out his earbuds.

"Michael!" He seemed to make a point of meeting my eyes. Wasn't that something people did when they liked a person—tried to meet and hold their gaze? Maybe my friends were right and Gil *did* have a crush on me. His red hair and freckles made him suddenly very interesting as he added, "What's going on in Penrose-land?"

Cooly, I said, "Same old stuff."

"Birthday on Friday, yeah?"

I blinked at him. He remembered!

"Yeah. Friday. I told you about my party, right?"

"Totes in my calendar."

Maybe my intuition *was* off. *Could* the secret admirer notes be from Gil?

He leaned on the desk, bringing himself closer to me so I could smell something on him, some citrusy spray coming from his collar. Pale stubble dusted his chin and his lips looked very soft. But I also had the distinct feeling of being…well, larger than him. I felt conscious of my longer legs, my bigger hands. Still, stealing glances into his face as we talked, I wondered what it would be like to let my thumbs touch the freckles beneath each of his eyes.

"How old will you be?" he asked.

"Eighteen. The big one."

"Rad! Now you're a legal adult who can't really do anything different from before."

"I can vote."

He rolled his eyes. "Because that was the first thing *I*

thought of when I turned eighteen."

"You're already eighteen?"

"Since November."

"Well, happy belated."

"And happy early. What can I bring?"

"Yourself." Then I added so I wouldn't come off looking like a creeper, "And a date, if you want. I mean, I guess I don't know if you're dating someone, so, if you are, bring, um, him."

His smile got bigger. His teeth were perfect. "No, no one to bring. Just me." He bit his lip, almost as though he had to do something to keep his grin from wrapping around his head and meeting at the back.

I grinned myself. And felt embarrassed. Gil seemed nice and normal—an athlete, which was different, but not an ass-faced jock. Still…did I find him *more* than just physically cute? He was definitely different than the guys I usually liked.

The bell rang and Mr. Lincoln, the Gov teacher (no end of jokes about that), started to quiet us down, glowering at the students straggling in late.

At the end of the period, Gil gave me his number so I could text him my address for Friday. Maybe it was shallow, but talking with Gil and knowing he would come to my party had me in a good mood by lunch.

Brent and Calista sat at our usual desks in Mrs. P.'s room. Brent looked worried, almost afraid, that I would either not show, or that I would. Calista only studied me. Obviously, they'd been talking.

I slid into a chair. "Muskequeers Two and Three!" I said.

Calista scowled. "Don't talk about yourself, babe. *I* am Muskequeer Number One."

Brent looked suspiciously at me. "You're in a good

mood. You haven't been talking to your finger like that kid in *The Shining*, have you?"

"I can't build a bridge?"

"You don't usually."

"Ouch."

Calista said, "Brent told me about the note in your locker."

I said, "It's nice to be admired," unable to keep from resuming my grin.

"Don't read too much into it," she said, like a parent saying, *Don't forget to vacuum.*

I told them about my conversation with Gil, and sadly, my friends seemed more excited about him coming to my party than I was…mostly because I wasn't sure I really cared if he came or not. I didn't feel much in the way of sparks. At least, not yet.

We stopped talking when more of our friends came in and gathered around. However, when the room got particularly loud, I leaned toward the two of them and said, "I *am* sorry about this morning. It just surprised me to find you're both on the Donick Walsh train. It's okay. He's not my friend—never *will* be—but that doesn't mean he can't be yours. It's good that he apologized for being an ass."

Brent said, "He's really not so bad."

I shrugged. "I wouldn't know about that."

Calista picked at her salad. "He's going through stuff," she murmured. "I decided that this could be a good experience for him. Like we talked about that day at your house, theatre people can be either really welcoming, or the nastiest bitches alive. I know which of the two I want to be. Besides, holding onto my resentment over old news will just become poison inside." She met my gaze. "I'm sorry about the stuff he did to you, Michael, but I can't hate someone for you."

I sat silent for a second. "I don't want you to," I then said. "I'll try not to bash him."

"Don't just try," she said. "Stop. I can see already that your bad feelings about him are becoming toxic. You're edgy and not particularly excited about the Revue. And you've been acting mad at us. We've never been mad at each other before."

I looked away, wanting to argue. Except she was right.

"I'm not saying suddenly get over it," she added. "But you need to start building that bridge you mentioned. If Nick needs to be a different person, let him. That boy who hurt you and called you names may not exist anymore. Don't be the kind of guy that forces him back into that role. Besides, letting it go is better for your own sanity."

I could only sigh out, "You're right. Keep pressing him to come to the party. I need to get used to being around him. We'll never be friends, but I don't have to hate him."

Some of our buds were beginning to give us irritated looks for whispering together.

I quickly said, "Love you, guys," and we joined back into the conversation, which was about the complicated dance-routines of some K-Pop group.

Mrs. P. approached us with the trashcan toward the end of lunch. Everyone tossed in their paper bags and apple cores.

"Michael," she said. "I want to talk to you after school. That fine?"

"I'm supposed to try on some costumes today," I said.

"I won't need more than a minute."

"Then, sure."

When Mrs. P. carried the trash to the other side of the room, Calista grinned at me and said in a sing-song voice, "I bet it's about your solo."

"I *am* nervous about what I'll get."

Brent scoffed. "Bitch, please. You'll get nothing!"

"That's true. I do suck."

"Like a chode."

Calista groaned. "Ugh…penis-floorshow."

After the final bell, I paused at Mrs. P.'s desk. With the last of the students trooping out the door, she sank into her chair, looking tired.

"Sit." She gestured at the nearest desk. "Are you having fun in rehearsals so far?"

I thought of Donny's seemingly eternal presence, no matter where I went or what I did. It gave me more anxiety than I liked to admit, but the last thing I needed was to get a reputation for being a whiny snot about casting decisions.

So I said, "I've been looking forward to being a senior in the Senior Revue for years."

"Good! I wanted to talk to you about the show, specifically your solo."

"Uh-oh," I said. "Should I be scared?"

"Well, I have a bit of a different idea about what I want you to do. You always pick beautiful ballads for your auditions. You're really strong on those kinds of songs. But I want to give you something that's going to challenge you, that'll be very different for you, give you some growth. I want to give you something comedic. You remember the routine you, Brent, and Calista did in the talent show, right? It was fabulous, and very different for you. I want to see some of that comedy in the Revue."

"Okay…"

"But I wanted to talk to you first, before you looked at the rehearsal schedule. I'll start passing it out today."

"What do you have in mind?"

She hesitated, biting her lip. "I want you to sing 'Popular'."

I frowned. "'Popular'," I repeated. "As in, Galinda with a guh, 'Popular'?"

"I have this great idea for it. Instead of having one girl singing the song to another girl, I want it to be *you* singing it to Calista and Brent. I know Brent's only stage-managing, but I'll see if he'll step in, just for the one song. Mr. Hardy's going to change the key so it's more comfortable for you to sing. In the gaps between some of the verses, I want to bring out that Vaudevillian comedy. Create a sketch where you're trying to make-over your friends, but with bad advice."

I sighed, trying not to let her see the idea wasn't impressing me. I felt sick to death of that song. She must have already had this idea for it though, otherwise it would never have been on the set-list.

"I wanted to run it by you," she went on. "But don't worry. I have a duet for you also, and that one *will* be a ballad. You'll be able to sing your heart out."

I don't think I looked particularly convinced, but it wasn't my business to be dissatisfied with her choices. I had to trust the director's vision.

"It's cool," I said. "I want to be a better performer. This is part of that."

She got to her feet. "Audiences love that song anyway. They'll be surprised to see a guy singing it."

I gave her an awkward smile. "I'll do my best."

Mrs. P. had to go to her car for something, so I walked toward the theatre alone. There was still another fifteen minutes or so before dance rehearsal began. When I passed the studio, a lot of barefooted dancers milled in the doorway, mostly girls securing their ponytails. A quick glance inside showed no sign of Donny. I really did need to stop psyching myself out about him.

The theatre could be entered from a side-door—what we students called *The Artistes' Entrance*—the costume-lab just inside. A little courtyard lay outside this door, and as I passed into it, a wave of ice-water seemed to douse me. Standing there by himself, holding one of those square paper-cup holders, was Donny, dressed in his dance clothes, flip-flops on his bare feet.

A hummingbird's heart might have replaced my own. Instinct told me to do an about-face, to dash away, yet he turned his head and saw me. He blinked once or twice and I thought his cheeks went pink. His hand lifted, touching one of the cups in the holder to steady it.

A surge of dislike coursed through me. I shifted my gaze and resumed walking. Still, he struck me like a magnet. I could feel his presence drawing and repelling me all at once.

In a small, low voice, he said, "Hey."

I said it back, snapping the word, unsure if it had even come out. Why couldn't he simply leave me alone?

He had to then ask, "Have a good day?"

Again I snapped out, "It was fine," too angry with him, too surprised at his asking at all, to care about being polite. I barreled passed him, and just as I reached the door, it swung open. A girl in dance clothes all but knocked me down.

She exclaimed, "I'm so sorry!"

I shook my head. "No big. My fault too."

It was Jackie Skarupa. Though she had danced in a few of the shows I had done with Mrs. P., she and I had never really gotten to know each other.

Trying to smile, I asked, "Costume fitting?"

"Yeah. You?"

"Yup. Well, have a good rehearsal."

She moved to go, but the sight of Donny slowed her feet. I was already stepping through the doorway when I saw him approach her.

Too intrigued to mind my own business, I moved far enough into the hall for the door to almost close, leaving just enough space to peer out. Though I scolded myself for eavesdropping, I tilted one ear toward the crack. The sound of music playing from the costume-lab drifted to me, along with the voices of my friends. I wished I could tell them to can it so I could better hear what was happening outside.

Donny said, "Hey, Jackie," in a tight, hesitant voice. "Can I talk to you for a minute?"

What did Donny want with Jackie? If I didn't know better, I would almost have thought he was about to ask her out. I had only ever seen him date cheerleader types with resting bitch face. Jackie was *not* that kind of girl, with her lazy eye and thick limbs.

"Uh…yeah," she said. "I—I guess." She sounded less than thrilled.

"This is for you," he said. "I figured I owed you one. Soy chai latte, right?"

"Y—yeah." Now the anxiety was gone from her voice, leaving only surprise.

"I owe you, like, a hundred," Donny added with a self-conscious laugh. "I just…what I owe you is a *huge* apology too. For that one time…with your drink." His voice quavered a little. Hearing what he said made my dislike stab all the harder. His voice had grown so small, I almost couldn't hear what he said next. "That was a really horrible thing I did."

She murmured, "I don't really know what to say."

"You don't have to say anything." His tone was kind. "I don't expect you to forgive me. I don't deserve it. But I still wanted to let you know that I wish I could go back and do it again. I mean—*not* do it again. Do it over, I guess I mean, and *not* do it. What I did. To you."

She stuttered as well. "I guess I…appreciate hearing that. I just don't—I mean I…don't know why…"

He sighed. "I have a lot of things I need to make up for. Things I feel rotten about. I'm not trying to apologize to make myself feel better. I'm apologizing because it wasn't right, what I did. And I wish I could make *you* feel better about it." A long pause. I almost thought they had gone and I hadn't heard their footsteps. Then he said, "I also wanted to say I think you're an amazing dancer. I'm really lucky we're partnered together. I'm sure you're not happy about it, and I don't blame you, but I still think you're great. If you'd prefer we didn't talk at rehearsal, or if you want me to turn the other way when I see you coming at school, I'll do it."

She said, still in that soft little voice, "Thanks for the tea. It means a lot."

His voice came very small now. "So…can we be cool?"

Now I *could* hear the sound of feet moving away from the door. "I'm actually happy to be partnered with you too," she said. "It's hard dancing with a guy who doesn't know what he's doing."

Donny's laugh, this time, didn't sound awkward. "We're a good match then."

Their voices faded. The last thing I heard was Jackie asking, "How did you know I like a soy chai latte?"

I stood there, infuriated. His apology, however sincere, pissed me off. And Jackie? Another one easily able to overlook whatever crappy thing some jerk had done to her. My resentment suddenly felt every bit as toxic as Calista had described. The throb of it in my veins had me wanting to savagely grin and burst into tears all at once.

DONICK

"And if I'm flying solo, at least I'm flying free."

I THOUGHT I WOULD die when Michael almost guest-starred in my apology to Jackie. Then I almost echoed the very words I put in the new note I pushed into his locker. Why *had* I stuck another note in there? It was dangerous! But I guess I did it because he said he thought I sounded fine when I sang. More guilt weighing me down…more longing for my old friend. My old *uncomplicated* friend I didn't have to be anyone but myself with.

All the ways we screw up our own lives…

Dance rehearsals are much more fun now Jackie and I are cool. She and Liam are good friends, so I'm welcomed into their midst like I wasn't before. It isn't lost on me how kind Jackie is to forget the past—like Brent, like Calista—because one day, someone won't want to forget and I'll be stuck with *that* guilt forever.

Classes are boring, each hour of the day dragging until I can be at rehearsal. While there, I actually feel happy. This music is like nothing I've ever listened to and I'm loving it. I download the songs at home, playing them on repeat when Pop can't hear—knowing he would say something if he heard ABBA and a bunch of showtunes coming from my bedroom. Maybe I'm a bit of a masochist, but I even hunt up the song Michael sang at his audition; then I can't stop listening to *that* on repeat as well.

The singing rehearsals are still a trial. It's Michael's turf, so I mostly keep to myself. It's difficult though. I would really like to hang with Brent and Calista. Calista especially. I've told her about me—the first person ever. My walls can come down around her. If I could spend more time with her and Brent my experience in the Senior Revue would be perfect. But, because of Michael, I stay clear.

We learn more and more songs, including a showtune-ish version of that Pink song, "Get This Party Started". It'll be the next big dance number we'll learn, Chalice says. The vocal parts will go as solos to the dancers who sing…and suddenly I have my first solo part. It's only one line, yet it makes me almost nauseous.

Then I look at the rehearsal schedule and that sick feeling intensifies. Because there, halfway through act two, is my name—and my name *only*—printed next to a song called "I Can't Do it Alone".

I approach Mrs. P. She laughs at my petrified expression.

"Had a good look at the schedule, huh?"

"I can't do a solo," I stammer.

"Sure you can. Besides, it's more a dance solo than anything. But you'll still have to sing. How's your stamina?"

I could forget about the fun I'm having and drop out this instant! Screw graduation!

In a tiny voice, I say, "Seriously?"

"It's a great number. Have you seen *Chicago*? Chalice really wants to show off your dance training. She *requested* we add the song to the set-list after you came to auditions. She's excited about it. You should be too."

I'm not excited—I'm not even afraid now. There's no word for how terrified I am. I don't say this, of course. I don't have to. I'm positive I look like one of those shivering chihuahuas.

I SEE RYAN AND Josue every day, but we speak to each other less and less. Where we once used to mostly trash-talk anyone and everyone, I now work on homework at lunch (I haven't quite worked up the courage to start going to the library every day yet) and try to block out their acid-tongues. Still, sometimes they start talking and I can't help listening, feeling, well, dirty.

For example: we've had this running gag since freshman year called Sack-Tap Day. It's cruel, and I participated without thought. We made it like a game—Ryan, Josue, Scott, and anyone else in our group who wanted in on it. The rules were simple: each player had to whack three guys in the balls at some point between the start and end of the school day; to get it done without being caught you had to be creative, but that was part of the…well, fun; another player picked your targets for you; if you were caught, you were disqualified; if you didn't get all three, you were disqualified. There wasn't even a prize if you made your goal. You simply had the "satisfaction" of knowing you had made it through another Sack-Tap Day.

I'm appalled to hear my "friends" talking about wanting to do this before Spring Break, which is in a couple of weeks. There hasn't been a Sack-Tap Day all school year. I had hoped they had buried that crap. I guess not.

Josue jerks his chin across the quad. "We need to get

that one," he says. "What do you think, Nicco?"

When I look, to my horror, it's Liam he's referring to. Liam—small, brown-eyed, laughing Liam. Today he's walking toward the drama-room with five or six other members of the Revue's cast, Michael included.

I shoot Josue a disbelieving look. He's bating me. He remembers my talking to Liam the other day. This is like a test of my loyalties.

I look back at my English notes. "Really stupid, Jo."

"I think that fag'll be *your* first target, *güey*."

"You think I would play that dumbass game?" I ask. "Ryan almost ruptured that kid last year. I figured that was our warning to quit while we were ahead."

"Don't play then. We'll just pick that *joto* for someone else."

Quiet has fallen at our end of the table. I send daggers at Josue through my eyes. "You're *not* planning another Sack-Tap Day."

Josue snorts. "Maybe *you're* the one who'll need to guard his nuts."

Ryan mutters, "Dude…" but falls silent, watching the way Josue and I glare-spar.

I gather my things, at last. "You know," I say, "the library is beginning to look like the perfect place to spend lunch from now on. I won't have to listen to this garbage anymore."

"Yeah? Deuces, *güey*!" Josue almost shouts. "Get the fuck out! Go hang with your *joto* drama buddies."

Scott elbows Josue and murmurs, "Chill, bruh."

But Josue's eyes are snapping with anger. "We'll get you, *güey*! You won't know who it'll be, but you'll be tapped, you self-righteous dick!"

I'm walking away even as he's shouting after me. I would like to launch myself at him and crush his nose with my fist. I only press my teeth into my tongue to keep from saying something I'll regret, and continue on my way.

It took twenty seconds.

I'll never eat lunch with them again, won't see them on weekends, won't text them, won't talk in class. I never expected our friendship, such as it was, to dissolve as quickly as it did, but I know, as I turn my back on them for the last time, that that friendship is gone. It's no surprise—that restart-button I'm so desperate to press necessitates casualties. To sit silent, looking away as they act like douche-nozzles, would make me a hypocrite. I can't do it anymore.

There's a lyric in a song I've heard sung at rehearsal that says, "And if I'm flying solo, at least I'm flying free". Walking away from my friends, and for good, this line plays itself through my head. I *am* free, and it's a relief.

RIGHT UP UNTIL Friday morning, I'm still leaning toward not going to Michael's party. Liam and Jackie (and a bunch of other dancers) have all been pressuring me to be there. Even Brent and Calista keep giving me not-so-subtle reminders. But I'm thinking about Michael and his family. Being in Michael's presence most every day is bad enough, I don't know if I can face the rest of the Penroses after what I did to their son.

Yet it's running into Josue during passing period that decides me. I see him coming. He sees me. We're both alone and walking toward each other. He suddenly lunges. His hand is cupped upward in a fake-out bid to do exactly what he threatened the other day—sack-tap me. He sneers as he keeps from doing it at the last second, malice filling his eyes. In my knee-jerk reaction to freeze and tighten, a thin knife of pain throbs through my shoulder. I groan and tears prickle at the unexpected clenching of the muscles around my mostly metal rotator cuff.

Barking laughter, Josue says, "*I* wouldn't tap you, *pendejo*! You'd fucking expect it. When it happens, you won't see it coming." He leaves me with the sensation that my balls have found a new home up inside my gut. I'm fighting the need to clutch my shoulder and massage the ache away.

I duck into a bathroom, locking myself in an empty stall, just to catch my breath and let the pain pass without anyone watching me.

That damn asshole! If Josue had really been my friend, ever, he wouldn't do something like that to me!

Yet I had hurt Michael terribly once—it's his birthday today!—and he had been my *best* friend. The new friends I'm making in the Revue…they would never do anything like that, I know—even after the terrible things I've said and done to them. Even only just getting to know me, they've been kind and welcoming.

Then, all of it—my desire to start over, my wish to make amends, these tentative new friendships—it all seems enormous, *huge*! It feels beyond anything I'm capable of! There are tears in my eyes again and I breath hard to fight them back. I think of my confession to Calista; I think of helping Brent measure out pieces of plywood as he told me about living with his grandmother and what a kook she is, though she's growing very forgetful and it worries him how once in a while it seems to take her a few seconds to remember who he is; I think of Jackie and her forgiving heart; I think of Liam—how a portion of every dance rehearsal we spend going over choreography. He works so hard, and always laughing.

I want to invest my time in *them*—not assholes like, well, myself. I want to be around the cast of the Revue because they make me feel happy, even after only a few short weeks of knowing them. They'll all be at Michael's birthday party tonight—and in an instant, I know that's exactly where I want to be too, with my new friends, even if I have to run the Penrose-gauntlet.

WITH NO FRIDAY rehearsal, I'm home right after school, glad Pop is still at work so I can think up a good lie for where I'll be tonight. He can't know I'll be at Michael's house. Pop won't ever forget Michael. To say I'm within two yards of him would give my father an aneurysm. So I fret in my room, looking through my clothes. What should I wear? I'm anticipating walking in and all eyes turning to me, shocked I would actually show up. Is it a jeans and T-shirt sort of party? Or should I wear shorts? Michael had mentioned people could swim, but I would rather cut off my entire arm than hang out in a bathing suit. Why do I care what Michael might think of my clothes anyway?

I can only hope Pop is in a good mood when he gets home. He doesn't usually say no to me going out with friends. I haven't gone out much lately, though sometimes he asks about Ryan or Josue—mostly wanting to know how they're doing in football. The best thing will be to say I'm hanging out with them. He won't care about me taking the car, so once I'm gone, I can go anywhere.

He's still not home by six o'clock. Though I text him,

he never replies. He must be out of range somewhere; or he's in a meeting with his phone turned off. Even if he's carrying one of the half-dozen phones he has lying around, I wouldn't know what number to use.

At last, as seven o'clock approaches, I send Pop another text and say I'm going out. I don't think he'll be mad—it's Friday night, after all. Maybe he won't question my whereabouts and he'll assume I'm with some girl, trying to get laid. Gross.

I dress carefully, in jeans and a shirt with buttons, knowing I'm being fastidious and…gay, I guess. But my anxiety over this party is strong. I know I'll have to greet Michael when I get there, and I want to at least look put together. Satisfied, I grab my phone and my keys, heading out the door into a night that's kind of warm for mid-March. I set my iPod playing some of the songs from the Revue once I'm in the car—for courage—and pull out of the driveway.

For the first time in six years, I'm going to Michael's house.

MICHAEL

FRIDAY MORNING—MY BIRTHDAY—GIL handed me a jewel case with a CD inside, MICHAEL'S B-DAY MIX written on it in purple marker. I eyed the printing for similarities to the print in the secret admirer notes. They didn't look the same. I smiled though, my ears hot. Gil looked unfazed when he said, "I know you're mostly into musicals or whatever, but there're some songs on there I think you might like. If you can even play it. CDs aren't really a thing anymore. Think of it as me pretending it's, like, 2002 or something. Besides, I'm broke. I can't buy you a real present. This way I won't look like a dink at your house."

"No presents allowed," I said, "so no worries."

He lifted his doubtful gaze to the trio of mylar balloons hovering above my head. They were either emblazoned with "HAPPY BIRTHDAY" or a big "18"—day-long embarrassment courtesy of my Muskequeers.

"Do those count?" Gil asked.

"No, because it's school. No prezzies at my *house!*"

"So mine doesn't count then?"

The heat in my ears spread to my cheeks. "Yours can totes count. And thank you. I like the vintage feel."

I knew now, for sure, Donny would be there, and I hoped Gil's presence would counterbalance the badness.

After school, Calista offered Liam a ride home (his apartment being in the same complex as her's), so we four crossed campus together. Brent chattered away about what he would do with his hair for tonight, coaching Liam on what he should wear. Calista played with her phone, grimacing when the other two got too loud. I, meanwhile, struggled with the balloons. I appreciated the gesture, but felt sick of trying to keep the damn things from tangling. The sooner I could shove them into a corner of my bedroom, the better. They could take every second they wanted of the forty-seven years it would require to deflate.

Then, out of nowhere, at the edge of the parking-lot, someone ran into Calista, almost knocking her down. Her phone went flying from her hand. The four of us jostled together, even as I braced Calista to keep her on her feet, balloon-ribbon drifting right and left. We glanced up and saw one of the football players—the big jerk who looked like a zeppelin.

"Jesus, Ryan," Calista said to him. "Don't you know how to walk?"

Ryan—well, now I knew his name, at least—had some stonery-looking guy with him, the obvious musk of weed drifting from his flannel.

Stoner smirked and said in a vacant way, "Lezbi-honest, Ry, these four girl-dudes might kick your ass if you don't say sorry for almost knocking the dyke down."

Ryan said, "I got distracted by all the pansy balloons.

Happy birthday, queer!"

"Much obliged, dude," I said, trying to sound unruffled.

"Something smells penisy!" Ryan said with a sneer, turning to Stoner. "You smell that?"

"Fag breath?" Stoner suggested, and guffawed. His eyes were squinted almost to nothing.

Though Brent just stared, looking tired, Liam seemed to dim, like a light turned low. He wouldn't lift his eyes. It irked me, to see him so beaten down. I made a face at the zeppelin. "Still just your own BO," I spat.

A dry hitching laugh came from Stoner's mouth. Ryan glared at him. Then his eyes, small and all but lost in his face, shot back to me. "Watch your balls, fag," he hissed. "We got a tap coming. I'll be looking for you."

Then they were gone. I sighed, muttering, "Fathers protect your daughters."

"I can't stand them," Brent said.

In a voice like a mouse, Liam added, "I hate when I have to go anywhere near them." He bent and retrieved Calista's phone. "They're such buttholes."

"Till the end of time," she said. Then she cursed. "Oh, come on! They cracked my screen? I just got this phone last month! My mom is gonna freak! Frigging Ryan! What a drain-trap!"

We went on our way, crossing the lot and arriving at Calista's Hyundai, even as she ran her fingers over the shattered phone-screen as though she could mend it with her touch.

"What did that mean?" Liam asked, once we were all crammed into the car. He and Brent were squished into the back seat. They were both so small it wasn't that uncomfortable for them, though my balloons floated about their heads. "They've got a *tap* coming up?"

Calista scowled, starting the engine. "Phone-breaking-dumbass-speak. Who knows?"

"The big one is Nick's friend, right?" Liam went on. "How does he stand them? I mean, I know Nick has had, like, issues with people before, but he's just so different from guys like that."

I clenched my jaw. The spreading quiet in the car made me feel Brent's and Calista's silence all the more. How could I keep from feeling anxious about my old not-friend being in my house in a few hours? My perfect senior year moments were all becoming lousy with Donick Walsh.

Calista caught Liam's gaze in the rearview mirror. "Well," she said, and summoned a smile, "if he's becoming friends with people like you, maybe he'll stop needing to be around foreskins like that."

Liam smiled back. "That's what I think!"

Brent said, "Listen to her using the word foreskin like it's a bad thing."

"Have I mentioned how crazy-excited I am about the party tonight?" Liam went on. "I know, I know. Like, six hundred times. But I've heard stories about parties at your house, Michael. I'm happy I'll get to go to at least one before you graduate and leave." His tone grew sad as he finished. Then he brightened, adding, "I'm really glad we convinced Nick to come too."

Brent giggled. "Li, you aren't getting a crush on Nick after all, are you?"

Calista turned her gaze to me for a very brief moment, then eyed the mirror again. I remained unspeaking, finding the idea of Liam having a crush on my old not-friend extremely unpleasant. How fitting would that be? Someone gay falling for a homophobe. Not exactly poetic.

"No way! No crush on Nick!" Liam cried.

"You talk about him a lot," said Brent.

"Nick's too tall for me. Besides, he's straight, right? That way lies complications. Why go there?"

"Good attitude to have," I put in.

Brent said, "Because sometimes even just being able to look is enough. I'm not a corpse. I'll appreciate the hotness where I find it."

"I second that!" Liam said.

Calista just looked thoughtful and went on driving in a silence to match mine.

She dropped me off first. Probably better, so I could relieve Brent and Liam of possible suffocation by mylar. I waved as Calista drove away, then pulled the mail from the box before entering the house. No one was home yet, so I went to the kitchen and sorted the envelopes, pausing when I saw that one of them was from USC. Suddenly the quiet of the house seemed very loud.

How thin the envelope was. How…inconsequential the whole thing looked. An acceptance letter would be bigger, I told myself, comparing it to the letter from CalArts—the *rejection* letter from CalArts. This one, and that one… they looked exactly the same. Happy birthday to me, I thought, my heart dropping into my shoes.

Unable to stomach it, I left the letter unopened on the counter and climbed the stairs to my room, the balloons floating in my wake like a good mood left behind and trying to catch up. If I saw that another school didn't want me it would put a pall over my whole night.

I shoved the balloons into one corner and tossed my backpack on the bed. Remembering the CD Gil had made me, I took it from the bag and slid it into my laptop, letting the disc import into iTunes. There were a lot of 80's songs, and it was interesting, thinking of getting to know someone through the music they liked. I sat at my desk, letting the songs play, not thinking about much except Gil's face and how he had sounded asking if his gift counted. Maybe he really did like me. But could I like him?

Doors opening and closing downstairs pulled me from my thoughts. The ridiculously loud voices of the twins as they charged through the house came to me. Their little feet stomped on the stairs and then they were suddenly at my door, grinning hugely, dashing in to leap onto my lap (their knees always managed to find their way into the most imperfect of places, making me wince).

"Happy birfday!" Topher shrieked. "Happy birthday!" Cady seconded, their piping cries grating against the other's and making me alternately grin and grimace, fearing for my ears.

I squeezed them to me and kissed their faces, strands of their pale hair catching against my lips.

"We drew you pitchers!" they cried together. "We drew you pitchers! At school!"

They each held rumpled sheets of paper.

"All right, let's see," I said.

The three of us knelt beside my bed as though we were going to pray. Topher shoved his picture under my nose first.

"Is that us?" I asked. He nodded, grinning, flashing his little gapped teeth. "All of us? Momma and Daddy.

Georgie and Topher and Cady?"

Topher looked very serious. "And you!" he said, pointing. "Look!"

"Oh yeah. Looks just like me. What are those big red things over all our heads?"

"Roses!"

I laughed. "Of course they are. Topher-Rose, Cady-Rose, Georgia-Rose, and…"

"Ninja-Rose!" Cady chimed in and stabbed at my stick effigy.

"What's this tall skinny black thing in the background, Toph?" I asked.

"Our house."

I made my eyes very big. "That's what out house looks like?"

"In my head."

I kissed his brow. "It looks like the top of it would touch the sky."

"It does. I saw it in a dream. Now Cady! Look at her pitcher!"

Cady held her picture right to my face, forcing me to lean back. While Topher's picture was legible, Cady, in her usual display of impatience, had simply swirled a bunch of colors in broad circles.

She lisped out, "It's a storm like Elsa makes, only it's made of rainbows."

"Fitting, huh?" Mom stood in the doorway, half-laughing. "Happy birthday, my baby boy!" She came forward to sweep me into a hug. The twins started jumping on the bed. "Stop that!" she told them but without much feeling, then went on hugging me. "My baby is eighteen today," she crooned, rocking me. "Eighteen years ago right now I was entering labor-hour thirty-two!"

"Ma!" I cried, extricating myself and sitting back in the desk-chair.

"You two!" she said to the twins. "Go downstairs! You can play with your tablets for a little while. But *only* a little while! You're spending too much time on them. Your brains will turn to mush."

They thrust their pictures into my hands. "You hafta hang them!" they said, almost in unison, then darted out chanting, "Mushy brains, mushy brains!" to the tune of "Let It Go".

"How was work?" I asked. "You smell like an alpaca."

"How was school?" she countered. "I see your friends got you balloons."

"We do that for each other every year. No big."

"But it is! These are for your eighteenth! My baby! Eighteen!"

I hurried to change the subject. "Where's Georgie?"

"Already at Belle's so she'll be out of everyone's hair tonight. Though you know the twins will be tough to keep upstairs."

"I don't think anyone will care."

She sat on the edge of the bed. From the pocket of her scrubs she pulled the envelope with the USC logo in the corner. "You didn't open it."

I felt cold at seeing it. "I know what it's going to say."

"No you don't."

"It looks like the other one."

"Will it upset you too much?"

"I don't know. You can open it if you want."

"What if it's good news? You could have more than just

your birthday to celebrate tonight."

"Go ahead, then. Open it. Read it for me."

"You sure?"

I'm certain I looked anything but, yet I shrugged and she tore the envelope. She pressed open the letter and skimmed it. The small smile that had touched the corners of her mouth faded. Her eyes turned to me and she said nothing, only gazed at me, looking disappointed. Though I had expected the rejection, it still stung.

"Maybe we *should* have waited until tomorrow, huh?" she said.

"It's okay. I'm not surprised. I guess that officially means staying in California is out. I want to go to New York though. I only applied to USC because that's where Dad went."

"I know," she said, her voice laced with sympathy.

"Besides," I added, trying to sound cheerful, "tonight we party. I won't have a spare second to think about it."

She laid the letter on the desktop, giving my knee a squeeze with one hand as she did so.

"Everyone'll start arriving around seven," she said. "The four hundred pizzas should get here at seven-thirty, Dad is stopping at the store on the way home to pick up chips and dip and sodas and stuff. I've got balloons and streamers. I picked up the cake too, after I got the twins. Come downstairs and look."

In the kitchen, an enormous pink box dominated the counter. Inside was a giant slab of icing with my name and a huge bubbly HAPPY EIGHTEENTH written in acid-colored frosting. A bag nearby carried smaller boxes full of cupcakes to be sure everyone would get their share.

"You like?" she asked, studying my face.

"I totally like," I said, and I did. Only, my brain felt like a rock all of a sudden. I blurted out, "Donny is coming tonight after all."

"Really? That's unexpected, isn't it?"

"It would be if my friends hadn't pressured him."

"Why would they do that?"

"Because suddenly Donick Walsh is the new thing. Don't you know?"

"How are things going for him in the show?"

"Swimmingly. Mrs. P., Chalice, Mr. Hardy…they all love him. He sings tolerably well, even has a solo. He's getting along with everyone, making all kinds of friends, including *mine*. Now he's coming to my birthday party."

"It won't be so bad."

"It'll be awful. How am I supposed to have a good time knowing he's here?"

"You don't really have to talk to him. We have a ton of space. Your friends spread out across the house and backyard at these parties. If you don't want to, you won't even have to see him. I'm sure he'll be happy to avoid you also."

"Except for him suddenly being everywhere at school. Why does he have to be at my house too?"

"Because you're a kind person who wouldn't have invited everyone in the cast except him."

I scoffed. "Being kind sucks."

She clicked her tongue, but she hugged me again, going so far as to stand on tip-toe to kiss my cheek. I wondered when it was I had grown so much taller than her.

"Do me a favor?" I asked. "When he arrives, will *you* be the one to open the door?"

DONICK

"Here in this teenage battlezone…"

I ARRIVE AT THE Penrose house exactly at seven, then get nervous. I sit in my car until seven-thirty, watching partygoers get dropped off, or park and go in carrying overnight bags. It's a nice house, because Michael's family has money. Pop does okay, but he isn't a teacher at a private school, or a vet, like Michael's parents.

At last, a car pulls up and a guy carrying an enormous stack of pizza boxes approaches the door. I take a deep breath and decide it's now or never. I get out and approach the house too, walking like a sloth, gripping my keys tight enough to stab myself.

The pizza guy is returning, pocketing a wad of cash. He throws me a curious look as we pass, and I feel a weird satisfaction. He's cute—black hair and small rimless glasses, maybe in his first year of college. He glances into my face with interest, giving a little smile and a "What's up?"

"Not much."

"Sounds like a good time in there. Have fun."

This guy is *interested* in me! I can tell! His eyes linger, his smile designed to be disarming.

I smile back, made awkward, not only by his interest, but by my satisfaction with it. "We'll see how it goes."

"Take it easy," he calls, walking backward a little to keep me in his sights, then vanishes into the night.

My nerves, gratified that a hottie thought me cute, jump again as I stand before the door. All kinds of noise and thumping music drifts from inside. I press the doorbell, immediately thrusting my balled hands into my pockets.

It'll be Michael who answers, and what will I say? *Happy birthday?* Or, *Thanks for inviting me?* I anticipate the dark look that will cross his face.

But it isn't Michael. His mother opens the door.

Noise shoots into the air like something struggling for freedom as she gazes at me. She looks almost exactly like I remember her. I spent years nearly a part of her family; she had been something like a mother, considering I never really had mine. The sight of her fills me with so much guilt, I suddenly don't think I can do this—go inside—after all.

"Jeepers!" she says, her tone pleasant. "Donick Walsh! I haven't seen you in ages. Come in!" I step into light and noise, glancing about for familiar faces. The ruckus is coming from the kitchen—where the pizza is being devoured, I suppose.

She sweeps me into a hug, shocking me. I stiffen, feeling unworthy, undeserving, of her affection. Images of Michael's eyebrow sheeting blood into his eye fill my head.

"You're all grown up!" She gives me a squeeze. Her tone turns motherly. "I'm really glad you decided to come."

I feel myself sort of hug her back, wishing I dared embrace her for real—like I used to. But what she gets from me is more an awkward pat on the back. Thank God

Michael isn't in the room.

"I was so sorry to hear about your accident," she says. "But how exciting about the Revue! Michael tells me you're an amazing dancer."

Michael said that?

"Thanks," I mumble, wanting to be anywhere else. Her kindness is horrible.

A pair of children (four years old, maybe five…or six—what do I know?) come barreling from the kitchen, screeching, clutching slices of pizza with which they've already painted their grinning faces. They dart up the stairs. Following close behind comes Mr. Penrose, shouting at them to use plates. He looks almost the same too, a little heavier, the hair about his temples grayer, but it's still him: a man with a totally different vibe from my own father—a patient, kinder vibe.

He pauses for half a second. "Donick!" he exclaims. "Golly, you've gotten tall. Excellent to see you! 'Scuse me a sec." Then he takes the stairs two at a time.

Mrs. Penrose sighs. "Tomorrow morning I'll be scrubbing tomato sauce off my walls."

I blink toward the stairs. "Twins?" I ask, stunned.

"Yup. Turned five in January."

Something sad swirls in me like one of those sea-snakes. "I had no idea you'd had…I mean…after Michael and Georgie, I—I didn't know that—that you and…"

"Yes, indeed. Twins. Topher and Cady."

If I do the math, that means Michael's mom ended up pregnant not long after he and I were no longer friends. I really *don't* know anything about him, do I? That sad sea-snake twists again. He's eighteen today, yet has a five year old brother *and* sister. How they must love him. Everyone does…

"Anyway," Mrs. Penrose goes on, "the house is already full, and more are arriving every second. But I'm sure you remember your way around. Nothing is off limits. Hang out upstairs, in the backyard—there's the pool and the fire-pit—hang in the garage or the kitchen, wherever. Pizza just arrived. There's plenty. Make yourself at home." She gives my arm a pat. "Like you used to."

Oh hell, why did she have to say that?

She moves up the stairs after her husband while I pass through a wide sitting-room. It's filled with couches and easy-chairs. God, the memories! I helped Michael and his family decorate their Christmas tree in this room once. On that coffee table, he and I would play Skipbo and drink Coke Slurpees from the 7-Eleven near our elementary school. The fireplace is ablaze, the orange light gleaming from the finish of a baby grand piano situated right in the window. Mr. Penrose would sit there in the evenings, playing Chopin and Mozart while Michael and I smirked, wishing we could hear the TV or our video games better. From the room's corners burst arrangements of balloons—those garish mylar ones made in the shape of eighteens, like the ones I saw him carrying around school today, only bigger.

The kitchen is full of chatter and bodies, some already in bathing suits. Streamers drape the walls, balloons batting through the air like volleyballs. The smells of cheese, garlic, tomato sauce are very strong. It's a sea of paper plates loaded with pizza, potato chips, veggies, splotches of dip.

I know right away that Mrs. Penrose greeted me at the door on purpose. Michael is staring, watching for my entrance. He instantly looks away when our eyes meet and continues talking and eating pizza, but I sense his discomfort. Still, I can't keep from smiling as a burst of voices call out my name. It's mostly dancers, but Liam darts at me; and Brent, holding a pink balloon by its knot in one hand, waves it from where he's sitting on the counter. Calista is standing there too, Michael between them. She doesn't smile—that's not really Calista, I'm learning—but she jerks her chin in a *come here* gesture.

Liam, however, is hugging me (getting hugs like this from other guys is awkward as hell, but also kind of awesome), followed by Jackie and a few other girls. They chorus different things at me, mostly about how I need to go into the backyard with them. Did I bring my swimsuit? Am I spending the night? I make my way through the bodies, happy that my presence doesn't get me those frightened looks anymore.

I slip into a pocket beside Calista at the counter, saying hello as she gives me a one armed side hug, sliding a pizza box in front of me. Brent hands over a plate.

"Fashionably late, I see," he says

My hands are shaking—Michael is very close, staring down at his food, trying not to look aggravated—as I start loading my plate. I jokingly say, "I got lost trying to get here."

Michael frowns at me. My hands seem to have passed their shaking on to the rest of me. "Kidding," I say, trying to smile. "Happy birthday."

He doesn't smile back. "Thanks," he says, then looks away.

"You guys have a good day?" I ask, hating the smalltalk.

Brent starts to speak but Calista interrupts. "Nick, who's that stonery-looking amoeba that hangs out with your friends?"

The bite of pizza I've taken threatens to choke me. I long to say, *They aren't my friends.* But I manage, "Scott Blair?"

"That his name?"

"He's the only stoned amoeba I can think of."

"Blonde hair," Brent puts in, "and a serious case of the squints?"

"Sounds like Scott. Why?"

Calista shakes her head. "Just wondering."

"Why wonder about someone like him?" I bump her elbow with mine and let a joke come out of me. "Not thinking of dating him, are you?"

She shoots me a look, like she's surprised. Honestly, I'm surprised too. I almost blush. And I could kick myself. *Don't start getting comfortable, Walsh!* I scold myself. Yet her face becomes amused. "That's exactly it," she says. "How did you know?"

"Wild hunch. Seriously. Why ask about that waste?"

Her answer is a sigh.

"What?" I press.

"It's nothing," she says. "We just ran into some of your friends after school today. I know who Ryan is, but didn't know Scott."

"They didn't do anything, did they?"

Michael speaks, looking angry, not lifting his eyes from his plate. "Broke her phone."

"They broke your phone?"

Calista twists her mouth, almost like a shrug. "Ryan bumped me and knocked it out of my hands. Broke the screen, though I can still use it. I'm just pissed because I've only had this phone for, like, five minutes." She pulls her phone out of the pocket of her khakis. The screen is a spiderweb of very fine cracks. I trip one fingernail over them.

"Well," I say, "my dad works for a bunch of cell companies.

I can probably get him to have this repaired. It's an iPhone. He's always testing Apple products. He's got connections."

Her whole face brightens. "Seriously? You'd ask him?"

"Sure. I'll let you know what he says on Monday."

"That would be amazing!" She gives me another of those one armed side hugs. "You're the best!"

I blush. It's curious, knowing Michael dislikes me so much, yet wanting him to hear words like that so he might change his opinion. I dart another glance at him. His profile is as unmoving as a face on a movie poster. It's his birthday, I remind myself, and my being right here, talking to his friends, is spoiling it.

I mutter, "Don't mention it," and pick up my plate. Liam has begun waving me toward the sliding-door. "I'm being summoned," I add. "Michael, again, happy birthday. Thanks for having me over."

He says nothing. Calista and Brent exchange looks, but I press through the other party guests and make my way into the backyard, holding my plate over everyone's heads. Liam is waiting for me, grinning as usual.

Memories hit me again. Running through the grass during summers, Michael and I barefoot and in swim-trunks, our toes stained by grass, our boyish shoulders peeling from sunburn. Winter vacation sleepovers gathered around the fire-pit in the cold dark, which burns like a beacon even now, silhouettes in lawn chairs ringing it. The pool light is very bright, sending wavering water-lines dancing over everything. It's much quieter here, though kids are getting back into the water and calling to one another. I see scattered coolers, lids open to reveal mounded ice and sweating soda cans.

I follow Liam toward one end of the pool. In an alcove, the jacuzzi is like a boiling pot. Liam is barefoot, wearing a pair of board-shorts and a T-shirt. Jackie and the other girls with us wear towels fastened about their chests. The cloying scent of hot chlorine is almost a cloud as we sink into chairs and loungers. Liam sits at the spa's lip, dipping his legs into the water. I let them do the talking. I'm still not sure what I have to contribute to these new friendships.

"You should have brought your suit, Nick," Liam says. "We're all going in."

"It's fine. I'll just watch."

Jackie says, "I bet Michael has something you can borrow. Or maybe his dad. You should ask."

Horrible idea! "I'm not big on swimming," I say. "It's cool."

Talk turns to rehearsals and the Revue. Liam, plate in his lap, utters a curse now and then when a carrot or a stick of celery rolls into the water. Once it's even a coin of pepperoni. I'm the only one involved in the singing portion of the show and they ask questions about how it's going, what the voices are like, what songs are being worked on, how bad some of the singers are when they're given movement. I say nothing disparaging because the non-dancers are working really hard to pick up their choreography, the same way I'm working hard to learn how to sing.

Once they're done eating, plates get tossed aside and towels come off. The girls slip into the spa. I've never had any interest in looking at them in their suits, yet try to pass off my averted eyes as some sort of gentlemanly display. When Liam gets to his feet, however, water running through the faint hair on his shins to trickle over his toes, I have to work hard not to stare. His shirt comes off and he's surprisingly lean beneath it. He's pale, hairless, slight, but he's got a flat stomach and nice, broad shoulders. I'm glad when he hides himself in the water. I'm not attracted to Liam, but that doesn't mean I don't find him attractive.

Jackie giggles. "Li, you should call Gil over. Maybe you can convince him to swim in his underwear or something."

I frown. "Gil? Gil who?" I only know of one Gil.

Jackie says, "Gil Hamilton."

My mouth drops open. "Gil Hamilton is here? Why?"

Liam snorts. "Because he was invited, genius."

"I'm just surprised."

"What's wrong with him?"

"Nothing. I played football with him in ninth grade, before he switched to wrestling. He's cool. I don't really know him very well, this just doesn't seem like his kind of party."

"Is this a jock thing?" Liam quips. "Because I wouldn't say this is *your* kind of party either."

Jackie comes to my defense. "It didn't used to be."

Liam smiles hugely. "I wonder if Gil's a boxers or briefs guy."

The girls giggle. I laugh too, but uncomfortably.

An Asian girl named Reese says, "He's my type for sure. I love red-heads."

Liam sighs. "My type too."

I've never listened to a guy talk about another guy like this. I'm intrigued. I almost wish I could bring up the pizza guy that had given me the eye outside.

I ask, "*What's* your type, Li?"

He bites at his lip, thinking. "Kinda small, like me, I guess. But a nice body!"

A girl named Tamika with her braids piled in an

enormous bun on top of her head says, "Who doesn't want a nice body?"

Liam smirks. "I would have one if I didn't eat so much pizza."

He's quickly splashed with a face full of jacuzzi water. In a few seconds, he starts again.

"I don't really care about, like, hair color or anything like that, but Gil's all compact and…hard, I guess."

"Hard?" Tamika snorts.

Now Liam flicks water. "Not like that!"

"Are you sure?" Jackie asks.

Before I can stop myself, I'm laughing, adding, "Yeah, Li, what *did* you mean?"

How out of place I should feel. And how unreal is this conversation? But I'm enjoying hearing him talk about boys, and I'm enjoying this simple teasing. It's so different from Ryan's or Josue's malicious jeers.

"Have you *seen* Gil Hamilton in his wrestling gear?" Liam asks. "Add a cape and he'd look like a superhero or something."

Reese turns her head toward the fire-pit. "Don't talk so loud. He'll hear you."

Liam grins. "I want him to hear. I'm interested. He should know."

I smile, but shake my head. "I hope you find someone great, man, but you won't get anywhere with Gil. Straight as an arrow."

They all look at me, blinking.

"What planet have you been on?" Liam asks.

I look at each of them, puzzled. "What?"

"Gil is gay."

I frown, on edge, waiting for some sort of punchline. "Yeah, right. Gil Hamilton? Wrestler Gil Hamilton? He's—"

"G-A-Y!" says Liam. "He's been out for, like, a year or something. How did you not now?"

I stare. "You're serious? Gil is gay?"

Tamika snorts. "You're, like, the last one to know."

My brain is reeling. A good portion of that is jealousy. How did he do it? How did he have the nerve? How could he keep wrestling? How did his team, his friends, accept him?

At last, I shrug and say, "Well, good for him. I hope he's happy."

"Anyone is happier when they're being themselves," Liam says. Though he's said it almost dismissively, each word weighs ten pounds, settling inside my ribs.

The conversation ends when Tamika grimaces. "Ew! Liam! There's a piece of onion in the water!"

I want a soda, so I offer to toss everyone's garbage. A cooler and a garbage barrel sit near the fire-pit and, not going to lie, I have this desire to see if Gil Hamilton is, in fact, sitting there. I know this huge new thing about him and it strikes me as totally impossible, regardless of what I've been told.

I lean over the cooler, squinting against the firelight. There are three people sitting in the chairs, and sure enough, one is Gil Hamilton. I pluck out a can of something—I'm not even sure what—then take a few steps closer.

"Gil?"

He turns his face, breaking into a grin.

"Nick Walsh!" He gets up and gives my fist a bump. I

had forgotten just how *not* tall he is. Still, Liam is right. Despite Gil's lack of height, he's broad shouldered with a killer chest and arms. He's wearing a sweater—not a sweatshirt, or a hoodie, but a real sweater, the knit kind with a v-neck that shows the hollow of his throat. The swaying light from the pool water paints his face and his red hair looks almost a normal boring brown. "Good to see you, man. What are you doing *here*?"

"Hey, don't say it like that." I laugh. "I can hang. What are *you* doing here?"

He shrugs. "Even gingers get invited places."

When he stood up, an enormous drift of scent—fruity and sweet—had washed into me. I make a face, half-amused, half-grossed out, fanning a hand through the air. "Dude! What are you wearing?"

He stretches his lips in a comic grimace. "Too much? I was a little spastic while getting ready to leave the house."

"Don't get too close to the fire. What kind of spray is that?"

"Actually," he says, almost hesitant, "it's some chick spray."

"Why?" I can't keep from sounding a little appalled.

"Because no other guy is gonna smell like me, get it? I'll be memorable. Mostly no one notices. Except I was a dumbass tonight."

I suppose his preference for smelling like a girl might have something to do with being gay, but Lord knows I don't know much about what makes someone gay or not, other than the obvious. I also wonder just how it is that Gil knows Michael. Is that a gay thing too? They all know each other? Or, it's not something…well, *bigger*, is it? Like, he and Michael are more than friends?

I try not to stutter as I ask how he knows Michael.

"We have Gov together." He gives me a curious look. "How do *you* know him?"

I swallow through an intensely dry throat. "I don't know him," I say. "Not really. I mean, I've known him since we were in elementary school, but we aren't really friends. He invited the whole cast of the Senior Revue, so, I guess that includes me."

"Oh yeah. I heard you were doing the show. I never took you for the theatre-type."

"I guess I'm not. Or I wasn't. I sort of *have* to do the show. But I'm actually having fun."

"I'm still shook though. I mean, you're spending time with these guys. I know they're not really…your crowd."

I give a dry laugh. "I'm not really sure what my crowd is these days."

"Bro, come sit. Fire's great. Let's palaver."

Palaver?

Gil returns to his chair. When I fall into the chair beside him, the guy and girl sitting across from us lean together and start kissing. Gil makes a face. I grimace, pop the top of the soda in my hand and swig from it. Dr. Pepper…gross.

"Sorry to hear about what happened last year," says Gil. "With football, I mean. Bad news, dude."

"I'm whatever about it."

"Yeah?"

"Wasn't really feeling it anyway. I just wish I hadn't had to miss so much school. My grades got really screwed. I know I'll be able to graduate, but it's been pretty close."

"Feel you, man. I'm stoked about graduation. Can't wait to get outta here."

"Where you going?"

"UCSB."

"Nice. Congrats."

"Thanks. Not sure what I'm gonna major in yet, but… you know."

"I don't know what I'm gonna do. Maybe community college? Who knows…"

"Cause of the no football thing?"

"Pretty much. No scholarships now. I wouldn't know what to study either."

"Check it out, bro. I've been hearing through the grapevine that you're, like, a tight dancer. Do something with that."

I laugh, self-conscious. "I never thought I would use dance for anything other than football training. Now I'm learning how to vogue every day after school."

"No way! That's dank, dude! Back in the day, that was a tight style."

The sliding-door opens, spilling noise from inside, including the strains of someone playing the piano. A group of people are even singing along. Partygoers step out, shut the door, and the sounds cut off.

"I wish Michael would come out," Gil says. "I haven't been able to talk to him much."

I hope desperately that Michael *won't* come out. He acted so irritated when I talked to his friends in the kitchen. I wonder if Calista knows Gil is gay. I have the sudden desire to gossip with her about him, to tell her that Liam has the hots for him. And the pizza guy flirted with me outside the house.

"There're a lot of people here," I say. "I'm sure Michael

will make his rounds."

"I just thought…oh, I dunno. I had hopes, I guess."

I give him a questioning look. Then I realize he's hinting toward my suspicion. "Oh!" I say. "You and Michael?"

"There's no me and Michael," he says, chuckling. "But…I think he's sorta cute."

The whole idea strikes me as awful. I rationalize it as jealousy toward Gil being comfortable enough with himself to give his attentions to Michael, and Michael being comfortable enough with himself to receive them. I may have liked the looks the pizza guy gave me when I arrived, but I would have peed myself at the simple idea of *really* flirting back, let alone in a setting where people could see.

I clear my throat. "How long have you been…I mean… Sorry, man, I didn't even know you were…into guys, I guess, until tonight. I—I don't know what to say."

"It's all good. I've been out since junior year. Why waste my life? I'm only young once. I wanted to finish high school on my own terms." He sits up straighter and gives me a very serious look. "Dude, Nick, that doesn't freak you out, right? I mean, I sorta know how you feel about that kind of thing. Which is why I was surprised to see you here. This theatre crowd…you know."

I shrug. "I'm not freaked. I just never pegged you as, well, like *that*?"

"Gay." He grins. "You can say it. I'm okay. Surprisingly no one has really cared."

"Not your friends?"

"They wouldn't be friends if they did."

"Your parents?"

He wrinkles his nose a bit. "Well, that was kinda

interesting. I mean, they're totally fine now, but when I first told them…it was my mom who freaked a little. My dad was cool. Then again, he hardly knows much about me and isn't too interested. Too caught up with his other family. He made all these jokes about understanding why I was into wrestling though."

"*Isn't* wrestling kinda weird?"

Gil snorts. "No! Trust me, there's nothing sexy about competitions. That's gay porn fantasy shit. Competitions and practices are all business. Did you ever have the time or energy to think about chicks in the middle of a football game?"

"No," I laugh out. "I never thought about chicks when I was playing football." I stare at the flickering fire. Gil, in a way, is the me I want to be. How is he—how are people like him—so brave?

Liam's voice suddenly cries, "Nick! Where'd you go?"

I call back, "By the fire!"

There's laughter from the jacuzzi and Gil asks, "Who's that?"

"Liam. Hidalgo? Do you know him?"

Gil shakes his head.

"A new friend of mine. Met him in the show. Really nice kid. Sophomore."

There's the slap of wet feet. Liam materializes beside my chair, still shirtless, but with a towel around his waist. His hair is sleek with water. Steam actually rises into the chilled air from his shoulders.

"Whatcha doin'?" he asks. His eyes flick to the boy and girl still making out on the other side of the fire-pit. He glances at Gil as though he doesn't care who he is.

"Just talking," I say. I gesture at the couple. "I think *that* became one person about five minutes ago. But this is Gil."

Liam holds out his hand for Gil to shake, his fingertips visibly wrinkled with pool water. "Pleasure, kind sir."

"All mine," Gil replies.

When Gil looks away, Liam raises his brows at me. The couple, who heard what I said, mutter under their breaths and leave their chairs.

Gil murmurs, "Try not to fornicate on your way into the house."

"We're gonna go inside," Liam says. "Tamika says Michael's dad is playing the piano. People are singing. Don't wanna miss out. It's like those lunch karaoke things."

"I'll come in soon."

Liam smiles at Gil, says, "You smell good. Anyway, nice to meet you," then pads away.

Gil twists around to see that Liam is out of earshot, then he grins at me. "Your new *gay* friend?"

I feel startled. "What?"

"He thinks I smell good? I didn't think you were comfortable enough with gay dudes to actually make friends with them."

"Liam's a good guy." I feel defensive.

Gil shakes his head. "I didn't mean anything. This is just different for you. You have a bit of the homophobe reputation."

"I'm not a homophobe."

The slider opens and closes, then a jarred feeling rushes through me when I hear Michael's voice. He crosses the yard, coming toward the fire. "Yo, Gil!"

Gil straightens in the chair, flashing his teeth at me. He

calls back, "Yo, Michael!"

"You been out here all this time?"

"Yup yup."

Michael comes into the light. He smiles at Gil, but the smile falters when he sees me.

Gil shifts over in the seat and pats the chair's arm. Michael perches on it, looking disconcerted.

Gil asks, "Having a nice birthday?"

Michael nods, and though he smiles, his dismay is as clear to me as the fruity musk rising from Gil's pores. He gazes into the fire, the flames making his eyes seem to be any color, or no color. He's pointedly not looking at me.

"I hear your dad is playing the piano," says Gil.

Michael scoffs. "That's what parents are for, right? To embarrass the crap out of you."

"I dunno. You got a lot of singers here."

"True. Theatre peeps are ginormous hams. Brent just sang 'Michael in the Bathroom'. I think he might be looking at something from *Legally Blonde* for an encore. 'Bend and Snap' maybe. He's not a great singer."

Gil raises his brows. "I feel like you just spoke a different language."

Michael laughs. Then they look at each other. Something passes between them during that half-second of silence. I sense it, and I want to claw it to ribbons with my fingernails. I feel like a left out little boy, simply wanting to belong.

I get to my feet. "I'm heading inside."

Michael doesn't look at me when he says, "Don't leave on my account."

Gil doesn't sense the acid in that sentence. He says, "Yeah, man, stay."

"It's cool. I'm getting cold." Then I add, teasingly, "Besides, your spray is giving me a headache."

"Total party foul, right? What was I thinking?"

Michael says, "You smell good, just, you know, don't get too close to the fire."

Gil barks out laughter. "That's what Nick said!"

Michael looks confused for a moment, his lips tightening.

"I should probably go find someone to drink this gaggy Dr. Pepper anyway," I say. "Don't wanna waste it."

But before I can make another move, the slider opens again and it's Brent shouting, "Michael! It's your turn to sing! You got a fan-club waiting to wave their phone-screens at you!"

"That's my old man's doing, I bet," Michael murmurs. "It wouldn't be a party without the crippling embarrassment."

Gil says, "I've never heard you sing." His voice is soft, sounding as though he would like nothing better. "Don't keep your adoring fans in suspense."

He gets to his feet and actually gives Michael his hand. Michael takes it and Gil pulls him up. I detest the gesture with every fiber of my being. I'm certain that in better light the crimson in Michael's cheeks would be clear. He starts toward the door with Gil in tow. I follow after and Gil turns to me, flashing his teeth again.

"Now *I'm* the nervous one," he says.

In a brainless moment, I say, "You don't have to be. Michael's amazing."

I dart a glance at Michael's back, wishing I could un-say the words. The only reaction is a minuscule twist of his head, as though he wants to dart me a glance.

"Another adoring fan," says Gil. "What're you gonna sing, Michael?"

"My dad'll pick," Michael replies as we reach the door. "He always picks. Usually a song we've been working on."

The kitchen is deserted, the counter wrecked with pizza boxes, vegetable trays, spilled ranch dressing. Open cans of soda stand everywhere and a bowl of potato chips has overturned beside the sink. Brent stands back to let us in, eyes gleaming with amusement at the sight of Michael and Gil together. Does everyone know that something's going on between the two of them?

We enter the sitting-area at the front of the house where every one of Michael's party guests are seated on the sofas and chairs, sprawled on the carpets, or perching on the brick hearth. As soon as Michael appears, Mr. Penrose's fingers summon piano chords and the whole room is caroling out a deafening rendition of "Happy Birthday". I join in, watching as Michael smiles self-consciously, making his way to the center of the room. An enormous birthday cake with ridiculously colorful icing sits on the coffee-table. Candles bristle from its frosted surface, tiny flames winking and swaying against the air. Mrs. Penrose is standing near the piano with one of the twins—Cady, I remember she called her—lifted in her arms. The little girl looks sleepy yet determined, much too big to be held that way, but seeming to insist on it nonetheless. Her twin brother is sitting on the couch in Calista's lap.

Once the song ends and the clapping and cheering stills, Michael, blushing, kneels beside the coffee table. Someone shouts, "Make a wish, Penrose!" Another voice tells the first speaker to shut the hell up. Michael leans forward, his face yellow in the glow of the candles, and breathes them all out. More shouts and clapping, tiny wisps of smoke drifting upward from the snuffed wicks.

"Did you wish, Micuh?" his little brother asks, playing with his own ears.

Michael ruffles his hair. "Yup!"

"What for?" the girl twin cries and shimmies out of her mother's arms. The room laughs. Michael puts his arm around her as she leans into him.

"Not allowed to tell," he says to her. Someone in the room shouts, "It won't come true!"

I have a moment when I feel as though I'm not truly standing here in the Penrose living-room. I think I must be in a pod somewhere, like in *The Matrix*. I find myself lurking in the arch between the kitchen and sitting-area, leaning there (my gross Dr. Pepper left amidst a jumble of abandoned cans), just observing, feeling more of an outsider than ever. And why? Because I can almost see what this party would be like if I had never done that awful thing to Michael so many years ago. It could be me sitting on the couch with little Topher in my lap. It could be me kneeling on the floor beside Michael, grinning and cheering and clapping with all the rest, never doubting that I belong here. Maybe I would even be working to bring Michael and Gil together, like Brent and Calista must surely be doing, instead of feeling jealous over their building connection, wishing I dared to be as courageous.

Michael's father suddenly flourishes the piano keys. He speaks loudly, typical of a teacher commanding a room full of children. "All right! Time for the birthday boy—sorry, birthday *man*—to give us a song!"

Michael makes a face.

But many voices have risen to second his dad's request, even Cady and Topher piping out, "Sing, Micuh, sing!"

"Do I have to?" Michael asks the room in a cheesy I'm-going-to-sing-but-I'll-pretend-to-hesitate way. There are cries of "Do it!" and "Don't be a pussy, Michael!" (Mrs. Penrose shakes her head, darting a glance at the twins.) With a theatrical groan, Michael steps to the piano. "Fine!"

Calista rolls her eyes. "Like there was any doubt."

Michael sinks onto the bench beside his father, facing the room. He says, "What'll it be, Dad?"

"'Gold in Them Hills', how about?" Mr. Penrose says.

The room quiets significantly. Michael darts a look at Gil crouched down at one end of the sofa, watching intently.

Michael speaks to the room. "Okay, so, 'Gold in Them Hills'. This isn't a song from a musical or anything. I first heard it on that old TV show *Queer as Folk* when I watched it on Netflix—a few years ago when my parents probably wouldn't have wanted me watching it." Mr. and Mrs. Penrose shake their heads. Michael continues, "Anyway, I thought it was really beautiful. I looked everywhere for the sheet music and couldn't find it. So, I gave a copy of the song to my dad, and for a Christmas present this last year, he basically wrote the sheet music for me, so, think of this as a world premier or something," he finishes, chuckling. "All right, Dad. Ready when you are."

The sitting-room gets very still. The piano is instantly beautiful, sweeping everyone under the introduction's spell. I can't look away from Michael as he begins to sing, as he lights up the room. Melody, lyrics, the silence underscoring both his and the piano's voices…they mingle and drift over me, causing the hairs on my arms to shiver.

AN HOUR LATER, cake and cupcakes have been distributed. Michael's parents put the twins to bed (protesting), then retire themselves (not protesting), though they announce they're upstairs watching TV if anyone needs anything. Then the party resumes.

Music blasts from someone's iPod, a crowd dances before the fireplace like a tribe of pagans. Others return to the fire-pit or the jacuzzi, some are drawn into the garage by a dartboard and a ping-pong table. When I peek in I see they're playing beer-pong, and I wonder where the beer came from, and if Mr. and Mrs. Penrose will care that there are kids slowly getting drunk in their house. But maybe that's the point of the sleepover. Michael's parents seem like the type who would allow underage drinking, knowing they can't really stop it, as long as those imbibing stay the night. More partygoers are sitting on the stairs, drinking from red plastic cups. On the landing, a girl has pulled out a deck of tarot cards, kids gathered around as she gives readings. A group has taken over the kitchen table, getting aggravated over a spread of Phase 10.

I wander around, not stopping long in any one place. I'm actually enjoying observing, talking to anyone who'll talk to me. Mostly I keep an eye out for Michael, being wherever he is not—though his inner social-butterfly is out in force. Seeing how happy he looks actually makes me smile a little. Gil *isn't* with him most of the time though. I wonder if that's a mutual decision not to be too clingy, to maybe keep gossip down. Mostly Michael is with his Muskequeers. People press me to dance, but I'm not comfortable enough for that. Besides, Michael's face keeps appearing amongst the pagans whenever a song is particularly good. Despite one or two awkward moments, I'm actually having a very good time. Parties were never this...*relaxed* when I hung out with my football friends.

Around eleven o'clock, I find myself upstairs sitting in the hallway with two or three of the Revue singers, listening to them tell stories about shows they've done. I leave them to use the bathroom and another sense of unreality sweeps me. As I wash my hands, looking at the toothbrushes in a cup beside the sink, I think the green one must be Michael's. The green towel hanging on the shower's door-rack has to be his too—maybe to match his eyes. Georgie seems to have a thing for pink and yellow. Though I suppose the green might be Georgie's.

I spy Michael's glasses on the counter beside a bottle of contact-solution. I remember him *always* wearing glasses, and suppose he must now only wear them at night before bed. I wonder how it would feel to see him in them now, grown up and as handsome as he's become, and not that thin little boy with the hair under his arms, beginning to grow out of his hands and feet, the glasses almost bigger than his face.

I'm right here in his home, he's only been feet away all evening, yet the Grand Canyon might as well separate us. How could I have treated Michael, our friendship, as though it all meant nothing? How will I ever find him again? How can I ever get him to *let* me find him again? Because...I miss him.

Leaving the bathroom, my eyes fall to Mr. and Mrs. Penrose's bedroom door, slightly ajar, their voices murmuring beyond it as a TV flickers. I'm not sure what my object is but I approach, gulp like a cartoon character, and knock. Their voices quiet and Mrs. Penrose says to come in.

A bedside light flicks on revealing the pair of them lying in their bed atop the covers, not yet in their pajamas, but with their shoes off. Mr. Penrose mutes the TV and they peer at me, a little surprised to see who it is.

"Hey kiddo," Mr. Penrose says. "What's up?"

"Did you need something?" Mrs. Penrose asks.

"I—" I begin, and then falter. I thrust my hands into my pockets again. "I'm not sure, really."

They look amused.

"Are you enjoying yourself?" she asks.

I nod. "Thanks for having us all over. For having…*me* over."

Mr. Penrose says, "You're always welcome."

"Always have been," Mrs. Penrose adds, smiling.

My throat feels unbearably tight all of a sudden. "I think I wore out my welcome years ago," I say.

"If that were true," she replies, "you wouldn't be here now."

"I guess. You've both been really nice to me tonight. After what happened with Michael…I just…I dunno."

I've been hovering near the door. Mrs. Penrose leans forward and pats the foot of the bed. "Come sit for a minute."

Thinking I might trip over my own Converse, I step forward to sit near her feet. I'm finding it hard to look squarely at either of them.

"I just mean…thank you," I murmur. "I shouldn't be here, I know. It makes it weird for *him*. I'm invading his space, like, crazy amounts."

"I've never understood," she says, "how two boys who were such good friends could suddenly just *not* be friends anymore."

I hurry to say, "It's my fault. I suck. And…I'm so…I mean, he's, like, your son, and I was really horrible to him." I pause, swallowing. "That has to be hard on parents, right? Makes it worse that the person being horrible…you both welcomed into your home and…" I clutch my phone and my keys in my pockets as though they're life-lines.

Out of the corner of my eye I see Mr. and Mrs. Penrose watching me. They don't look at each other, yet I can sense that grown-up parental connection communicating silently. I wonder if my own parents would have had that, if my mom hadn't died…

Summoning courage I don't think I have, I look at them and say, "You treated me like I was your son. I forgot about that for a long time. But I remember now. And I'm grateful. For back then, and tonight. I owe you both an apology for what I did."

Mr. Penrose's face is kind, but he stays silent. Mrs. Penrose gives my shoulder a squeeze.

"We appreciate hearing that. I've always thought it was silly, and friends fight sometimes."

I shake my head. "It wasn't just a fight. I…I terrorized him." My voice shakes. "I hurt him because I knew how."

"The truth is, Donick, it's *Michael* who needs the apology. Not us. You know that. Yes, he was hurt. You were his best friend and then you just…"

"I turned on him."

She doesn't agree, but she doesn't tell me I'm wrong.

"I don't think he wants my apology," I add. "If I gave it, he wouldn't accept."

"Listen, kiddo," Mr. Penrose puts in. "I know my Ninja."

I smile; it's been a long time since I heard Michael's nickname. "He's got a temper on him, and when he gets mad, he gets *really* mad. Imagine a toddler like that… But once he's been able to hash out his stuff, then he gets over it. Maybe he just needs time to get used to having you around. You were there, and then you weren't. You were important to him, and yes, maybe you did some crummy things, but Ninja's never been able to deal with it—and I mean deal with it by having an outlet. You weren't exactly there for him to be angry at. It's hard to make peace with something when the object of the chaos isn't around."

I think about that for a few seconds. "Calista and Brent think maybe he'll never be able to forgive me," I say.

"It's possible you'll never be able to be friends again, that's true," Mrs. Penrose says. "Sad, but true."

I take a deep breath. "That'll have to be okay. Michael doesn't owe me anything. It's me that owes him. More than I'm capable of paying. But I can try. Somehow."

Suddenly my phone is vibrating in my hand. It startles me a little. I pull it out, glancing at the screen. Dismay stabs at me.

"It's my dad. I need to answer." I get to my feet, but give them a tentative smile. "Thank you. Again. It's been really nice seeing you. I know it's kinda late, and I wish I'd known before, but congratulations on the twins. They're really cute."

Mr. Penrose snorts. "They're really loud."

Mrs. Penrose sighs. "And really demanding."

I chuckle, and they smile at me. "I hope we'll see you again, Donick," Mrs. Penrose tells me. And Mr. Penrose adds, "Looking forward to seeing you in the Revue, kiddo."

I hurry out. In the hall, I answer the phone. Before I can

say anything, Pop's voice almost shouts from the speaker.

"Where in hell are you, Nicky? I been texting and calling you for hours!"

I'm suddenly anxious. How I hate when his voice sounds like this. "Sorry," I stammer out. "I didn't feel my phone go off."

"You shoulda waited for me to get home before taking it on yourself to go out!"

"I didn't think you'd mind."

"I mighta needed you to run an errand for me, or maybe I needed the other car. D'you think of that? Never mind the fact you could be dead somewhere and I'd have no idea!"

"I'm fine, Pop. I'm sorry."

"Well? Where in hell are you?"

Embarrassed, I dart a glance at the kids still sitting on the floor nearby. I cross the hall, pushing open the door to Michael's room, and slip inside. The music is loud from downstairs, but it's much quieter here—plus I'm about to lie and would prefer no one know. I remember that it's Michael's room, of course, but in the burst of panic I always feel when Pop gets angry, I don't pause to think about *massively* overstepping my welcome.

"I'm at Josue's," I say. "A bunch of the guys are here. We're just hanging out."

"You drinking, Nicky?"

"No." The way I say it sounds petulant because he thinks I'm going to lie to him—I can hear it in his voice.

"Next time you wait 'til you talk to me before you go anywhere."

"I tried to text you. I even called but you didn't answer."

"Beside the point! You don't get my permission, you

don't leave the house. Got it?"

I sigh with my lips away from the phone so he won't hear it. "Yeah, Pop."

He's always like this. There's never any consistency. Sometimes I have more freedom than I know what to do with, then there are times like now. I can never figure him out, aside from the simmering irritation always below the surface.

"It's eleven-thirty," he says. "Home by midnight." And *click*, he's gone.

I clench my teeth, heaving a sigh. I push the phone back into my pocket and stand there for a minute, rubbing at my eyes.

Then I look around.

Michael's room…

It looks just as I remember it—yet, different. The overhead lamp is off, but a string of white Christmas lights drape the top of the window, casting the room in a dim, mellow glow. Instead of a narrow boy's bed, a queen without a frame sits against the wall. The bedspread is green, like his towels—to match his eyes, I think again. In one corner float the balloons I saw him with earlier. The television atop his dresser is newer, and where once there were shelves of DVDs, blu-rays have taken over.

I step closer to the bookcase, because the top shelf is devoted to Michael's favorite movies and TV shows. All seven seasons of *Buffy the Vampire Slayer* sit there (they used to be his parents', I recall). The extended editions of *The Lord of the Rings* are side-by-side with all eight *Harry Potter* movies. Here are the *Alien* films too, along with *The Walking Dead* and *Game of Thrones*. Another shelf is loaded with anime. I lean down to read the titles. *Attack on Titan, Ninja Scroll, Ponyo, Deathnote, Fruits Basket…* His usual eclectic mix. He always did like a little of everything. There are also shelves of manga—*Battle Royale, Inuyasha, Fushigi Yugi,* and what looks like everything CLAMP every wrote. I never remember Michael reading books much, but there are a lot of those too. There are action figures everywhere, even hung on the walls—Superman, Legolas, a complicated-looking anime robot, Buffy and Angel, Pennywise the Clown, Sailor Saturn, and even the big creepy looking Queen Xenomorph from *Aliens.*

Posters cover the walls. *The Rocky Horror Picture Show; Edward Scissorhands; The Goonies* (that one hung there in my day), Henry Cavill in his *Man of Steel* costume on the back of the bedroom door (I smile, wondering what Michael would think of my computer's desktop screen and my secret folder of man-crushes). There are also posters for *Hamilton* and *Newsies,* while a *Wicked* poster signed by Joel Grey is to one side of the bed. Over the headboard is an anime wall-scroll showing a pair of male ice-skaters. I stare at this one for several seconds. Above the desk are two bright posters—one, the original version of *Sailor Moon,* and the other, *Sailor Moon Crystal.* Here and there around them he has tacked up a handful of his old *Pokemon* cards. I may not broadcast my nerd-tendencies, but I watch Crunchyroll when I'm alone. Michael would be surprised, I'm sure, to know how familiar I am with all this stuff.

A sheet of glass covers the desktop, and beneath it, all sorts of photos have been arrayed. Lots of his siblings— though the balance falls in favor of Cady and Topher, all the way back to when they were newborns. I smile at a photo of the entire Penrose clan obviously standing in Harry Potter World at Universal Studios, Michael decked out in a beanie and scarf striped in yellow and black, one arm around Georgie, Topher clinging to his free hand. Elsewhere, Brent and Calista grin up at me, and many, many have Michael himself with them. Some photos of him are old enough to be the Michael I remember best. *My* Mikey.

I don't intend to look, but the sheet of paper lying on one corner of the desk draws my eye, and though I don't touch it, its folded edges are open enough that I can see it's a letter from USC. A *rejection* letter from USC. I frown, feeling sad for him, wondering if this is troubling him, weighing on his mind, even as he tries to enjoy his birthday party.

But I forget the letter when I glance up and see, pinned to the wall beside the *Sailor Moon* posters, the two secret admirer notes I left in his locker.

He hung them up! Did they matter to him that much?

If he knew they were from me, well, I picture him snatching them down and holding them, one by one, over a burner on the kitchen stove. Still, he pinned them here, where he can see them when he's doing homework, where he can see them from anywhere in the room. All the anxiety I've carried over whether or not I should have put them in his locker vanishes. They've mattered for some reason, and gladness sweeps my anxiety aside, bringing out a smile…which falls from my face instantly when I hear footsteps in the hall and Michael's voice calling back to someone down the stairs.

For the first time, I know what it means when someone says their blood runs cold. I'm in Michael's room, without permission, and he's about to catch me. Why did I linger after Pop ended the phone call? Stupid, stupid, stupid!

Michael pushes the door open. He sees me and stops dead. His brow corrugates.

"What are you doing in here?"

His voice is strange. He sounds curious, but with resentment beneath. He doesn't raise his voice, yet I think if he had screamed at me I would have been less disarmed.

I sputter a bit. "Sorry. My dad called. I needed a quiet place…I'm sorry. I shouldn't have—"

His eyes tick to the desktop, to the college letter, and something shutters over his face, closing off. He says, "Are you looking through my things?" and all but stomps toward me, snatching up the letter and stuffing it into a drawer.

My face gets hot. "No," I say, taking a step back. "I promise. I—I wouldn't—I mean, I was looking at the pictures was all." I want to stare suddenly at the secret admirer notes. That crooked red heart seems to want my eyes desperately. "Your twins—I—I didn't know about them."

"Yeah well, you wouldn't, would you?" His nostrils flair. He won't look at me. When he speaks again, his tone is flat. "Phone call over?" I don't trust my voice, so I nod. "All right, then get out," he finishes and crosses to the dresser.

Feeling flayed, I take a few silent steps to the door, then pause. I can't explain why I don't go.

I say, "Your room's the same."

His reply is quick. "Why would it change? *I* didn't."

I feel the sting. "I know," I say. "Mikey—"

"Don't call me that!" he spits. He turns toward me, face angry now. His eyes almost glow with fury as the twinkle-lights over the window catch in them. He's pitched his voice low so as not to shout, yet I feel the force of his words all the same. "I haven't been Mikey for a long time."

"Sorry."

"What are you doing?" he suddenly asks. His expression is fierce. I hate seeing his features twisted in anger. Maybe because I know I deserve it. "Why did you come here tonight?"

"I just…I wanted to spend time with everyone."

"Typical self-serving bullshit."

A flare of irritation sweeps me. "What else should I say? That I came to celebrate your birthday with you? You haven't exactly hidden how much you *don't* want me here."

"You're right, I don't."

"Then why extend the invite?"

"Because I had to."

"Wrong. You didn't *have* to do anything. You could have invited the entire cast except for me. We both know I would know why." His jaw is working, the muscles jumping beneath the skin. But he doesn't say anything. I add, "I would have understood."

"Then answer the question," he says. "Why come at all?"

I can hear the waver in my voice when I reply. It shames me, knowing he's aware of how close I am to tears. "Because I'm trying…I'm…trying."

"Great," he says, yanking a sweater out of a drawer. "How about keeping the social experiments away from me." He goes to the bedside table and plugs in his phone.

My anger spikes again. This isn't some social experiment, this thing I'm attempting. I want to change, to start over, to reset. Hearing him put such an ugly spin on it, cheapening it, the hardest thing I've ever done, makes my own jaw clench.

I say, "Don't treat me like some asshole, Michael."

He rounds on me, and almost shouts, "You *are* an asshole, Donny!"

"Don't call me that! If you're not Mikey, I'm not Donny! I haven't been Donny since we were friends."

"Don't I know it."

"What's that supposed to mean?"

"It means you're a poser! You do everything because someone told you to do it. You feel things that people tell you to feel. You haven't had an original thought since your balls dropped!"

"At least I have a pair."

Michael actually laughs. "Nice come back. See? There's still a part of you that remembers what it was like to shove my face into that locker."

He may as well have punched me in the nose. "I'm not..." I try to say. "I'm not...*him*. That asshole who did that to you. I'm not him."

"What? Not anymore? You've always been him, *Nick*." He crosses toward me as he speaks until we're face to face. I have to work hard not to retreat. My eyes are drawn to that comma of a scar beneath his eyebrow. The frail light makes it just visible. "You can apologize to them," he says in a low, cutting tone. "You can make them your friends. You can try and take mine. You can change what they all see. But your insides? I know that they're the same."

"They're not. *I'm* not. I am *trying*—"

"Sure." He smirks. "You're different. We all are. I take back what I said. I'm different too. But all of us...we're changing into the people we want to become. Whatever you're turning into? I don't know what that is. And I think it'll be as ugly as what you were before."

In that instant, I could kill him. My hands are in fists. The fear that lurks within me—that I can never be better than my past, that I'll fail in this attempt to make things right, that I'll discover my outer layer isn't the only part that's rotten, but the very core of me also—has just been framed in speech.

Michael moves to the door. When I open my mouth, thoughtless words dart from me, coming from the wound he's inflicted. I want them back before I've even finished speaking them, but they hover in the air, all but painted in letters made of fire.

"Sometimes," I say, "I hate you, Michael."

"Perfect," he replies. He doesn't turn around, speaking with his back to me. "The feelings we have for each other are mutual."

My anger dissipates at this, and again I feel flayed. This conversation was nothing like I had wanted it to be. So many things have come off my tongue—so many untruths. I *don't* hate Michael, yet in saying it, I now know that he, really and truly, hates *me*.

I call his name, not knowing what I'm going to say, yet not wanting to leave our first real conversation in all these years—such as it is—on this note. But he doesn't let me speak.

"Show yourself out," he says. "I don't want you in my house anymore."

Then he's gone.

A million things flow into my mind like waves beating sand: an uncomfortable sense of déjà-vu, a feeling of worthlessness, of futility. I had felt I had made so much progress these last weeks, yet Michael so easily shattered all of it. I'm struggling against tears, bottled emotions battling for freedom, but I won't break down here.

It slams into me that for the last few weeks, since the day of the auditions, this attempt I've been making at starting over, at righting my wrongs, has been for Michael. Not really for me. The one person I betrayed by allowing the rot in me to take hold, is the one person I want most to make amends to. Yet that one person hates me.

I feel foolish, mortified. I need to be gone. Pop is watching the clock, yes, but I can't stay here, even if Michael hadn't ordered me out. I want to get away from everyone so I can hurt in a place where no one will see. That sense of déjà-vu—it's almost as though it's chasing me through the house.

I'm able to get out the door without being stopped, thank God, keeping my head down and hoping the tribe still gyrating in the sitting-room are too distracted to notice me slipping out. When I get into the car, my ears ringing with the sudden silence, I sit, eyes burning, all but willing the tears back and away.

I won't cry! I tell myself. *I won't!*

As I start the car and begin to pull away from the Penrose house, I notice another car parked across the street, its windows thoroughly fogged. I want to sneer at the dripping glass, thinking about that couple making out by the fire-pit. I hadn't seen them again after they had walked away. Now I know where they went. Just then, my mood is so dark, I feel so broken, I can't keep from thinking that that couple are the two most pathetic people in the world. After me, of course.

I remember the song Michael sang; I think of its lyrics as I drive. "*Though our troubles seem like mountains, there's gold in them hills…*" Suddenly I feel surrounded by mountains—great, tall mountains filled, not with nuggets of gold, but rocks and dirt. Nothing at all, except rocks and dirt.

MICHAEL

*H*AVE YOU HEARD from Gil at all?" Calista asked as she, Brent, and I sprawled on my bed Sunday afternoon. Empty Slurpee cups and a bag of Funyuns littered the floor, *It Follows* running its ending credits over the TV. (They had humored my horror movie love for once.)

"He messaged yesterday to say thanks for inviting him over and that he had fun," I said, feeling disappointed. "That was it."

Yes, he had been at my party, and yes, we had had a couple of instances of talking together. But we hadn't danced in the living-room, or even hugged at the end of the night. I had been confronted with the last person I ever wanted to be alone with instead, and right here in my bedroom.

I didn't like remembering the look on Nick's face when I startled him by coming through the door. I had said some pretty horrible things. Some I had meant, but not all. By saying I hated him, knowing that was way more harsh of an emotion than I actually felt, I had the guilty suspicion I had lowered myself to the level of people just like him. Or, at least, people like his friends. Because truthfully, Nick *was* acting different, and, as he had said, he was trying. But trying *what* exactly?

I hadn't told my friends about ordering him from the house. Brent looked for him, and I felt too much like a jerk myself to admit Nick was gone because of me.

"I have the feeling," I added, "that Gil seeing me being a dork with my friends might've been a turn off."

"He looked like he was having fun," Brent said. "You should've seen his face when you sang."

I shrugged. "Gil didn't exactly give me much to work with. We talked, but we always talk in class, and pretty much about the same surfacey stuff. He *did* give me that CD, but he loves music and talks about it all the time."

"He came to your party though," Calista said. "And let's be real, babe, the crowd here wasn't exactly *his* crowd."

"It wasn't Nick's either," said Brent. "So weird how he just disappeared."

"Yeah, but Nick is *becoming* part of the theatre crowd—sorry, Michael—and he pretty much knows most everyone that was here. Now. But Gil? Come on, he had never even heard you sing. This was not his scene."

"So you're seconding my theory about his having been turned off by seeing me in my element," I said. "Thanks, pal."

"Gil's nice, but face it. He's super far to one side of the spectrum (sports), and you're super far to the other (the arts)."

"That should mean we could meet in the middle."

"Doesn't really work that way, babe. You need someone already in the middle. Avoid people on your side of the spectrum like the plague. No more Joels or Dillons. You need to steer clear of all theatre nerds."

I huffed, irritated by the suspicion that she might be right.

Her phone suddenly pinged. "Who the hell is it?" she muttered, peering at the screen, trying to read the message through the cracks. "Everyone who texts me is here."

On the heels of her phone, I heard the buzz of mine against the glass top of the desk. I crawled across the bed and reached for it. Brent gazed morosely at the TV. "No text for Brent?" he mumbled. "Brent can't be popular too?"

"*I'll* text you," I said, chuckling, "right after I see who it is." The look he gave was dark.

Calista spoke, and a coldness crept into me. "It's from Nick, speak of the devil."

"Devil is right," I snapped.

"Did Nick text you too?" Brent asked me.

"Yeah, that's it. We're on our way to becoming besties again." I favored Brent with a grimace and glanced at the phone screen. And frowned. "Don't know the number. Someone from the show maybe…"

Brent spoke in a high falsetto. "Oh, Michael, you wonderful, tall, green-eyed tenor! Do you remember who's called for rehearsal tomorrow?" He snorted.

Calista's face broke into a broad grin. "Listen to this. Nick says he asked his dad about my phone, and his dad is totally down to get the screen replaced."

"All right, Nick!" Brent grinned. "Way to do a solid!"

"He'll take it to his dad and his dad will have it back, good as new, in a day or two!"

She started texting back, careful of the glass. True, Nick had come through, something I was surprised he had even offered, which irritated me further. It also made me feel slightly rotten after the way I had spoken to him.

However, my thoughts became an instant blank when I swiped open the text message on my own phone.

I told u 2 enjoy ur b-day week, the message read. *How did that work out?*

My eyes might have popped from their sockets, they opened so wide. I think I even stopped breathing. I lifted my gaze to the secret admirer notes tacked to the wall. The second, from my locker at the start of the week, read: I HOPE YOU HAD A NICE WEEKEND! ENJOY YOUR BIRTHDAY WEEK!

I breathed out, "Holy smokes…"

My friends turned. I held my phone out and they squinted at the screen.

"So?" Calista said.

I tapped the second note on the wall. "It's him! Or… her. It's my secret admirer!"

"Unknown number?" Brent said. "Not Gil?"

"Totally not Gil."

"How do they have your number then?" Calista asked. "It's gotta be someone in the show. We have a contact-list. Check it and see if the number's there."

I scrambled for the list. It came out of my backpack rumpled and creased. I smoothed it on the desktop, then hunched over it, comparing the number on the phone with the numbers beside each cast member's name. Brent and Calista came to crowd me.

"Is there a match?" Calista pressed.

Excitement making my heart thump crazily, I checked number by number until I reached the end of the list. Not one had matched.

"Is anyone missing?" I asked. "Someone who might've

been overlooked?"

Calista shrugged. "Not that I know of."

"What are you gonna reply?" asked Brent. "You gotta find out if it's a guy or girl. If it's a guy, find out if he's gay. Maybe he's got a crush on you."

Calista clicked her tongue. "A theatre person. Another Joel or Dillon."

"Don't jump the gun," I said. "It's probably like you said. Just some friend being nice."

"But you have all your friends' numbers. Anyone else would be on that list, wouldn't they? I take back what I said. This is some secret admirer ish."

"I second that," Brent said.

"Well?" I watched their faces. "What should I say?"

"How about, 'Yes, I had a great week.' Or even, 'No, my week sucked.' Something." Calista paused, looking very intently at me. "Or, and I'm going out on a limb here, babe, you could ask who it is."

"That's good! Play dumb! I like that." I began tapping into the phone. "How's this? 'My birthday was decent. But sorry, I don't know who this is.' That work?"

"That's not *playing* dumb. You *don't* know who it is. Just ask, *Who the F are you?*"

"But you know," Brent put in, "*not* rude."

"I'm sticking with this," I said. After a tiny hesitation, I tapped the little green arrow, then released a breath.

"Wait, what if it's some creepy stalker?" Brent suddenly said.

"*Now* you point that out?" I cried.

The phone buzzed in my hand. A finger of ice trailed between my shoulder blades. I checked the screen—same unknown number—and swiped open the text.

"'Do you really not know who this is?'" I read aloud. "'I figured quoting from that second note I left would give it away.'"

"Just ask who it is," said Calista.

Grinning, I typed, *Thank you for the notes. I really appreciated them. But do I know you?* then sent it.

Calista's phone went off then with another text from Nick. She focused on it while Brent went to take the movie out of the blu-ray player.

But I felt like my friends were no longer in the room. Everything had shrunk to the size of my phone-screen. I made a show of setting it aside when I really wanted to clutch the thing, hanging on for dear life, awaiting the next text.

When the reply came, it only brought a frown to my face. It said, *Id rather not say.*

I typed, *Well, do we have any classes together?*

The same reply came with the same lack of apostrophe. *Id rather not say.*

Can you at least tell me if I'm talking to a girl or a guy?

Id rather not say.

I sighed, and typed, *Now you're just being irritating.*

Sorry, was the reply. Then, on the heels of that: *Doesnt knowing stuff about me sorta defeat the purpose of a secret admirer?*

Well, will I ever know who you are?

Probably not.

Then I was left to puzzle over that. "What's the point of a secret admirer," I said, "if they never intend to reveal themselves?"

Calista shrugged. "Maybe it really is about staying secret and just doing something nice. For a secret admirer to reveal their identity, well, that seems self-serving or something. Makes it about them."

Brent sighed. "I'm heading home. I have calculus homework due tomorrow and working on that will be more fun than watching you both stare at your phones."

"All right, you big whiner!" Calista said, getting to her feet and grabbing her keys. "Let's motor. I promised my mom I'd be home for dinner anyway. Sunday night— family time. You know."

I made a face of apology. "Sorry, guys. Didn't mean to get all distracted."

"Please, even *I* know it's more fun hanging out with your phone right now than us," Brent said. "I'd do the same, bitch. See you tomorrow."

They vanished into the hall. My twin brother and sister made a war-zone of noise downstairs, shouting goodbyes as my friends left. I merely sat in the desk-chair, swiveling back and forth, thinking. I hadn't responded to my mystery correspondent yet, but I wasn't sure what to say.

At last, I typed, *Are you willing to tell me anything, anything at all, about yourself?*

A moment later, *Sure,* popped onto the screen. Then half a minute after that came this: *I think ur amazing & talented & I admire u. U inspire me.*

I felt the smile stretching my mouth. I replied, *It sounds as though you know me. To think those things, I mean. But you've already said you'd rather not say.*

Nope.

Well, whoever you are, I appreciate the notes. I know you

can't know how much they mean, and maybe it doesn't really matter that much to you, but I'm going through some stuff, and it matters a lot to me. So, thank you.

Ur welcome. I understand.

You understand?

About going thru stuff. If u need a mysterious & metaphorical ear, if u trust me, reach out any time.

I didn't want to think that whoever was on the other end of the texts could not only be a creeper, but maybe a colossal jerk playing a joke—like Nick Walsh and his friends. I truly had appreciated the notes in my locker—I was staring at them on the wall, at that moment—and with my stress about colleges, and grades, and the Revue, my resentment at not being able to relax at rehearsal, thinking that this secret admirer was somewhere and, well, admiring me, smoothed the ragged edges of all that stress. I hoped that if, for any reason, I *couldn't* trust this person, I would feel it. As my Muskequeers had pointed out; this could be *anyone*. Yet somehow, I felt no apprehension— only a tentative, happy feeling.

Thank you, I typed. *And if you trust me, the same goes for you.*

DONICK

*"Take me through the darkness
To the break of the day."*

DURING SOPHOMORE YEAR, when I had just made the varsity football team, a senior invited me to a party at his house. He was varsity too. Wanting to feel part of the team, when he dared me to invite "some loser" to the party, I didn't hesitate. I convinced some dorky AP student I wanted to make friends, invited him to a "cool-kids' party", then humiliated him by telling him to get lost in front of an audience. Once the poor guy with the mortified eyes had slunk from the house, I had dissolved into laughter with my friends and the girl I had been dating at the time. I never felt a twinge of remorse about it, not even when I ran into the guy at school.

I hadn't thought of that poor kid in a long, long time. The memory might never have resurfaced if it wasn't for Michael ordering me from his party. I suddenly remember now—that kid is a senior, like me—and have the added burden of guilt to weigh on me, along with my hurt feelings.

The depressing thing is I had been dared to do it again to another poor kid, last year, right before the ruination of my shoulder. So, again, I did it. If a crushed rotator-cuff and all kinds of screws holding it together are the beginnings of the price I must pay for being so cruel, then I truly deserve every bad thing that happens to me. There has to be a balance; I should have been kind to so many people, yet I was the complete opposite. Nothing separates *me* from *them*, not really.

Still, I can't say I only feel hurt, or contrite, after getting kicked out of Michael's house. Driving home, I suddenly feel angry. I can barely sleep once I crawl into bed—never mind the argument I have with Pop first. I know I have no right to act butt-hurt. I've inflicted pain on Michael over and over, yet faced with his retaliation, I can't handle it. Typical of an asshole-coward-bully.

Saturday morning, I go to my dance-studio to teach the little four and five year olds their ballet positions, then how to make noise with their tap shoes. It's only thirty minutes for each class, but I like it (and it's a bit of a paycheck for me). It's nice to see some of my teachers and the staff. I'm not in class during the week like usual because of rehearsals for the Revue.

Once I leave the studio, dark clouds settle over me—Pop has basically grounded me for the weekend. The rest of the day is spent chained to the house, mowing the front and back lawns (though there isn't much grass…I mow the weeds, I guess). Then I have to clean the kitchen, and Pop would have found something else if I didn't tell him I have homework. This is true, I *do* have homework, but I don't plan on doing it. I want to hide in my room and think.

Michael has left me shaken.

And remembering things that suck. Can't forget that.

Yes, I was angry last night. I fought back tears even as

I almost ripped the steering-wheel off the column while driving home. Fighting with Pop sort of deflated me, as it always does—it's exhausting. Then I simply felt hurt. It's easy to remember crap when you're feeling that way, and Michael's righteous anger accentuated that guilt as though it had been honed with a blade.

I plug my earbuds into my laptop, launch Crunchyroll and search for that anime I saw on Michael's wall— the pair of posing ice-skaters. I remember the title, and in seconds, I find it: *Yuri!!! on Ice*. Boy, that's a lot of exclamation points. Making sure to have my school books open and some random document ready beneath the internet window (in case Pop might poke in his head), I start the first episode. Then move on to the second. And the third. Before I know it, I've been watching for hours. I've never seen an anime quite like it. I understand why Michael must love it so much—because in all honesty, he's never far from my mind the entire time I'm watching.

I'm jolted by the opening song, because I'm singing it regularly at rehearsal, and it embodies the entire theme of the Revue. But there's such a refreshing light cast over these male ice-skaters and the drive to do what they love and feel passionate about, without the stigma of what other people think. Then there's the two main characters—Yuri and Victor. The romantic relationship going on between them is subtle and hardly addressed, because it doesn't need to be. They happen to be falling for each other and no one makes a scene, no one questions it or them. They're just a couple of guys. Guys who feel more than friendship for each other. And the scene with *the kiss*! Wow!

The joy of this anime is overwhelming. I can't stop

smiling. I watch through it almost in one sitting, and when it's over and night has fallen, Pop wanting me to make him dinner, I feel completely different than I had when I began. I feel hopeful.

As I work in the kitchen—Italian sausages with onions and red, yellow, and orange bell peppers (yes I can cook—I *had* to learn to make Pop happy) I'm thinking about my conversation with Michael.

I'm not angry anymore. I'm feeling determined. He doesn't believe in me, and that's okay. But I know who I am, inside. That person hates himself for what he did to his best friend, and now that former best friend is a person I admire, a person I think is amazing. I mean, that song he sang at his party… Holy crap! And the notes I left for him...or Secret Admirer left for him…he hung them on his wall! If knowing someone admires him from afar makes a difference in his life, then I want to be that secret admirer. He doesn't ever need to know it's me.

I go into Pop's office after dinner, open the drawer where he keeps all the old tester cell-phones, pluck up an ancient Razr flip-phone (because it's green, the color of Michael's eyes) and take it to my room. I'll contact him from this cell with its random number. He'll never be able to find out who it is. I'll let him know the texts are coming from his secret admirer, and…well, I don't know yet what exactly I plan to do, but opening a window of communication seems wonderfully attractive. Especially because we might be able to talk like we used to. Before I screwed everything up.

I'm so nervous, I don't even do it that night. I'm still dithering on Sunday.

Then I remember Calista and what happened to her

phone. Approaching Pop about that, even though he's been pissed at me, is easier than texting Michael.

I creep into his office where he's sitting behind his desk at the computer. He looks up over the little reading glasses he wears when he's sending e-mails and stuff.

"What is it, Nicky?" His tone is still a little frosty, but he doesn't *feel* as angry as he did yesterday. With a dad like this, a person learns to read emotional weather.

"So, a friend of mine cracked the screen on their iPhone," I begin. Then I hurry to say, "It wasn't their fault. Someone ran into them and knocked it out of their hand."

He squints at me. "Which friend is this?"

"Ryan." I wonder if I've said it too quickly, or if my eyes look shifty. I add, "It happened at Josue's on Friday night." I drop my eyes and look embarrassed. "It was me, actually, who ran into him. We were in the backyard throwing the ball around…well, they were throwing it, since I can't really, and I was running to catch it and didn't realize how close Ryan was to me. *Boom*! Phone on the ground. I feel really bad. I was hoping maybe you'd be able to get it replaced?"

I wait, trying to stay composed. Pop looks at me hard for what feels like a full minute. "How'd that shoulder feel catching?" he asks.

I put on a disappointed expression. "Not great. It was really sore yesterday, just from playing with the ball for a few minutes."

I'm getting the usual appraising look. Am I lying? He never trusts me, and suddenly, for the first time in my life, I'm justifying that distrust. Years of honesty with him, even as he thought me a liar, and now I'm totally lying about a bunch of things. But if I said it was Calista's phone, he would ask who she is, and then I would have to lie some more.

"Too bad," he says at last. "Yeah, I can probably get it replaced. Depends on how damaged the screen is. I'll have to see. Bring it to me tomorrow. Shouldn't take more'n a day, maybe two."

I brighten. "Thanks, Pop! Big help! I'll text him right now."

He only looks back at his computer screen; the sounds of his fingers on the keyboard follow me out.

So this is how I decide I'll handle it. I'm going to write the text to Calista (I have her number from the cast-list), then write the text to Michael. I'll send them both at the same time. If they happen to be together, it'll look less fishy if the texts come in all at once. Or so I rationalize it. I'll have to be very careful. Anything to keep the suspicion off me. But what to say to Michael?

I tell Calista to wipe the memory from her phone, just in case my dad looks through it. I would really need for him to find pictures of Michael in there, or any of the photos Calista has been taking of people in their costumes during fittings—including me!

And for Michael's text, I decide to ask about his birthday.

As evening begins to fall, I lay both phones on my desk, and simultaneously hit SEND on each.

It takes several minutes to get a reply from either of them. When Calista responds, it's to tell me thank you and that she thinks I'm awesome (makes me smile to read it). But it's Michael's response I'm waiting on.

I lay on my side on my bed, the green Razr flipped open and dark. When it lights up, I suck in a breath. We message back and forth for a minute or two (how irritating it is to type with just these number keys—I have to abbreviate everything to keep from going nuts), Michael playing coy like he doesn't know it's his secret admirer texting him. Though he then begins asking about me, I steadfastly tell him he can't know. But I reiterate how amazing I think he is. It's another one of those surreal moments (like being at his house), typing these things, knowing he's on the receiving end. Not even two months ago, I only thought about Michael to dislike him. Now I would give anything to be his friend again.

Then he sends this: *Well, whoever you are, I appreciate the notes. I know you can't know how much they mean, and maybe it doesn't really matter that much to you, but I'm going through some stuff, and it matters a lot to me. So, thank you.*

He must be talking about the rejection letter I saw on his desk. Or maybe…and this is a horrible thought… maybe he has boy troubles…something to do with Gil? And maybe, just maybe, me, Donick Walsh, making friends with his people and being around him most every day really is making him miserable. I don't like the idea of Michael being upset by stuff. I sit there on my bed, holding the Razr in slack fingers, gazing at the wall, wishing I could do something for him. But it's not my place. To him, I'm just some rando.

I type, *Ur welcome.* Then, after a moment of hesitation, I add, *I understand.* Because if anyone understands going through stuff, it's definitely me.

You understand? he replies.

About going thru stuff, I write. Then I type the following, delete it, and change my mind, typing it again: *If u need a mysterious & metaphorical ear, if u trust me, reach out any time.*

I send it, nerves tight as a spring. I flip open the screen when it buzzes again, hoping he won't say he thinks I'm some weirdo.

Thank you, he replies. *And if you trust me, the same goes for you.*

I'm suddenly so happy, I have to close the phone and process. I remind myself it's not really *me* he's talking to, which melts my smile, so I push that thought down. It's enough to just be talking to him. I'll get to know him all over again—*this* Michael, the one I forfeited my right to. Only, I'll have to be careful about when I text him, and where. It's a very fine line I'm walking.

THERE ARE THREE things I plan to do with my Monday. I can do all three while I'm at school, so my Monday already feels like it's beginning well, despite the anxiety one of the things gives me.

I take my laptop with me, cradled in my backpack. Some of my classes are becoming increasingly useless—typical senior year stuff—and I'll have time to accomplish the first thing while sitting, doing nothing, as the rest of my peers talk about grad-night at Disneyland and prom.

I had an idea after texting Michael. It'll be late, of course, but I want to get him a birthday present: a custom phone case. I've used this particular website before, so I know just what I want for him. I search the internet for artwork from *Yuri!!! on Ice*, saving the pictures I find (not only for him, but for myself too) in my secret folder of man-crushes. I'm specifically looking for a picture of Yuri and Victor together, and settle, at last, on one of them in costumes, embracing with their hands laced, showing off the gold rings on their fingers. I import the picture to the site, position it on the phone case mockup, then place the order.

I cross Task #1 off my mental check-list. Task #2 will be harder. My belly squirms just thinking about it. But it must be done.

The boy I played that asshole party prank on in sophomore year is named Wyatt Isenberg. He was short and scrawny then, and he's short and scrawny now. I think we football players picked on him because of how funny we thought he looked. He had large glasses perched on a pretty big nose, his chin pointed and weak. I see him sometimes on campus, and throughout our time at Kliewer High I've had more than a few classes with him. He looks pretty much the same, except his cheeks are always bristly with beard stubble now and he's already losing his hair. This semester though, I have no idea where I might find him, let alone when his last period is. Since my classes go until the end of the day, plus rehearsals, I'm on campus for the long haul. Ideally, I would like to be able to find him before he goes home.

So I poke my head into the guidance office during nutrition break, hoping to talk with Mrs. Moes for a few minutes.

"Hiya Nick!" she says, gesturing me inside. "Door open or closed?"

I hesitate for a second, then close it. I sit nervously in the chair across from her.

She's in her late thirties, very short blonde hair, with a tendency to wear flowing ankle-length skirts. I never had occasion to talk with her much before the end of junior year. But after my football debacle, and the troubles with my grades, I began to find my way into her office fairly often. I've never minded much—I like her just fine. She has a pretty deep speaking voice and always talks softly, smiling the whole while.

She pushes the computer keyboard aside and clasps her hands atop the desk. Her wedding band is set with an enormous diamond, popping from her finger like a wayward knuckle.

"How are things going with the Revue?" she asks.

"Fine."

"Having fun?" I nod. Then my face gets hot when she adds, "The teachers are raving about you. Too bad we couldn't get you into the arts department sooner. Or at least under different circumstances. No stress to your shoulder?"

"None."

"Good. So what brings you in today? No issues with classes, right?" She glances at her computer-screen. "You're grades are holding steady."

I guess I shouldn't be surprised she's been keeping tabs on me. I'm juggling a lot of academic balls. One slip and graduation and myself will exist in different realities.

"You aren't feeling overwhelmed by things, are you?" she asks.

I shake my head. "I actually feel like I have more free time now, even with rehearsals. No football games or anything like that."

"How about things at home? Everything all right there?"

She's met my father, had long phone calls with him about my attendance after my injury. She knows what he can be like and I've always found her sympathetic. He's a good dad, and I think she knows it, but he can be very intense, and I think she knows that too.

Suddenly, I feel like I'm being interrogated. She asked me why I needed to see her, then followed it with another question. I don't want to talk about grades, or my dad. I shift in the chair, beginning to bump my knees.

"My dad doesn't know about the Revue," I tell her.

A line dips between her brows.

"He…my dad doesn't understand about stuff like that. He won't…"

"I thought that with all your dance background he would be supportive."

"He only okayed the dance classes because they came recommended as football-training. His opinions about… well, art and dancers, actors…they're not…so great, I guess you could say."

"Will you not tell him *ever*?"

"I'm gonna try to keep it from him as long as I can."

"What does he think you're doing after school?"

"Helping out in woodshop."

"Oh. I'm sorry you think you can't share this with him."

"Totally can't."

"Well, what can I do for you?"

I dart my eyes around the room, trying to buy time. If I don't get to the point, the anxiety might not let me speak at all. So I force it out.

I tell her about Wyatt Isenberg; I tell her what I did to him. It's not easy—I feel nothing but shame, knowing she's watching me so carefully, her looks disapproving, almost angry. It's only made worse when I tell her I pulled the same trick again on a girl named Erin Smallwood. It's hard to so baldly paint myself as capable of such cruelty, but I tell her everything—about my reputation, about my guilt, and about what I want to do about it.

When I finish, she doesn't speak for a moment. She

looks troubled.

At last, she says, "I'm not the only councilor who's had to listen to their students talk about the bullying they've received at the hands of the varsity players. Your name has come up often over the years."

"I know."

"You do realize those students are too terrified of all of you to ask us to do anything about it? They're afraid they'll be picked on worse, maybe even hurt."

"Trust me," I say, "I don't need the reminder. I can't stop thinking about any of it. I can't stop feeling bad. I don't *want* to stop feeling bad. I don't want to forget it. Forgetting is like not caring. And I acted like I didn't care for too long. I'm working on myself here. Or trying to. To fix things. Which is why I'm hoping you'll help."

"Help with what?"

"Wyatt Isenberg. And Erin Smallwood. I owe them a huge apology. I'm not sure there are many things worse than humiliation, but that's exactly what I did—I humiliated them. I wasn't alone in pulling that prank, but I can't do anything about the other guys. Some of them are already graduated anyway. I just...I need to tell Wyatt and Erin I'm sorry. If they have something to say to me, if they want to be angry, or tell me how much they hate me, I owe it to them to hear them out. That's all." I pause and rub at my forehead. It feels sweaty, oily. "It's all so stupid," I mutter. "I wish I'd never been friends with any of those guys."

"Well," she says after appraising me for several seconds, "if you're serious about this, Nick, that's very big of you. What kind of help do you need from me?"

"I don't know where to find either of them. I was

hoping you might be able to give me some clues. I know that's probably not something you can share, but I don't know where to look. And this is something I *have* to do."

"Erin is one of my students, so I can tell you that she's part of a strings ensemble that meets Tuesdays and Thursdays after school."

"Strings ensemble?"

"She plays the cello."

I nod. The band-room. All right.

"And Wyatt?"

"Wyatt is not one of my students, but…" She fiddles with the computer for a second or two. "Wow, lots of AP classes. Oh! Track!"

"Wyatt Isenberg is on the track team?" I ask, disbelieving.

"That's what's on his schedule." She catches my eye. "I really shouldn't give this info. But I understand what you're trying to do. I'd like to see how it turns out. Come by again and tell me how it goes, yeah? I'm trusting you, Nick. Don't let me down."

Mrs. Moes's belief in me is the complete opposite of how Michael made me feel. It's amazing to know someone trusts me to do the right thing. "I will," I say. "Thank you." I stand to go, but she waves me back.

"Bell already rang. You're late. I need to write you a pass."

A T LUNCH, I visit Mrs. P. to talk to her about possibly being late for rehearsal the next couple of days. I suspect my conversations with Wyatt and Erin won't be quick. She says it's no problem (because she's cool that way). Still, standing by her desk, I feel the force of Michael's presence across the room, like fire licking at my back. As I turn to go, I dart looks toward the Muskequeers and their circle. Liam isn't there today, but Brent waves and Calista flashes a peace sign.

"After school?" she calls out, holding up her phone.

I give her a thumbs up.

"I'll stop by the dance-studio after I'm done in the costume-lab."

I'm heading back to the door when Brent shouts, "Where you going? Stay and eat with us!"

I try not to notice Michael's expression, which is stoney, but sort of odd, like he's thinking really hard. Whatever the expression, it's not welcoming. After all, he hates me—told me with his own lips—before throwing me out of his house. I've carried the green Razr in my backpack all day and suddenly feel it dragging at me like Frodo's Ring. Michael's going through stuff, I think, and remember his birthday present coming in a few days.

"I can't," I say. "I've got some place to be. Thanks though."

Brent shrugs. "See you later then."

As I slip out the door, I almost run straight into Gil Hamilton, walking in with his fruity scent much more subdued than when I last saw him. The tinny whine of music comes from his earbuds.

"Yo! Nick! How's it hanging, man?"

We bump fists and I chuckle. "None of your business. I'm in a rush." Then, feeling uncomfortable, I summon the courage to say, "Have fun with Michael," and speed away.

The last few school days, I've spent lunchtime in the library. This way I can avoid all the fools I used to consider friends. Also, I can get schoolwork done. It surprised me to find that Gabby Rosen spends her lunches in the library as well, sitting at a table with a group of other girls, all half-working, half-giggling. She waved to me the first time she saw me, seeming surprised I would be in the library at all. I smiled, because it was she who gave me the idea about making over my soul.

Now I have a favor to ask. I go right to her table.

"What's up, Nick?" she asks, that sweet smile playing over her face. Her friends all look a little embarrassed and giggly at my presence, but I keep my attention on her. She's surrounded, of course, by her monstrous pile of books.

"Can I pull you away," I ask, "for, like, two minutes?"

The eyes of her friends go wide, their giggles not very contained. Gabby rises from her chair.

"Yeah, where?"

"Just in the stacks over there. It's no big deal. I need to ask a favor."

We make our way down an aisle of books, pausing as musty smelling biographies close in on us. She tucks the gold curls of her hair behind her ears, and I imagine some boy somewhere will go nuts with wanting to run his fingers through it.

"What favor?" she asks.

Now I'm a little dithery. This whole situation will come off more gay than I'm comfortable with yet.

"You totally don't have to do this," I say, "but I thought I would ask. You were the first person I thought of actually."

"Oh?" I'm amazed she doesn't look distrustful, only curious.

"I have a birthday present for someone. Except this person can't know it's from me."

"Why not?"

"Long story. So I have this gift—or at least I will once it

arrives—and I don't want him to know—"

"Him?" She sounds startled.

I pause, flushing. "It's not what you're thinking," I stammer.

She shakes her head, lifting her hand to her mouth to hide her smile. "I'm not thinking anything."

"He's an old friend," I blurt out, "and I don't want him to know. It's a surprise."

She doesn't look convinced. If I try to say anything, to lie about my sexuality, it'll be a total giveaway. I would rather say nothing at all.

"I'm hoping," I go on, "that you'll be willing to deliver it for me."

"Sure," she says, like it's nothing at all. "To who?"

I'm relieved for half a second, then nervous as hell. What if she knows Michael and automatically assumes a gift from me means I have a crush on him? Oh God! What am I doing?

"Do you know Michael Penrose?" I ask.

"Yeah, but not really. We did *Joseph* together last year. It's more like, I know of him, or know him in, like, passing or something. I doubt he remembers me. That's who the present's for?"

"His birthday was last week and I'm a little late with his gift. It's really important he not know it's from me. *No one* can know."

"Won't he think it's weird I'm giving it to him?"

"You won't be. You know where Mrs. Peebles's classroom is, right? We'll figure out a time when you can take it there. Give it to her, say someone wanted you to deliver it, and she should give it to Michael Penrose when she sees him."

We arrange the possible drop-off for later in the week,

then I have nothing left to do but thank her.

I walk with her back to her giggling friends. They give us highly interested looks but I just wave at them and find my usual out-of-the-way table. I prepare to pull out my schoolwork, but the green Razr is in my hand instead. I turn it on. I've kept it off since texting Michael last night. What to say though? Suddenly, I know.

The phone, however, goes off in my hand!

The text-alert is insanely loud in such a quiet place. Eyes turn toward me. The librarian frowns at me (she frowns at everyone) and I roll my eyes. I switch the alerts to vibrate, then stare at the text message on the screen. It's from Michael, sent this morning. It says, *Weird thinking that I'll be at school with you, but I'll have no idea who you are. This is like something out of a rom-com. Lol.*

I blink at that. Rom-com? My texting with Michael isn't romantic! He doesn't even know who I am! I could be some lovesick girl! Why would he say that?

I debate on sending a direct answer to this text, but decide to go with my original intent. I type out, *I know ur birthday is already over, but I just bought u a present. U should have it by the end of the week!* Then I hit send.

In seconds comes his reply: *A birthday present? You don't have to do that!*

I know I dont have 2, but I want 2. I hope u like it!

Suddenly, it's like I've forgotten where I am. That feeling of having missed him all these years is so strong, I can't help but sit happily gazing into the phone, feeling as though I'm far away from the library and the school.

Okay, well, I'm really excited! he replies. *That means a lot! I think u'll love it.*

How do you know?

I just do.

But how? Do you know me or something?

I sit, undecided, then type, *I know more about u than u'd think.*

Ooh! Now you sound like a creeper! Scary!

I am. Im a scary, stalkery, creeper.

Well, you've given me two very nice notes, and not only can I actually talk to you now, but you're giving me a birthday present. If that's scary, stalkery, creeper stuff, then I'm okay with it. But who are you!?

Smiling to myself, I type, *Nope, not gonna happen.*

A full three minutes go by while I chew my lip and drum my fingertips on the table. At last, this appears on the screen: *If I tell you a little bit about the stuff I'm going through, will you tell me some of what's happening with you? I can't really talk to my friends about some of it.*

I swallow. *Y not?* I ask.

Because it'll just irritate them.

Yes, but what if Im 1 of those friends. U could b saying stuff 2 the exact person u wouldnt want 2 hear it.

Lol! First of all, my friends are with me right now and I know they aren't the ones texting me. Secondly, I'll risk it. I feel like I can trust you.

He can, I think. He *really* can. Because I've lost his trust once before, and I won't lose it again.

Except, he would never have sent those words if he knew it was Donick Walsh he sent them to.

I think for a minute, then type. Then I delete. Then type again. At last I send: *U can tell me whatever u like. Im happy 2 listen. Whatever u've got 2 say will stay w/ me.*

The bell rings then, startling me, signaling the end of lunch. I pack up and head to the first of the two English classes that end my school day, wondering what Michael will reply. But I don't hear from him for the rest of the day.

It's hard to think of him though. I've got Wyatt Isenberg on my mind.

After school, I stow my stuff in my locker and make my way across campus to the playing-fields and the track. I'm wishing every step of the way I could talk myself into calling an apology to Wyatt a loss. This will be different than apologizing to Calista or Brent, or even Jackie. I have to be around them every day. Wyatt I never have to see if I don't want to, yet I'm hunting him down anyway. I guess it's proof of how important doing this is to me. Plus, how would I face Mrs. Moes after her vote of confidence.

Once I reach the track, I scan the runners pumping their legs around its perimeter, sweat glossy on their bare shoulders. There's an encircling ring of chain-link and I pause, leaning my elbows on it, waiting to catch a glimpse of Wyatt. I study him with interest when I spy him come around the curve.

He's still pretty skinny, barely five and a half feet tall, but in his tank-top and running-shorts he looks wiry and quick. His nose seems as enormous as ever, even without his glasses, and the poor guy's forehead is very broad, the scalp visible through the crown of his hair. But all in all, he looks like he knows what he's doing. I'm impressed. It just goes to show that everyone, even those we've previously viewed with disdain, have something great about them.

As he draws near I make out the sound of his breathing. I steal myself and call out. He squints, running shoes slowing a bit.

"Who's that?" he pants. "Can't see. Don't have my glasses."

I say, "It's Nick Walsh," and watch as a dark look clouds his face. He pauses, breathing hard, hands on his narrow hips. He glances around as though waiting for something to happen.

"What do you want?" he finally asks. His tone is not friendly.

I feel myself recoiling from him, from what I need to do. But I suck in a breath and manage to say, "Can I talk to you?"

"I'm busy right now." He takes a jogging step or two along his lane.

"It'll just take a minute."

"What?" he says, stepping nearer, exhaling a harsh breath. "Another party invite?"

If this were easy, I think, *it wouldn't be worth doing.*

"That's actually what I want to talk to you about," I say. "Please?"

Wariness fills him, shooting through every part of his body like the racing of his blood. I can almost feel his distrust. Yet somehow, maybe through curiosity, there's also a sense of relenting. "Fine," he says. "Walk a lap with me so I don't cramp."

I smile—awkwardly, yes, but I do smile at him. He only eyes me like I'm a tarantula. He's already begun walking so I fall into step beside him.

After a second I say, "You look good out here. How long you been running?"

"Cut the crap, Nick. What do you want?"

That recoiling feeling nudges me again.

"Basically," I say, "to apologize. For what I did to you— inviting you to that party, humiliating you like that."

"Succinct word—humiliating."

"I know. I have no excuses. I just wanted you to know, I *needed* you to know, that I regret doing that to you. I should have invested all that energy in being a better person, or at the very least, being your friend. Instead of being a jerk."

"Being *cruel*."

I sigh. "Being cruel. Something similar happened to me recently. Totally deserved, of course."

He utters a dry laugh. "You? With all those popular gorillas for chums?"

"Well, that crowd and I…we've sorta parted ways."

"Since when?" He sounds disbelieving.

"A few days ago, really. But it's been a long time coming."

"Why? Because of getting hurt in football?"

I throw a look at him. He isn't as angry suddenly, more curious than anything. "That's part of it," I tell him. "But mostly they're awful and I can't hang anymore." I fumble for the right words. "It's like there's all this new stuff in my brain. Things I've done, I guess, that I don't want to keep doing. Hence the apology I owe you. I don't expect you to accept it or anything. I don't deserve that. I just thought I also owed it to you to let you have your say. It's awful to be silenced when you have something to get off your chest."

"You're an asshole! And a dick!" he blurts out without an instant's pause. "I've thought about slugging you a hundred different times these last couple of years. But you're still kind of a big meathead-looking guy, and I'm just a rack of bones."

"Not anymore," I say. "I'm still amazed seeing you running like this. You look good, man."

"My folks are amazed too. My mom always says she has no idea where a brainy Jewish boy like me got sudden athleticism." He falls silent for a moment or two. Then he says, "I guess…thanks. For saying sorry. It helps."

"Not enough."

"Doesn't matter anymore anyway. A few more months and this high school nightmare will be over. I'll be able to forget all the felchers who gave me a hard time and go on with my life."

"You'll go to college, become a doctor, get a hot wife, lots of money, then you can buy and sell our asses."

"That's the plan!" He grins for the first time. His teeth are pearly white and perfectly straight.

"Well, I hope it works out. You deserve it, dude." I hesitate, then say, "And I hope you'll remember that at least one gorilla meathead who gave you a hard time wished he could have been your friend."

He squints into my face—checking my sincerity, I guess. He must see it because he says, "I appreciate that."

"And hey!" I say, slowing my steps as I find a break in the fence. I do have a rehearsal to get to, after all. Besides, despite his acceptance of my apology, I still sense that we're not friends. For him, just like he said, it really doesn't matter anymore. *I* don't matter anymore. But I'm happy I talked to him just the same. "Good luck with this track stuff," I finish. "You're really fast."

"Good luck with the Senior Revue," he tells me, turning to resume his run. He calls over his shoulder, "People are talking about your dance-skills, man."

AT HOME THAT night, after handing Calista's phone over to my dad, I'm sitting on the floor with my schoolwork around me. I feel like English 11 is kicking my ass, which blows since I'm already feeling like I'm barely getting by in English 12. At least my grades are holding steady, as Mrs. Moes said—it's just that they're holding steady at barely passing. At least I have good tunes to listen to. It's weird to think of myself enjoying "Dancing Queen", but I can't seem to get enough of the songs from rehearsal. Of course, the music is solely coming to me through my headphones—no way would I get away with listening to Madonna, or all these musical songs, without Pop saying something rude.

And the green Razr? It's sitting beside me as I await another text from Michael. I can't stop wondering what private things he wants to share that he can't tell his Muskequeers. I had waited all through the rest of school and checked it every break in rehearsal, but nothing. I'm almost wondering if he's decided not to text at all. Maybe the situation—communicating with a mysterious stranger who won't say anything about him or herself—has at last convinced him to call it quits.

But then the phone buzzes and I snatch it up. My heart, which had suddenly raced, seems to halt in my chest. It's a long text, coming through the Razr in chunks (God, I forget how convenient my iPhone is) and reading through it almost makes me not want to respond. I should have suspected what Michael would want to talk about. Yet I had forgotten for a moment that it isn't "me" he's talking to.

Somehow I text back. Then, in spite of my heightened emotions, my bedroom disappears as easily as the library had earlier today. I feel like I'm alone with him—just Michael and me.

Hey, Secret Admirer! he sends. *Sorry to take so long to text, but I had a busy afternoon. Anyway, about my pals and why I can't talk to them. At least about this one particular thing. Years ago I had this friend. His name was Donny. He did something really terrible to me. He's actually a complete jerk and has done terrible things to a lot of people. We were best friends once which makes it worse. Anyway, this not-friend is sorta back in my life… NOT by choice! Trust! He's started making friends with my pals and they seem to really like him. I'm having a hard time with it. I can't really talk about it with them anymore. They've forgiven him or whatever, and I have a hard time with that too.*

I send: *I can c how that would b hard 4 u.*

It's not just that, though. I had a birthday party over the weekend. Maybe you were there and I don't even know it. But my not-friend was there (long story), and I got really irritated with him and basically kicked him out. I also told him I hated him.

Harsh. I understand u were upset, but that doesnt seem like u.

That's the thing. It's not. But having this not-friend around all the time, even though I try not to have to talk to him, has me feeling shook. I sorta hate myself for losing my temper. I treated him no different than he treated me.

U cant help how u feel. Especially when a friend hurts u. Its that whole love & hate thing being related.

And I really did love him once. He was my best friend.

A fist seems to sit around my throat when I read this. But I reply: *I still think hating some1 doesnt seem like u, but I guess Ive never been hurt that badly b4.*

I don't think I DO hate him. I instantly regretted saying it. But he said he hated me first and it just slipped out.

Maybe HE didnt mean it either.

He talks to my friends but doesn't really talk to me unless he has to. I see him almost every day in rehearsal and he mostly acts like I'm not there. Typical asshole.

Thats rough.

But there's something different about him now. I mean, he's making friends with all these people he never used to give the time of day to. In fact, he used to be really awful to them.

People like ur friends? Ur Muskequeers?

You know about that?

Every1 knows about that. Like, the whole school.

Did you see our talent show routine?

No. But I wish I had.

That was in 10th grade. You know I'm a senior, right? I mean you must. What grade are you in?

12.

Wow! You told me something about you!

I shouldnt have.

Why?

B cuz I said I wouldnt. But…I guess I feel like I can trust u 2.

I'm nearly sweating at what I've revealed.

I'm wearing you down! he texts. *I gotta get you to tell me more!*

I wont budge! I write. *But Im sorry about this not-friend of urs. I wish I could do something 2 make it better.*

Getting to talk about it with someone helps. Thank you.

Any time.

He's not so bad, I guess. He's kind to my friends, and that's a big deal for him. I mean, my friends are all gay, and he's got giant gay-fear!

Gay-fear? Thats not a thing, I bet.

You know I'M gay, right?

Yes. Have a boyfriend?

No. At least, not really. There's this guy who sometimes seems into me. He came and ate lunch with me today but acted mostly like a friend. I don't get him.

So u have not-friend troubles AND boy troubles.

Haha! Yes, boy troubles. Amongst all the other issues which I won't bore you with.

Ur not boring. Talk 2 me bout whatev.

Do YOU have a boyfriend, Secret Admirer?

Lol! Nice try. But that wont work. Whatever answer I give will either mean Im a girl, or a gay guy. U'll still b left guessing.

I'll at least have a hint. For sure I'll know you're not a straight man.

Im not a straight man.

And I about *die* from having actually sent this!

He writes: *Woo-hoo! A clue! A clue!*

Lol! Not much of 1.

Well, I'm guessing you're probably a girl. Girls can do this secret admirer thing as just friends without making it into anything else, since you know I'm gay. If someone gay acts like a secret admirer to another gay person, it turns everything into crush-territory, you know? And I don't get the sense that you have a crush on me. Unless you're not out.

U've been thinking bout this a lot.

I'm curious about you.

Im nothing special.

I think you are. Because talking to you is easy, and thinking about the notes you left me has brightened a tough day…or twelve! Even knowing there's a friend out there who thinks I'm AMAZING means tons.

Its true tho. I do think that.

And I think YOU'RE amazing for thinking I'M amazing. Not many people do.

There ur wrong. Every1 thinks ur great! Im sure there r

plenty of people who wish they could b ur friend & feel like they cant. Ur uber-talent intimidates them.

Hey! I'm approachable! Anyone can be my friend! Even you!

Even ur old not-friend?

He doesn't want to be my friend. Gay-fear, remember?

But he's friends w/ ur Muskequeers.

I'm different. I think I'm all the reasons why he's a homophobe. We kissed once, when we were in sixth grade. He never spoke to me again except to call me names.

The plot thickens! U made the moves on him, huh?

I guess I must have. If he'd made the moves on me, we might still be friends I guess. Anyway, thanks for letting me talk about him. He annoys me so much!

Any time.

It's getting late. I've got to go pick up my sister from her friend's house, then I've got homework to finish. Can I text you tomorrow?

Of course. Then again, I might text u first & then what?

Then I'll be in a crazy good mood. On the heels of this comes: *Goodnight, Secret Admirer!*

Anxious over what's been said, yet smiling, I reply: *Gnite, Michael.*

MICHAEL

*E*MOTIONALLY, I WAS all over the place throughout the next week. I looked forward constantly to texting Secret Admirer (the name I assigned to his/her phone number). Whoever they were, they were a distraction from my growing fear over the remaining three colleges I still waited to hear from. Not to mention homework piling up, almost daily rehearsals, plus all the other piddly crap making me crazy.

Somehow though, Secret Admirer grounded me. It wasn't that they shared much about their life. It only felt easy to say I was scared I wouldn't get into any of my dream colleges. I could talk about Gil Hamilton and how, for all his friendliness, he never acted that into me. Though liberal with his hugs, his interactions with me were the same as with anyone else. He didn't try to hold my hand; he didn't text unless I reached out first. I had texted Secret Admirer and received responses with Gil sitting right next to me. For sure, Secret Admirer wasn't him. Secret Admirer only ever texted me at school during lunch, never at rehearsal. Leading me to believe he or she was, for sure, in the show. Even then, most contact happened in the evening while I was at home.

Yes, somehow it felt safe to say (or text) things to a faceless, mysterious stranger I wouldn't communicate to anyone else. I couldn't explain it. When I had said I trusted them, I had meant it. The odd thing was, Secret Admirer said they trusted me, but I wished they really would. I wished they would tell me more about who *they* were.

Calista and I were walking toward Mrs. P.'s room on Wednesday during lunch. Calista had her face in my phone so she could check her e-mails, waiting for a response from some rando on Craig's List about vintage clothes from the 70's she was trying to get ahold of for the show. I zoned out, thinking about this birthday present Secret Admirer had promised. Not so much concerned with what it might be, I wondered if he/she would reveal who he/she was and deliver it him/herself?

Reaching Mrs. P.'s door, we were just entering when Gil came barreling out. He wore an Ariana Grande T-shirt with THANK U, NEXT printed on it.

"Sorry guys," he said. "I was gonna hang today but I gotta get home."

"That sucks," I said. "I like when you hang." I blushed a little to say it. Was I really flirting with him? Would it matter? He was too wishy-washy to let me know where I stood with him.

"I've liked hanging," he said with a smile. "But my mom's pissy. I have to let the dog out. Playing appeasing-son is a must or I might end up grounded over Spring Break. I'll see ya!"

He leaned in to hug me, though I had to bend some, being so much taller than him. That orange scent filled my nose, then his mouth came close to my ear.

"Wanna do something Friday night?"

I blinked, grateful Calista had gone inside and wasn't there to see my expression.

She also had my phone. What if Secret Admirer sent a text while she looked at the screen? I hadn't been very forthcoming with her or Brent about how often I texted that mystery person.

But wait! Gil? Asking me on a real date? I pulled back, feeling flustered.

"Yeah, for sure," I stammered. "What do you have in mind?"

He shrugged. "We can talk about it later. I'll text you."

He bumped his fist against my shoulder and went on his way. Somehow, I wasn't as elated as I thought I would be. I chalked it up to nerves. I hadn't been out on many dates. Dillon and Joel had been hang-out-at-school boyfriends almost exclusively.

"What a bitch," Liam was saying as I came in. "Can you believe it?" All eyes were on him, even a very interested Calista. She handed me my phone as I sat.

"What bitch?" I said. "There's a bitch? I wanna hear about the bitch."

Liam huffed. "Fine, I'll start over. Have I got a tale to tell!"

One of our friends, a girl named Joey who could neither sing, nor dance, and therefore wasn't doing the Senior Revue (she was a fantastic little actress, though), waved her hand. "Li, you were just getting to the good stuff. Jesus Christ, Michael. Your timing blows." She laughed to show she wasn't serious. But it was hard to tell with her, being a bit of a bitch herself, even on the best days. Still, we loved her. She was a lot like Calista, only Calista had a softness to her that Joey lacked.

"Okay," Liam began again. "This is a story about Nick Walsh!"

I groaned. "All your stories are about Nick Walsh. Hire new writers."

My Muskequeers shushed me. I could see by their faces that their new friendship with my old not-friend had them pretty well invested.

I began checking my phone. No text from Secret Admirer.

"So I heard this from Miranda Beck," Liam went on, "who's cousin, Cassie Jones, is in band. Yesterday after school, Cassie showed to some practice-thing in the band-room and Nick came to talk to some chick."

"A band geek? Nick usually dates cheerleaders," said Brent, popping the wad of gum in his mouth. "Maybe this is a side-effect of hanging out with drama-kids."

Liam said, "Just listen! God! So Nick comes to talk to this girl in band. Cassie said the girl looked *pissed*, and Nick, like, had a weird look on his face. She went outside with him and after, I dunno, like, thirty seconds—" Liam startled giggling, his face full of amused disbelief, "—the bitch started yelling at him at the top of her lungs! *Everybody* heard it! She was all, 'You're a fucking dick! It doesn't matter what you say, you're still an asshole!'" Liam guffawed now. "Can you believe it? Talk about a crazy bitch!"

Joey smirked. "Well, what did Nick say to her? He *has* been a porn-sized dick in the past, you know."

I couldn't keep quiet. "I second that."

Calista looked thoughtful. "What else could it be? One of these apologies he's been making, I bet."

"Totes," said Brent. "But what was he saying sorry for?"

I grimaced. "Probably for the same garbage he's done to all of us. Calling us names, spreading rumors, being an all around asshat."

"Well, it stands to reason," said Calista, "not everyone will be so forgiving."

Liam shrugged. "Nick's been completely nice to me. I know people always say he's a jerk, but I never saw it. I think it's sad. If he did something mean to that girl and she responded to an apology like that, that makes her a bitch in my book."

"She's not a bitch," I said, feeling my anger simmering. "Nick's hurt a lot of people. Calista's right. Not everyone will be able to forget that."

"Cool it, babe," Calista said, eyeing me.

I grimaced and sat back in my seat.

"I think it sucks too," Brent said. "He tried to make it right and that girl acted like a slag."

"That was her choice," Calista put in. "I mean, Nick was pretty terrible to me for, like, *all* of high school, but I'm pretty chill with him now. Even against my initial instincts. I didn't want to hold on to some grudgy bullshit," she added, pointedly looking at me. "I feel better for it. That girl won't be able to say the same...sad for her."

Again, Calista was right, but I would never admit it out loud. Keeping my anger toward Nick kindled was becoming a challenge. I didn't know if a guilty conscience about my party bothered me, or if other things counterbalanced my resentment—like a date with Gil, Spring Break, or Secret Admirer texts. It felt like anger at Nick and the prospect of good things in other parts of my life just couldn't co-exist.

It had become increasingly difficult to pretend he wasn't there, not when rehearsal put us in such close quarters. From the moment he had walked into the dance tryouts, I felt his presence whenever he was near, like something caught in a tooth when the tongue can't leave it alone. I had to *grudgingly* admit he was doing a great job. He had a good voice, and his dance training lent him a stage presence that made me want to watch him. I told myself I hated every minute and stared so hard in order to find fault. But…I had to admit, he was good. As the days passed it became clearer and clearer that the teachers, our fellow cast-members, my friends, were beginning to love him.

"I still think she's awful," said Liam. "It makes me want to find out who she is and slap a bitch."

Calista grinned at him. "That protectiveness toward Nick rearing its head again, Li? You're sounding more and more crushy every second."

Liam flushed. "No, no! I told you! Nick isn't my type."

I scoffed. "Yeah, he's got serious gay-fear!"

Calista looked irritated. "Knock that crap off already. Christ!"

I sat silent while Liam said, "Besides, I already have a crush on someone, and it's not Nick."

Brent's mouth fell open. "Praise holy things! Who is it?"

"Just someone."

Joey cocked an eyebrow. "*You?* You've been making time with someone?"

"Nothing like that. I just really like him."

"One of the cutie dancers in the show?" Brent asked.

Liam was suddenly red as a tomato. I suspected Brent had made a pretty good guess.

"Look at your face," I said, laughing. "Whoever he is, does he dig *you*?"

"We're, like, making out all the time, everywhere!" Liam said in a rush.

"That's so gross!" said Brent. "Because I'm jealous!"

Calista shook her head. "Get real, babe, you're making out all the time too. Just, you know, with strange guys in the backseats of their cars."

"Ouch!" Brent pasted an outraged look on his face, but it melted right away. "That was pretty good actually."

I snorted. "And true!"

Joey, looking across the room, suddenly whispered, "Speak of the devil…"

We followed her eyes, and I felt my teeth lock. Donick Walsh stood in the open doorway. He began making his way over.

I murmured under my breath, "What the hell does he want now?"

"Don't be a chode," Calista whispered back, then, louder, "Hey Nick! Gonna eat with us today?"

He looked embarrassed, and something between wanting to stay and wishing he could be anywhere else. I felt hard pressed not to show my frustration with him.

"We were just talking about you too," I said, then wished I had kept my mouth shut. The uncertain light that came into his eyes, sensing maliciousness in my tone, reminded me of the way he used to look years ago when his dad became particularly teasing, when the jokes might or might not have actually *been* jokes. It also brought Friday night to mind. Guilt punched like a fist in my chest.

Sometimes I hate you, Michael.

Perfect. The feelings we have for each other are mutual.

His embarrassed laughter brought me back to myself. "Talking about me, huh? I'm afraid to ask."

"We heard about that girl yelling at you yesterday," said Liam.

Nick's ears went pink. "She had to get some stuff off her chest. I had it coming. You know."

I could see real concern in Liam's eyes, and in the faces of my other friends. How did Nick Walsh deserve their sympathy?

"It's no big deal," Nick added, yet I could see from his dropped eyes and the way he began fumbling at his backpack zipper that he was troubled. He looked lost suddenly. "But hey," he went on in a brighter voice, "I only stopped by so I could bring this."

He pulled out an iPhone box, handing it to Calista. Her look of surprise mirrored itself on most of the encircling faces. Even I was surprised. He had actually come through for her.

"It's new," Nick said, "even though it's been opened. My dad said it was easier to just grab a new one. Got everything up and working. Just transfer your stuff from your computer-backup."

"Holy crap!" Calista said. "This one is a newer model than mine! It's got a twelve-hundred dollar price tag!"

Joey smirked. "Careful Nick, or everyone is going to ask you for favors."

Nick grimaced. "I can just see my dad's face. Keep it on

the DL, please."

I could remember his dad's face well enough—especially when rage contorted it as he called me a little queer.

"Thank you so much!" Calista said. "I seriously owe you! This is incredible!"

"Not even a thing," said Nick, hooking his thumbs into the straps of his backpack. He looked crazy uncomfortable when Calista got up and hugged him. It took me aback. She wasn't a hugger.

"Seriously," she said. "Stay. Eat with us."

For an instant, his eyes skipped to me. Then he shook his head.

"I've got assignments due on Friday in both my English classes. You know, the sprint before vacation. I *really* need to work on them. Thanks though."

"Raincheck." Brent pointed a finger at Nick's face. "You can't brush us off forever."

Nick only smiled tightly at that and (with one last glance at me) arrowed for the door.

*G*IL DIDN'T TEXT like he said he would. Thursday morning in Gov, he simply said, "Let's meet after school tomorrow. I'll come back when your theatre class is over and pick you up. We can go from there. I already know what we'll do."

Thursday afternoon's rehearsal Mr. Hardy allotted for working on solos. He called only a handful of us, and Nick, thankfully, was not there. It came home again just how little I could relax with him around. I almost felt like I was back in my element.

After singing through "Popular" a few times (I wasn't

sure if it would ever *not* feel strange to be performing that song) Calista and I took an hour drive to the home of the rando from Craig's List. Then, with her backseat and trunk full of musty smelling outfits straight from *Saturday Night Fever*, we drove back to school to leave them in the theatre. She would have liked it if I started trying on outfits right then, but I put my foot down. Not until they'd aired out some. Nasty!

Most evenings I either did homework or tried to focus on reading *Pride and Prejudice* for English…or stared at the TV. I never was much of a phone-aholic like most of my peers, but every night since the first time Secret Admirer had contacted me, he/she and I had texted until one or the other of us went to bed. I couldn't seem to let my phone get too far from my hand.

They were long conversations, and easy. I talked about my day, about Gil and our approaching date. I talked about my family and how I looked forward to seeing my twin brother and sister react to Easter morning. And, no, I couldn't seem to lay aside the subject of Nick for long, but Secret Admirer never made me feel that I should be guilty for being resentful. Even in the face of the mystifying turnaround happening with Nick, I was annoyed. It wasn't just that band girl he had apologized to so disastrously, or his becoming friends with Calista and Brent. I began to hear things around campus: his sudden kindness toward students he had bullied and called horrible names; tracking down people he had harassed in some way and asking for their forgiveness. It all seemed so bizarre, and re-reading the messages between Secret Admirer and myself showed me just *how* resentful it had me feeling.

Still, not knowing anything about the stranger I texted frustrated me. Whoever they were, they were kind, and thoughtful. There were often rather wise responses to my grousing. This Secret Admirer was rapidly beginning to fit the bill of a best friend, and I could only wish the conversations didn't have to be so one-sided. I thought I might give anything for just a *little* bit more information about them. Yet they had said I would probably never know who they were.

However, I went to school Friday with my mind full of nothing but Gil and our date. He had said he knew what we would do already, so I had plenty to wonder about. Where would he take me? Would there be kissing involved? I couldn't say for sure whether that had me excited or not. But again, what did I know about real dating? All day I watched the clock for the end of school, anticipating. I couldn't muster much interest in anything.

Until something happened after last period that left my mind pretty much useless for the actual date.

My Muskequeers charged out of the drama-room, heading to the theatre with Mrs. P.'s keys to open the costume-lab. The campus, however, grew deserted fast with all the students eager to start their vacations. I dropped by my locker, then began making my way toward the doors at the end of the almost empty hall. I had just glanced at my phone to see if Gil had sent any texts, my nerves beginning to *really* get jumpy, when someone shouted my name.

But it wasn't *Michael* that echoed from the walls. It was a jarring, panicked, "Mikey!"

I glanced up just as something knocked into me, sending me sideways into a row of lockers. I hissed in pain as my arm went numb, a lock punching into my shoulder. I would later find a bruise the size of an orange. I flinched, startled by the sudden tussle of bodies beside me. A sharp noise, like a cry and a cough all mixed up. My mouth dropped open as Nick Walsh slumped against the lockers beside me, his friend Josue leering at him with a Pennywise-smile. The big guy—Ryan—who had broken Calista's phone, stood back, expressionless and silent.

Josue sneered out, "Knew you'd come running like a little bitch! You think you can fuck with me and get away with it, *güey*? Huh? You ain't any better than this faggot!"

Hearing myself called that triggered something— something shame-filled. I could only stand mute, wanting to crawl inside myself, even as I wished I had the nerve to stick my fingers into this asshole's eye-sockets.

"I'll mess you up, Nicco!" Josue carried on, flecks of spit flying from his lips. His fists were knuckle-studded knots. "Think I'd end up with a Saturday school 'cause of you and not come after your ass? Tapping your nuts was the easiest fucking thing when you're so quick to rescue a pansy like Michael Penrose! And I saw you hugging that fairy at lunch! You a faggot too, Nicco?"

He all but spat the last words. I went on staring, bewildered, my arm throbbing, my backpack slipped from one shoulder. Nick slid down the lockers until he crouched on the floor, groaning, his own backpack twisted up behind him. Head lowered, he cupped himself between the legs.

Horrified, I somehow found my voice. "You hit him in the balls?"

"You might not escape it next time, fag!" Josue spat at me. So much hate glared out of his features, it left me speechless.

"Dude," said Ryan, "let's get outta here. You got him.

It's over."

Josue grimaced at Nick. "You're a piece of shit, Nicco, you know that? I should do worse. You're lucky I don't. Trying to pretend you're better than all of us."

Again Ryan said, "Let's go! This is stupid! And, like, a teacher might see!"

With one last "Dickless *puto*!" directed at Nick, Josue followed Ryan down the hall and out the doors. The muscle in my shoulder smarted and throbbed.

Nick made a sudden choking sound, coughing and gasping. "I'm gonna ralph!" he wheezed out, struggling to rise. I saw at once his face appeared almost green. Without thinking, I grabbed one of the gray garbage barrels with its mouth of knotted plastic bag. Just in time. Nick leaned over it and vomited, making me wince. He was oddly quiet about it. I eased his backpack from his shoulders and set it aside. His arms were pliant as noodles. He coughed a little, sniffled, but after half a minute, I could only hear his gasping breaths.

What had just happened?

Lifting one arm to swipe at his mouth, sniffing hard, Nick straightened a little.

"Wait," I said. "Here." From my backpack, I fished out a half-empty bottle of water. He gazed first at it, then at me, eyes streaming, lips wet. I heard him swallow. Then he reached for the bottle, uncapped it, and swigged from it, swishing the water in his mouth before spitting. He drank deeply then, grimacing as he swallowed. My brain seemed to have slowed. I thought I must be staring at him as though he had sprouted a horn from his forehead.

He slumped against the lockers, breathing hard, one hand clutching the bottle, the other falling into his lap, sliding unselfconsciously over his groin again, as something like a hitching sob bubbled in his throat.

Again I watched him, trying to make sense of the last ninety seconds.

Finally I asked, "Was that sack-tap meant for me?"

"I thought it was." His voice was full of agony. He let his eyes fall closed, head against the locker at his back. "I should have known."

"What do you mean?"

"Don't worry about it."

"You thought they were going to do that to me?" When Nick gave a nod, I said, "You called my name—"

"I called you Mikey. I know you don't like it. It just… popped out. I didn't think I'd make it in time."

I knew the pain he was in, yet he worried about offending me? I almost wanted to shout, *What's the matter with you? I don't understand anything about you anymore!* but instead I found myself kneeling beside him. He opened his wet eyes, grimacing with his discomfort (and what a weak word that was for the kind of pain he was in), or he might have been grimacing at my proximity. He met my gaze, then looked away, as though he didn't want to be seen like this.

Again he sniffed. "Thank you for the water," he muttered.

He put the bottle to his lips and drained it. Perspiration made his forehead shiny, and his eyelashes were wet. A pale dusting of bristles, faint, stood out above his upper lip where he drew at the bottle's mouth. I took it from his shaking fingers and tossed it into the garbage can. Color had returned to his cheeks, only it was hectic and very, very red.

Another surreal moment swept me—for his features

were my old friend's. After all we had been through, how was it that I was here, with him—not just in this situation, but *at all*? He looked more grown up now, of course, his jaw defined, nose more prominent. And that light fuzz on his chin… His hair was longer than I had seen it in years, falling in damp strings over his brow. I wondered if he had always worn it so short before because of football. I suddenly felt I had been seeing him for the last month without really looking at him.

When the silence began to be awkward, when I thought myself studying him too closely, I asked, "Why'd you do this?"

He shook his head. "Dunno."

After another pause, I said, "They got me before, you know. Sophomore year."

He darted a sharp look at me, pain still clouding his eyes, but regret filled them too. His lips twitched, then pressed into a hard line. He said, "I didn't know."

"Would you have cared if you did?"

"It probably wouldn't have fazed me. Back then."

He let his eyes drift to the patch of floor between his Converse. There came another audible swallow and a small fit of coughs.

I reached for the trash barrel. "Gonna hurl again?"

He shook his head. Then he turned his face toward me, his expression confused.

"What are you doing?" he asked.

"What?"

"Why are you staying with me?"

I felt my cheeks get hot. What *was* I doing? I had a date I was running late for. But all I could do was recycle what he had said moments before.

"Dunno."

I settled on the floor, leaning, as he did, against the lockers.

"You don't have to," he said, looking further shocked to find me sitting beside him. Hell, I was a little shocked myself. Now it was my turn to glance away, self-conscious. He sighed. "I mean, come on. You hate me, so…"

That guilt-fist again. I *had* said that, yes, yet he had come to my rescue just the same—or whatever this had turned out to be.

"I don't hate you, Nick," I heard myself say, staring at the lockers across from us.

"You said you did."

"You said *you* hated *me*."

Silence.

"Well," he said at last, "I don't. Sometimes I thought I did. But I never really have."

"Could have fooled me."

"I know." He paused again. "I said some really horrible things to you, Michael. I've *done* horrible things to you."

"I remember."

"I've wished I could take them all back."

Something stirred in my chest. If asked, I would have been hard pressed to say whether I had been waiting for years to hear those words, or if my resentment sometimes felt so strong they didn't matter. I couldn't look at him, though I sensed the weight of his gaze.

It was my turn to stare at the patch of tile between my feet. I said, "You can't."

His face turned away. "I know," he said once more.

I wasn't sure what to say next. He twisted his arms to

hold his belly, which I felt sure must still be roiling. He had done that for me. After how I had treated him…

"I was pretty mean on my birthday," I said.

"I deserved it."

"Not then. I'd had a long, sort of crummy day. Which sucks extra hard considering it was my birthday. Still, I took it out on you."

Once more our eyes met. His narrowed, something dark coming into his expression.

"What is it?" I asked.

His gaze locked just above my eye. "I gave you that," he said, lifting one hand, fingers moving toward my eyebrow, toward the six-year-old scar. I almost expected he would touch it, and I found I didn't feel the impulse to tilt my head away. Nick, however, stopped his fingers about an inch from my skin, dropping his arm across his belly again. He looked away, cheeks flaming with more color than ever. He murmured, "You were my best friend."

"You were mine," I replied.

His throat rippled as he swallowed. "You *should* hate me."

"For a long time I thought I did." I looked away. I hadn't known such words were going to come out of my mouth, that I would suddenly be feeling kind toward him. Something older stirred again, however, something resentful. I said, "I'm still not sure I *like* you though."

"Join the club. I don't like myself."

I thought of Brent and Calista, Liam and Jackie. I thought of the girl that had yelled at Nick when he had apologized to her. I recollected then what he had told me in my room the night of my party.

"But you're trying?" I said.

I think his darting look checked for mockery in my face. He nodded slowly and murmured, "I'm trying."

"I've been wondering lately," I then said, "if your dad was a different kind of guy, if we would have stayed friends."

"What do you mean?"

"Come on," I said, blushing myself, laughing awkwardly. "That day? What he said? The way he treated me?"

"Don't remember it. It was awful."

"I learned a lot about myself that day." I smirked. "I guess we both did."

He gave another slow nod. "I guess we did."

"If your dad hadn't caught us," I pressed, not looking at him, hearing myself say the words and marveling at my own nerve, "or had reacted differently…do you think we would have stayed friends?"

He stared at the opposite lockers for a second or two, seeming to muse on the question. I could sense something building in him, something he wanted to express but didn't know how. His lips twitched, and just as he appeared to make up his mind to talk, my name echoed through the hall again.

"Michael! Jeez, there you are!"

It was Gil.

Nick and I turned toward the hall-doors and watched him stride toward us, looking impatient. The sight of him irritated me. I had forgotten all about him these last few minutes. I found I hadn't been ready to end this conversation. But how could it continue now?

I scrambled to my feet. "My bad," I said. "We had… um…an emergency, I guess."

"I've been looking everywhere. I went by the theatre, and was on my way to the drama-room when I saw you sitting here." Gil's eyes fell on Nick, who lifted a sweaty, curiously colored face. "Hey, Nick. What happened?"

I rushed to say, "Someone hit him where they shouldn't. Psychos. I didn't want to leave him alone."

"That sucks. Sorry, man. I know how that is from wrestling."

Nick shook his head. "I'll be all right. You two should get going."

Gil said, "You sure?"

Though Nick nodded, I didn't feel right about leaving. He still looked so battered.

"We can wait a few minutes more," I said. "It's no big deal."

But Nick said, "No, really. I'm fine. I'll be up in a few. You guys got plans. Do your thing."

"Solid, bro," Gil said and actually took my hand, lacing our fingers together.

Nick saw the gesture, and something passed behind his eyes—disgust, I felt sure. Yet, somehow, Gil's hand felt too small in mine, awkward, not quite right. I told myself it was just Nick's presence and the clear indication of his disgust rearing its head again. It irked me, especially after the way we had been talking.

Gil smiled. "Let's head out then, Michael."

I nodded, but went on throwing looks over my shoulder as we passed down the hall, watching Nick get smaller and smaller, becoming a formless shadow slumped on the ground.

MICHAEL

"And on the beach at sunset,
When we're walking hand in hand…"

THREE BAD THINGS…

The first: my date with Gil. I wasn't really fair to him at the start. I was far too distracted wondering about Nick. However, the regret I felt at not really being present would have been massively assuaged if I had known how the date would end—what Gil would do.

To begin, he drove us to Zuma Beach in Malibu. I tried to think it romantic and sweet, but honestly, I hate the beach. All that cold water, sand everywhere. Plus, the beach usually means bare feet and I hate mine and never want anyone to see them—they're too big, I think, and too bony. Still, Gil had a blanket and some bags of snacks, and being a good sport, I took off my shoes and socks along with him and we tromped through the sand, set out the blanket, then sat and watched the sun set. The weather was nice for the end of March and the clouds were beautiful.

We talked about prom. We talked about coming out and past boyfriends. (He even wanted to know if I had ever hooked up with Brent or Liam, but I could only say, "That's like incest! They're practically brothers to me!") He told me about his home life: his mom was an RN; he had an older sister who lived in Arizona with a dude fifteen years older than her; his dad had run off with "some bitch" when he was eight—they rarely spoke, and though Gil hadn't seen him more than two or three times since he left, he sent fat checks at birthdays and Christmas. Gil was going to go to UC Santa Barbara but wasn't clear on exactly what he would study. He had no intention of wrestling again once high school was over. He asked me where I wanted to go to school and about theatre and my singing. I told him I had only ever dreamed of being an actor and a singer my whole life. The idea of having to do anything else because, well, dreams don't always come true, was not something I wanted to entertain. Though I had to admit I wouldn't mind teaching theatre, like Mrs. Peebles. It was easy conversation. Yet…it wasn't any different from our talks in Gov every morning. Then he brought the conversation back to relationships. I had to admit I had never done more than make out with a guy, though Gil, like Brent, seemed to be a pro at hooking up.

It didn't impress me.

My thoughts wandered back to Nick.

In my ears, I heard the sound he made. What had his friends meant when they said they had seen him hugging somebody at lunch? He had probably been accosted by Liam or Brent. Except Brent had been with me. I remembered how small and defeated Nick had looked hunkered on the floor as Gil had swept me down the hall—swept me from a talk that had felt like ridding myself of an over-tight sweatshirt I had been wearing for much too long. I wanted desperately to tug out my phone and text Secret Admirer about what Nick had done.

Suddenly I remembered: my late birthday present…it had never come. I waited all week but had thought so much about my date with Gil the present hadn't crossed my mind. Had Secret Admirer lost interest in my friendship?

From the beach, Gil drove us back toward home and we stopped at a movie theatre.

"One of those fancy ones that serves dinner," he said. "You pick the flick. I'll see anything."

Of course I picked the scary one, and though I enjoyed myself (mostly) Gil jumped and hid his face and looked miserable. He didn't try to hold my hand and I didn't try to hold his. It didn't feel like any more of a date than seeing movies with my Muskequeers.

On the ride home, he kept saying, "I don't know how you like movies like that! I won't sleep tonight!"

I didn't tell him that all the scary movies I loved so much troubled me more than I let on. I didn't sleep well much myself, that string of Christmas lights over my window staying lit every night because I didn't like the dark.

Still, I loved horror movies—and clearly, Gil didn't.

"My buds don't like them either," I said. "Only one person ever liked watching them with me, and he—"

I cut myself off. My thoughts had tumbled backward. Donny and me: watching all those scary movies on sleepovers, trying to freak each other out, often succeeding.

My pause had Gil darting a glance at me. "He? Who?"

I shook my head. "An old friend. From elementary school."

Then things went bad, quick.

Gil pulled up before my house. He turned his face and smiled. Shadows played over his features, except for a glimmer in his eye from the near streetlamp.

"Have fun?" he asked.

I nodded, tugging my backpack up from the footwell and clutching it in my lap. I was suddenly nervous, wondering if Gil and I were going to kiss. I wasn't sure I wanted that. I hadn't had any exceptional time on our date. And, I discovered, I didn't *feel* anything exceptional.

He studied my face, catching his bottom lip with his teeth. He leaned forward a little. "Come here," he murmured, and holding my breath a little, I let myself lean toward him.

My nose filled with citrusy scent, then his mouth pushed at mine. His lips were dry, but open. The sudden pushing of his tongue against my teeth startled me, and though I kissed him back, a kiss like that caught me unprepared. In a very few seconds, I pulled away. He only gazed into my eyes and licked his lip.

"You're a good kisser," he said, almost a whisper.

I thought, *Am I? Are* you? *So much tongue!* But I said, "You too."

I waited for a spark, a bell, fireworks—and felt nothing.

I didn't want to kiss him again. Yet when he tugged me toward his face once more, I told myself I felt so little because of how distracted I had been all night. I was on a date with a really cute guy who liked me, and all I could think about was Nick Walsh vomiting into a trash barrel, looking like a wilted piece of lettuce. How aggravating.

This time the kiss lasted longer, though Gil's tongue stabbed with no less persistence. His fingers slid to my shoulder. His other arm circled round my neck, drawing me nearer. His hand brushed along my arm, dropped to my thigh and pressed, squeezing.

He exhaled against my mouth, muttered, "I'm hard," and suddenly his hand slid over the fly of my jeans. He might have poured fire-ants into my lap. I practically leaped out of my skin, grabbing at his wrist, pulling his fingers away, turning my face from his mouth. I shrugged his arm from my shoulders.

"My family's, like, fifteen feet away," I said as an excuse. Crap, how fast he moved!

He grinned. "They aren't gonna see. We don't have to have sex or anything. There're other things we can do. Make it look like we're just talking."

He leaned toward me again, and our mouths almost met, but I felt completely repelled. I leaned away, my backpack against me like a shield—I saw myself, with a surge of mortification, as some prudish Victorian maiden, but I couldn't help it. I bumped my shoulder against the door and felt a stab of pain, a reminder of my collision with the lockers at school.

This time when Gil sat back, it was with a frustrated sigh. "What the hell, Michael?" he said. "Gimme a break!"

"It's too fast."

"Are you kidding?" Now his tone was impatient, irritated.

I frowned. "What? Me not wanting to have sex in your car in front of my parents is asking too much?"

He sighed again, chewing the inside of his cheek. "Sorry, okay. I didn't mean to push. It was a nice night, I just thought—"

"It's a big deal," I said. "I know it doesn't seem like it is anymore for people, but it is for me."

A coldness had come into my voice. I was irritated with him now, and he could sense it. He tried to give me a placating smile, but it didn't mask his own irritation.

"Look," he said. "My bad, okay? I had a good time tonight. Don't be mad."

"I'm not."

"Okay."

There was a space of silence, the car full of awkwardness.

"I should go," I said at last. "Thanks for the movie and dinner. And for driving."

I opened the car door, but he put his hand out, drawing me toward him. I thought he would kiss me again, to really take the sting out of my rebuff, yet he gave only a hug, orange-scented and quick.

"'Night, Michael," he said.

Then I stood outside the car, hoisting my backpack onto my shoulders. I had barely closed the door when the car lurched forward, swerved a hasty U in the street, and sped off, leaving me taken aback.

Because it was Friday, the twins were up later than usual—I could hear their high-pitched voices, even from the sidewalk. I turned to the house, unwilling to go in yet. It would be all noise. It would be Mom and Dad wanting to know how the date had gone. Georgie making kiss-faces. It would be my baby brother and sister bombarding me with their hugs, their foreheads perfectly in line with my groin now so every unexpected embrace made me wince.

Pain to a lesser degree than anything Nick had experienced today. I knew. I had spoken truly when I told him his dumbass pals had sack-tapped me before. But I had never been hurt so bad I needed to vomit. And again, why in hell *had* Nick gotten in the way? Why come to the rescue? Had I really told him I didn't hate him? He said he didn't hate me—hadn't for a long time, maybe ever. He wished he could take back what he had done. He said it. An apology. The ball lay in my court: forgive him, move onward and upward, or hold on to my resentment, my anger.

Suddenly everything overwhelmed me…

And I did bad thing the second:

I tugged out my phone, pulled up Secret Admirer's number and dialed it. I listened to it ring and ring, never stopping to think what would happen if he or she actually answered. Oh God! What would I do when I heard their voice for the first time? But I needed someone to talk to badly, and not just text messages. I wanted the one person I had been the most explicit with about my resentment toward Nick and my weird confusion about Gil.

The ringing went on and on until at last there came a *click!*

Followed by another *click* as the call ended.

I felt my already low spirits sink further. I could only stare at the phone. *I need you*, I thought. *Why can't you just tell me who you are?*

Then a text message lit up the screen. *U know I cant answer ur call, Michael*, it said. *Im sorry.*

Too disappointed to want to text everything I had on my mind, I simply replied, *I know. Worth a shot. Just needed to talk. I'm fine though. Goodnight.*

Then I turned the phone off completely and went into the house, plastering a smile on my face.

THE NEXT AFTERNOON a letter arrived for me from the Carnegie Mellon School of Drama.

Another no.

Bad thing number three.

DONICK

SO MANY BAD *things today*, I think as I drive home. By the time I get there, it's almost dark.

"Whatsa matter, Nicky?" Pop asks when I come through the door. He's peeking out at me from the kitchen, prepared, I think, to be angry. When he really looks at me, he comes into the entry-way. He's been home for a while because he's not in work clothes and he's barefoot. "You're walking funny. Look sorta pale."

He's genuinely concerned, but in Pop's usual fashion, it's a concern that doesn't know how to comfort. It's the standoffish interest of a man who's never understood how to raise a child alone when the love of his life had to leave him on his own. My turmoiled emotions and thoughts have almost let me see that for the first time.

"Got hit," I manage to say. "You know where."

He almost laughs, a gut reaction born from his awkward concern. "That ain't good. How'd it happen? Hey, I got dinner on the stove."

I had begun to make for the stairs. I can smell something cooking, but I'm desperate to lay down, to be alone so I can make sure anything is left below the belt. Besides, the thought of food makes me want to blow chunks. Again.

"Not hungry, Pop."

"So?" he prompts. "How'd it happen? In the shop? That why you're late? I thought maybe you went off on your own again. I was already thinking of chores for you to do all weekend."

I have no patience for this sort of ribbing—the truth disguised as jokes. And if he knew I had been sack-tapped because I protected Michael Penrose?

What I say is, "Yeah," in that same strained voice. "Woodshop. Another kid was goofing off and stepped on a board. It flipped up and…you know."

"Rang your bell but good, eh?" I summon a completely fake smile and start to make for my room. Pop calls after me. "You need anything, Nicky?"

Maybe the hospital, I think with a prickle of fear, remembering that kid whose testicles were almost ruptured after the last Sack-Tap Day. I only mutter, "Ice or something."

"Some Friday night. Spent sitting on a bag of ice-cubes."

I know he wants me to laugh with him, to think his jokes are funny, but right now I don't have it in me to play the game of ignoring our shallow relationship, or that he's angry all the time—and that I have to ignore that too.

I drop my backpack to the floor once I'm in my room, then lock the door. Pop doesn't like locked doors because he can't open them whenever he feels like, but I don't need him barging in now. I strip off everything and in the mirror on the closet door I can see, with a wince, that yes, there's some swelling—on one side more than the other. I guess *any* swelling is too much, but it could have been worse. For once I'm thankful my legs are so thick—the muscles of my inner thighs kept Josue's knee from doing emergency-room damage.

I tug on a pair of basketball shorts and, after unlocking the door, I ease onto the bed, stretching out with my knees apart, trying to catch my breath. Every move I make has me holding the air in my lungs. Thank goodness I don't have to see anyone for a week. I've never been more grateful for Spring Break.

Thirty seconds later Pop comes in, a squishy blue icepack in one hand, a bottle of ibuprofen in the other. A water bottle is clutched under one arm. The desk acts as a make-shift bedside table and he sets everything down.

"Take some pain killers," he says. "I'll leave dinner out if you get hungry."

I barely register that he's gone again, so thankful for the marvelous cold of the icepack as I literally cup it between my legs. I swallow five ibuprofen, then close my eyes.

I doze, only it's like being half-awake in a nightmare because my thoughts won't shut off; I don't know when I'm awake or asleep; it's just bad things bad things bad things. The whole day just went…wrong!

MICHAEL'S BIRTHDAY PRESENT had arrived on Thursday. I swooped it into my room as soon as I got back from school (no rehearsal for once), glad Pop wasn't home yet to wonder what was in the package. I unboxed the phone case and examined how it turned out. It looked exactly how I hoped, and I knew Michael would love it!

I re-boxed it and pulled out a few sheets of lime-green construction paper from an old box of drawing stuff I used as a kid. I wrapped the present in that instead of actual wrapping-paper, which I didn't have. But also…it reminded me of Michael's eyes.

The only hitch in the plan was that I hadn't seen Gabby in the library since Tuesday. On Thursday I finally asked her giggly friends what was up and they told me she was sick. I stared at the green package on the corner of my desk all Thursday night, listening to a recording of the song I'll be performing for my solo in the Revue, even as I absently worked on vocabulary for *The Awakening*. If Gabby wasn't around, how would I get the present into Michael's hands? If I couldn't do it Friday, I would have to wait until after Spring Break. Friday or nothing!

It was bad enough Michael wanting to spend the evening texting me—well, secret admirer—about his coming date with Gil. Something jealous-like crawled through me. I thought again of how envious I am of them—comfortable with who they are and, for the most part, accepted by the people around them. Well, except for assholes like Josue and Ryan—and *me*…as I used to be.

I took Michael's present to school this morning, fingers crossed Gabby would be there. If I could hand the box off to her, she could get to Mrs. P.'s room before last period when Michael and his Muskequeers had their theatre class.

But right from the start, the day was full of bad things.

By some miracle, I happened to be in the right place at the right time. Between first and second periods, I witnessed one of the varsity players—a bleach-blonde dude named Anthony Frobisher who has the guy-equivalent of resting-bitch-face—pass a gangly-looking freshman boy, flick out his hand and bop him one right in the crotch. Anthony Frobisher's face actually formed an expression: he looked constipated, holding in laughter as he booked it, losing himself in a crowd of students exiting a classroom. I wanted to chase after him—use my fists like a troll-hammer—but the kid he targeted had doubled over, holding himself, looking supremely uncomfortable.

I approached slowly because he looked afraid *I* would attack him next. "You okay?" I asked.

He moaned in a little voice, "No…"

"You need the nurse? Sometimes those jerks sack-tap too hard."

He grimaced, attempting to stand straight. The yelp he had made had drawn some attention, but not much. Most kids had kept on their way. It amazes me that not one person had tried to stop jerkass-Anthony after he had done the damage, let alone check on this poor freshman.

The kid shook his head again, and I could do nothing but say, "Sorry, man. Listen, don't keep quiet about this. Tell the principal or your councilor or something. Other guys are for sure in line to get tapped today. It's this thing those morons do."

"I'll be fine." His voice sounded strained, face pale. "No big. He didn't get me very hard."

Another one willing to keep quiet. Mrs. Moes had been right. People were afraid to stand up to those losers. But I wasn't. I had been one of them once, to my shame, and I wasn't afraid of what they might do to me. I had told Josue and Ryan if they attempted to play this idiotic game, I would stop them. So, I would do just that.

Which set me up for the biggest bad of the day.

Mrs. Moes, in a meeting with a student, had looked impatient at yet another of my interruptions. I waited for her to finish, then sat before her desk. It was my turn to be impatient when she asked me how things had gone with Wyatt and Erin. I answered quickly and then, once again, I psyched myself up to display a little more of my shame and told her all about Sack-Tap Day. I couldn't squarely meet her eyes. I then related my argument with Josue about it.

"I told him if he didn't lose the idea, I would stop them from playing. Well, I just witnessed Anthony Frobisher tap some kid a few minutes ago."

Mrs. Moes looked tired, sighed, shook her head. "Some *game...* Who exactly will be participating in this?"

"For sure I know about Anthony, but also Josue, Ryan Pollard, probably Scott Blair too. The rest I'm guessing are the usual varsity guys. I don't even know which ones. It's so fucking stupid." I had muttered this last under my breath, then gave Mrs. Moes an apologetic look.

She exhaled again, pushing herself to her feet. "All right. Thanks for telling me. I'll report it to one of the admins and see if we can stop this nonsense before it gets too far off the ground."

I turned to leave, feeling satisfied—already imagining the faces of my my stupid ex-friends when confronted by one of the assistant principals—but she stopped me.

"You need another hall-pass, Nick."

I DIDN'T WITNESS ANY of the guys getting a talking to, but the few times I saw Josue and Ryan in passing they didn't look happy. I didn't see any other sack-tap victims though, so I could feel satisfied. I felt pretty damn smug about it, actually. I wanted to get in Josue's face and say, "See, dude? Told you I would stop it!" I settled for smirking at him.

Whatever glimmer of a good mood I had been in died as soon as I arrived in the library at lunch. Gabby wasn't at her table. I got the same report from her girlfriends: still out sick, she might have bronchitis!

"Tell her I asked about her," I said. "That I hope she'll be better soon."

I wandered back outside. Bronchitis…pretty serious. Most likely she'll be sick all through Spring Break. I really do hope she'll be okay, but at that moment, I was also thinking selfishly, wondering what to do about Michael's present. I promised he would have it by the end of the week, and here it was, lunchtime on Friday, and my delivery-option was no longer an option. I couldn't deliver it to Mrs. P. myself—not in a million years. That would place me too close.

Then I thought, *Donick Walsh, you doofus!* because I never really needed Gabby to begin with. Liam Hidalgo could play carrier-pigeon for me! Why hadn't I thought of him before? He's close to Michael, but not so close as to raise suspicions. Besides, I trust Liam. If I would have to tell him more than I might like, I felt confident in his discretion. But where to find him? Drama-room? I decided to check the dance-studio first. I mean, why go to Mrs. P.'s room and run into the Muskequeers—run into Michael— if I can avoid them? Delivering Calista's new phone earlier in the week had been hard enough. And would I really want to see a potential scene between Michael and Gil as they planned out their date? No, thank you!

It's odd walking across the quad now. Before, when I

glued myself to the usual table with all the football jerks, it seemed to be our own small world—football players and cheerleaders and the occasional stoner like Scott Blair. Beyond, a sea of fodder for bullying. Once I stopped sitting with Josue and Ryan, lunches became solitary while I studied in the library. Now though…there aren't many tables or groups sitting under the trees that don't have some kid I've gotten to know in the Revue. My brain can't cope with their hellos and their waves. It embarrasses me, and I was happy to get away from the quad.

Before I reached the dance-studio doors, however, Liam himself had come darting from the direction of the boys' locker-room. "Hey," I said. "I was just coming to find you."

He paused, looking hurried. He jerked a thumb over his shoulder. "Just throwing my jazz shoes in my locker. I had class before lunch. I'm heading to Mrs. P.'s room now."

"Can I walk with you?" I felt a little hesitant; he didn't look particularly happy to see me, but maybe he only felt rushed. "I wanted to ask you something," I added.

"Sure, let's go."

He looked a little less hurried now, and we walked back the way I had just come.

"What's up?" he asked.

"I need a favor."

"Who's drink of choice is it now?"

"Nothing like that. It's… I mean, there's not really time to explain right now. Plus, too many people around."

"Mysterious much?"

"No, I just—I really can't ask you to do this thing for me until after Spring Break now, anyway. But I'd still like to run it by you ASAP. Are you busy tomorrow?"

"I've got a rehearsal here in the morning at nine. After that I'll be free."

"Rehearsal? School's out."

"It's the only scheduled day over break. Chalice and Mrs. P. are working on "The Mirror-Blue Night" with some of the singers and dancers. They're using freshmen and sophomores for lyrical dance stuff in the background. They asked me to be in it!" Liam's face lit up.

"That's great," I said. "I've been learning my song, but Chalice hasn't had me in to choreograph it yet. I think it's on the schedule for the week we come back. Scary stuff." Talking about it like that made me feel less nervous, because it still boggles my mind to think I'll actually be singing and dancing all by myself in the show, without a group to hide in.

"You got this," Liam said. "So, about tomorrow…"

"Yeah, so, would you want to meet up after your rehearsal? Grab lunch or something? My treat."

Liam's smile got bigger. "This must be some favor!"

"Kinda is. I have a couple classes to teach at my studio in the morning. I'm usually finished around noon. How 'bout I come here and pick you up. If you're not done yet, I'll wait."

"You sure?"

"The surest."

"Sweet! I'm *über* curious now!"

"It's not a big deal, really," I said, but thinking, *To anyone but me, that is.* "You've got my number. Text me if something changes, yeah?"

"I will. Thanks!"

We were at the edge of the quad. I paused there. "I'm heading to the library," I said, "so I'll let you go."

"You're awesome, Nick," he said, and I was thrown

a little off balance when he abruptly hugged me. In my shock at how public we were, I sort of stood like a piece of rock. Then my arms came around him and gave him a squeeze, self-consciously patting his shoulder.

In the theatre crowd I've suddenly become immersed in, everyone, guys and girls, are always hugging each other, and while it's taken some getting used to, it's something I've come to like. But in a theatre-setting! The quad suddenly seemed full of watchful, hostile eyes. Yet, I think Liam is great, don't I? He *is* my friend, after all, and just because he shines his gayness like a sun, and I hide whatever part of me that's the same behind a blackout curtain, it doesn't mean I can't hug him back, right? Who cares what all these people think? Or so I told myself, as I relaxed in the embrace.

Though the hug lasted just a few seconds, I had time to think, *Girls don't smell this good!* Because close to Liam like this, whatever he wore at his neck came to my nostrils, and I wondered why I had never noticed before that when a guy smells nice like this, it's actually pretty sexy. Well, at least when they don't drown themselves in scent like Gil did at Michael's party.

All around, that hug from Liam, there for all the world to see, felt definitely not bad.

"I'll see you tomorrow," he said, pulling back. "Thanks in advance for lunch."

Then I had wandered back to the library, debating if I should text Michael and say he wouldn't be getting his birthday present this week after all. I wanted to text him regardless—talking with him is something I've looked forward to every day. Though our conversations aren't exactly deep, it's the sort of small-talk that tells me a lot about who he is now: musical-theatre loving, anime obsessed, manga reading, horror-movie watching Michael, who loves his little sisters and brother like a dad; and the Michael who resents the hell out of Nick Walsh, irritated that his friends are giving that same Nick Walsh the time of day. But I try not to dwell on that. As the days pass, as I find out more about him, I'm realizing I never had a best friend like Michael. I doubt I ever will again.

This thought depressed me and I decided not to text him, but to focus on my schoolwork until lunch ended.

Cue the bad-things-train.

Stoner Scott Blair is in my English 12 class; my last period of the day. He stopped me on my way out the door. I waited for him to say some jerkoff thing about my ratting them out over Sack-Tap Day. He looked pretty dim, but his eyes weren't as glassy as usual.

"Hey bruh," he said. "Thought I'd give you, like, a heads up."

"'Bout what?" I know I didn't look very friendly. In fact, I think I probably looked pretty distrustful.

"The guys are pretty pissed about the sack-tap."

"I told that stupid-ass he'd better not try anything. That shit is tired."

"Yeah, I kinda agree. Takes, like, too much work, you know? Anyway, they're pretty pissed. They're gonna get back at you by, like, getting one of your friends. Today. After school. Like, *now*. They talked about it at lunch."

I thought of Jackie, of Liam. How would my old asshole pals even know who I've been spending time with? They don't know me anymore. I don't see or talk to them now, and they certainly don't see who I'm hanging with at rehearsal.

"What do you mean," I asked, "*getting one of my friends?*"

"They're gonna sack-tap him, I think."

"Who?"

"Some kid you used to hang with. They said you've been hanging around with him a lot or something."

They were talking about Michael! But that made zero sense. I hadn't been hanging around with him. Anonymously texting him, yes, but definitely not hanging out with him.

"If it's who I think you're talking about," I said, making a face, "what the hell? He's not my friend."

"Guess they heard you went to, like, some party at the dude's house?"

"Oh shit…" I muttered. I remember thinking that all of this assholery felt beyond exhausting.

"Yeah, bruh," Scott said. "Your locker's, like, near his or something. It'll be easy to make sure you see it happen. They're, like, really pissed. We all got Saturday school."

"Why tell me then? Aren't you pissed too?"

"Eh, I can be wasted at home, or wasted here. It's, like, all the same, or some shit. It's a bitch-game anyway. Who likes having their nuts slapped around?"

I wasn't really hearing Scott anymore. I felt a dancing sort of hurry crawl into my feet, like the pause before a sprint. *Now*, Scott had said, *after school!* I couldn't be wasting time here! I had to stop them from hurting Michael!

"Thanks," I then said, already beginning to dash away, calling over my shoulder, "you did a solid. Sorry for getting you in trouble."

Then I had gone charging toward my locker, thinking,

It's Michael they've targeted! Michael, of all people! And why? Because of a rumor I went to a party at his house? I'm never with him at school, never around him even in passing. Of all people, it's Liam I would expect those asshats to target. But Michael?

He's not going to get hurt because of me again! I remember thinking, and then it started spinning through my thoughts like a mantra, over and over, as I charged with a speed I don't think I had ever displayed on a football-field, down a flight of stairs, across the quad, aiming like a bullet for the hall where our lockers are.

And it wasn't Michael they even wanted. It was me. I walked right into a trap, running through the school like some kind of hero, chanting Michael's name in my head. Then it all became confusion, and pain, and Michael acting strangely caring, confusing me and almost making the pain worse. Then there was Gil with his overwhelming orange scent, come to collect Michael for their date. I was left like a deflated balloon, watching them vanish, leaving me alone, unsure if I really did do what I had just done.

I stayed, hunched on the ground, for almost an hour, my butt feeling numb and cold from the floor, wishing like hell my balls felt numb and cold. Instead, they sent dull stabs into my gut every few seconds. I seemed to feel them like ostrich eggs. I kept my eyes closed, and mercifully, I wasn't thinking about anything in particular. It felt like the answer to a prayer, to be so thoughtless. I simply sat and felt nothing—aside from the sickening pain.

The quad outside had no longer been as bright when I got to my feet, scooping up my backpack. I thought I might hurl again when I first stood. Or cry like a baby. Yet I took deep breaths, grimacing every third or fourth step, and moved sluggishly toward the doors, using one hand on the lockers to brace myself.

It was when I paused just before the doors of the hall, stealing myself for the long walk to my car, that my thoughts kicked in again and my discomfort drifted to the back of my mind. Beneath my hand, the texture of the locker's paint felt different. I stared at it, almost unseeing for fifteen or so seconds. Then it was like I had X-ray vision: swimming up from beneath the paint, I could see the words FAT WHORE in big black letters.

Because I had written them…two years before.

IT'S COMPLETELY DARK when I come fully awake. At first I think it's the throbbing in my groin that's brought me from sleep, but it's the sound of buzzing, persistent and loud in the silence of my room.

That's not my iPhone—*that* phone is never silenced unless I'm in class. It's the sound of the green Razr going off…and not a text message! Michael…*calling* me! No. Calling his secret admirer. Still, Michael actually calling, even though I've said several times we can only ever text. Why? He's supposed to be on his date with Gil. Can this day get any stranger?

Almost not feeling the pain between my legs, I stumble over to my backpack, crouching, digging through it until the Razr is humming like a green hornet in my fist. MICHAEL flashes in the little glass window. In a gesture as quick as the flick of a thumb, I have the phone open (which answers the call), then closed (which immediately hangs it up).

My lungs are tight, watching the light in the Razr's square of a window until it kills itself.

I flip it open again and type out, *U know I cant answer ur call, Michael. Im sorry.* As I hit send, I wish more than anything that I *could.* What I wouldn't give to be able to talk to him right now—as *me* and not his secret admirer.

His response is immediate. *I know,* it says. *Worth a shot. Just needed to talk. I'm fine though. Goodnight.*

I want to say, *I really need to talk too!* I want to ask about his date with Gil, but I'm afraid he'll actually tell me and I'm not up to hearing about it tonight, not feeling as crummy as I do. I'm unbearably lonely all of a sudden. Lonely and hurting. Michael has his Muskequeers, and now Gil for a boyfriend; I don't have friends anymore— they were the ones who put me in this pain, after all—and I wouldn't even know what to do if some guy somewhere were interested in me, or I were interested in *him.* Never mind that Pop would probably lose him mind.

I reply with: *Everything alright?*

Though the last thing I want to hear about is what a wonderful night he's had, and how crazy about Gil he is, I can't help feeling as though I've let Michael down by hanging up on his phone call. I'm further troubled by the fact he doesn't text me back. His *Goodnight* suddenly seems so final.

DONICK

"In this world so full of fear,
Full of rage and lies,
I can see the truth so clear…"

MY PAIN IS much more manageable the next morning, though walking isn't particularly comfortable. It's best I call out of teaching at the studio. I smile at the regret in the owner's voice as she adds, "We never see you anymore, Nick. You're missed." Once the Revue is over (something I'm beginning to dread—I'm having so much fun), I'll come to class again and they'll see me most every day. "I'm gonna miss the kids," I say, "but I'll be back next week."

I down more ibuprofen, then after a shower, put the ice-pack back in the freezer. It sat in my crotch on and off all night, but whatever.

Pop hears my movements and calls from his office, "How you feel, Nicky?"

"A little better," I call back.

"Eat something! You skipped dinner! You have work?"

I lie. "I'm leaving for the studio soon." There's no way he needs to know I'm having lunch with a friend who's so openly gay.

I hear him laugh. "You sure you should teach with crushed nuts?"

I roll my eyes (because he can't see—I would never do it if he were watching). "I feel well enough to teach. None of the kids are older than six. It's not too strenuous." This is the same argument he used while I recovered from my shoulder surgery. Should I be teaching, let alone dancing, when I can't play football?

I figure I'll drive over to the school and wait for Liam to finish his rehearsal. I'll be really early—like, hours early—but I plan to sit in the car and think about yesterday. Specifically, I need to think about that mismatched locker-paint and the black lettering I know is hidden beneath.

I park in the shade of some trees once I reach school and roll the windows down. The day is nice and there's a breeze. Only one or two other cars can be seen near the open gate outside the dance-classroom. The campus is otherwise deserted with everyone cleared out for Spring Break.

I tug out the green Razr. Michael still hasn't replied since his final text last night. I hope he's all right. The more I think about him trying to call the one person he knows he can't call, the weirder it seems.

I text him again. Starting casual, I type, *Happy 1st day of spring break!* then add, *Im really sorry bout last night. I wish we could talk. I wish I hadnt had 2 hang up like that, but its better this way. Dont b angry w/ me. Please.*

Then I pull a notebook from my backpack, find a blank page, and start writing. I pause frequently, frowning through the windshield, dredging up old sophomore year memories. My mindset isn't great today and remembering these things doesn't help. Once I'm done, I have a list of names—and it's long, about twenty people. I also feel kind of emotional. But I keep reminding myself, *It's not easy, but it'll be worth it.* Then I stow the notebook back in my bag, ready to bring it out on the first day back from break when I go bug Mrs. Moes again.

I wish Michael would text back. What if my not answering last night made him never want to text me again?

I see dancers leaving the studio, cars beginning to pull into the lot. No Liam though. I wait a few minutes. It's almost noon, yet there's no sign of him. Curious, I get out and cross toward the open gate. Maybe he stayed home and forgot to let me know.

I poke my head into the studio, stuffy with sweat-smell. Chalice is by the sound-system, talking quietly with Mrs. P. They glance up, then exchange a funny look.

"I'm looking for Liam," I say.

"Haven't seen him," says Chalice, "though he was supposed to be here."

Mrs. P. adds, "He didn't call and no one could get ahold of him."

"Weird," I say. "He was really excited about today. I've been waiting for him. We were gonna hang."

"I wish we had known you were around," Chalice says. "You could have stood in for him. We didn't have any of the dance captains to learn his part."

Not that I could have done much dancing, with this fire burning in my groin, but I tell them to give me a call next time. Then I add, "I guess I'll head out. I'll call him and see if everything's okay."

"Actually, Nick," Mrs. P. says, "I'm glad you're here. We were just discussing you."

As usual, anxiety ripples through me. Maybe it's my eternally guilty conscience, or the feeling of always being on guard around Pop. I join them at the sound-system.

"We were wondering something," Mrs. P. adds.

"Have you ever done any choreographing?" Chalice asks.

Surprised, I say, "I guess. Saraswood Dance Center is my studio, but I've never been able to participate in their concerts. My teachers would have me choreograph some, like, small numbers for their classes. I don't know if they were any good."

"I can already tell you make a good teacher," Chalice goes on. "You're so helpful to everyone, and you have an eye for steps. We were wondering if you'd be interested in choreographing something in the show."

I blink, embarrassed. "In the Revue?"

Mrs. P. nods. "I think we went a bit too ambitious with some of our numbers this year. We've fallen behind. Not a lot. But enough to make us antsy."

Chalice adds, "Between the amount of work we've put in on 'Vogue', the *Mamma Mia!* medley, the other group numbers, not to mention they all need polishing, I'm stretched a bit thin. I've got smaller groups yet to work on, and we haven't been able to work on *your* number at all."

"And I've got another song I want you to look at too—a duet," adds Mrs. P.

"You learn so fast though," Chalice puts in, "we know we don't have to worry about you. The other dance captains will be getting some extra credit by choreographing smaller numbers as well."

"Once we're back from break, performances will only be a month away," Mrs. P. says. "You'd be doing the show an enormous favor."

I feel flattered, a grin breaking out on my face. "I'd be happy to," I say. "Have I heard the song yet?"

"It's called 'Cover Girl'." Mrs. P. plucks up a paper sleeve with a CD inside. "It's a New Kids on the Block song from when I was a kid. Always have been a sucker for those boys. Has a real 60's pop vibe to it. This disc has all the songs from act two. We want four guys singing boy-band style, accompanied by four girls. The girls will sing the *following* song with the guys accompanying *them*. It'll only be the senior singers."

"The ones not involved in 'Vogue'," Chalice adds. "There's no way for, say, *you*, Nick, to be ready for 'Cover Girl' after just finishing the previous number."

"What are you looking for?" I ask.

"Something fairly simple," says Mrs. P. "Think 50's and 60's doo-wop. Four mic-stands with the guys singing at them."

She and Chalice then give me minute details about what they'd like. I can't help feeling excited. It sounds right up my alley. I ask when they would like to start and Chalice tells me right after we return from break.

Mrs. P. says, "Rehearsals basically become an everybody-is-called-every-day sort of thing." She pantomimes praying. "Hopefully everyone will be there like they're supposed to be!"

"At this point," Chalice shrugs, "the ones who are there get put in the numbers. If they're not around, the space gets filled by someone who is. The time for goofing off is past."

"There'll be something for everyone to do at all times. You'll see, Nick. Every available space in the entire performing-arts building will be utilized in some way."

"We need to remind Calista about getting the masks made for the masquerade," Chalice says as an aside to Mrs. P. "I want the dancers to have them to wear as soon as possible. It's going to change some things for them. You know how it goes."

Mrs. Peebles says, "Go ahead and listen to the song, Nick. Get some ideas. We might see what we can get done on the first day back from break, okay? Just remember—nothing too complicated. They're singers, not dancers. And we don't want you aggravating yourself over this."

"No worries," I say. "Thanks for asking me."

They have some other things to discuss, so they ask me to shut the door on my way out. But before I can leave completely Mrs. P. calls out, "Oh, and Nick? The duet I'd like you to work on is on that CD too. It's a song from *Pocahontas*: 'If I Never Knew You'. Really beautiful, kinda sad, but it'll be perfect right before we bring the audience back up with the finale. We aren't changing the key, so you can learn the guy's part straight from the track. We'll have you practice with Mr. Hardy ASAP."

I shut the door and head back through the gate, wondering which girl I'll be performing this duet with, nervous all over again. But it's also sorta cool—the amount of stuff I have to do in the show. I'm in all the big dance numbers, I've been added into a few smaller groups as both a dancer and a singer. Now I'll be choreographing a number all on my own. But maybe busy is better; I won't have time to psych myself out with nerves.

My feet slow when I see Liam standing on the curb, gazing after a departing car. He starts when I speak, spinning to face me with the same harried expression I saw on his face yesterday.

"What happened, Li? I was worried."

He looks sheepish, cheeks going pink. "I overslept. Alarm didn't go off. Then my ride was late. I got here as soon as I could. I know I missed rehearsal. I hope they won't be mad."

"It's probably no big deal. You sure you're okay?" He must have been in a huge rush. He looks rumpled, like he can't relax.

"Totes okay! Still good for lunch?"

"Fully. Come on." I start walking toward my car.

Liam asks about the CD in my fingers and I explain about choreographing for the show. His harried look disappears and a big grin replaces it.

"No way!" he almost squeals. "I wish I could be in that number!"

I unlock the car and we slide in, me with care, hoping he won't notice my pained expression. "Well, don't miss any more rehearsals," I say, "or Mrs. P. and Chalice will stick someone else into your numbers."

"I've been, like, flakey this week, I know. But I've had reasons!"

I start the car. "Like what?"

His cheeks pink again. "Nothing big," he hurries to say, but something tells me that might not be true. Whatever it is, he's embarrassed and I don't want to press.

I pull out and drive toward the exit, saying, "If you need to talk, I'm a willing ear."

He changes the subject. "So where're we gonna eat? I'm curious about this favor you need to ask. Sounds mysterious."

As I drive, I notice Liam's smell again. It's the same scent I noted when he hugged me at lunch yesterday. I have to laugh at myself, thinking about all the stuff I never knew, or admitted about who I am. I like it, this scent coming from another boy. In comparison to all the sweet perfumes any of my girlfriends ever sprayed on themselves, I like this way more. Only, it would be nice to smell something this compelling on a guy I could really fall for.

I LET LIAM PICK where he wants to eat. We end up at this build-your-own-pizza place called The Pie Stone, smelling overwhelmingly of yeast and dough, and laugh together over the toppings he picks: Kalamata olives, extra garlic, basil, blue-cheese, bacon, and lots of pepperoni.

He grins. "I'm not kissing anyone today—no one'll care!"

"I'm thinking about your family later tonight."

"We've got a dog who's a gas-machine. I can blame it on her."

I chuckle, thinking, *Gay or not, guys are still guys.*

Liam digs into his pizza straight away as though he didn't get breakfast. Or dinner the night before. His eyes avid with interest, he asks again about The Favor—he says it like that, as though the words are capitalized.

"Look," I begin, fighting the urge to dance around the point, "this is a big secret. Like, *no one* can know. I'm seriously trusting you on this."

"Mystery! What's the big secret?"

"I have a gift for someone."

"Anyone ever tell you what a *big secret* actually is?"

"It's a birthday present. I don't want the person to know it's from me."

"Who's it for?"

I stare at the cheese on my pizza, my appetite receding.

I'm about to voice the secret, hoping and praying I really *can* trust Liam.

"Michael Penrose," I say.

Liam's eyebrows shoot up. "Really?"

"I didn't get him something for his birthday. Then I found the perfect thing and, well…I got it for him, but he can't know it's from me. Seriously! He *can't*! Like, ever!"

"Why not?"

"Because," I start to say, then sigh. "Because Michael doesn't like me very much. But, I guess…even if he doesn't, I still…" I shrug, then mumble, "I dunno…"

Liam sucks oil from his fingers, studying my face. Then his brows shoot up again.

"Oh my God!" he hisses. "Are you Michael's secret admirer?"

Even had I thought of a way to deny it, the opportunity flees when I feel as though my face could cook the pizzas. My mouth works soundlessly. Then I only slump in my seat.

"How do you know about that?"

"Holy crap, Nick! You? That's wild!"

"He and I were friends once. A long time ago."

"So I've been hearing."

"And I feel bad about some things. I wasn't a good friend but…I'm trying to make up for it."

I can't meet Liam's eyes. This is mortifying and I haven't even gotten to the favor yet. Still, I should have known it would be this way. Liam *is* Michael's friend.

"So it's you," Liam muses. "The notes, and the text messages?"

"You know about those too?"

"Totally. He compared the phone number to everyone's

in the Revue. How'd you work that? Even I got your cell number from the contact-list."

"Spare phone. God, Li! You *have* to keep this to yourself. Please! I didn't want anyone to know about all this other stuff. I'm *seriously* trusting you."

"And you can. I won't say anything. I know how to keep a secret." He pauses, sipping his Diet Coke. Suddenly, he's snorting, then full on laughing.

"What?"

"Nothing, nothing. It's just…and don't get mad at me for saying this, but this whole situation is *so* gay! If I didn't know better, I would totally think you were a big 'mo!"

He laughs to himself again. But the strangest sensation, like a hole opening somewhere around my lungs, has my shoulders slumping and tiredness overtaking me. The throb in my groin is beginning to feel uncomfortable again. My ears burns. Liam quickly falls silent. When I glance up, I see his eyes are so huge he might be an anime character.

"Holy shit," he murmurs. "You are."

I lean my forehead into my palms, squeezing my eyelids shut, wanting to really be lost in the dark, not sitting here, admitting to yet another person that I'm not the guy I've worked so hard to be for so many years. I wonder if anyone, even after admitting the truth about themselves, truly feels ready to let go of the persona they hid behind.

"Well?" Liam presses. "I'm right, yeah?"

I force my head into a nod.

"Holy shit!" he says again. I hear him shift in his chair. "Am I the only one who knows?"

"No. Calista does."

"You told her? That's crazed! Everyone thinks you're,

like, a homophobe and stuff. But you're tribe."

"I'm what?"

"Tribe. You know, part of the team."

"It feels like I'm playing solitaire here."

"Aw, Nick…" His voice gets pitying. "Don't. There are a lot of people who love you. If you just told everyone—"

I shake my head, alarmed. "No! I'm not ready for that!"

"Chill. I won't say anything. But I'm glad I know. If *you* need an ear, I've got two."

"Thanks." I try to smile. "None of this has been easy. I've been such an asshole."

"Explains about the dancing though."

I blink. "What?"

"How about The Favor? Michael Penrose, remember? Birthday present?"

"Oh, yeah. I just need it delivered. I was hoping you'd hand it to Mrs. P. when we're back from break. Have her give it to him."

"Why can't *I* give it to him?"

"Because he knows you and I are friends. He *can't* trace it to me. I asked someone else to do it, someone he would never suspect, but she couldn't."

"I'll give it to Mrs. P. and have her give it to Michael— check! And she never saw me." He begins laughing again.

"What now?" How I wish I could take back telling him. The truth about myself keeps getting more and more real.

"Nothing," he answers, then giggles. "It's just…I mean, come on! You've got a crush on Michael Penrose, don't you?"

I feel hot from the base of my neck all the way into my hair. "No!" I cry, loud enough to be overheard by the other diners. I duck my face. "Jesus, no," I mutter. "I already told you. He and I were friends a long time ago—"

"Yet you've been sending him little love notes? You made a point of getting him a birthday present?"

"They weren't *love notes!*"

"The first one had a big ol' heart on it!"

"That was…*accidental!*"

"Sure."

"It was! I only sent those because…I guess…I want him to know that I—or *someone*—appreciates him. I didn't when we were friends and I regret it. I—"

"—admire him?"

I'm feeling insanely awkward. I can only sigh and nod.

Liam says, "But in secret?"

"Yeah."

"Sounds crushy to me."

"It's *not* a crush!" My voice rises once more. "Mikey— *Michael* and I, we—"

"Look, there's no shame in it. He's totally great. I mean, have you *heard* him sing? See? You think he's great too. I mean, you've practically already said it."

"I do, but—"

"And let's be real. He's good-looking. You think he's good-looking, right?"

Again my lips move but nothing comes out. The trajectory of this conversation sucks. I give Liam an exasperated look and almost grudgingly say, "Yes, I think Michael's good-looking, but—"

"No buts! Just answer the questions. Believe me, I know crushes. Do you follow him around the room with your eyes?" He actually bats his eyelashes.

I grimace.

"Seriously. When he's around, do you watch him?"

I pause, frowning. Because I have to answer, "Yes. But I've known him for—"

"Only yes and no answers! How about at rehearsal, or even his birthday party? Do you always seem to know where he's at?"

Now my answer comes out grudging. "Yes…"

"How about this: when you think about him, like, when you sent him those notes, or text him, or when you imagine how he's gonna react to the present you got him, does it make you feel happy?"

"Li—"

"Does thinking about him make you smile?"

I'm having difficulty thinking at all, because it's all striking a little too close to some sort of bullseye. I'm growing more and more agitated.

I mutter, "Yes. I guess he does." And acknowledging it makes my lips twitch a little, wanting to do just that— break into a smile.

"Okay," Liam says. "Almost done. How about this one. Can you imagine yourself *kissing* him?"

My eyes skip away. I want desperately to squirm. I murmur, "Wouldn't be the first time."

"Huh?"

"Long story."

Liam shrugs and says, "Okay, finally, does Michael make you feel…I dunno." He squints at the ceiling, thinking. "Just, does Michael make you *feel?*"

"Li…"

"Answer! It's just you and me here. Consider this one of the first big steps to being comfortable with who you are."

"Fine!" I say, groaning. "Yeah, okay? I feel all kinds of stuff about Michael. We've known each other since kindergarten. But that doesn't mean—"

"Like what kind of stuff?"

He's not going to let me off the hook. So I decide to answer honestly, even if just for the sake of getting him off my back.

"Sometimes, when he's around, or I watch him in rehearsal, or pass him in the halls…I get sort of…I dunno… like I can't breath or something. He makes me nervous, you know? We have a lot of history, and I've been a dick, so…"

Liam shakes his head, his mouth curving in a goofy, lopsided grin. "You, sir," he says, "have a crush. On Michael Penrose."

I'm smirking in disbelief. But then I think of how it felt to see the secret admirer notes tacked to his wall; how happy it made me to come up with the perfect birthday present for him. I think of our text messaging and how I wish I could do so not just as his mystery admirer. I remember my jealousy at the idea of he and Gil Hamilton together, and suddenly it isn't just jealousy at how open they can be, how free they are to be themselves, it's jealousy at the thought of Gil having access to Michael in a way I never can. Lastly, as I feel the ache between my legs, reminding me of the sack-tap I took for him—to protect him—I see the truth in Liam's words. My smirk becomes an equally goofy and lopsided smile.

I almost whisper, "I have a crush on Michael Penrose," as though testing it out. Liam's smile grows enormous, and seeing it, mine does too. "I have a crush on Michael," I say again, almost laughing at the absurdity of it, the *rightness* of it. "Oh my God, Li. He's so freaking talented.

And cute! You're totally right, he's *way* good-looking!"

"Told ya."

"I've never had a crush on a guy before."

"How's it feel?"

I shrug, saying the only thing that comes close to describing it. "Freeing."

"So, what'll you do now?"

"What do you mean? What *can* I do?"

"It's super easy, sister. *You're* into guys, *he's* into guys. That's, like, ninety-five percent of the battle done and over already."

"No way! Michael doesn't like me. Like, *at all*. Not as a friend, not as anything. Hence the secret admirer. It's the only way I can—"

"Get as close to him as you can while still playing it safe? I see how it is."

"No! I'm telling you. He'll never forgive me for the shitty thing I did to him."

"Maybe. Either way, you're still doing something cool. Keep up with it. Show him that he's not the only one who's a catch."

"I'm an asshole, not a catch."

"Nah. You're pretty great too. I would crush on you myself if you were my type."

This type-thing again…

"We know what yours is," Liam adds. "Amazingly talented actor/singers who are tall and have dark hair."

Though I'm embarrassed as hell, I'm laughing with him. It's so completely absurd and unbelievable, yet *true*!

"All along," I say, "it's been him. Ever since we were kids. It's probably why I drove him away. It's always been my own fault, and now it's my own fault I've got feelings for him and they won't ever go anywhere."

"Never say never." He throws a chunk of pizza crust at me, smiling.

Suddenly I'm ravenous. I drag my pizza toward me and devour it.

I DROP LIAM OFF at his apartment and give him Michael's present—I brought it in my backpack. Then I drive home.

My head feels like there's been an earthquake—a brainquake—inside. Over and over, like a hamster running its wheel, I keep thinking, *I have a crush on Michael!* What's left in the wake of this knowledge is chaos. I don't know what to do. This crush is the first real crush of my entire life! Not quite eighteen yet and for the first time I know what it's like to have feelings for someone. How pathetic is that? Though I know it won't go anywhere, it also makes me feel elated somehow, like I could run ten miles without slowing.

Once I'm home and walking through the door, I'm so dazed (not to mention aching in the groin—I'm dying for more ibuprofen) that I have no mind for Pop's presence right there in the hall. A thundery scowl paints his face as he stands with arms crossed over his chest. He might have been watching for my return. I pause, instantly on guard, sensing his mood is not a happy one.

"Hey, Pop."

"Where you been?" His words come out clipped.

I force my eyes to stay on his because they want to skip away as a lie leaves my mouth. "Class."

"I had to run an errand at the T-Mobile store down the way from your studio."

With those words my belly rolls over. I feel the blood drain from my face.

"The car wasn't there," he goes on. "I checked."

"The lot was full," I'm quick to respond. "I parked on the street."

"I went inside, Nicky."

None of the years of training in keeping my features passive will save me now.

I stammer, creating on the fly, "Yeah, well, I got there and wasn't feeling so hot after all. I was in a lot a pain, actually. I could swallow a bottle of pain-killers right now."

He squints at me. "You decided not to teach after all, huh? Where'd you go? You didn't come back here."

"I went to lunch and worked on some homework instead."

"Oh yeah? Where?" He's not buying it, and I feel myself regressing to ten years old, ready to cry because he's angry with me. I've done nothing, really, to warrant his suspicion. Why is he always like this?

"The Pie Stone."

"You been there all this time?"

I nod.

"Alone?"

"Not the whole time," I decide to say. "I ran into a friend and we ended up talking for a while."

"Who?"

"No one you'd know." Frustration begins to lace my words. "What's the big deal, Pop? You're acting like I did something wrong."

"Watch your tone."

"Seriously," I say, of course not doing what's good for me—which is what he told me to do: watch my tone.

"Why are you interrogating me? So I didn't teach today. So I had lunch with a friend? What's the BFD?"

His eyes narrow behind his glasses, taken aback at the heat in my voice, not to mention my words. His arms uncross and one palm turns over, held out toward me.

"Gimme your car keys."

"Oh come on, Pop, it's Spring Break!"

"*Give* me your keys."

I half-sigh, half-groan. The keyring is in my hand and I all but slap it into his palm.

He begins fiddling with it, working the biggest key off the ring until only the house keys remain.

"You are grounded, you understand? You ain't leaving the house until break is over. We can talk later in the week about whether or not you'll be teaching next Saturday. Maybe anymore."

"Give me a break, Pop! The whole vacation?"

"And you may not get the car back after that."

"How'm I gonna get to school?"

"You got feet, doncha? Use 'em." He slaps the remaining keys back into my hand hard enough to sting.

I give another half-sigh, half-groan, moving to brush past him and stomp up the stairs. Why does he have to be such an asshole sometimes? No wonder it's always been so easy for me. I don't know any different.

"You're lucky I don't take away your phone too," he calls after me.

"The car *and* the phone?" I pause on the stairs to glare back at him. "I had lunch with a friend and you're mad enough to do all that? That's BS, Pop!"

He stalks closer to the bannister. His teeth are clenched.

"You watch your mouth, Nicky. You're toeing a fine line here."

"I didn't do anything wrong!"

"Oh yeah? Last weekend?"

I roll my eyes, frustrated enough now to let him see me do it. "Yeah, fine. Great. I went out without clearing it with you first. I'm a horrible son."

"You're deceptive is what you are."

I stare at him, my brow tensed. "Why don't you just say what you mean, Pop. You think I'm a liar!"

"I never said anything about you being a liar, Nicky. You're deceptive. A deceiver. There's a difference."

"What does that mean?"

"I know you weren't at Josue's last Friday night."

I can only stare, at a loss for words.

He smirks. "Didn't think I'd find out, huh?"

I sigh, shaking my head. "I don't care." I start to turn away but he speaks again.

"You never do. You open your mouth and prove over and over again I can't trust you."

I turn back. "What's this about, Pop? Like, *really*? When have I ever done anything to make you think you can't trust me?" He opens his mouth and I cut him off. "*Aside* from the usual stupid teenager crap everyone does."

"Where were you last Friday night, then, hm? Not at Josue's. I gave his dad a call when I got home this morning. No party there last Friday night. You weren't even there hanging out. So? Where were you?"

"I *was* at a party."

"*Who's* party?"

"A kid from school."

"What kid?"

"Some kid I met in woodshop. Jeez! Third degree much?"

"This is why you're deceptive, Nicky! You tell me half-truths, or you withhold information! How can I trust you when you pull this shit on me?"

I shake my head, putting all the frustration I can muster into my face. I grind out, "Just get off my back already!" and go on up the stairs, seething.

He shouts after me, "Stay up there, Nicky, for the rest of the weekend! Got it? Bathroom and kitchen, that's all! I don't want to see your face any more'n I have to. And if you keep mouthing off under your breath, I *will* take your phone away! In fact!" I hear his feet on the stairs, and though I'm nearly to my bedroom, I know better than to barricade myself inside. I stop and wait. He again holds his hand out. "Gimme your phone after all. Maybe you can have it back on Monday."

I don't make a sound; I keep my face expressionless. I dig into my pocket and pull out my iPhone, laying it in his palm. I turn toward my room and vanish inside, closing the door behind me.

Then I stand there, fists clenched, belly aching, wanting to heave my backpack through the window. Instead I set it on the desk, unzip the pocket and pull out the green Razr. Pop can keep my iPhone forever for all I care. I don't have friends to text on it anymore, no one to call. I didn't have Spring Break plans anyway. Who would I hang with? (Keeping the phone on and looking through it would be something he would absolutely do. Thankfully, when it comes to my iPhone, I have nothing to hide.)

This weekend I need nothing but the green Razr. The only person I could possibly care to talk to right now is Michael.

My crush.

MICHAEL

"While I'm alone and blue as can be…"

I WAS BUMMED OUT all through break. I wanted nothing more than to stay in my room until school resumed, in pajamas, watching scary stuff that wouldn't help my mood. I watched everything from *Sleepaway Camp* to *The Ring* to all the *Final Destination* films.

Everyone left me alone, thankfully, and when my Muskequeers tried to text me, I either gave one word responses, or didn't reply at all. I even ignored a couple texts from Secret Admirer, because my date with Gil was sure to come up and it embarrassed me to think of reporting how lousy it had been—especially the end. I also wanted very much to talk about Nick Walsh; I couldn't stop playing what had happened on that last Friday in my head. I kept thinking, *If Nick and I could talk again—talk like* that, *just him and me with all the other crap removed—serious, truthful—maybe I would understand him, and why he did what he did.*

I even went so far as to write Nick a text message, trying to broach the subject with something like humor. It said: *How are your…you know…?* But he never responded.

I wondered what Secret Admirer would think of what

Nick had done—and that I had texted him after all my professions of dislike.

At last, two nights before Easter, as I lay in bed, I took up my phone. *Hey, Secret Admirer!* I typed. *I'm really sorry I'm been AWOL these last few days. And I'm sorry I tried calling. Things have been rough. I guess you could say I've sorta been in hiding.* I sent it, hoping I would get a response—hoping I hadn't royally screwed up this friendship.

The response came pretty quick, and relief at not being ignored loosened my chest.

Secret Admirer: No worries. Im having a shitty break 2.

Me: Too bad we can't hang out. We could have had a shitty break together. Maybe it wouldn't have been so shitty then.

Secret Admirer: Wouldnt have mattered anyway. Ive been grounded.

Me: That IS shitty. What did you do?

Secret Admirer: Nothing. Parental figures can b whack. Spent the last 2 days confined 2 my room w/ nothing 2 do but homework & watch CrunchyRoll on my comp.

Me: Gasp! CrunchyRoll!? You're an anime fan? How have you never told me that?

Secret Admirer: I havent told u a lot of stuff. And u dont exactly ask.

Me: Because I know NOT to ask. There're all kinds of things I wanna know about you. But I'd rather let you stay mysterious, AND AROUND, than push too hard and have you go away.

Secret Admirer: Thx. Id rather B around 2.

Me: So, anime fan…what have you been watching all weekend?

Secret Admirer: Sailor Moon Crystal. Ive never seen it. I needed 2 catch up.

Me: I like the original better.

Secret Admirer: Me 2.

Me: Did you finish it?

Secret Admirer: Havent started the 3rd arc yet.

Me: Nice! Secret Admirer is an anime fan! It's weird, knowing more about you all of a sudden. I like it.

For the first time in days, a real smile touched my face. Several minutes passed while I waited for a response. At last, the phone buzzed and I read the reply, my smile getting wider.

Secret Admirer: U can ask me 3 questions. Any 3 questions. & I promise 2 answer 2 of them. W/ complete honesty. BUT!! No asking what my name is. Only stipulation.

Me: REALLY!?

Secret Admirer: Really.

Me: Ooh!!! Possibilities! Okay! Are you a guy or girl?

Secret Admirer: 3 questions. Thats only 1.

Me: All three at once?

Secret Admirer: Yup.

Me: Why? So you can chose which two you wanna answer?

Secret Admirer: Precisely.

Me: Boo!!! Fine. Question 2: Are you in the Senior Revue? Question 3: Do we ever hang out at school?

Again several minutes passed. I was on pins and needles. At last a reply came through, followed closely by a second.

Secret Admirer: We DO NOT hang @ school.

Secret Admirer: Ur secret admirer is a GUY. R u freaked out?

Flashes of hot and cold darted through me. No, I wasn't freaked out. I didn't know *what* I was feeling. But if Secret Admirer was a guy, then the further implication…

Me: You told me before that you weren't a straight guy. But since you're a guy after all, that means you're not… well, a STRAIGHT GUY.

Secret Admirer: Nope.

Me: What does that mean? Gay? Or bi?

Another lengthy gap before the reply came.

Secret Admirer: Gay.

Me: Cool. Me too. Though you already know that.

Secret Admirer: Every 1 knows that.

Me: Well that cuts down a lot of variables. I'm in the GSA. I know pretty much all the gay kids at Kliewer.

Secret Admirer: Not all.

Me: You aren't out?

Secret Admirer: No.

Me: Wow! Like, no one knows?

Secret Admirer: Not really. Only 1 or 2 ppl I trust.

Me: Did you just figure it out or something?

Secret Admirer: Ive known 4 a long time. But Im

trying 2 get used 2 it.

Me: You should hang out with all of us then. You'd get used to it real quick!

Secret Admirer: MuskeQUEERS, right?

Me: Lol. We're pretty gay, but not, you know, GAY gay.

Secret Admirer: GAY gay?

Me: Like flaming.

Secret Admirer: What about Brent? Hes pretty flaming.

Me: Is that a bad thing?

Secret Admirer: Not @ all. I wish I was brave like him. Like u.

Me: What's stopping you?

Secret Admirer: My family wont understand. & my friends wont either. Its scary.

Me: I know. But if they don't understand, if they hate you because of it, then they don't really love you, you know? Or if they do love you, and still hate you for being something you can't help, that love isn't healthy.

Secret Admirer: I think ur rite.

I thought for a moment before replying. My secret admirer was a guy, and gay! A gay guy being the secret admirer of another guy must have something romantic mixed in it somewhere. I started typing.

Me: So if you aren't out, and even though you say you've known you were gay for a while, how can you be so sure? You've never had a boyfriend, never kissed a guy before. So?

Secret Admirer: Ive kissed a guy b4.

Me: No way!? Who?

Secret Admirer: Just this guy looking 2 try something out.

Me: And?

Secret Admirer: & what?

Me: Did you like it? Come on! Deets!

Secret Admirer: I know I wanted 2 kiss a guy again. That count?

Me: Totes counts!

Secret Admirer: U told me about ur boyfriends. Dillon & that other 1. Did u know u were gay b4 dating them?

Me: U know I did. I told u. I knew when I was in, like, 6th grade.

Secret Admirer: Well me 2. I just didnt know what the feelings meant.

Me: So? What about guys you like? Now that you DO know you're gay, are you interested in anyone?

Again, a pause. I sat, covered in my blanket, TV droning in the background, while Secret Admirer's reply seemed to take forever. At last the screen brightened; something inside me brightened too.

Secret Admirer: Yes, there IS some 1. I guess u could call him my 1st crush. Ive never had 1 b4. @ least, not like this.

Me: Is this crush on one of the people you've come out to?

Secret Admirer: THAT I dont want 2 answer. Srry.

I bit at my lip. I had hoped to maybe trap Secret Admirer into answering yes, because technically *I* counted as one of the people he had come out to. Perhaps, just perhaps, this guy I had been talking with, who had been sending me notes for weeks, who liked so many of the things I liked, who made these text conversations so easy, who I thought about constantly, might have a crush on *me*. Of course, I couldn't think what I would do about it. Like Calista had warned, he might be a creeper. Knowing for sure now that he was a guy, *and* gay, didn't change that. Still…

Me: I understand. No need to apologize. But I hope that one day, and maybe soon, you'll feel less afraid of coming out to everyone. I'm here if you need to talk about stuff. And whoever the guy is that you're crushing on, he's very lucky. I wish you his gayness and returned feelings!

Secret Admirer: Of his gayness Im 100% positive. Of his returned feelings Im 100% positive its a lost cause. But having feelings 4 some 1 like him is amazing all by itself. I have no room 2 complain.

Before I could reply to this, another text came through.

Secret Admirer: About ur birthday present. Srry it no showed. I promise u'll have it the day we come back! My delivery system fell thru. Lol.

Me: Knowing so much more about you completely makes up for it. But thank you. It's getting late and I need to sleep. Talk tomorrow?

Secret Admirer: Yes, definitely. Thx 4 letting me share. Talking 2 u makes me feel less alone, Michael. Gnite.

I didn't text back, only shut the phone off, whispering, "Goodnight, Secret Admirer," before setting it aside.

Burrowing into my pillows, I laid there, unable to sleep for a long while, thoughts tripping over our texts, recollecting everything I now knew about my mysterious correspondent. Whether a creeper or not, the truth was, these last several weeks would have been unbearable without him.

SECRET ADMIRER AND I texted on and off almost every day through the rest of break. Knowing for certain he *was* a he, and a *gay* he, kept a little inner smile coming and going from the moment I woke up until I went to bed each night.

Easter over and school back in session, Gil acted like we had never been on our date at all. He smiled at me, talking about nothing as though it was any other day in Gov. But I didn't care. The end of the date somehow overshadowed everything that had come before it. I didn't expect to see him in Mrs. P.'s room at lunch anymore, which was fine by me. So I wouldn't finish high school knowing I had had *one* good boyfriend. If Gil was the option—peace out to that.

During nutrition break, as I paused at my locker—Calista and Brent hovering at my shoulder but arguing together over the pros and cons of *The SpongeBob Musical*—I spotted Nick, head down, shoving things into his backpack. Something like gratitude stirred in my chest. I left Brent and Calista to their discussion and made my way to Nick's side.

Surely it was the remembrance of what had happened in this very hall before break that had his face first paling, then growing pink.

"Hey," he said in a faint voice.

"Hey." I paused, unsure of what to say next. "Good break?"

"It was fine."

"Nice Easter?"

"Didn't do much. My dad's been sort of upset with me. And Easter isn't a big thing for us."

"I sent you a text…um…last weekend, I guess it was."

He looked away, as though his locker's insides were highly interesting. "Sorry," he mumbled. "My dad had my phone. I, um…"

"No worries," I hurried to say. I already felt out-of-place and awkward; his obvious discomposure wasn't helping. "I just wanted to check on you. Make sure you were okay. After that Friday, I mean."

He nodded. "I got your message this morning."

"So…how are…"

"My balls?" His cheeks grew redder.

Now *my* cheeks flamed. "Well, I was gonna say *you*, but…yeah, that works too."

His movements became almost frenzied as he finished loading his bag. Still he wouldn't look at me. "Lots of ibuprofen, some ice, I'm good as new. For the most part."

"Good. I wanted to be sure you hadn't needed the hospital or anything. You looked really bad, so I thought—"

"I have to go, actually. I'll be late for class. Sorry. I have to get across campus is all. I'll see ya."

Then his locker was shut and he was loping through the crowd, twisting his arms into the bag's straps. My usual irritation toward him niggled. Had I been given a brush-off? Why was he the one that got to act like he didn't want to talk to me? *Asshole-ish-ness dies hard*, I thought. I wanted to think what had happened embarrassed him—it would explain his face getting so red—but it felt to me like more of Nick Walsh being Nick Walsh: a jerk! So much for our conversation. There would never be a repeat, I was sure. But why should I care? I didn't need to try and understand him. Once a jerk, always a jerk!

At lunch, however, I had no one to think about but my mysterious Secret Admirer!

Somehow Mrs. P., looking amused, had a slim box wrapped in green paper to hand to me when I walked in. She stayed tight lipped about where it came from, and all I could do was slide into my usual seat with Calista, Brent, and some of our other friends looking on as I opened it.

The *Yuri!!! on Ice* iPhone case inside almost made me squeal as loud as the twins! It was prefect! *Perfect!* I wanted to shout, *How did he know?* but I was too busy smiling like an idiot, all but ripping my old phone cover off to replace it with the new one.

All Calista could do (though she was amused, smiling in spite of herself) was mutter, "Oh *Lord*! So gay!"

I nodded in agreement.

DONICK

"Will I ever tell you?"

A SPRING BREAK GROUNDING gives me plenty of time to binge-watch anime and listen to that New Kids on the Block song over and over to get choreography ideas. I jot notes and work out a few steps in my bedroom. Mostly I'll choreograph on the fly—like Chalice does. I'll be ready once I get back to school.

However, on the first day back, I don't have much brain-room for choreography, or even irritation at having to walk now that Pop has taken away the car. He's left my iPhone on the kitchen counter, and when I turn it on, one—and only one—text comes through. A text from Michael, checking on me after the incident on the last day before break. We texted quite a bit over the Easter weekend on my secret Razr, and, holy *crap*, how nervous he suddenly makes me. Even just to *think* of him! I couldn't stop myself from sharing way more than was safe in our texts. My new feelings for him seem to steal my good sense. Yet this checkup text is to *me*, not his secret admirer. Though his consideration gives my heart a squeeze, I can't bring myself to text back. I'll run into him at some point during the day, and I'll deal with him then. I think I need emotional preparation.

And I do run into him, which is sufficiently awkward and sends that thought: *I like this guy! I* like *like him!* repeating in my head. I can barely look at him. Then I *don't* deal with him because I all but run away. How can I talk to him, look at him, when I can't stop thinking about him? When I can't stop thinking about how, once upon an early middle school time, he had given me my first kiss? When I can't stop wondering what kissing him *now* might be like?

My excuse to get away is that I have to get to class, but it's nutrition break and I have more time than I need. What I really want is to go see Mrs. Moes again. Until I found it in my backpack, I pretty much forgot about the list I made in my notebook while waiting for Liam the day we had lunch. I suppose it was easy to forget it when other things distracted me all through break.

In the counseling-office, I make a lunchtime appointment. At least I have something else besides Michael to think about during the next two periods. And that thing is: how exactly am I going to tell the story of the locker paint to Mrs. Moes?

I KNEW RYAN FROM middle school but met Josue in tenth grade. We all three played football and palled around together, doing exactly what I've been saying we did—acted like asshole-jerks. Obligated to begin ninth grade amongst the football masses, all my training under my dad's watchful eye soon displayed itself and I joined the varsity team sophomore year. Though neither Ryan nor Josue would join me until a year later. Having me as their friend enabled them to start hanging out with the other varsity players. Sack-Tap Days happened every few months, we had choice names and nasty slurs to give to anyone we viewed as beneath our notice, and we egged each other on when it came to devising ways to "get" students we hated—even if we hated them simply because they were loners, or awkward…or gay.

Tenth grade. Back-to-school night. A variant of Sack-Tap Day.

The quarterback I would end up replacing, a senior named Eliel Lantz, came up with the idea. Instead of choosing boys we would knock in the delicates, we would pick for our targets any students we didn't like. Finding their lockers, we would use black permanent markers to write things about them on the doors after dismissal on the day of back-to-school night. Then, when the parents of those kids walked around campus, they would see these messages.

It's hard for me to think about what a kick we got out of this idea. For a week, we sat around at lunch, talking trash and thinking of choice names and messages to write. Eliel himself provided the Sharpies—great big fat markers. Such a disgusting prank, and back then it amused me to no end. Somehow or other, I got my second girlfriend out of it, a relationship that would last into the summer, until I didn't care to keep in contact with her and she dumped me.

I picked out four kids. The first three were in my own grade. Kristina Layne, Nan Gray and Roddy Thomson.

Kristina was at least 100 pounds overweight, and at the start of tenth grade she had cut her hair very short, which accentuated the roundness of her face. Because she always dressed in baggy clothes—at least back then, thinking to hide her figure—she came off looking very much like a boy. The same thing I called her to her face was what I spelled out on her locker door in thick block letters—FATASS BULL-DYKE.

Nan was a shy, introverted girl with black hair that hung to her waist in an oily scraggle. She never quite acted normal, and I later found out she suffered from Asperger Syndrome. All I knew then was that she picked at the skin around her fingernails a lot and had some weird eye-ticks. Why would someone like her become a target for me? Because I had passed her in the quad one day in the middle of class when I had taken a bathroom break. She had been out there pacing back and forth, overseen by an aide who kept a little distance, watching. Nan mumbled to herself, occasionally letting out these wailing screams. The supreme foreignness of her behavior was enough for me to make her a subject of laughter and derision at lunch—therefore, how could she *not* be perfect fodder for Eliel Lantz's game. On Nan's locker I wrote: WASH YOUR HAIR, PSYCHO!!!

Roddy was a boy I had known since elementary school—in fact, both Michael and I used to play four-square and tetherball with him. In eighth grade, Roddy had begun to get pimples. By the start of high school, his face had become an eye-hurting mass of blackheads and angry eruptions that literally gave him the appearance of a person who had been beaten. He grew his hair out, hoping to hide his skin, but that made it worse. He stopped talking if he could avoid it, sat at the back of class, and rarely raised his hand. It was usual to hear all kinds of people saying things to him like, "I've got a paper bag you could put over your head!" or "Try not to smile! You'll pop and get pus all over me!" Sometimes, particularly cruel people even posted things like this on Facebook, or tagged him in pimple-popping videos on Instagram. I could have picked plenty of nasty things to write on his locker, but I chose to print ACNE CORP below the number plate in bubble letters, framing it in a box as though it were a logo.

Then there was the fourth kid: Dinah MacFarland. She began high school in the same grade as me, but, like Josue, got held back a year. She…

Never mind…I can't think about her right now. I haven't mentioned Dinah until this point because every time I *do* think of her, I force the memories away. I can't talk about her. Not yet.

Anyway, the other guys on the team, and a few of the cheerleaders too, all had similar targets and similar things to say. Some of the messages were a lot worse than what I wrote. But I remember nearly all of them.

It was easy to linger on campus the day of back-to-school night. Less than ten minutes, and we carried out Eliel's plan, my nose stinging with the sharp scent of the marker. Once we had finished, knocking each other's knuckles, we parted ways and went home, only to go on laughing about it for weeks afterward; even as kids murmured and whispered, some of the targets walking about with their heads hanging lower than ever. No one was caught; no one even questioned us. Whether anyone suspected us, I never found out. It was just another thing on a long list of shitty things we did, and because of that, I quickly forgot all about it.

I'm awful for forgetting.

At this point, Roddy is home-schooled, and Nan left last year to go to a special school that can better work with her needs. The only two left are Kristina (who's lost a ton of weight and no longer even resembles the girl we all made fun of) and Dinah.

And as I already said, Dinah I need to put off thinking about for a little bit longer…

AT LUNCH, ON my way to see Mrs. Moes, I pass Josue in the quad. I'm surprised to see he's holding hands with some blonde girl. She's a very heavy-looking girl with a hawk-like beakiness to her face. She's never eaten at the varsity table before. Where the crap did he met her? Also, I wonder what he sees in her. Not Josue's style at all. It must be a prom-thing—it is coming, after all.

He sneers when he catches sight of me. His head turns and he mutters something to her. Though she grins (if someone so dishrag-looking *can* grin), I try very hard to keep my eyes trained ahead, to not see them. As we cross paths though, he suddenly makes a lunge at me, snapping his hand out toward the fly of my jeans. He doesn't connect—never meant to, of course—but my abrupt recoil, the stiffening of my stomach muscles, rekindles a little of the pain and nausea. I grunt as though he *has* connected, my hands twitching toward my groin. His gleeful smile reminds me of the Grinch. He snorts with laughter, as does his heavy-looking girlfriend.

I grimace and say, "Saturday school coming up, Jo?"

His eyes flash with hatred. "Where's your car, *güey*? Saw you walking to school. Maybe you can get a ride with your *pendejo*-faggot friends now."

He's laughing again, he and his girlfriend moving toward the table, leaving me fighting my queazy stomach. He joins Ryan and the others—Scott included, looking squinty and vacant even as he snorts and guffaws.

Assholes.

Mrs. Moes is free as soon as I walk in, so I'm in the chair right away, facing her desk as she looks expectantly at me.

"Anyone give you trouble," she asks, "after that juvenile ridiculousness before break?"

I wish I had the nerve to report Josue and the others for sack-tapping me. But I would feel like a narc. It was one thing trying to stop them from hurting someone else, but running off to say, "Josue is being mean to me!" would sound too much like I'm seven.

So I shake my head. "No, no trouble. Except..."

"What now?" Her tone is teasing, but a little exasperated too.

I tug out the folded piece of paper I had torn from my notebook and pass it to her. She frowns at it, then glances up.

"Sophomore year," I say, and my voice quavers slightly. "The defacing of the lockers..."

"Oh boy..." She sighs, lifting her hand to rub the bridge of her nose. I have trouble raising my eyes to her. "All right, Nick," she says. Her gaze is cold. I've disappointed her. "What's the list for? Why are you bringing this to me now?"

"Look," I say. "The guy whose idea it was isn't even here anymore. Along with a few of the others who participated. And that list is incomplete. I left off anyone who's graduated, or who I know transferred out or whatever."

"And?"

"And...I guess I need to do something about it."

She taps the paper. "Please tell me this list wasn't *all* you. There are about twenty names here."

"Only two are mine. Now, anyway. The rest were targets for other guys...and some girls."

"This is enough to get you kicked out of the Revue, you know."

The thought of that could bring me to tears, but I only nod.

"You need to be thanking your lucky stars," she goes on, "that this nonsense is more than two years old. *And* that you need the Revue to graduate, so it doesn't really count as an extracurricular for you. Also…" she sighs, "…I admire what you've been trying to do. But I need to know what your plan is for fixing this," another tap to the list, "before I can agree to whatever help you need. That is why you're here, right?"

The rest of our conversation doesn't take long. I leave Mrs. Moes with the list, then head out, making my way to the library.

Gabby is back and I'm glad to see she's well. I take my usual table, then pull out my books, pausing to check the secret Razr. My heart gives a jolt when I see Michael has sent a text.

I love it! I love it! I love it! it reads. *Best birthday present ever! Good thing I know you're gay now! It won't be weird if I say that I love my prezzie so much I could KISS you! Thank you, thank you, thank you!*

My mind goes blissfully blank. Josue, the old locker messages, being grounded—all gone. How can I remember any of that when I'm grinning like that derpy cat in *Alice in Wonderland?*

I'M EXCITED TO see Liam at rehearsal so I can tell him *Job well done!* and maybe even hug him. But once the loud and giggling cast is assembled, I crane around, frowning, because Liam is nowhere to be seen. He's missing another rehearsal? What is going on with him?

Half-listening to the teachers giving their speeches, I try to keep my eyes from the curling black mop that is the back of Michael's head. He's with his Muskequeers a few rows in front of me, occasionally lifting his phone to gaze at its new case. Again, I struggle against that Cheshire Cat grin. He said he could *kiss* me...

Then I'm starting a little, blinking, when I hear my name mentioned.

"In addition," Chalice is saying, "Nick has also agreed to help out. He'll be choreographing 'Cover Girl'."

Whispers ripple, heads turn my way. Even Michael shifts curious eyes, meeting mine for an instant before I glance away.

"Here's the plan," Mrs. Peebles chimes in. "First hour we're all together—reviewing blocking for 'History Maker', then staging 'Let Me Be Your Star'. I trust everyone used their break wisely and knows their parts. Second and third hour we'll send 'Cover Girl' peeps into the lobby with Nick. Sara, you'll grab the girls for 'Diamonds Are a Girl's Best Friend' and start working here on the stage. Mr. Hardy will work solos and duets in the tech-booth with anyone left over—specifically, Dejohn Hewlitt, we want to go over 'Dream a Little Dream of Me' with your guitar, hear how it's coming; Becca, we haven't heard 'Another Suitcase in Another Hall' yet. We want the two of you first."

Calista's hand goes up. "Those not doing anything," she says, "come see me in the costume-lab. I have plenty of stuff for the cast to try on. I also haven't measured one or two of you yet. And it's time to start making your masquerade masks. I've got all sorts of tchotchkes out, and plenty of glue."

Brent, the stripe in his hair the color of a blue Otter Pop today, calls out, "And if you *still* need something to do, there's set stuff to help with."

"We don't want to see anyone sitting and doing nothing," Mrs. P. adds. "Be productive!"

Chalice says, "I also want to take another look at the dancers for 'The Mirror-Blue Night'. We need to add…" She squints around. "Is Liam here?" Eyes dart from face to face, but no one says a word. Chalice and Mrs. P. exchange a look. "All right," Chalice shrugs, "he's not here, he's out of the number. I'll think of a replacement."

"We need everyone here, guys," says Mrs. P. "If you have to miss, you risk losing parts in the show, as we've said. We're beyond the place of excusing absences. I understand there are emergencies, but we've still got a show to put on. There are only a handful of weeks left. We have zero time to goof off."

I check my iPhone hoping for a text from Liam, but there's nothing.

Then we're beginning Mr. Hardy's vocal warmup. Standing with the other tenors, I have to fight against my own eyes. They want to be on Michael, my *crush*. I want to watch him sing. I'm near enough to see the smattering of freckles beneath his lashes, the way the work-lights make his eyes look like emeralds. His chin and lip sport fine dark hairs, and suddenly (weirdness of weird), picturing him shaving has me feeling sort of funny.

I'm grateful he never looks my way. Still, when I turn my eyes, I catch Calista's gaze from amongst the altos. Her expression as she watches me is a sort of thoughtful frown. *She knows about me!* I say to myself. *If she notices me staring at Michael, she'll come to the same conclusion Liam did!*

I force myself to concentrate. Thankfully, the first half-hour passes quickly; I'm too busy remembering where I'm supposed to move on this lyric or that. It's the second half-hour when Chalice and Mrs. P. are setting blocking for "Let Me Be Your Star"—a great song from some TV show I've never heard of—that things get dicey. The number begins with the girls, entering singly or in pairs while singing their solo and duet lines, moving to stand in different formations, the guys waiting in the wings. It's just like Liam said: I'm hyper-aware at all times of where Michael is. He's standing alone now, in the shadow of the curtain, watching what's happening on stage. He's smiling a little (probably watching Calista), yet he has an air of intensity about him—he's taking this rehearsal business very seriously. I frown at myself inwardly, because I'm staring at the way his T-shirt pulls tight across his shoulder-blades, the way his butt looks in his pants. I have to rip my eyes from him in confusion.

It's not until the cast breaks apart to work in smaller groups that the true reality sets in. Michael will be in "Cover Girl". Meaning *I'll* be teaching him his choreography.

The four guys in the number carry mic-stands into the lobby to use in our rehearsal. The four girls who will be their partners mill around, waiting for their parts. As I begin explanations and demonstrating steps, I keep my eyes averted from Michael as best I can. I feel suddenly like a bumbling moron. Looking that way in Michael's eyes is the last thing I want.

The four guys harmonize amazingly. They know the song cold, thank goodness. I'm impressed with all of them, because words marry to choreography almost right away. Within two or three run-throughs, they've got it locked in. By the time rehearsal is nearing completion, the number is more than half done—the partnership portion I have in mind to be saved for another day.

And through it all…Michael, Michael, Michael! I don't know how I accomplish anything when sometimes I feel like it's only him and me in the lobby—even as I pointedly keep my eyes away from him, joke and laugh with the others, and address them all when *he* specifically asks a question. I'm scared he'll glance into my face and my feelings will burst from my eyes like tears.

Just before we call it a day, Chalice and Mrs. P. come to watch what we've accomplished. As the singers run through it, I record them with my phone so I can e-mail them the video.

Because I'm watching through the screen, I allow myself to keep my eyes on Michael. He really knows how to sell it. He performs as though there's already an audience, and I think, *I don't make him nervous at all. He would never be able to perform like that if he was as aware of me as I am of him. Then again, I have the crush, which makes his presence that much worse. He feels nothing; at least nothing like that.*

Lord, how depressing is that? I've known my crush on him won't ever go anywhere, but in this moment, faced with that knowledge in this specific way, it's enough to make me feel like a hollowed out piece of wood.

Chalice and Mrs. P. applaud, beaming smiles. They make one or two suggestions, but overall I can see they're impressed. I'm proud of myself, but wish there weren't so many people around to hear their praise. When they go back into the house, I linger in the lobby, stowing my iPod in my bag, winding the cord of the portable speakers we used to play the song.

"They're right, you know," Michael says, and I jump, heart knocking into my ribs.

"Jeez, wear a bell," I joke, but I still keep my eyes averted.

"Sorry." He's got his hands clasped around the pole of his mic-stand, scuffing the round plate of its foot with his shoe. "I just meant about the choreography. It's really good."

I must look tense—I *feel* tense—but manage to say, "Thanks."

"I had no idea you could do anything like this."

I shrug, not knowing how to reply. My hands are shaking. "There's a lot of stuff we don't know about each other," I manage. "We haven't been friends for a long time." There's a pause. I want to swallow my tongue when I pop out with, "How was your date with Gil?"

He's silent for a moment.

"Fine," he then says. "It was…fine."

"Good." Though I don't feel good inside.

In a hesitant sort of way, he asks, "Can we talk for a minute?"

"Isn't that what we're doing?"

He chuckles. "I meant after rehearsal."

I think my very atoms might spin apart. I can't, *can't* be alone with him. It's too confusing, too *rending*. How is it that for months all I've wanted was the chance to be Michael's friend again, to repair the damage I inflicted, yet now, viewing him through the lens of a crush, I want nothing more than distance?

The truth comes to my rescue. "I can't. I need to get

home. My dad is really on me right now. I don't have my car so I have to book."

He looks doubtful. "All right. Maybe tomorrow or something." He carries the mic-stand back into the theatre, leaving me alone.

I'm about to follow, when I glance out the lobby-doors.

And almost do a double-take!

There's a car parked at the curb right outside, and Liam is leaning down into the open passenger-door. He's saying something, but I can't see much of his face. Whoever the driver is—his mom, I assume—is lost in shadows inside the vehicle. Rehearsal is almost over. Why is he even bothering to show up?

I push open the doors and lean out, just as he shoves the car-door closed. He watches from the sidewalk as the car peels away, jumping and rattling over the speed-bumps. It's so like the Saturday before break when I watched him waving to this same car, it's like falling backwards in time.

"Hey," I call. He whirls around, grinning when he see me. "Another no show, dude," I say as he comes up the steps.

"I know. I need to talk to Mrs. P."

"They took you out of that number."

"Shit."

We stand in the lobby now, talking low so we won't disturb anyone in the theatre.

"You might be able to beg back into it," I say, "but it's not looking good. No more missed rehearsals anymore." He sighs, looking agitated. I ask, "Is everything all right? You were so excited about the show. Now…"

"I'm being a total flake. I know."

"Just don't miss anymore."

He's still looking preoccupied. Then he grins at me. "Mission accomplished, bee-tee-dubs."

I shush him and glance toward the theatre-doors, but I'm grinning too. "I noticed. Thanks for playing delivery-boy. How'd it go? Mrs. P. didn't get weird about it, did she?"

"No. But she probably thinks I have a thing for Michael now." Liam pokes me in the belly. "And the reality is, that's *you!*"

I shush him again, feeling my ears get hot.

"You're adorable, Nick. You owe me a hug now." Liam leans in, hugging me like he has before, only with much less awkwardness on my part. This close to him, I smell his scent again—that guy-smell—only it's suddenly very strong, drifting from his neck and his pale brown hair.

And all at once I know the smell.

Oranges.

Liam smells like…

Still I might not have pieced it together—Liam's sudden flakiness, his harried behavior, suddenly smelling this scent on him when I've never noticed it before.

I say, "That's weird. You smell just like Gil Hamilton." Liam's face suffuses with the brightest blush I've ever seen. His expression doesn't even try to be subtle. My mouth drops open. "Li?" I press. "Why do you smell like Gil Hamilton?"

Mischief sparks in Liam's eyes. He bites his lip. "Damn it," he almost groans. "I hoped no one would notice."

I feel like my face must be fixed in horror. "Notice what?"

He looks embarrassed. "Gil and I…well, you know…"

"No. What?"

"We've been…hanging out. Since Michael's party."

"Hanging out?"

"You know. We've been…hooking up." Liam's voice drops on the last words. "I mean, we saw each other almost every day during Spring Break. Like, damn! I had a *good* vacation."

"You and Gil…"

He nods. How happy he looks all of a sudden. "Don't tell anyone. I keep your secret, you keep mine, yeah? But it's so nice to be able to talk about it. Finally!"

"Since Michael's party?"

"You introduced us, remember? He followed me around for a while after we had cake, and we talked by the fire some more, and then…" Liam chuckles. "Then we pretty much made out in his car for the rest of the night."

I blink again, feeling like a monster bonehead. *Not* the kissing couple from the fire-pit fogging the windows of that car outside. Liam and Gil! Making out a dozen feet from me. Michael's…what? Boyfriend? Talking about liking him while we sat by the fire. Coming to look for him that Friday so they could go on their date. And all the while, for weeks, he and Liam…

I make a small sound of disgust, shaking my head. "This is like something on the CW," I mutter.

"Am I freaking you out?" Liam frowns. "I thought you'd be okay talking about this. I mean, since this sort of thing doesn't bother you after all. You've been nothing but nice to me. I don't want to make you uncomfortable or anything. I mean…I just thought, after what we talked about, that—"

"No. No, it's fine," I say, but the cogs of my brain are turning very slowly.

"Anyway, it's why I've been missing rehearsal so much. I want to see him, and we've had to sneak around. He doesn't want anyone to know. I think part of it is because he's a senior and I'm a sophomore. He's embarrassed."

"That doesn't bother you?"

"Totally no. He's hot! You should see his abs!"

"No thanks."

"And for someone so short, he's got a—"

"Don't finish that sentence."

There's a sudden rush of noise from inside the theatre. Voices escalate as the cast makes their way out. Liam and I step to the side. A hectic moment passes when I'm being waved at, said goodbye to. Liam has people giving him puzzled looks. "Where've you been?" and "Good, you're not dead!" fly at him as he smiles sheepishly.

When the exiting kids are only a trickle, he murmurs, "I also think he doesn't want anyone to know because I'm not eighteen. And, you know, he is."

I think I must look appalled again. "You guys are…"

"Only a couple times." Liam's features soften. "He was my first."

"Oh boy…" I mutter. "And he's…available? Like, he doesn't have a boyfriend or anything?"

Can it be possible Michael hasn't talked about Gil in front of Liam? Or that either Calista or Brent haven't spoken out of turn, even accidentally? How can Liam not know that Gil and Michael are basically a thing?

"I guess *I* sorta count as a boyfriend now," Liam says.

"I just meant, I thought he said something about being into someone, or dating someone. At Michael's party, I mean."

"Nope. Free and clear."

Another rush of voices fill the lobby and the Muskequeers appear. I feel suddenly like I'm about to be crushed by two walls sliding together. Calista and Brent pause, then join us, wanting to know where Liam's been and if he's all right. Michael eyes me, then Liam, looking funny. I feel his presence all over again like pins being pushed against my skin.

"I gotta head out, guys," I say, already moving toward the door, even as Michael steps into the circle we've formed. "I'm running really late. My dad's gonna have an embolism."

Liam, Calista, and Brent wave ("I'll text you later, okay?" Liam says). But Michael stays silent, watching me go, looking…well, almost hurt.

Night is already falling as I begin the walk home, and though it's true I'm running late, I have no room in my head to think about Pop being angry with me. I can think only of Michael, having feelings for a guy who says he likes him, who takes him on dates, yet all the while is a ginormous dirt-bag.

Whether I'm talking to Michael as myself, or as his secret admirer, how can I keep something like this from him?

MICHAEL

"I tried to dance with the devil on your back,
And given half the chance would I take any of it back?"

I FEEL LIKE LATELY we haven't been able to talk much," Calista said, eyes on her hands where she worked a needle through the holes of a button, affixing it to some fancy-looking orange coat with shiny green braid. She wore her big goofy glasses again, as if she needed them to see her stitches.

We sat at the back of the theatre, just her and me. A similar coat lay across my knees, and though I wasn't fastening buttons to it, I was re-enforcing the existing ones, since most dangled by a thread. She had taught me how to do this, yet still I worried I did a piss-poor job.

In the front row, Mr. Hardy played his electric piano beside Mrs. P., running through a few numbers featuring a men's barbershop quartet made up of ninth and tenth grade boys. They looked ridiculously small and child-like, despite their big voices. They were going over "Lida Rose", a song from *The Music Man* (which had been our fall musical when I was a sophomore). I smiled to hear it. In that production, I had been one of the River City men's quartet. Sometimes I still crooned the song to my sister, changing the words to

"

Georgia Rose. Mallory Beaumont, a senior, waited to begin her part as the quartet segued into "Will I Ever Tell You?".

Chalice wasn't in the theatre today because she had taken Nick into the dance-studio to choreograph his solo. I had to admit I was fidgety with curiosity as to what his solo would be like. Bad enough I was so bothered by Nick acting like I wasn't there yesterday. Our "Cover Girl" rehearsal had felt like it had been him and everyone else. Why did he act as though talking to me was such a big deal? As if he had any right to feel that way.

I was replaying our conversation from before break, puzzling over his behavior, when Calista asked her question.

"You and I talk," I said. "We're all just busy. Rehearsal and stuff. And homework. Everyone is starting to talk about prom too. Have you thought about who you're gonna go with? Don't just go with Brent."

"I don't want to talk about prom." She sounded impatient, like she sensed I brought up unimportant nothings to avoid sharing. "I want to talk about how weird you've been the last few weeks. Both Brent and I feel like you're not telling us something."

"What's there to tell?"

"That's the question. You've never *not* shared with us before."

I kept my eyes on the needle. It was safer to act like I didn't understand, because I *had* been sharing (almost) everything, only with Secret Admirer, not my Muskequeers.

"Okay, look," she went on, "it's just me asking. Brent doesn't notice anything. Love that sister, but he's all flamboyant in his self-involvement. I know you're worried about colleges and stuff. Is that it? Are you depressed about it or something?"

"I'm not depressed," I said. Though that wasn't entirely true. I *was* bothered that three out of five schools had rejected me, and I was anxious every day as I waited to hear from the last two—the major two: New York! Still, I thought I had been acting normal, saving my blues for when I was alone at home.

"Okay, maybe not depressed," she said, "but you're *something*. I just can't understand why you're keeping secrets."

"Keeping secrets?" I repeated, sounding cynical.

"Call it whatever. You told us that you and Gil were going on a date, but you never said anything about it afterward. You were MIA all through break too. Then there's the secret admirer thing. You were talking a lot about that, and suddenly nothing. I thought it had fizzled out. Then this birthday present…"

I sighed. "My date with Gil sucked, all right? He ended up all hands and it made me uncomfortable. I'm not like Brent. I can't just hook up with someone."

"Well, Gil sucks, and I'm sorry. But why not call me? Or have us over for a bitch-fest. Pizza and lame anime, or scary movies. We could've talked it out."

I thought, *Because I wanted to talk to* Secret Admirer, *that's why.*

I shrugged. "I wasn't all that upset, honestly. I know you guys were really pushing for Gil and me, but I don't think I've really liked him all that much." I paused. "There's a lot going on, is all. I guess my mind is overloaded."

"With what?"

"Rehearsal, schoolwork, college stuff. And…" I paused again, knowing I was supposed to hold back, that she wouldn't want to hear this, but *this* was different from what had irritated her in the past. So I said, "And I'm really frustrated with Nick."

"Here goes," she groaned. "Yes, I know. You hate him so much. And now he's choreographing this number you're in and—"

"I don't hate him," I interrupted. Then I frowned at her. "And if you want to know why I'm not keen on sharing, maybe it's because you told me not to."

She answered my frown with one of her own. "You don't hate Nick Walsh? Since when?"

"Since ever. I've just been mad. And I'm not that mad anymore."

"What changed?"

"I was kind of mean at my party," I muttered. "I felt bad. And then…"

I bit my lip and stared at the coat's buttons. This part would have been okay to share, yet I had kept it to myself; I couldn't understand why. I began telling her about what Nick had done for me. I wasn't explicit about our conversation, but I did tell her that he had given me something of an apology. Then I told about how I had texted him over break with no response, tried to talk to him twice yesterday, and he practically ran each time.

"*I'm* the injured party here," I finished. "*I'm* supposed to be the one who ignores or not, but he won't even look at me. It's almost worse than it was before."

She looked thoughtful, her sewing now forgotten. "He really did that? Wonders. But I guess not so much. We've been saying he's a nice guy. He wasn't before, I get it, but he is different now."

"He's trying…I know. Because I've seen it. I just don't understand him."

She returned to her buttons. "*I* didn't see him ignoring you yesterday. Actually, he seemed to be staring at you a lot."

"He's probably re-thinking what he did that Friday, looking at me like I'm wearing a bunny-suit or something."

"Still don't know why you didn't tell me about that." She busied herself stringing her needle.

"I guess I didn't know what to make of it. I wanted to talk yesterday, but he said he couldn't, yet there he was running his mouth with Liam."

"What did you want to talk about?"

I shrugged. "Just wanted to talk. See if we could be friends again. Nothing like it used to be," I hurried to say. "That sort of friendship with him is long gone. But, you know, not where things are as awkward as they've been since rehearsals started. Only now, it's like knowing he's said he wishes he could take back what he did to me has made things super extra awkward."

"I'm glad you're not so angry anymore. It was worrying me. I've never seen you so pissy before."

"I was being a little bitch, I know. Besides, I think it's been this secret admirer thing that's really helped."

She gave me serious eyes. "Michael, be careful with that. I keep saying."

"I know."

"You don't! You're clueless about what this person wants."

"And he could be a creeper, yes. You've said it often."

"He?"

I felt my cheeks heat.

"Wait wait," she said. "What's this *he* crap?"

"Yes. He." I tried to say it like it was no big thing.

"Your secret admirer is a *guy*?" She stared. "How do you know?"

"He told me."

"He *told* you? When?"

"Over break. He actually opened up a lot. Told me about himself."

"He was all zip-lipped for weeks and now he's talking?"

"I guess, yeah. He told me he's a guy. He said he likes anime and horror movies. And…he said he's gay."

Calista dropped the coat. "Yeah, all of that isn't a coincidence or anything!" she hissed, trying to keep her voice low so the singers on stage wouldn't hear. "He's basically *you* texting you and leaving you presents. That's stalkery."

"He's *not* like me," I blurted. "He's not out. It's a secret, I guess."

She stared at me for a second or two, then gazed off over the seats of the house. She tried to stifle a sudden huff of laughter as she went back to her work.

"What's funny?"

She shook her head, mouth twisting against the laughter. "Careful, babe," she said. "The way you've been talking about your secret admirer, only to find out he's some closet-case, you're all set up to fall for him—a dude you might dislike royally if you ever actually met him. This guy could be anyone, and it's always the last person you want it to be."

"I don't have feelings for my secret admirer," I said, but I was beginning to wonder. So much of my confusion lately had to do with him. Last night we had texted until one in the morning—talking about TV shows, books, our favorite movie soundtracks. He had opened the flood gates about himself and more and more information came pouring out. Not necessarily anything that could give his identity away, but stuff about his interests that spoke volumes about the kind of person he was. I met Calista's eye and said it with more firmness. "I *don't* have feelings for my secret admirer. Stop looking that way."

"It's none of my business if you do or not—after all, I question whether you'd actually tell me. I just wouldn't recommend it. It'll be disappointing. Now, are you done with those buttons? Can I give you more?"

I stayed quiet for a second. Then I said, "I'm sorry I didn't say anything. I know how you've felt. But also…I dunno. It just…I guess I've felt like it's mine. Something…a person, I guess, who's just mine."

She watched me as I spoke. Then she shook her head and muttered, "So *gay*."

AT HOME THAT night, Secret Admirer and I were texting—our almost nightly ritual now. I apologized to him for telling Calista some of the things he had shared about himself, yet I had to admit I felt relieved at telling her. It was unusual for the Muskequeers to keep things from each other and on the drive home I gave Brent the overview.

I sent: *Brent thinks our texting is romantic or something. His inner romance novel heroine is showing herself. He's started calling you my soulmate. He tells me I need to bug you about meeting up.* I sent this with a teary-eyed laughing emoji. Secret Admirer's response (*Eh, u dont wanna meet me! Id only disappoint!*) didn't leave much room to keep the subject going. Discouraged, I started talking about Nick instead.

Secret Admirer wrote: *Im happy to know u arent as mad about this dude anymore. It wasnt good 4 u 2 hold on 2 ur anger. U say u think hes trying 2 turn over a new leaf. Maybe part of that is being nervous around u or something. After all, u were friends once. He might b afraid u'll hate him again. & who'd want that? Ur kind of awesome, u know.*

I smiled to myself. *If I was so awesome,* I replied, *he would't have stopped being my friend.*

Let him do what he needs to do. U were best friends once, it shouldn't b hard to b friends again. Maybe have some patience with him. U may not feel like he deserves it, but it does seem like hes trying. Dont let him cop out just becuz hes a little scared of u.

I replied with: *LOL! I'm the least scary person on the planet!* But I thought Secret Admirer might be right. Maybe Nick and I *could* be friends. It might mean a little effort on my part, and as hard as it was for me to believe I could actually feel that way, I thought I might be up to the challenge.

I decided that the next day in rehearsal I would act like his avoidance of me hadn't happened the previous two days. I would go out of my way to be friendly. After all, we would be back to working on "Cover Girl". If he could laugh and joke with my fellow singers, he could laugh and joke with me too.

But that rehearsal…

It was like a trip back into the worst part of our past.

THE PLAN IS pretty much the same as Monday," Mrs. P. told the cast, laying out the numbers she and the other teachers wanted to review. "We'll split up again during the last hour: 'Diamond' girls in the lobby this time, 'Cover Girl' singers on stage. Dancers, get on your shoes! We're looking at 'Get The Party Started' first. Singers, let's warm up!"

"Get The Party Started" was mostly a dance number with live singing, so I was able to stand in the wings and watch all the parts get pieced together. Today, the dancers were singing full-out for the first time, working the choreography without marking. I had to admit the way they handled it impressed me. Singing and dancing at the same time is never easy. I could understand why pop singers felt the need to lip-sync sometimes (or all the time, depending on the pop star).

And, yes, Nick was doing very well. His voice had grown in strength since the first day. He sounded good. Combine that with the way he moved, it was a lot like watching Justin Timberlake or Usher. Frustration and irritation can't seem to exist in the same place as admiration, and watching Nick sing and dance his way through the rest of the song made it stupidly easy for me to forget. Maybe I couldn't do that this last month or so because I wasn't ready. I wanted to make the effort and try now, just like he said he was trying. If I had to push a little harder than I already had, I would do it.

When it came time to separate, the stage emptied of everyone but Nick, myself, and the other "Cover Girl" singers. We began by running what we had learned on Monday to work out spacing.

"Nice job," he said to me. "You remembered it perfectly. But I'm not surprised."

Even if he wouldn't look at me long enough to see it, his words made me smile.

What we had learned Monday, though, was the easy part. We were now moving into a section of the song that was relatively short, but complicated. The girl I would partner, Anoop Divya, wasn't much for this sort of ballroomy style. Once Nick began to break down the steps, she seemed to suddenly lose coordination. To be fair, she wasn't the only one. I had times when it was hard to tell my left foot from my right, and the other cast-members were needing Nick to move extra slow, breaking down who stepped left or right, forward or back.

"Don't feel bad, ladies," Nick said. "Ginger Rogers always said her parts were more difficult than Fred Astaire's. She had to do them backwards and in heels."

The guys had it difficult enough. We had to sing at the same time. Still, I could tell that the number, up to speed and without its performers acting like idiots, would look great. It was frustrating and tense, of course, all of us concentrating hard, but we were having fun.

Then, at one point in the combination, when Anoop grew close to tears over not being able to figure out her half of our steps, Nick did something necessary, but shocking. To me, anyway.

"Here," he said to her. "Stand behind me. I'll walk through your part slowly while I count it. Stop me if I move too fast."

Suddenly Nick stood right in front of me, all but in my face! His arms were up, he was pulling me toward him, my arms lifting to mirror his. One hand on my shoulder, the other against my palm, my arm slipped around his ribcage without thought. Then our proximity struck me like a brick, and the muscles of his back felt like baked earth beneath my fingers. My face might have gone numb. A little moment elapsed when he met my eyes, seemed to realize what he had done, and blushed brighter than a fire engine.

"Sorry," he muttered.

I shook my head, swallowing around something that felt like a peach-pit.

"Okay," he said, louder. "Anyone else having trouble, follow along. Michael knows it, so any guys needing help, stand behind him. Girls, behind me. Five-six-seven-eight!"

It was only two counts of eight, yet it felt like it lasted two hours. My face burned, Nick's face burned, we avoided each other's eyes. I could feel the pads of his fingers digging into my arm, even as my hand cupped his shoulder blade. I feared my palm was sweaty where his pressed against it, and I had to remind myself to breathe. My heart, in my nervousness, seemed to leap over beats.

"Keep going," Nick murmured to me as we got to the end of the second eight-count. "I wanna do the dip."

"Go for it," I said. "I promise I won't drop you."

"I trust you," he replied, then turned, arching back against my forearm, knees bending to help with balance. I leaned with the dip, marveling that Nick, someone who weighed as much as I did, if not more, could feel so light. But he knew how to distribute his weight.

In that second or two we held the position, I took in the fall of his blond hair across his forehead and about his ears, how bright his brown eyes looked under the overhead work-lights, and I thought again, *Who is this? I don't know this man.*

My nerves must have been firing a dozen times per second because I felt suddenly like I had drunk too much coffee. I brought him back up and we parted quickly, me barely hearing anything he went on to say. I only knew that Anoop was back in my arms and we were doing it again.

She said to Nick, "Do it with Michael one more time, will you? But, like, do this entire section with the music so I can see it up to speed."

I blinked at him, even as he nodded and came toward me again, calling for the kid in the tech-booth to let the track play. This time, however, he seemed more aware of me, as though he had acted too quickly the first time to register how close we were. I wondered if the idea of dancing with me again troubled him, knowing he was about to have a guy's arms around him—a gay guy's arms. I thought I felt the damp hand that clasped my own shaking. I, myself, might have become an overtaxed tendon.

"Anyone else who feels they know it well enough," Nick added to the others, "go ahead and give it a shot."

The music started and Nick again counted us in.

This time it wasn't just two counts of eight. It was much longer. But I tried very hard to concentrate on the steps, and not on how I could almost smell his sweat, feel his exhalations against my chin. He knew the part well, and not to be unfair toward Anoop, it was nice to be able to do the combination full-out with a partner who was sure of their feet. A smile wanted to come to my lips, but when I glanced into Nick's face, he looked…well, not *miserable*, but something in that ballpark.

My awkwardness this time around (and maybe his awkwardness too) made itself felt when we got to the dip. I leaned a bit too far and felt our balance go off. I didn't drop him, and we didn't fall, but he gave a startled jerk. The arm about my shoulders tightened. His other pinwheeled, then reached for me. The singers around us darted forward, but I had lifted Nick enough for us to regain control, though not before our arms were around each other and we were almost embracing.

It had happened in the space of two, maybe three seconds (the kid in the tech-booth pausing the music straight away), and in the silence, even as I muttered, "Sorry sorry sorry!" at him, my ears and neck on fire, he started to laugh. It seemed very loud in the silent theatre, and it suddenly affected me too. I laughed with him, saying, "This is why you're the dancer, and I'm not," which made us laugh more. It wasn't exactly funny, but I think the breaking of our awkwardness had burst the floodgates. As our laughter dwindled and we separated, I had a confusing moment where I remembered how solid and lean he had felt under his shirt, and was back to not wanting to meet his eyes.

Mrs. P. sat grading at the back of the theatre. I glanced toward her, wondering if she had been watching.

Then I saw Nick's dad standing just inside the theatre's doors.

Mr. WALSH STILL made me think of a simmering pot. That impression seemed to go hand in hand with his expressionless face, because his expressionlessness was somehow full of appalled ire. Dressed in slacks and a polo, the front of his shirt swelled over his belt buckle in a more pronounced way than I remembered. Though he looked a bit older, he was still little and wiry, still bearded, the glasses perched on his nose at once amplifying and masking the anger in his eyes. But why? *Why* did he look so appalled? It couldn't have been Nick's dancing—Nick had been doing that for years. It had to be because Mr. Walsh had seen his son dancing with a queer.

Nick noticed my expression and turned to look. Silence fell, a mumbled whisper of "Who's that?" from someone coming as loud as a thunderclap.

I seemed to hear, reverberating through time, the words, *Get your fairy friend the hell outta my house!* I remembered this man calling me a *faggot*, even as I felt all but chased, terrified, into the front yard.

As Mr. Walsh began to move with deliberate steps toward the stage, I glanced at Nick. He looked white as a sheet, breathing in quick whips of breath. He wouldn't, or couldn't, take his eyes from his dad. I wanted desperately to do something, but felt that small twelve year old within me making me quail.

Mr. Walsh paused near the edge of the stage, his gaze cold. In a low, almost dead voice, he said to Nick, "Home. Now."

Then he turned, walked back through the theatre, and out the doors.

Mrs. P. had watched the exchange, puzzled. Now she started to make her way toward us. The gathered singers were turning to Nick, who hadn't moved. "What was that about?" I heard. And, "Was that your dad?" Mrs. P. stepped onto the stage, crossing toward us. "Is everything okay?" she asked. "Nick, was that your father?"

Nick's larynx bobbed as he swallowed. He nodded his chin like a robot, then murmured, "I have to go." It was almost a whisper. He wouldn't lift his eyes to any of us. He began gathering his bag, shoving his shoes inside, zipping it with stiff jerks. "I'm sorry. I have to go," he said again. His voice shook. Turning deaf ears to Mrs. P.'s questions, keeping his gaze lowered like a beaten dog, Nick darted away, following his father's path out of the theatre. I watched him go, beyond confused.

Then a thought I had never had before surfaced in my head.

We were all just copies of our parents. Our parents taught us how to act, who to be. Nick had been handed a bum deal—his mother gone before he could remember her, and a father genetically predisposed to being an asshole. And somewhere in there, *his* father had probably been an asshole. It didn't excuse Nick's past behavior, but it wasn't all his fault. I could see that. Kids who had been screwed up by their parents had basically been robbed of their choices. It made me love my mom and dad all the more.

DONICK

MY MIND IS racing a million miles a second as I make the thirty minute walk home. Pop didn't even wait for me. I came out of the theatre to see his truck speeding away. So I started walking, not thinking about how I'm still wearing my dance sneakers, ruining the soles on the concrete. I can't think of anything but the look on Pop's face: unabashed disapproval, and anger. How much had he seen? Did he watch how I danced with Michael? See the way my arms went around his shoulders, the way we laughed together?

What will I do when I get home? How will I defend myself when it's now clear what I've been doing after school every day? And what was Pop doing there? Why would he come into the theatre? Did Josue or Ryan rat me out?

By the time I reach home, I'm sweating. In the driveway sits Pop's truck (the second car—my car—locked away in the garage). I approach the porch, then push open the unlocked front door, my pulse rushing in my eardrums. Pop has never hit me, yet I'm suddenly so terrified of him I feel myself bracing for a blow. Too frightened to make a sound, I close the door as softly as I can, standing rooted just inside. Where is he? What will he say—or yell? No amount of quick thinking (which I don't have in me at the moment) is going to get me out of this deception I've created.

I take a step toward the kitchen. The entire house might be holding its breath.

His voice stabs the air, as low and measured as it had been in the theatre.

"Upstairs," he says. I jump a little, and see him on the landing, framed in the entry to his office. He turns and vanishes inside.

Every step is heavy as I climb the stairs. My feet feel as though they're sinking through the carpeting. I pass into the office and find Pop standing at the window. The light is fading outside, the room in deep shadows. His arms are crossed over his chest as he stares down into the backyard. I wish he was in his desk-chair. I'm more than half a foot taller than him, yet when he stands like that, angry with me, I feel as tiny as a fly. He doesn't look at me, only speaks to the glass.

"What did I just see?"

That same even, frosty voice, the chill in his tone more jarring than a shout.

"It's—it's nothing, Pop. Just—"

"Nothing my ass." His head twists toward me, hands falling to his hips. "What do you think you're doing? Dancing like that with—"

"I don't have a choice, Pop."

"Hell you don't!"

"You know without football I don't have enough credits

to graduate. My councilor told me if I worked on the Senior Revue I would get the PE credits I need."

"And the woodshop story?"

I swallow. "I have helped…a little. But I only told you that—"

He scoffs. "So much deception…"

"Because I knew you'd react this way."

"Then why do these things, hm? Why do the exact thing that's gonna piss me off?"

"Football's the only thing that *didn't* piss you off!" I cry. "That's why! You haven't stopped making me feel bad that I can't play! You'd rather see me permanently injured than doing something—" I cut myself off. I had almost said: doing something that would actually make me happy.

"Watch your tone, Nicky." The eyes behind his glasses look very intense. The child within me wants to cower, but I try hard not to back down.

"What did you do?" I ask. "Come to check up on me?"

"With good reason. As deceptive as you been lately, I thought I'd make sure you weren't feeding me a load of garbage again. Truth always comes out, Nicky. Always. No matter how hard you try to hide it." Pop says this very pointedly, stirring a flame of anxiety within me that has nothing to do with the Senior Revue. He moves toward his desk. I hope he'll sit, yet he merely stands behind the chair, hands gripping its back. "I went into the office to ask where I could find you," he continues, "wanting to know where the woodshop was. Imagine my luck at running into your councilor. In the theatre is where I'd find you, is what she said. And boy howdy, did I find you! *You*, prancing around the stage like some kind of *faggot*!"

"Don't call me that, Pop."

He shakes his head in disgust. "I knew I shoulda put a stop to all that dancing bullshit of yours years ago. This is where it's lead. But you know what? No more. It stops now. I'm not paying for another class, and you sure as hell ain't gonna be teaching."

"You can't stop me."

One blunt finger levels at me. "Rotten ice, boy. That's what you're on." He leans forward, that finger now stabbing the surface of the desk. But no. It's not the surface of the desk. It's a laptop—*my* laptop. I think, *Perfect, he's taken the car, now he's taking my computer, next he'll be asking for my phone again.* "You got a lot to answer for," he adds, "and you better be mindful where you're stepping."

I grit my teeth, even as he studies me with an expression I can't begin to read.

At last, he says, "You ain't doing that thing no more— that dance performance or whatever. Today was your last day. Got me? You're officially dropped."

My mouth falls open. "Pop, I *can't* drop the show! They're counting on me!"

"They can count on someone else."

"I won't graduate without it!"

"I'd rather see you a high school dropout," he spits, "than prancing around like a queer with all those other— those other—"

"Pop!" I shout, appalled to hear how ugly he can be when I thought myself used to it. My raised voice stops him. He stares. "I'm happy," I say. "For the first time in my life, I'm happy. Does that count for anything with you? Do you even care that football made me miserable?"

"You're one of the best players I ever seen!"

"I'm a good dancer too. And I'm happy doing it."

"Yeah, I bet. Don't think I didn't see who that was you was with."

My stomach drops. He *did* see. I play stupid. "Who?" I ask, as though I'm stalling for time.

"That homo kid you used to hang around. That's who."

"Michael? How do you even remember him?"

Pop sneers. "A man don't forget the queer that put the moves on his son. Looks like it's happening again."

"Jesus, Pop. It was just a rehearsal. I was helping all of them with their steps."

"What it looks like to me is that he had his arms around you. You wouldn't be getting close to that boy again, wouldja? Enjoying his company?"

"No."

It's not strictly a lie, is it? But, as usual, Pop's gaze is full of distrust.

"Really?"

He comes around to the front of the desk, perches in the edge, dragging my laptop onto his knee. I see the light flare onto his face all too fast as he lifts the screen, because he hasn't needed to turn it on. I don't keep it password protected, any more than my phone, because I know Pop wouldn't allow it. He turns the screen around to face me and jabs his finger at the mouse. My file folder is there—my *hidden* file folder—full of my secret pictures. My lungs feel clotted with wet leaves.

"Explain this then," he says. A photo of Hugh Jackman looking ripped and pissed off as Wolverine appears on the screen. "And this?" Jason Momoa. "And this. This.

This!" More photos: a shirtless Ryan Reynolds, Michael Fassbender kissing himself in *Alien: Covenant*, Channing Tatum and Matt Bomer from *Magic Mike*. Pop keeps clicking, more pictures filling the screen, even a few fan-art drawings I found of characters like Deadpool and Spiderman in beefcake poses. At last, the series of pictures I found from *Yuri!!! on Ice*: Yuri and Victor with their arms around each other. "Care to explain *this*, Nicky?"

I say, weakly, "It doesn't mean anything. I like superheroes and…" Then I trail off.

"I see this garbage on your computer, catch you in a theatre with all those artist types, even as you lie to me about it. *And* you got your arms around that old fag pal of yours. Makes me wonder, Nicky. Makes me wonder…"

Hearing my father talk about Michael like that sparks something in me. I'm scared enough to tremble, but somehow I find strength to speak, to almost yell.

"Wonder about what? If your son might be a fag too?"

"*Are* you, Nicky?" His voice is like iron. There's disgust beneath it, as though entertaining the thought will make him ill. "You wanna be very careful about what you're gonna say."

All of my impatience with his homophobic bullshit spirals up inside me. The exhaustion of being afraid of who I am, mixed with the stress of making amends for all the hurt I've caused, clenches like a muscle. I bite out, "What if I was, Pop?"

There's no way to describe the look he gives me except to say it's *dark*.

"Then we'd have a *serious* problem."

I shake my head. "You're unbelievable."

"Are you saying what I think you're saying? Did that

kid turn my son into a faggot?"

I grimace. But it matches the grimace he's giving me. God, I'm so, *so* tired. If he decided to fly at me and wring my neck, I don't think I would have the strength to fight back. My voice comes out hoarse, almost choked.

"That kid didn't turn me into a faggot, Pop. Don't you know? Faggots are born that way."

My laptop is pushed back onto the blotter as he gets to his feet. His teeth are clenched, the muscles in his jaw jumping through his beard. "I won't have it," he spits. "You understand me?"

"What'll you do about it?"

He pauses, staring as though I've just vomited on him. Then he says, "I'm glad your momma's not here to witness this. She would be so ashamed."

Liking my father hasn't always been easy, but I've loved him as best I can. Yet for the first time, hearing him say that, I hate him.

"Mom wouldn't be ashamed of me for being something I can't help," I say, and talking through the lump in my throat feels impossible. The image of him standing at the desk blurs and runs like rain on a windshield as I fight tears. "Mom would pity me. She would feel sad for leaving me alone with an asshole like you."

He's across the room in three steps. He slaps me hard, his calloused palm jerking my head sideways, stinging enough to make the tears fall. I suck in a breath and gaze back at him, too stunned to move, to even lift my fingers to the smarting bit of fire that has become my cheek.

His voice trembles with rage. "When I come back, you will not be in this house. Do you understand?"

Then he's leaving the office, pounding down the stairs and out the front door. It slams hard enough to shake the walls. I'm still standing where he left me when I hear his truck's engine rev and then the whistle of the wheels. Tears are scalding my cheeks, burning hotter than the place where he slapped me—the first time he's done anything like that. I think I might start to hyperventilate.

When I come back, you will not be in this house.

So he's kicking me out? And why? Because now he knows his son is gay? But where am I supposed to go? I don't even have the car to sleep in.

I move sluggishly to my bedroom. My thoughts are a tornado. I'm pulling out the old battered bag I used for my football gear, trying to think of all the things I'll absolutely need, all the things I have to leave behind. But thinking is so hard!

God help me, but it's *really* out there now! I'm gay! I've admitted it to my father—and he hates me for it! I think of those poor kids who commit suicide because they feel unaccepted, and though thoughts like that are foreign to me, I can understand them now. How many kids at school are just like me? Struggling to live some semblance of a happy life, even as outside forces conspire to drown them. And the shame shame *shame* of having been one of those outside forces to any number of kids I could have been a friend to.

I'm sniffling, snot running from my nose, tears dripping from my chin. I can barely see what I'm doing. I stuff clothing haphazardly into the depths of the bag. Thank goodness it's pretty large. In the bathroom, I sweep in deodorant, razor, toothbrush, whatever I think I might need. Then I'm dashing for frivolous stuff—the chargers for both my iPhone and the green Razr, my iPod and earbuds, even going back into Pop's office for my laptop. No way am I leaving it. If he doesn't like that I've taken it… I think, *Come and find me.*

But there's so much I'm leaving. Photos of my family when we were three, not just two. All the books and DVDs and blu-rays I turned to when I felt overwhelmed by life… Well, life is overwhelming me right now, and I'm leaving them behind. What can I turn to now? *Who* can I turn to now? Where am I going to go?

All my school stuff is in my backpack lying by the front door. I drop the football-bag at the bottom of the stairs, stepping into the kitchen. Sucking in a shuddering breath, I slip the house keys off my keyring and leave them on the counter. Then, working my arms into the straps of my backpack, pulling onto my shoulder the football-bag containing all I have in the world, I exit the house. I lock the door behind me before trudging across the twilit lawn to the sidewalk.

I stand there for a full minute, swiping tears from my cheeks like some five year old, wondering which direction I should go. I have no idea. There's nowhere for me *to* go. The only place I ever had is at my back, the door locked, and I no longer have a key.

MICHAEL

THE REST OF rehearsal was sort of bewildering. Other members of the cast just shrugged their shoulders over Nick's sudden departure. But me? Seeing Nick's father, after all these years, was disquieting. Still, I futzed through the rest of rehearsal as best I could, though there wasn't much to do with Nick gone. When Calista found out what happened, she gave me even more to think about.

"His dad didn't know," she said. "Nick was keeping it secret because he knew his dad wouldn't like it. I hope he won't have to leave the show."

When she dropped me at my house, even as I toyed with the idea of sending Nick a text to ask if everything was okay, I was surprised to see all the lights off inside. Opening the door, I saw a scribbled note lying on the half-moon table where we all dropped our keys. *At Dad's band concert tonight. Georgie with us, twins with Uncle Rex. Love, Mom. PS Leftover stir-fry in the fridge if you need dinner. Also, bring in the mail.*

I took the mail from the box, then shut the door, snapping on lights as I passed into the kitchen. I put the Tupperware container with the stir-fry into the microwave, then sank into a chair at the table and sorted through the stack of envelopes and coupon circulars. We had been listening to *Songs for a New World* in Calista's car, and I was absently humming "I'm Not Afraid of Anything" when the melody died in my throat. My hands actually started to shake.

I found, first, an envelope with The Juilliard School stamped on it, then a second envelope reading New York University. The last two. And at the same time.

I suddenly felt afraid of everything.

The microwave beeped, its hum dying away. I put my hands in my lap, as though the pair of envelopes were slivers of glass and I might cut myself.

Like the previous three, these two were much too thin to be good news. Or so I already told myself. Something within my ribs wanted to rise to the ceiling, my head feeling fuzzy, achey.

I darted out my hands and ripped open the flaps one after the other, quickly, like ripping away a bandage.

Thank you for your application… we regret to inform you… your auditions were… most difficult of decisions…

I hardly needed to skim the print on either letter—I knew the details by heart now.

"That's it," I muttered. "All five…"

Suddenly I would have given anything to say that I had gotten into UCLA or CalArts.

Just like that there were tears in my eyes. I breathed hard, fighting a sob, thanking God I was alone, that my parents were out so they wouldn't see me struggle not to break down.

My auditions; songs and monologues I had rehearsed and rehearsed; traveling to visit campuses. I laid my head in my arms on the kitchen table, sucking in air, yet the rock that seemed to fill my throat felt almost painful in its enormity.

I sighed out, "And I thought today couldn't get any worse. Holy crap…"

The sound of the doorbell made me want to scream. I could have hammered my fist onto the table.

But I got up, hoping to find a late Amazon delivery or something, fully aware that the misery on my face couldn't be hidden, wanting to see no one. When I swung open the door, all the air in my lungs found its way passed that rock in my throat and escaped me in one huge rush.

Donick Walsh stood on my doorstep.

I couldn't do it. I just couldn't. The sight of him with the porch-light gilding his pale hair, looking at me so funnily, overwhelmed me. I burst into tears.

MIKEY?" HE SAID, worry crossing his face. "What…"

I swiped at my wet cheeks, mortified, even as I shook my head. "Sorry," I managed to say. "Really bad day."

"You too?"

I stared at him, my eyes continuing to well. His backpack and an enormous sports-bag were slung over his shoulders. He was still dressed for rehearsal, including his dance sneakers. Then I realized why he looked so strange, now that I paused to really see him. His eyes were red-rimmed, his cheeks blotchy and raw.

I muttered, "You've been crying." He didn't say anything. I sniffed. "Things got bad with your dad?" He nodded.

"I should go," he said, dropping his eyes and beginning

to turn away. "I shouldn't have come here. I'm bothering you. I'm sorry."

I sighed, wondering at myself. "Don't be a moron. Just come inside."

Now he looked hesitant—the door might have been the entrance to Shelob's lair. But he came in. We stood, made awkward by the unspoken wrongness in out separate lives, even as it was so obvious we could commiserate with each other on some level.

I swiped at my face again, feeling as embarrassed as he looked. "Have you had dinner?" I asked in a congested voice. He shook his head. "I'm heating something up. There's enough for two. Come on."

He set down his bags and followed me into the kitchen. I silently took the stir-fry from the microwave and began to dish it onto plates.

"Oh God," he murmured. I turned and saw him at the table, looking down at my last two rejection letters. He had glimpsed one before, in my bedroom the night of my birthday party, yet unlike that time, I couldn't find it in me to care. "This is why you're upset?" he asked.

"Yeah." I brought him his plate, setting my own on the table. He slipped into a chair while I went for forks. I shoved the letters out of the way, wanting nothing more than to ball them in my hands and toss them in the trash. "Last two. Looks like I'll be matriculating at a junior college."

A lifeless quality touched his voice when he said, "I'm sorry."

I sat and we began to eat—if anyone could call it eating. We mostly pushed vegetables around our plates.

"So," I said at last, "that's my crisis. What's yours?"

He didn't answer right away. I glanced at him, wondering if he had heard me.

Then, in that same lifeless tone, he said, "I had nowhere else to go. I didn't know what to do."

"What do you mean?"

I watched his eyes swim, but he blew out a breath, staring at the ceiling to keep the tears from falling. I had never seen him cry before, never seen him look so stricken. I would say he looked beautiful if he didn't have such misery on his face.

"My dad told me to leave." He almost whispered it.

I stared. "What?"

He sniffed, playing with his fork. "I can't go home. I took everything I could, but I don't know where I'm supposed to go. It was stupid to come here. I'm sorry. I just…"

"He kicked you out? Why? Because of the Revue?"

Again Nick's eyes lifted to mine; he seemed to think for a moment, before something behind his gaze deflated and he went on staring at his food.

"He said I needed to drop out. Ordered me to. I told him no, that too many people are counting on me. He said if I didn't drop out, then he wouldn't have me living in his house." Nick shook his head. "You know how he is. About people like…well, like…"

"Like me?"

Nick only hung his head, stabbing at water-chestnuts and pea-pods.

My problems seemed to pale in comparison, yet it was difficult to believe Nick had been kicked out of his house just because he wanted to dance in a school musical. Then again, knowing what I did of his father, maybe it wasn't so hard to believe.

"I'm sorry," he said again. "This is stupid. I'll go. I—"

"Get real, Nick," I said, even as he began to rise from the table. "Where are you going to go? Just sit down."

He did, though with no less hesitance than before.

"I hope you don't mind my saying," I added, "but your dad's always been a bit of an asshole."

"A *lot* of an asshole, you mean." He scoffed. "It was pretty ugly."

"Well, you should talk to my parents. They'll be back in a couple hours."

"You'll let me hang out?" he asked, surprised.

"What else're you gonna do? We can sit in the living-room and watch TV. I've got homework but I don't think I'll be able to concentrate."

"Tell me about it."

We both seemed to be done with our dinners, though the plates didn't look much different than when I had dished them up. He hovered awkwardly by the table as I dumped the leftovers, then rinsed the dishes. I gave him a soda from the fridge ("Still a Pepsi man?" I asked), then we moved into the living-room.

"My eyes are all irritated," I told him. "I need to take out my contacts. I'll be back in a minute."

I left him there with the television remote while I went upstairs and locked myself in the bathroom. I removed my contacts, set them in solution, pushed my glasses onto my face, then stared at myself for two or three seconds. I saw a stranger in the mirror. My eyes were red, my face pale. I seemed to wear a dazed expression, as though the death of my anticipated college days hadn't sunk in very far. Combine that with how confusing it felt to have Nick Walsh in my house, again, and I looked like I wasn't playing with a full deck. I took off my glasses and splashed water on my face, dried off, replaced them, then went back downstairs.

Nick was perched on the recliner when I came in. I fell onto the couch. He couldn't relax, that was obvious, sitting like he had rebar for a spine. His brows were creased with worry. I needed some reassurance myself, yet oddly, I felt like I wanted to do something to take away his anxiety. Sympathy pains, I guess.

We barely exchanged five words, but the bizarreness of the situation wasn't lost on me. A few weeks ago I had ordered him to leave my house, yet here he was, saying he had nowhere else to go, even as I fed him dinner and sat just a few feet from him, definitely made awkward and embarrassed, but also somehow comfortable too. We had seen each other at our worsts. And also our bests.

As mindless television played (reruns of *The Golden Girls*) we simply sat and stared at the screen, waiting for my parents to get home.

At close to nine-thirty, I heard the rumble of the garage-door, then the hum of Mom's minivan pulling in. Nick's back stiffened even more. He cast a look at me.

"I'll talk to them," I said. "Run up to my room. Give me a few minutes."

He nodded, uncertain, but left the living-room.

"Wait," I called. "Take these with you. I don't want to explain them to my parents yet."

I handed him my rejection letters.

I met Mom and Dad bustling in through the garage-door. Dad wore his tuxedo, the loose ends of his bowtie hanging from the open collar of his shirt. Mom's hair was up and she wore her pearl earrings, her black dress in danger of becoming rumpled by the boisterousness of Topher and Cady. Georgie was with them, chattering loudly into the mouthpiece of her earbuds, talking, no doubt, to some friend she had just been with.

Both Mom and Dad started to say something to me, but I interrupted with, "Nick is here."

They froze. "Donick?" Mom said.

"He's upstairs. It's…not good."

Dad said, "Georgia Rose, keep the twins inside. We'll be in the garage with your brother for a minute."

We trooped into the garage's silence, broken only by the ticking of the minivan as it cooled. The outside door hadn't been shut yet and I could see the beams of the headlights on Dad's black Mustang parked at the curb. They flicked themselves off, even as I watched, like an animal going to sleep.

"What's going on, Ninja?" Dad asked.

So I explained—about rehearsal, Nick's father showing up, how angry he had looked, and then finishing with Nick's appearance on the doorstep and what he had told me.

Mom's face wore a mask of pity. "That poor boy," she murmured. "And damn that man. Even after all these years he's just the same."

"Nick is in your room?" Dad asked.

"I told him to wait there while I talked to you."

"And he said he has nowhere else to go? Oh boy."

"Do you think it's strange?" I asked. "The reason he gave for his dad kicking him out? Doesn't that sound…I dunno…it doesn't sound like a very good reason."

"We all know what his father is like," Mom said. "I wouldn't put something like this past him."

Dad said, "And Nick isn't eighteen yet, is he?"

I shook my head. "Not until June."

"Well, his father can't kick him out then. He's still a minor."

"I don't think something like that would stop his dad," I said. "But I mean…what now?"

My parents looked at each other, then at me.

Dad mused, "Why would he think of us—of *you*, Ninja? You haven't been friends in a long time. He has other friends he would feel more comfortable turning to, don't you think?"

"I'm not sure. Something he said recently, about his friends…maybe he can't go to them. Everything is so weird."

"Well," said Mom, "we can't just turn him away."

I nodded.

"How do *you* feel about it, son?" Dad asked. "It's sort of your call. Would you be okay with him staying here for a day or so, until we can get things straightened out?"

"Yeah, I guess. I mean, if he has no place to go, then he *should* stay. In a way, I sort of…owe him a favor."

Mom looked at Dad. "Then he stays?"

"Of course," Dad said. "Where'll we put him though? We don't exactly have guest rooms anymore."

"Living-room couch?" said Mom.

"He can sleep in my room," I said with a sigh. "He always camped on the floor next to the bed when he slept over when we were kids. He can camp there now."

"We can pick up an air-mattress tomorrow," said Dad. "Too bad the twins wrecked the last one."

"Let's ask Donick where he would prefer to sleep," said

Mom. "He might want to crash on the couch rather than your floor, Sweetheart." I read the unspoken meaning in her words. Nick might not be comfortable sleeping in the same room with me—either because of our past, or other reasons. Still, I shrugged and the three of us moved back into the house, the rumble of the closing garage-door following us.

Noise and havoc filled the kitchen and living-room, Cady and Topher yelling and shouting, Georgie barking at them to be quiet. I wondered what Nick must be making of it upstairs.

"Bring him down," said Dad. "Let's have a little chat."

I found Nick in much the same way I had found him in my room on the night of my birthday party—standing awkwardly, staring around him at the stuff on the walls.

"They said you can stay," I told him.

"Really?" Something like relief replaced his stricken look. But not completely.

"Yeah. Come down."

He followed me back to the kitchen. He looked as sheepish as ever, facing my parents, but Dad smiled.

"Hiya, kiddo!"

Mom came and actually hugged him. The expression on Nick's face was almost fearful. His ears reddened and he darted his eyes at me.

Mom said, "Michael told us you and your dad had a bit of a fight. I'm sorry to hear that. But you're always welcome here. We can try and figure something out this weekend. In the meantime, I'm afraid we don't have the room we used to, so your choices are: stay in Michael's room, or sleep on the living-room couch."

"Neither will be particularly comfortable, sad to say," Dad

said, "but I'll stop at the store for an air-mattress tomorrow."

Now Nick looked horrified. "Please, don't do that. I'll sleep wherever."

Dad smiled at him again, then said deliberately, "I'll pick up an air-mattress tomorrow." He kissed Mom's temple. "I'm going to change out of this penguin suit and jump in the shower. Nick, welcome to Penrose Manor." Dad shook Nick's hand, gave the back of his neck a squeeze and headed for the stairs.

"So?" Mom prompted. "Where'll it be?"

Nick's eyes shifted to me again. "I don't want to bother Michael. So…"

"It's fine." My tone was brusque. I should have pushed him toward the couch, but some part of me seemed to want to know what it would be like, after all these years, and all we had been through, being in close quarters. "My room'll be quieter. Unless you *want* to sleep on the couch."

He shook his head. "No, your room is fine. Thanks. Kick me out if I get in your way."

"I won't think twice." I turned toward the stairs. "Get your stuff."

Mom followed, watching Nick hoist his bags onto his shoulders. She asked, "Is there anything you'll need, Donick?" When he said no, she added, "Well, if you find you forgot something, just let us know. Michael Sweetheart, grab linens and spare pillows, a couple of blankets from the hall closet, will you? I have to get the rugrats into bed. It's almost ten o'clock."

I left Nick in my bedroom while I went for bedding. I grabbed two or three blankets, thinking he might use them as extra cushion when he slept.

"Here," I said, setting everything on my bed. "Towels too. I usually shower before bed, but if you want first dibs, you can go. You know where the bathroom is."

"Are you sure?" he asked.

I gave him a nod. I actually wanted a minute alone, and getting him out of the way for a while was my real motivation.

"Feel free to use whatever of mine is in there. Shampoo, body wash. Georgie's stuff is there too, but you can't miss what's mine. I may not be much of a guy," I added, "but I don't enjoy smelling like lavender and peaches." I almost tagged on, *Or oranges*, but held my tongue.

"Thank you, Michael," he said. "I know I don't deserve it, but—"

"Consider us even for getting socked in the nuts in my place."

An awkward laugh escaped him, but it was half-hearted. The worry wasn't far from his face. He mumbled, "Thanks again," gathering up the towels and some things from his bag, and went out into the hall. A moment later came the sound of the bathroom door shutting.

I pulled out my phone and brought up the text-thread from Secret Admirer.

You'll never believe this! I typed. *Guess who's at my house right now?*

I sat in my desk-chair once I hit send. Nick had left the letters on the desktop. I didn't want to look at them again, so I opened the drawer and tossed the last two in with their poisonous mates. The sound of water running into the tub came through the wall, followed by the buzz of my phone.

Secret Admirer: Drama!! Have no idea. Who?

Me: My old not-friend himself! Nick Walsh!

Secret Admirer: Thats interesting. Whats he want?

Me: He's actually going to be staying over. For a couple of days. Maybe longer.

Secret Admirer: Doesnt sound much like a NOT-friend.

Me: He's been kicked out of his house. His dad's a complete jerk-hole. Trust me, I know.

Secret Admirer: But y come 2 ur place?

Me: He said he doesn't have anywhere else to go.

Secret Admirer: Wow!! & even tho u & he arent friends anymore, out of all the ppl he could have turned 2, he still came 2 u. C? U cant deny ur awesomeness. Its tru. Even Nick Walsh c's it.

I set the phone aside when the bathroom door opened. Nick came padding back into the room, his dirty clothes and dance shoes all knotted together in one hand. His hair was dark with water and he had draped his damp towel around his neck. He wore a clean T-shirt with the faded logo for *Stranger Things* on the front and too-large basketball shorts. His feet were bare. Seeing them was slightly jarring; they looked enormous and tough, calloused from years of sports and dance. It was odd to think I hadn't seen his bare feet since we were kids. The hair on his calves looked like threads of gold. His legs hadn't been hairy like that back then.

"She's all yours," he said. A tenseness hovered about him.

"You normally sleep in that?" I asked. "I just mean, I have extra pajamas. If you need."

He looked down at himself. "This is it. Thanks though."

"Feel free to set up your bed wherever. I won't be long."

I got up and kicked off my shoes and socks, pulling

pajamas from my dresser. As I moved toward the door, he spoke, and I paused, turning as he shook out the folded blankets and sheets, not lifting his eyes.

"I know we're not friends," he said. "And I know I don't deserve yours or your family's kindness. But I appreciate it. Just want you to know."

Now he did look at me. I didn't know quite what I should say. So I simply nodded and left the room.

I stood under the hot water longer than usual, letting the spray batter my face, trying not to think about the thousand things suddenly dumped on my plate. Come summer, should I start looking for a job flipping burgers? Was there any merit in going to a junior college? Even if I did, was there any point in trying to transfer somewhere? CSUN perhaps? And what in hell was Nick Walsh doing in my house, setting up a bed on the floor of my bedroom? He would be sleeping just a few feet from me, after all the bullying, the name calling, the blood pouring into my eye from my split eyebrow. I even paused before the fogged mirror and examined that comma-shaped scar, remembering the way he had lifted a hand toward it, as though he might have touched it, the day he had been sack-tapped.

When I came back into the room, I found him sitting cross-legged on the floor, staring at his iPhone. His bedding was laid out beneath him, alongside my own bed—where he had often made his bed on sleepovers—that is, when he hadn't fallen asleep *in* my bed, side by side with me. I had a queen-size, plenty big enough for the both of us, even though we were each six feet tall now and neither of us were particularly slight. Then I frowned at myself. I didn't want him in my bed, sleeping beside me!

"Your phone buzzed or something," he said.

"Thanks." I paused at the desk, my feet on his blankets, to pick up my phone and slip it into the pocket of my pajama pants. "Give me your towel," I told him. "I'll hang it in the bathroom."

He had folded it and set it atop his bag. He pushed it into my fingers and I returned to the bathroom, draping it over the shower rod to dry. I checked my phone. Sure enough, another text from Secret Admirer.

U'll have 2 tell me how things go, he wrote. *Im thinking of u. But I gotta get 2 bed. Talk 2morrow, yeah?*

I replied, *Yes, talk tomorrow. Night!* then slipped back into my room—where I seemed to feel my old not-friend's presence like a Horcrux.

Mom poked her head in at the door. "All set?" she asked.

"Yes," Nick answered. "Thank you."

"Try to be comfortable, Donick. We'll have an air-mattress for you tomorrow, so you'll only be on the floor for one night. I hope you survive it," she teased. "My creaky old bones would be screaming at me all day tomorrow if I was in your place." She gave me one of her mom-looks—one that said she was sorry for my awkward position, but also proud I had set aside my emotions. "Sleep tight, Sweetheart," she said to me, then blew a kiss in my direction. "Donick can get a ride to school with you and your friends tomorrow, yes?"

I nodded, though I would have to be sure to text Calista first thing in the morning. Once again, this huge thing had happened and I had texted Secret Admirer first.

"'Night, boys." She closed the door.

The silence in the room was suddenly very loud. Our eyes might have been billiard-balls—colliding, flying apart, colliding, flying apart.

I switched the lamp off and padded to the bed, the twinkle-lights hanging around the window giving off their usual mellow glow.

"I always leave those on. Will they bother you?" I asked.

He said no, then twisted himself onto the blankets, pulling a sheet over his legs. I fell into my bed, aware of him more than ever—aware of the sound of him breathing, shifting around. In a few seconds we were both still, lying there with the sound of my parents murmuring, Georgie's movement in the bathroom, the house settling. Downstairs, Dad's grandmother's old clock chimed—quarter to eleven.

Five minutes might have passed, then ten. I wasn't sleepy at all, too troubled for my brain to calm. I could hear Nick's restlessness and figured it must be the same for him.

At last I whispered, "Nick?"

"Hm?"

"It's weird…having you here."

"Sorry."

"I didn't—I just meant…I never thought you'd spend the night at my house again."

He was quiet for ten or fifteen seconds. Then he murmured, "There's a lot going on I never thought would happen."

Now my turn came to be quiet. At last, I said, "I'm sorry you've been going through so much crap lately. I'm sorry if I did anything to make it worse."

In an odd voice, he replied, "You haven't, Michael. Not at all."

We didn't speak again after that. But I stayed awake for a long time. It was hard to feel tired when a moment later I heard the sound of him softly crying. He would never want me to acknowledge it, so I could do nothing but listen to the sharp hitching of his breath, thinking there must be so much more going on with him than I could ever guess.

DONICK

IF EVER I had doubts about having, not just a crush, but *feelings* for Michael, those doubts would have swept themselves away after showing up on his doorstep. Where else *could* I have gone? He doesn't particularly like me, yet he's still there for me. All the times I've told him—as his secret admirer—how amazing he is, are evidenced right there with allowing me, someone who's hurt him terribly, to stay (because it's not really Mr. and Mrs. Penrose that allow it, I know). *And* he offers to share his room! What I've done to deserve his kindness, I'll never understand.

Yet laced through all my gratitude is the remembrance of how much it stung when Pop slapped me.

When I come back, you will not be in this house.

Are you saying what I think you're saying? Did that kid turn my son into a faggot?

I'm glad your momma's not here to witness this. She would be so ashamed.

Those last words seem to bounce off the walls of my skull. How that hurt—worse than the slap.

The next morning—my face feeling puffy from how much crying I did all night (I'm fairly certain Michael heard most of it)—he and I rise with his alarm and go about getting ready for school. We don't talk much, don't really look at each other. I'm feeling funny about Calista and Brent arriving to pick Michael up and seeing me with him. Maybe I should walk.

The whole house is awake. Mrs. Penrose, wearing scrubs, actually makes pancakes. We sit at the kitchen table and begin eating. She sets out a pair of smaller plates with the pancakes cut into pieces, and as though they have some sort of homing beacon between their ears, Michael's twin brother and sister scamper into the kitchen in their footie-pajamas and climb onto their chairs.

Ten seconds pass, then they both pause and stare at me with eyes Michael's identical shade of green.

The boy doesn't take his gaze from me, though he speaks to his brother. "Micuh, who zat?"

I guess they wouldn't remember me from Michael's party.

"That's Nick," Michael says. "Can you say hi?"

It's the sister who says it. Then she looks at Michael. "Who's Nick?"

Michael gestures. "Him."

"Who's *him*?"

"*Nick*, silly. Did you get syrup in your ears?" He tickles the side of her neck. She giggles and squirms, looking at him with adoration. I watch this with interest. I've never seen this side of him before.

The boy looks at me again. "Are you Micuh's fren?"

I glance across the table. Michael says, after a second or two, "Yes, Nick is my friend. Eat your pancakes, Toph, they're getting soggy."

The girl looks at me very earnestly. "I'm Cady. I'm five." She shows me. Her brother holds out all the fingers on his hand too. "*I'm* five!" he cries. "We're bowf five! We're twins. Know what that means?"

I smile at him. "Two at once, right? What's *your* name."

"Topher." It sounds more like *Tofuh*.

"Topher, huh? Is that short for Christopher?" He nods. I say, "I like your name. And Cady's too."

"D'you sleep here?" he asks.

"I did. Your brother let me stay in his room."

Cady chirps, "He has a big bed! We sleep with him sometimes and watch cartoons! Did you sleep with him?"

I feel my face get hot. When I look at Michael, his cheeks are pink too.

He says, "Just eat your pancakes, both of you."

Michael's mother drinks coffee and leans against the counter, asking about rehearsals. She gives me a surprised smile when Michael reveals I've been choreographing one of the numbers. He also tells her we have rehearsal on Fridays now since the show opens so soon.

She's saying, "Well, graduation is, what, five or six weeks after that? Don't get so busy you start slacking off on assignments. Either of you. None of this senioritis nonsense, got it?" when Georgia comes down the stairs, followed by Mr. Penrose.

Georgia, dressed in something of a school uniform—white polo-shirt and khaki-colored pleated skirt—gives me an interested look, and when she says hello, she actually calls me Donny, saying how she hasn't seen me since she was a little kid. I can't help saying to her, "You're all grown up." She smiles embarrassedly, even as Michael mutters, "Everyone calls him Nick now, Georgie, not Donny."

I shake my head. "It's okay."

Michael narrows his eyes at me. Then he looks back at his breakfast.

It's bewildering, sitting there, witnessing the Penrose morning routine. Georgia spreads jam on a pancake and munches it like a taco as she heads out of the kitchen, followed by her dad—once he's gone round the table, kissed both twins on the cheeks, saving Michael for last. He even gives my shoulder a squeeze. Is this how fathers are supposed to be? I feel sudden grief at having no idea. Even the pat on my shoulder accentuates how broad a margin there has always been between men like him, and men like Pop.

Georgia and Mr. Penrose head out the door (he calls out, "Hope my roses have a good day!"). Georgia attends the private school where her father teaches, so I suppose they always leave together.

Michael's phone buzzes. "Calista," he says.

We leave the table and Mrs. Penrose swoops at Michael to embrace him and kiss his cheek.

Then she hugs me, murmuring, "Try not to think about, you know, *stuff* all day. Focus on schoolwork, on rehearsal, if you can."

Getting this unlooked for mothering from her is awkward, but I nod and try not to show my embarrassment.

Topher suddenly begins chanting my name. I look back at him, laughing a little, and he says, "Come back, 'kay? We'll show you what our rooms look like!"

"No one wants to see those disaster-areas," Michael says, though it's good-natured. "Have fun at pre-school, 'kay, Toph? Love you both."

Their cheery (piercing) shouts of, "Love you, Micuh!" actually make me grin.

Michael must have warned Calista and Brent in advance I would be with him, because neither acts particularly shocked at seeing me. They're friendly though, which is a nice difference from Michael's coolness. I stuff myself into the back of Calista's little red Hyundai, Brent squashed against my side, and we drive off. Brent begins asking for details about what happened, and though I explain it the way I told Michael, I catch Calista's eye in the rearview mirror and suspect she has a clearer picture of what I'm *not* sharing.

Once we've reached campus and I'm out of the car, I give a forced wave and begin to move away when Calista calls to me, "You should come eat with us at lunch today. If you want, I mean." Brent seconds it. I glance at Michael. He just watches me, looking interested as to what I'll say.

"Thanks," I reply. "Maybe." Though I know (and I'm sure they do too) that I won't show. I'll be at my usual table in the library, doing schoolwork, and texting Michael at the same time. Besides, if I spent lunch in Mrs. P.'s room, Michael would surely notice the lack of texts from his secret admirer. I'm already anxious about how I'll keep up my communication with him now that his secret admirer is staying in his house. I really *am* like a stalker. Yikes, I'm a mess…

I carry an odd, displaced feeling throughout the morning. Having slept in a strange place, arrived at school in a strange way, and knowing I won't be returning home later, unsettles me. It's like going outside and discovering the sky is pink, or the shape of a circle is actually a square.

I'm pulled from my funk when I get a note from Mrs.

Moes during third period. It says to come see her at nutrition break. I remember the locker graffiti and the list of students I had made. I suppose now, more than ever, I need to carry on with this amends-mission I've given myself. I'm sure everything happening to me is karmic balance.

But it's still not balance enough.

Maybe hitting that reset-button and trying to start over is really about beginning from nothing.

*H*ERE YOU GO," Mrs Moes says as soon as I walk into her office. She's holding out my list of students. "It's a little shorter now—some of those kids aren't here anymore: homeschool and such. You've got a good fifteen names though and I wrote their current locker numbers next to each. Of course, some of them may not be using those lockers, but the majority should be where the computer says."

"Thanks," I say, glancing over the list. "This is great." I give her a smile, but it must not be very convincing, because she frowns.

"Everything all right?"

I shrug. "Yes. And no. A lot going on."

"I hope I didn't get you into trouble with your father. He was looking for you the other day and I told him where to find you. I know you didn't want him to know about the Revue but…"

"Don't worry about it," I say, shaking my head. "It's fine." I wave the list. "Again, thanks for this."

"Well…if you need to talk, my door is open. Oh, and Nick?" I've turned to leave, but pause. "Have you ever heard of *kintsugi?*"

"Ken who?"

"*Kintsugi.* The Japanese art of gold-repair."

I shake my head.

"It's like a philosophy. When a piece of pottery is broken, you know, like a bowl or vase, it's not thrown away. It's repaired with lacquer mixed with gold. It creates a new type of beauty, but also turns a piece of the pottery's history—a difficult piece—into a new strength."

Her mentioning gold makes me think of the song Michael sang at his birthday party. Unrequited crushes sure can make a person feel helpless. And I'm only making it worse on myself. Texting him, now staying at his house… How will I ever lay these feelings aside?

I say, "That's interesting," wondering why she's brought this up.

She smiles. "You might look it up sometime. There are some beautiful examples online."

I give her another puzzled, "Thank you," and leave the office.

*G*IVING THOUGHT TO the fifteen names on my list is a good distraction from everything screwed up in my life. I spend the rest of the day going over all the students written there, thinking of anything I can recollect about them. Some kids I don't know at all—they were, after all, someone else's targets—and I figure I'll have to think on the fly.

At lunch, I text Michael with the same false cheerfulness I used when texting him from the bathroom last night. (Picture me leaving water all over the Razr as I tried to reply to his texts with one arm sticking out of the shower, just to keep him off my trail.) It's disconcerting, because it's me he seems most to want to talk about. Thankfully, he only reiterates the "weirdness" of having his old not-friend (as he calls me) sleeping on the floor next to his bed. He could be bashing me, but in all the conversations he and I have had about me, he's never been downright mean—aside from occasionally calling me an asshole or a jerk. But I can't hold that against him. I *am* an asshole, and a jerk. Or at least I was. Anymore, I don't feel like I know what, or who, I am.

I apologize to the teachers at rehearsal for leaving so suddenly yesterday. I think some sort of word about what happened has spread through the cast because none of the teachers are upset; they actually look at me with sympathy. They allow me time to keep working on "Cover Girl" during the last hour of rehearsal. Otherwise, it's business at usual. All singers and dancers are together running and cleaning every number we can; Brent is all over the place, trying to help the tech crew bring set pieces onto the stage. Calista runs back and forth too, from numbers she sings to the costume-lab where she fits more people, including me.

At first I think it's a relief to be around her, until I find we're alone and she's giving me another one of those speculative looks. I tense up.

"I'm really sorry," she says, "about what's going on with you and your dad."

She hovers around me. I'm trying on a pair of too-long black shorts and she's hemming them so they rest just above my knees. I'll be wearing the white dress-shirt, black tie, and suspenders from the "Vogue" costume for my solo, only I'll switch out the black pants for these shorts, and wear my dance shoes with no socks. Also a fedora. It's a weird look, but one Chalice insists will go well with my number.

"Thanks," I reply. "Pop isn't easy to live with. Guess I don't have to now."

"It's *not* really the show, is it?"

I shake my head. "You know why."

"How did he find out?"

"The uncomplicated version? Some pictures on my computer."

She wrinkles her nose. "Naughty!"

"Nothing like that." I laugh. "Stupid really. Pictures of actors or whatever. Actors I've thought were…"

"Hot?"

"Pretty much."

"Like who?" She grins. "Who revs Nick Walsh's motor?"

My face warms. "Well, I had some pictures from *Magic Mike*, even though I've never seen it. Henry Cavill. I even had one or two of Kit Harrington from *Game of Thrones*. You know, from that resurrection scene?"

She snorts. "It's all Brent talked about when he saw it. Me? I'm partial to the scene with Jon and Ygritte in the cave. I'm all about girls who are kissed by fire." A couple of pins are pinched between her lips as she kneels at my side, her knuckles grazing my knee as she tucks the hem. She says, "Michael's got that Superman poster of Henry Cavill hanging in his room."

"I know."

"Michael looks like him a little bit, huh?"

"A little. But with green eyes."

"Notice his eyes, huh?"

She looks up at me and I can only blink, my mouth hanging open.

"You're his secret admirer, aren't you?"

"What?"

"Come on, don't deny it. It was something he mentioned the other day about his mystery phone-case giver. About how he's gay but not out. Michael has no idea he was describing you. But I knew."

I sigh. "Yes, it's me. Please don't say anything."

"I won't. I'm a secret keeper of the first order. Never fear." She pauses. "But why? *Why* be his secret admirer? That's what I don't get. With your guys' past..."

"I'm just trying to make it up to him. Let him know he's awesome. That he's special."

She scoffs. "So gay! What? You into Michael or something?"

I think she expects I'll blush and sputter. I think she expects I'll launch into denials and act offended. But I don't.

"Yes. I like him."

Her expression melts into surprise. "You like him? Like, *like* like him?"

"*Like* like him. Yeah."

"Since when?"

"I guess since we were kids. Since that time I kissed him in my living-room."

She's silent for several seconds, digesting this.

"Is that why you went to his house yesterday?" she then asks. "After the fight with your dad, I mean. Because you like him?"

"No!" I say. "I wish I had *anywhere* else I could have gone, believe me! You think liking Michael is easy? You think I want him right there as a constant reminder of how screwed up I've made my life? He may not hate me, but he'll never *really* like me, even as a friend. No,

I went to his house because I had nowhere else I could go. His parents were always nice to me, and the night of his birthday party they made me feel welcome, even when Michael didn't. That's all I kept thinking about. It's selfish, I know, going there when it makes Michael so uncomfortable. But I didn't know what else to do."

"All of this complicates things, you know. Michael feels close to his secret admirer—who is *you*—something I've been warning him against since that first note showed up in his locker. If he ever finds out, I think he'll feel just as betrayed as he did when you turned on him in middle school."

"I know," I say, my voice coming out small. "That's why I don't even want him to find out about me being…"

"Gay? Just say it. You're too funny, Nick. Say it out loud. Makes it real. And it is, isn't it?"

I grimace. "Fine. I don't want him to know that I'm… gay…because that'll be a betrayal too. He's always thought I turned on him because I knew he liked guys. It'll make me a hypocrite."

"Well, you sort of *are* a hypocrite." She smiles at me. "It's understandable to some degree, considering your dad."

"And God," I say, "now that I'm staying at his house, sleeping in his room—"

"*That* he did not tell us!"

"On the floor!"

"Still!"

"Maybe I should make his secret admirer disappear."

She sighs, getting to her feet. "As much as I've been worried about this whole secret admirer thing, now that I know it's you and not some skeezy creeper, I would say *don't* have him disappear. That would break Michael's heart. I just don't know what the solution is. Go ahead and change out of those shorts. I'll have them hemmed by tomorrow."

So LIAM KNOWS about my feelings for Michael, and now so does Calista. Extreme amounts of scary! But I have every reason to trust her to keep *that* information to herself as well.

I'm able to finish up "Cover Girl"—and any demonstrating of steps the singers require I do *without* stepping into Michael's arms again. However, it's at the end of rehearsal that another piece of my karmic ass-kicking falls into place. Mrs. P. and Mr. Hardy call first me over to the piano, then Michael. With the two of us standing self-consciously together, we're told that the "If I Never Knew You" duet from *Pocahontas* will be sung in the Revue by him and me—to each other.

DONICK

WE DON'T TALK about the duet on the ride home—not even to Brent and Calista; we don't talk about it with his parents when they ask how rehearsal went. In fact, I'm so uncomfortable with the idea of having to sing this song together—a bittersweet love song about two people who have left an indelible print on each other's lives—I try and force it from my mind. It's not easy. I had listened to the track after Mrs. P. told me to start familiarizing myself with it, but I had assumed I would be singing it with one of the girls—it is, after all, a duet written for a man and a woman. It had *never* crossed my mind I might be singing with another male, let alone *Michael!* God sure has a sense of humor...

Though Mr. and Mrs. Penrose are friendly, and Georgia talks to me like she has no idea what went on between her brother and I all those years ago, I still feel like an outsider in their family setting. Even the way that Topher and Cady want to hang on me and show off their toys doesn't remove my awkwardness. Still, I make it through the dinner they held off on eating until Michael (and I) got back from school.

Mr. Penrose bought a single-chamber air-mattress before coming home—an action that makes me feel strangely emotional. Michael tells me to bring it upstairs and set up my bed. He even fetches the battery powered air-pump from the garage. His dad and the twins hover near the door as I unbox and inflate it. Michael sits on his bed half-watching and half-playing with his phone. (I feel a jolt pass through me when the green Razr in my front pocket vibrates against my hip—but where and how can I answer his text?) Then, once I've got the bed all arranged, I stand back, unsure of what I should do now. *Now* is when I feel how unwelcome my presence must be—in these day-to-day life moments. My instinct is to find some corner of the house where I can focus on my school-work and not be in anyone's way.

Topher and Cady want to show me their rooms first, and all of their half-broken possessions, and how they can jump on their big-kid beds, and the extremely noisy karaoke machine they got from Santa Claus, and the pictures they drew in school, which are held to their walls by what seems to be almost an entire roll of Scotch tape.

"They've recently discovered scissors," Michael says from Topher's doorway. I hadn't known he was there. I was nudging tiny shards of paper flaking the floor like snowfall with one toe of my sock. I turn to look at him. "Those blunt kiddie things," he adds. "They cut up so much paper my mom doesn't bother vacuuming in either of their rooms as often as she'd like. They don't even really make anything. Just messes."

Topher and Cady seem to have forgotten either of us are here. They've grown distracted with little *PAW Patrol* figures they use as something like horses for tiny *PJ Masks* characters with rubbed off face-paint.

Michael says, "I'm going to be doing homework for a while."

"I have homework too."

Already awkward…then just more awkward with the second or two of silence that follows this.

"Anyway, that's what I'll be doing." He turns to leave and I follow him back to his room.

"Will anyone care if I use the dining-room table?" I ask, reaching for my backpack.

He's lowering himself into his desk-chair, but looks at me, a little surprised. "Oh. No, no one'll be there. But you can work in here. If you want. You don't have to leave."

I smile a false, tight smile and shake my head. "I don't want to be in your way."

He looks like he'll say something, then closes his mouth and shrugs his shoulders, turning to the desktop where's he piled his Government textbook and a copy of *Pride and Prejudice*. "All right," he says.

I carry my stuff downstairs and into the dining-room, settling into a chair and unloading my books. I actually don't have much homework to do, but I need to concentrate, because I have something more important to focus on.

First things first, I pull out the Razr and read Michael's text.

Michael: No need to tell you about how weird MY day has been! How was yours?

Me: Sorry it took so long 2 respond. Ive got a mountain of reading 2 do 4 English. Way behind. So, the old not-friend complicating ur life that badly, huh?

Michael: Not really. I just don't understand him, even when he's sleeping in my bedroom not three feet away.

Me: Whats not 2 understand?

Michael: EVERYTHING! He comes here with a story I don't entirely buy, saying he had nowhere else to go, yet he seems to want to make things as awkward as he can. Drives me nuts.

Me: Whats he doing now?

Michael: Homework or something.

Me: Whats awkward about that?

Michael: I said he could do his homework in my bedroom with me, but he insisted on using another room.

I frown. *Not entirely true, Michael,* I think.

Me: Whats the big deal? Maybe ur awesomeness will b 2 distracting! Haha!

Michael: Yeah, right. He just seems to be avoiding me. Which makes no sense since he's in my house and sleeping in my bedroom.

"Oh, Donick! I didn't know you were in here!"

I jump a little and drop the phone into my lap, glancing up with an expression I hope isn't guilty. Mrs. Penrose stands in the doorway to the kitchen. I feel a surge of affection for her, discovering suddenly I used to love Michael's family like they were my own. I feel more than ever what an idiot I was, throwing Michael away.

"I had some work to do and didn't want to be in the way," I say. "Don't want to overstay my welcome."

"Not possible." She sits across from me. "Did you hear

from your dad today?"

"No."

"Did you try reaching out to him?"

I shake my head. *That's* a terrifying thought.

"You should at least let him know where you are. So he doesn't worry."

I stare at my pencil. "He won't care."

"I know it seems like that, but you'd be surprised. Maybe think about calling him tomorrow. I know how I would feel if Michael were out of the house and I didn't know where he was."

"That's the difference though," I can't help saying. "You're different parents compared to my dad."

"Just think about it, okay?"

I nod. She stands and starts to walk out of the room, then pauses.

"Michael is glad you're here, Donick."

I blink at her. "How can you tell?"

"A parent, a *mother*, just knows. You two were very close once. It's good you two can spend time together. The bonds of friendship don't just vanish completely."

"I don't know about that."

Her smile is indulgent. "Well, you're *here*, aren't you?"

Then she walks away.

I lay the Razr back on the table and stare at it for half a minute. *Please let her be right*, I think. I want Michael in my life more than anything. He'll *never* be a boyfriend, no matter how much I may have feelings for him—because how could he *ever* think of me that way after all I've done. But it doesn't matter. I want him in my life in *some* way.

Still, maybe Calista had a point. This secret admirer

thing… Maybe I'm digging myself into a hole that will lose me even Michael's friendship. But would he really be so torn up if I just made his secret admirer go away? I rub at my eyes. Every way I turn I'm acting selfishly. Even when trying to do something nice for Michael, I'm potentially hurting him too.

I text him with, *Ive said it b4, I know, but I'll say it again: have patience w/ ur old not-friend. He might not know quite how 2 b ur friend, not if he feels guilty about hurting u. But he came to u out of all the ppl in the world when he had a crisis. He obviously cares about u after what happened the Friday b4 break. Maybe hes hoping u still care about him 2. The bonds of friendship dont just vanish completely.*

He didn't respond for a long while after that. When he did it was only to say goodnight. I had gone to find Michael's parents in the meantime. They had said if I needed anything to let them know. And I needed fifteen sheets of printer-paper, a Sharpie, and a roll of tape.

MICHAEL

"I am hiding,
But he's out there
Just ignoring all our history.
Memories get erased
And I'll get replaced..."

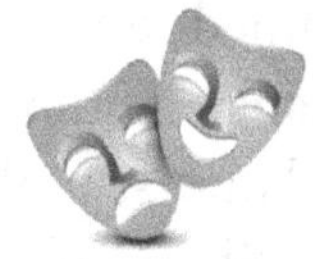

IN MY GROUP text message thread with Brent and Calista, I all but begged them to come over Friday after school, hoping they would hang for the night. Anything to avoid sitting at home with Nick for company on a Friday evening. What would we talk about? What would we do? I knew he wasn't hanging out with his asshat friends anymore, so I couldn't rely on him going out. Thankfully, both my Muskequeers were down to hang. ("LET'S GO TO IN 'N' OUT FOR DINNER, THEN WATCH A MOVIE!" Brent wrote in all caps. It felt like he was screaming at me.) I breathed a sigh of relief.

Friday's rehearsal everyone was again spread all over the place. The tappers were in the dance-studio working on "Always Look On the Bright Side of Life". Yay for a break from Nick; he seemed to be everywhere all of a sudden. I spent the first half of rehearsal going over "Popular" with

Chalice and Mrs. P., adding in Brent and Calista (the only number Brent would do, just for the sake of being The Three Muskequeers one last time). As much as I had had misgivings about being the soloist for that song, I had to admit the way we had arranged it, combined with Muskequeer-goofiness, breathed unexpected life into a tired number. I could hear the laughter of cast-members watching from the house. But it wasn't hard to have a successful number—not when I shared the stage with my two besties. Our chemistry could be seen in the dark.

The weirdness resumed once rehearsal ended. We made our way to the dance-studio to collect Nick before going to the car. The dancers, pink-faced and sweating, were just leaving, some still in their tap shoes. The humid air trapped inside drifted out at us, smelling…well, like a bunch of sweating teenagers.

Nick looked a little flustered, his shirt patterned with sweat so it clung to his skin. Brent's expression was appreciative. I wanted to scowl.

"I have something I need to take care of," Nick said. "I'll be a little while. Go on without me. I don't wanna make you wait."

"No big." Calista shrugged. "What's going on?"

"Nothing." His reply came quick. "Just something I need to do."

"It's almost dark," I said. "My house is too far to walk to."

"I don't mind. Seriously."

"We're swinging by In 'N' Out on the way," Brent piped in. "Muskequeer dinner-party!"

"It's fine. Really." Nick looked uncomfortable—at least I thought so. Probably at having been grouped in as a

Muskequeer. He added, "Eat something animal-style for me."

Calista and Brent tried to convince him again, but he went on refusing. I could do nothing more than stare at him, wondering what he had to take care of, and why he was keeping it a secret. He wasn't making a case for being particularly trustworthy.

We watched him walk toward his locker, dance shoes hanging from his fingers. The silver taps on the soles gleamed in the light of the setting sun. Brent made a muttered comment about his calves. Calista groaned and began walking to the car. As for me, I wanted to kick myself—I had already been staring at them with decided appreciation before Brent spoke up. Stupid stupid stupid!

Sitting in the drive-thru at In 'N' Out Burger, I grudgingly added a cheeseburger and animal-style fries to our order. "We can't just sit there eating and have nothing for him when he gets back."

Brent ignored me, no doubt texting some rando from the backseat. Calista, however, grinned, saying, "That's the spirit!"

"Knock it off," I told her, and though we lapsed into silence, the only sound coming from Florence + the Machine in the car's speakers, I saw her shooting me a look now and then. "What?" I barked.

"Nothing." She sounded like she might be suppressing giggles. "You're being nice to him. Not just anyone will take a kneecap to the balls for you."

"Oh shut up."

Her grin returned and I couldn't understand why.

The line at In 'N' Out was so long—as usual—it took us almost forty-five minutes to get through the drive-thru.

By the time we got back to my house, Nick had taken care of…whatever he had to take care of, and beaten us home by ten minutes. He looked startled when we set his food out for him. But he sat at the table with us and we started eating. We discussed rehearsal, and Calista and Brent asked Nick about his solo. All four of us marveled that the Revue was going to open the first of its two weekend run in exactly two weeks.

"Yowza," Calista muttered. "Two weeks from, like, right now. I have so much work to finish."

Brent said, "Think Gil will come?"

I felt uncomfortable. I darted my eyes at Nick. He only watched us talking. I wasn't in the mood to talk about Gil Hamilton and wished for an easy way to skate around the subject.

"To see the Revue?" Calista snorted. "I hope not. He's an ass."

Nick spoke up at last. "Why is Gil an ass? I thought—"

"He and Michael were—and forgive the air-quotes— hanging out?" cut in Brent. "Stress on the *were*."

Nick met my eyes. "You guys were going to hang after school. *That* day, I mean."

Brent spoke up again. "Well, Gil screwed up. I wouldn't mind getting my hands on him."

"I bet you wouldn't," Calista said.

"You know what I mean."

Nick suddenly looked weird. I almost stared as he glanced around the table, then studied his fries, picking at the cheese and onions.

My neck got warm. It was one thing for Nick to know about my sexuality, and another for it to be right in his face. He would move his air-mattress into the living-room tonight for sure.

"It wasn't working out," I muttered. "End of story."

Again Nick studied my expression. I thought, *Put the big scary homos in cages and all the douchey mouth-breathers will wear looks like that when they come to gawk at the freaks.*

Yet he surprised me when he said, "I'm sorry. That's too bad."

I looked away. "Wasn't that interested."

"What about you, Nick?" Calista put in. "Even I can acknowledge you're a hottie. Why no girlfriend?"

Nick blinked at her, then studied what was left of his food. "I've had a few." He made a face. "But they were stupid. Couldn't stand them any more than I could stand my friends."

"They weren't what you were looking for, huh?"

"Nope."

"Don't think you'll find it in high school?"

"I'm positive not." Nick paused. "What about you, Calista? Why no girlfriend for *you?*"

Now *this* was interesting—Nick Walsh asking Calista about being a lesbian?

She sniffed. "I'm saving myself for college experimentation. I can nab all the hot bitches who are looking for the inexperienced friend to try stuff with."

Brent giggled. "What kind of stuff?"

She flicked a fry at his chin.

"Besides," she added, "who the hell would I date? We've got more gay boys than gay girls running around campus. I'm sort of a lone-wolf by necessity."

"Makes prom look bleak, doesn't it?" said Brent. "It's soon. Two weeks after we close the show."

When Calista then asked Nick if he was going, he looked as though he had been thinking of something else. "Prom? Oh. No."

"Why not?"

"I never bought tickets."

Brent said, "They're sold out now anyway. Bummer."

Nick shrugged. "I was kinda distracted by other things for the last year. Even if I had bought tickets, I don't know who I would go with." He glanced at each of us. "You guys are going, yeah?"

Calista made a face. "Not my scene."

I narrowed my eyes at her. "Oh, she's going. She's gonna be *my* date. She can't use the no-tickets excuse because I've got 'em and we're going together. I'm not going to my senior prom without my best friend."

"Yeah, we'll see about that." She smirked.

"If she doesn't want to go," Nick said, "why not go with Brent? Or is the school not okay with that?"

Brent said, "Kliewer High is totally okay with same sex couples. But I'm not going with Michael. I *have* tickets and I'm going to use them."

"Have you decided who you're gonna ask?" Calista said.

"I'm thinking Liam."

Nick's brows went up. "Liam? Really?"

"Yeah. He can only go if a senior invites him, so I'm thinking I will. I think we would have fun. I'm so happy I got to know him this year. He's completely cute and I don't find him sexual at all."

"You'd certainly be little and twinkish and fab together," Calista snorted.

I shot her a look. "See? Brent's going. I've got tickets,

and I need a date. *You're* going with me. The end."

Calista just made another face and started playing with her phone.

"Still sad though," Brent sighed out. "No one goes with an *actual* date. We might as well be going with our siblings or something."

"We're all alone and pathetic." I shrugged. "No one graduates with a significant other. Big deal."

"I know I'm okay with it." Brent grinned. "I've got good friends and I'm not alone on a Friday night. I'm more than happy being here with you guys."

"I second that," said Calista, looking up and knocking her shoulder against Brent's. "Though this one would ditch us in a heartbeat if the random hot stranger he's looking for online were to hit him up."

He scowled. "Not true! Mostly. I just like having someone to make out with."

I said, "Well, I third the sentiment. Not the making out part. Mostly. I'm glad to spend my Friday night with you guys too."

I wondered if that were entirely true, and because I couldn't bring myself to look at Nick, I didn't look at Brent or Calista either. I just knew I was glad I didn't have to spend the evening alone with him.

Then Nick put in, "I know I'm glad. It's good not to be alone."

A S USUAL, WHEN it came to viewing material, I wanted to watch either anime or a horror movie. We crowded into my bedroom, Calista, Brent, and Nick sprawling on the floor with a bag of Doritos waiting to be ripped into and cans of soda near to hand. I fiddled with the remote, making suggestions, and heard them all get vetoed (I couldn't always insist like that day I had gotten them to try *Yuri!!! on Ice*). I *really* wanted something scary though, yet the only one who was down was Nick. The look in his eyes reminded me so strongly of the half-excited, half-nervous light that used to come into them when we were in elementary school, sneaking to watch stuff like *Friday the 13th* and *Halloween*, that I felt unsettled for a second. Having him here, hanging out with my friends, was the bizarrest thing. But somehow, it also wasn't.

At last Calista said, "Just put on *Sucker Punch*! It's anime-like, has horror elements, and, you know, pretty blondes in short skirts."

Brent scoffed. "Well, half the room will appreciate that part."

I watched Nick and Calista exchange a look.

In the end we all agreed against *Sucker Punch* in favor of watching *Labyrinth*, since we had all been hearing that David Bowie song so much in rehearsals.

I lay on my stomach on the bed, watching, but also zoning out. I was thinking about Secret Admirer. I had been texting him at lunch, telling him I would have friends over and couldn't really talk tonight, but I wanted to. I wanted that uncomplicated friendship which, by its very nature, compartmentalized itself away from all the drama in my life. I glanced at the three people leaning against the foot of the bed—my two best friends…and a spare—telling myself it should be *him*, Secret Admirer, here, hanging out. Not Nick.

As much as I liked *Labyrinth*, I detested that lame-ass

scene with those red puppets and their swappable heads. As soon as the percussion signaling their song began, I said, "That's my cue to hit the can," and rolled off the bed.

I all but ran into Mom in the hall. She still wore her scrubs, and looked tired.

"Just getting home?" I asked.

"Yeah," she sighed out. "Very long day."

I grinned. "You smell like walrus. Did you give a walrus a colonoscopy today?"

She flicked the end of my nose. "Funny man. You don't know how near to the truth that is. Everyone over?"

"Yup."

"Nick in there?"

"Yes," I said with a groan. "You don't have to sound like you're checking to make sure I didn't leave him out."

"I know you better than that. I need to talk to him is all."

"Well, I gotta pee."

I moved toward the bathroom, hearing her say, "Why, if it isn't my surrogate children!" as she entered my room, followed by Muskequeer chatter. I grinned and shut the bathroom door.

A minute later, I was back in the hall. I paused at the door to my room. Brent and Calista glanced at me. There was no Nick. I said, "I'll be back in a sec," then padded down the stairs. Whatever Mom wanted to talk to Nick about had me curious. He was sleeping in my room—I deserved to be involved in a discussion about him living in my house. Still, something made me pause outside the kitchen. I could hear voices in the living-room, and for once, wherever the twins were in the house, they were quiet.

"…still super angry, I'm sure." Nick's voice.

"I was surprised in all honesty," Mom said. "I haven't seen him in a lot of years, but he looks the same. And yes. Certainly angry."

"He wasn't mean to you, was he?"

"Oh no, nothing like that. He remembered me. It almost looked like he wasn't surprised to see me."

Mom had gone to Nick's house to see his dad?

"I wanted him to know where you were," she went on. "I didn't think you'd tell him yourself. You're angry. He's angry."

"I'm sure he didn't care. I'm surprised he didn't throw *you* out too."

"Actually, and you may not be ready to hear this, he looked a little relieved knowing where you are. But he *is* mad. And not just mad. He's feeling other things too. Considering."

A space of silence fell. I wondered for a second if I had made some noise and given myself away.

At last, Nick mumbled, "Did…did he…tell you about…"

"Yes. He told me."

"Oh."

Another silence. Then, making my heart skip a beat, Mom asked, "Michael doesn't know?"

Nick's reply was vehement. "No!"

"Anyone else but your dad?"

"Not really."

"Well, it stays with me. Just know, you have people in your corner. Okay? I only went to let him know we had you, so he wouldn't worry."

"He doesn't care."

"He's your dad. He's a hard-ass, even I'll admit that, but he *does* care. He was relieved to know you were all right.

That was plain."

Nick made a scoffing noise. "I can't ever go back. He won't want me there."

"Things are strained, sure. Maybe you two just need a break from each other. Even parents get sick of their kids sometimes. Believe me, I know."

"This is different."

"Change is always difficult to handle. Imagine Brent's poor grandmother. Every other day she has to get used to a new color streaked into his hair. But she does get used to it. Parents just need a little time to get accustomed to when their children change things up."

I wasn't breathing, straining to hear as much as I could. There was more to Nick getting kicked out than simply doing the Revue, just as I suspected. Was it not being able to play football anymore? Was it his dancing? Maybe even that he was choreographing that number? Nick's dad was definitely the type who would freak at discovering his son was a choreographer. Then again, maybe it had something to do with what his dad witnessed—Nick and I dancing together—that unguarded moment when we were laughing, almost embracing, even accidentally.

And what was I not supposed to know? What was *up* with Nick?

"My dad won't accept *this*," I heard him say.

"He might take a little longer, but he'll get there, I think." Mom's tone brightened. "For now, you're here. Concentrate on school and rehearsals. We'll keep you as long as you need to stay. And!" Her tone grew very pointed. "I know I don't need to say it but, well, we trust Michael, and we trust you. Do I need to say more?"

"No!"

What was *that* about? Drugs? Was Nick using something and his dad found out? God, I understood Nick even less now. And I had trapped myself. How could I ask Mom about this conversation when I wasn't supposed to have heard it?

The sound of movement came to me, and Mom saying, "Gimme a hug, mister. Then go back to your movie. Remember, you've got support."

I crept back to the stairs, taking them two at a time as I held the air in my chest, trying to move with cat-stealth. I was back in my room, settled on the bed and staring at the television screen as though I had been there all along when Nick returned. He carried a carton of rocky-road ice cream and a handful of spoons.

"I've been told we have to eat this or else."

"Ooh! Give it here!" Brent held out wiggling fingers.

We finished the movie passing the ice cream around, all while I played that conversation again and again in my head. Whatever Nick and Mom had been talking about, not only could I not ask *her* about it, I also felt hinky about mentioning it to Brent and Calista. Not even Secret Admirer. Nick didn't want me, or anyone, to know about something—something bad enough to get him kicked out of his house. Regardless of how confusing my thoughts were concerning him, I wasn't some gossip. At least not about something important like this.

But damn, my curiosity was killing me!

MICHAEL

A SLOW BURN OF talk rippled through school on Monday, beginning with the first bell and crescendoing by lunchtime.

All across campus, lockers were to be found with sheets of paper taped to them. Each sheet had been scrawled with black marker. It reminded me strongly of that time when someone had painted nasty messages on a bunch of locker doors just before back-to-school night. *These* were no offensive messages though; this time the messages were positive and uplifting.

YOUR SMILE IS LIKE LIGHT!!

BELIEVE IN YOURSELF AND MAKE MIRACLES!!

YOU ARE STRONG AND FEARLESS AND BEAUTIFUL!!

BE CONFIDENT AND REMEMBER YOU ARE AMAZING!!

YOU ARE KIND, AND SMART, AND COURAGEOUS!!

BE PROUD TO BE YOU!!

Sitting in the drama-room at lunch, we were all buzzing, knowing this wasn't some spirit-week gimmick.

I said, "Now we know Nick was one of the assmunches who wrote that back-to-school night crap."

"I guess we also know what he had to do on Friday after rehearsal," Brent added.

"It was a douchey thing to do back then," Calista said, "but honestly…having read a couple of those messages, and seeing the faces of some of the students who were bullied before…well, I can't help but think he's sorta awesome now. Kind of an amazing thing he did."

Nick had surprised me on Saturday morning by going off to his dance-studio to teach ballet and jazz to little kids—I had had no idea he instructed too. I smiled at imagining him teaching Topher and Cady to dance. They would probably get a kick out of it—they adored him already, running through the house chanting his name as soon as he came back. I thought of the sound of his breathing from beside my bed, almost a light snore as he slept. He tried so hard to keep out of my way, to not make waves in such close quarters. Somehow, I wasn't as inconvenienced as I thought I would be.

"Yeah," I murmured, half to myself. "He's trying… and it's working." I found there wasn't much of my usual grudging tone behind these words.

THERE WERE NOW less than two weeks before the opening of the Senior Revue. Rehearsals began running later and required more focus from everyone. Singers and dancers were all over the place; when we weren't running numbers, we were helping with sets, props, costumes. Bits of glitter and sequins and feathers were everywhere from decorating the "Vogue" masks. When the glue had dried and the dancers had claimed them, all the singers sat in the house and grinned at the spectacle. The number looked amazing!

Thursday and Friday had specifically been allotted for our *sitzprobe*.

Wednesday night, Nick asked me what a *sitzprobe* was. His expression amused me, as though he thought he must be the biggest moron for not knowing.

"It's the first time singers and orchestra work together. We'll run the numbers with the band so we can get the right tempos for choreography and quick-changes and stuff. The rehearsals will go pretty late, but we usually get fed. The week before opening is called HellWeek for a reason. That pretty much starts tomorrow."

For a lot of us, the two days of the *sitzprobe* were the first time we would be seeing each other's numbers. It was a good gauge for what sort of reaction we would get from the audience. I hadn't seen Calista perform her big number yet— "Diamonds are a Girl's Best Friend"—and kept irritating her with my professions of how much I wanted to see her acting feminine and wearing something skimpy—though since she had designed her own costume, that could mean skimpy *for her*. I had also seen nothing of Nick's solo. I had a sort of scared anticipation for Friday when we would be running the second act where "I Can't Do it Alone" was placed. I think a lot of people were curious about his number; he would be performing the only real dance solo in the show.

Then there was Nick's duet with me. We had fudged through it once with Mr. Hardy, but I told him Nick and I would have no problem learning it on our own with my dad's help. Nick had the male part of the song because it was a little more straight forward. The female part was mine because it was a bit more technically difficult. Dad sat at the piano and every day Nick and I sang through it, neither one of us particularly comfortable. I mean, come on! It was a love song! One that seemed to strike very near to the sort of bitterness our friendship had been invested with for so many years. Yet I also felt a little swept up in the song too. Nick sang it well. Dad and I gave him some coaching, and when he and I harmonized together, Mom would poke in her head and say, "You boys are giving me chills!" Still, Nick and I avoided each other's eyes when we sang it, and if I was uncomfortable, Nick had moments when he looked in positive agony. I would think: *There's that inner homophobe again, rearing its face. All because he has to sing a love song with another guy. Stupid!*

The *sitzprobe* ended up being very productive. There were a lot of great musicians at Kliewer High and the orchestra sounded great. We all sat in the house when we could, watching numbers, applauding and cheering.

Seeing Calista perform "Diamonds" was a trip! Her costume *was* pretty skimpy, in the vein of the rest of the masquerade section of the show. She surprised me with what good shape she was in, usually hiding herself in baggy, frumpy clothes. But there, playing with makeup and hair, singing her heart out, she blew me away. The teachers had found ways to push us all out of our comfort zones—Calista was perfect proof of that.

After running through "Cover Girl" and then its followup number, "Girl for All Seasons", I all but started shaking when Nick's number began. Standing in the wings where I had exited, Calista pausing beside me, I could see Nick's nervousness, hear the quaver in his voice. He was singing alone in front of everyone for the first time, hearing his accompaniment in full orchestra rather than just piano, his singing amplified by the snake of a microphone taped to his cheek. Still, he didn't miss a beat. When he started dancing, interjecting each combination of steps with the "she'd go" (now changed to *he*), then the "I'd go", my mouth wouldn't stay closed. It was one thing to see him dance in a group, but watching him perform alone (executing choreography that appeared to make him float, or contorting his limbs in ways I didn't think were possible from someone with his build) made me feel like I couldn't breathe. He darted and tumbled all over the stage and apron, using the stairs and platforms of the set. Seeing him in his costume, I had a moment when I didn't recognize him.

"Holy shit!"

Brent appeared, smelling like sawdust, his tee spotted with dried paint. His eyes were huge, watching Nick execute a series of spins for the last "perfect unison" part of the song.

"Look at how fast he spots his head! He's, like, doing a million forties!"

Calista smacked Brent's shoulder. "Forties? Their called *fouettés*, you chew-toy!"

He grinned at her. "Thank you for putting him in those

shorts, bitch."

I was thankful the wings were dim so my Muskequeers couldn't see my reddened cheeks. Yes, Nick's legs were something to see, and once again my appreciation of them unsettled me.

When he finished, holding his final pose with the last accent of the orchestra, screams and cheers echoed in the house. Even Brent nearly deafened us with sudden hooting and hollering. Nick, I knew, would steal the show every performance. A combination of relief and disappointment settled on me when he exited the stage into the opposite wings. After watching that, I wasn't sure what to say.

Truthfully, I wasn't *ever* sure from one minute to the next what to say to him. He lived in my house, brushed his teeth in my bathroom, slept next to my bed. Yet it was impossible to keep him compartmentalized in my brain in the same way I had for so many years. Not only had too much happened recently, but our lives were being lived almost on top of each other's.

One evening he started to leave the bedroom to do his homework, and I finally said, almost angrily, "Would you quit going into hiding like that? It's okay. You can stay in here. Use the desk, sit on my bed, sit on *your* bed, or the floor…just *chill*. You don't have to leave." It was almost as though he felt he *couldn't* leave after that.

So, mostly in silence we would hang in my room. Truthfully, there wasn't often stuff for either of us to do. A lot of our classes seemed to be being taught with a teacher's version of senioritis and homework was becoming slim. True, Nick was busier than me with his English 11 assignments, but still…

For the first time in a long time, I had someone to watch scary movies with; someone who looked as excited to watch them as me. I would make a suggestion (more like an I'm-putting-this-on-watch-with-me-if-you-want sort of thing) and then there we would be, him sitting in the desk-chair, or stretched belly-down on the air-mattress, me lying on the floor, or reclining on my bed, watching a movie together. Not much talking to each other, no, but it was good knowing he enjoyed himself as much as I did. It didn't stop at horror movies. I would put on some anime and he would watch with me. I would feel like a rerun of *Buffy* and he would suggest which episode to watch (leaving me marveling that, yes, he *had* gone on watching the shows we used to watch together). All around, it just seemed to get more and more surreal.

I thought I began to notice Georgie getting a little moony over him. She looked like some sort of Ginny Weasley when they were in the same room together and began to be afraid to talk. Cady and Topher started to haunt my bedroom more often than usual, wanting to hang on him and get him to play with them, and wonder of wonders, he *would!* I worried they might hurt him—his shoulder *was* screwed up—but he seemed to enjoy being a kind of surrogate big brother. It must have had something to do with him being an only child. Mom and Dad enjoyed having him around too, and in that respect, at least, it was as though Nick Walsh was still my friend Donny, never having gone away. I didn't know what to make of any of it.

After the first couple of days, it was impossible to crawl into bed, shut out the lights, then lay there in silence. Almost tentatively, we began to talk, not having to look at one another, the room bathed in the faint glow of the twinkle-lights.

At first it was easy stuff: the Revue, rehearsals, Brent and Calista (he was curious to know when and where I had befriended them).

Then the less easy stuff: I was curious about *his* friends and wanted to know why they had tricked him with that knee in the groin. I even wanted to know about his girlfriends, because with all the pointed ignoring of each other he and I had done these last six years, I never noticed him dating anyone. I felt taken aback when, after telling me about his girlfriends, he actually wanted to know about my boyfriends; further heightening the surreality, I found myself laying in the almost dark telling him about Dillon and Joel.

Then there was the hard stuff. He asked me about college, wanting me to talk about my clean rejection sweep (I still hadn't said anything about the New York rejections to Mom and Dad). I brought up the locker graffiti. I asked more about what he had meant when he said he was "trying". Though he started and stopped a lot, he told me all the ways he was attempting to make things right with the people he had wronged. I thought about the kids he had apologized to and done nice things for, and felt strange. It must be because I was finding a sort of respect for him, which I never anticipated *ever* feeling in a hundred million years. We talked about his dad (his voice wobbled a little and I hoped he wouldn't cry again), but he left things fairly vague about his "Pop". I couldn't blame him. I wouldn't want to talk about it either. But there was something there, I knew, that had to do with whatever my mom had learned when she visited Nick's house, something he wasn't telling me. As much as I wanted to ask, I held my tongue and tried not to dwell on it.

One thing we *did not* talk about, and that was our past. Whether I was averse to bringing it up, or he was, we never touched on our old friendship and how it fell apart. It seemed like the only hint we would ever have was our interrupted conversation the day of the sack-tap. I supposed Nick's guilt over me would be a long time in disappearing. Sometimes I would catch him looking at me and would feel the scar at my eyebrow as though it were a pimple the size of Mount Fuji.

I also never mentioned Secret Admirer. His notes hung above the desk, and sometimes Nick would gaze at them, and I wondered if he thought they might be leftovers from my all but meaningless relationships with Joel and Dillon. Yet he never asked.

I still texted Secret Admirer though—at school mostly, especially at lunchtime—and occasionally at night, but it was difficult. I was so busy and out so late at rehearsals, I wasn't always available to text him. In fact, he seemed to have taken a step back himself, which lent more credence to my theory that he was *in* the Revue with me. And if not, maybe he just didn't want me to feel pressured as I headed into the patience-trying stretch of HellWeek. But also, I didn't want to spend every evening with my face in my phone when Nick was around. I felt like it would be rude to begin with, but also, I was a little afraid he would want to know who I was talking to. Sharing stuff about Secret Admirer with Calista and Brent was one thing, but I felt far too possessive and jealous to think of sharing anything about him with someone like Nick.

I was dying to ask Secret Admirer if he would come see the show, but held back. I feared he might tell me he *was* in it (which would make his presence very real), or if he wasn't, he might say he wouldn't come out of fear of giving himself away. Half a dozen times I typed the question, and every time I deleted it.

Still…I was becoming comfortable around Nick. He didn't feel out of place in my house after awhile. Soon, talking with him didn't feel strained and awkward. He seemed to carve out his own space in the morning car ride to school with Brent and Calista, more so than Dillon or Joel ever had, or Liam, or anyone who had palled around with us. Though he minded his own business during the school day, he was often with us at rehearsal. I almost could have tricked myself into thinking he *was* my old friend Donny…except there was a wall—some impenetrable thing I couldn't name, couldn't push beyond, but which I always sensed there.

TECH WEEKS ARE known by their other name for a reason. The days leading to opening night were very long and tedious. We couldn't run numbers anymore because we wouldn't have the band again until dress rehearsal. The tech students were in and out of the booth at the back of the theatre while Mrs. P. sat inside working with the lighting designer. Various spots of illumination came and went all over the stage as the cast slowly walked through all the show's numbers. Calista had also set up racks of costumes and a continuous flow of people changed from one thing into another.

However, HellWeek also had its charms. A great deal of cast bonding happened because everyone felt like they were in a war-zone together. We talked (sometimes too loudly, silenced by increasingly grumpy teachers) or tried to cram in schoolwork. Sometimes we played games. But all in all, things went smoothly.

Nervous energy ran through everyone. I thrived on it. I loved the bustle; the jittery feeling in my limbs; the quiet moment sitting in the dressing-room at the makeup counter, working on my face in the mirror; waiting at the tech-booth to collect my body-mic, then securing it to my cheek, that damned mic-tape leaving a residue that seemed to take weeks to come off; slipping into my first costume of the show; focusing my mind on what it would feel like to step out onto the stage for the first time… It was all such a heady, almost religious experience for me—it was difficult not to think about the college rejection letters sitting in my desk-drawer. What was I going to do now?

Brent seemed to be the only one *not* feeling this sort of manic energy. He had done his job of completing the set and now he could hang out backstage, big clunky headset sitting over his hair as he listened to comments from Mrs. P. or the techies working all over the place. With his job now solely that of stage manager, he didn't have much to do until showtime (aside from his one number with Calista and me).

Then there was Nick. He sat across the dressing-room looking completely bewildered the day of dress rehearsal. I watched him in the mirror. I couldn't tell if it was nervousness or if he was scared. What would he be like tomorrow when the theatre filled with an actual audience? Noise surrounded us—someone's iPod playing the soundtrack to *Dear Evan Hansen*—the guys in the room laughing and joking.

I watched Nick pick idly through the small boxes of makeup supplies Mrs. P. kept the dressing-rooms stocked with. He glanced my way, meeting my gaze in the glass.

He didn't look away, only tried to smile. That slightly petrified look in his eye seemed to dim the last six years and I could see Donny in there—a hesitating little boy.

"What's the matter?" I asked.

His smile went crooked. He turned his gaze back to the makeup box. "I don't know what to do with this stuff."

I brought over the black bag I kept my own stage-makeup in. "I don't use the dressing-room makeup," I said. "Who knows how many faces it's touched. I have my own. You can use it. I'll help you. I won't make you look like a freak, don't worry."

His expression became a little strange, but he murmured, "I trust you. Thanks."

I stood beside his chair, tilting his face upward, using my fingers to brush strands of hair away from his forehead. I explained what I was doing as I went, trying to teach him something so he could do it himself the rest of the run. It was strange, examining his face this closely. He needed to shave, and a couple of almost unnoticeable pimples spotted his temples. I also had to marvel at how good-looking he was, his eyes the color of chocolate, his sort of perfect lips. I had touched them with my own once, in another life. Suddenly I blushed so badly I felt grateful I had told him to keep his eyes closed while I darkened his eyelids.

I stood behind him once I finished and he turned to face the mirror, nodding his chin this way and that to examine himself.

"It's a little thick," I said, "but it needs to be. You can't see that from the audience."

He smiled. "Here I was expecting I'd look like something from *The Rocky Horror Picture Show*."

I chuckled. "We could do that, though I think Mrs. P. might frown on it. But hey! *You* might end up liking it," I teased. He gave me a startled look, then lowered his eyes. I had to fight the urge to apologize. It was becoming all too easy anymore for me to forget who I talked to.

Suddenly Liam burst into the dressing-room looking buoyant. He had barely opened his mouth, exclaiming, "Dress rehearsal, y'all! Are we ready for this?" when Brent followed, almost on Liam's heels. He had lowered his headset so it hung around his neck like a big chunky necklace. He eyes were wide, dark blue dyed streak feathering his forehead as though he had been running.

"Did I just see," he cried, looking incredulously as Liam, "what I thought I saw?"

Liam's bright expression morphed into alarm. "What?"

"In the parking-lot," Brent said.

Liam's ears were suddenly tipped with red.

Beside me, Nick shifted in his chair. He started to say, "Brent, don't—" but Brent barreled over him.

"Did I just see you making out with Gil Hamilton?"

The rest of the dressing-room had fallen silent but for "Only Us" playing from the iPod. Liam glanced around, looking caught out. When I saw his expression, Brent's question at last sank in.

Nick stirred again. "Brent, come on. Don't do that."

Liam shook his head. "It's all right." He looked guilty now. Guilty, and somehow relieved. "Yeah. I was."

Brent didn't look angry exactly, but he glanced my way to check my expression. "Is this a new thing?" he asked Liam.

Nick said, "Li, you don't have to talk about it. Brent, cool it."

Again Liam shook his head. "No, I'm glad it's out there. I'm tired of having to hide it."

Brent's eyes went wider than before. "How long has this been going on?"

"Since Michael's party…"

I hadn't given much though to Gil in the last couple of weeks. After our date he had pretty much started ignoring me. There was nothing there—there hadn't been even when we went on our date, I had come to realize. But somehow it still made me feel crappy. Even that night, on our date, Gil and Liam had already been…

"Holy shit," Brent breathed out. "That long?" He checked my face again. Liam, however, didn't look at me in any special way. I thought: *He never knew Gil and I went out.* How that was possible with the times I had talked about him with my Muskequeers at lunch or at rehearsal, I couldn't guess. But I could see that that was exactly the case. Which made me pity Liam all the more for buying into Gil's crap.

I met Brent's eye and gave my head a little shake. Liam didn't deserve any kind of interrogation. It wasn't his fault Gil was trash. Nick must have seen the look I gave Brent because he said, "Brent, it's okay."

Brent turned to him. "Did *you* know?"

But Liam spoke. "Yeah, Nick found out. He promised he wouldn't tell."

I felt a further jolt somewhere in my midsection. I pasted a smile on my face though, and crossed to Liam, patting his shoulder.

"Good for you," I said. "Gil's a good-looking guy. Brent just likes to be in the middle of drama. He *does* need to cool it. I hope Gil will be more open about it. You shouldn't be anyone's secret, Li. You deserve better than that."

I sank into my chair and started fiddling with my character shoes, changing out my socks. Around us the other guys in the dressing-room were losing interest, turning back to their own preparations. Nick stood up and started easing Brent toward the door.

"See? It's no big deal, man," he said. "Now stop bugging us so we can get ready. If you keep your headset around your neck like that, you won't hear if someone needs you. Doesn't the show sort of belong to *you* now? Go do your thing." He lifted the headset and plopped it over Brent's ears.

Brent left the room, darting worried glances at me. I concentrated on my shoes.

"He seemed pissed," Liam muttered to Nick. "He doesn't have a thing for Gil or something, does he?"

Nick put his arm around Liam and led him to the chair beside his own. "No. It's just Brent. Michael's right. He likes to be involved in everything. It's why we love him, remember? Plus it's, like, a gay-gossip-line. He wants to know the latest. Sorry the secret's out of the bag."

"No, I'm relieved. Maybe Gil won't want to be so secretive now. I hope he won't be mad."

"He isn't worth it if he is."

A second later, Nick was standing in front of me, holding out my makeup bag. I had left it on the counter beside his station.

In a low, very quiet voice, he murmured, "I'm sorry I didn't tell you. I thought you and Gil were becoming a thing or whatever…and I didn't know how you'd take it, coming from me. After I found out you weren't that into him, it was a relief. Still, I didn't want you to know."

I found myself unwilling to look at him, because, honestly, I felt humiliated. The last thing I wanted was to look pathetic in front of an old enemy. "Might have been better if I did," I muttered.

"I know. That kind of thing hurts, even if you weren't that into him. He's still a complete hemorrhoid. I didn't want to see you get hurt."

I sighed, not knowing what to say. Nick had hurt me enough on his own. Why care about someone else hurting me? He had hated me, actually scarred me, then reviled me for years, just for being gay. Yet he had protected Liam, keeping a secret for him, *supported him*. Regardless of what Nick said about sparing my feelings, *that* seemed to hurt worst of all.

MICHAEL

IF ONLY SECRET Admirer hadn't left me another note in my locker on Friday.

I found it after school, and when I saw it sitting there atop the textbooks, my breath caught. Once more, a red heart traced the front. Inside, in the usual black lettering, it said: HAPPY OPENING NIGHT, MICHAEL!! NOW EVERYONE CAN SEE HOW AMAZING YOU ARE!!

If only he hadn't left it! It was the deciding factor in my decision to text him and ask if he would come see the show. That, or if he was *in* the show. If I hadn't done that, everything wouldn't have fallen to pieces.

Though our call-time wasn't until six o'clock, it was a Muskequeer-habit on show days to just hang out, with maybe a coffee-run in the mix. It ended up working out all around because Mrs. Peebles and Chalice wanted to see Nick right after school to run through his number a couple of times. (Something about wanting to tweak the lighting so the spots would hit him at the appropriate moments.) We had left all our things backstage in the dressing-rooms; then, while Nick rehearsed, Brent, Calista, and I sat in the house. I showed them the new Secret Admirer note. Calista took it and studied it for a minute or two, though Brent busied himself with staring at Nick, in his shorts, on stage. Without a word she handed the note back. I studied it myself, trying to decide what to say in my text.

"I'm Starbucks bound," Calista muttered, getting to her feet. "You two coming?"

"I'll hang out," I said. "I have something I need to do."

Calista frowned, but Brent stood to go. With them gone and Nick busy running his number, I meandered backstage into the boys' dressing-room where it was quiet and I would be undisturbed.

I sat at my station and pulled out my phone. What to say?

Thank you for the note. It means a lot. I really hope you'll be at the show.

No. I deleted that and tried again.

Thanks for the note. Will I see you at the show this weekend?

No.

Thank you for the note. I hope you'll be at the show. I know I can't know who you are, but I would love just knowing you're there.

I re-read this one a time or two and decided, yes, it was the one. (Could I have used the word *know* a few more times?) It would be vague enough not to assume Secret Admirer was in the show, but still clear that I wanted him to come.

I sent it and went to slip my phone into the pocket of my jeans.

And heard a dull, muffled buzz.

It sounded like a trapped fly. But I knew what it was. I think my heart must have slowed to half its speed.

It had to be a coincidence—some phone here in the

dressing-room vibrating just after I sent Secret Admirer's text.

Frowning, I swiped my phone on, typed and sent: *If you can come, please at least let me know the performance you'll be seeing, okay?*

Two seconds later, again, that faint vibrating hum.

No way… No *way*!

I got to my feet. I stared at my phone where it said **Secret Admirer** in bold letters above the text message thread. I hit the tiny circled *i* beside the name, then the little image of the telephone. It started ringing, and I strained my ears.

There it was, rhythmic and insect-like—a phone vibrating.

Now holding my breath, eyes shifting everywhere, I circled the room, listening hard.

Then found myself at Nick's station staring down in confusion at his backpack. The sound was its loudest right here. I heard the click from my phone as the call went to voicemail. The vibrating from Nick's backpack ceased.

With unsteady hands, I fumbled at the pocket-zipper. I felt frantic now. I jerked the backpack toward me and reached inside. My lungs seemed to have vacated my chest, leaving a gaping cavity. Because I tugged out not one cell-phone, but two. The iPhone looked lifeless, but the other, an ancient-looking green flip-phone, had a square of glass on the front with MISSED CALL glowing in it. I dropped the iPhone back into the bag and almost ripped the Razr open. There, on the screen, were alerts for one missed call and two new text messages.

I felt suddenly nauseous. The phone jittered back and forth in my shaking hand.

"Not him…" I whispered. "It can't be. He wouldn't. Please, not him…"

All at once the dressing-room door opened.

There Nick stood, slightly sweaty with his hair rumpled from his turns.

He started to smile when he saw me, but the phone in my hand was too obvious to hide; my face was too shocked, too horrified, to school into any other mask. I stared, watching Nick's features slide from surprise, to fear, then into a sort of devastated resignation.

"Please tell me," I managed to say, "that he's not you."

"Michael, I—"

"Tell me he's not you!"

Nick's eyes dropped at the force in my tone. He said nothing.

"He's not, Nick! *You're* not! You *can't* be! All this time?"

He sucked in a shuddery breath. "I never, *never* wanted you to know."

I felt myself grow weak all over, fearing I might fall if I didn't brace a hand on the edge of the counter. "My God…" came out of me in a whisper.

"Please let me explain."

"You left me those notes," I mumbled. "Even the one today." I dropped the green Razr onto his bag as though it burned. Then I saw my own phone, clutched in my other hand. I stared at it, at the phone case—at Yuri and Victor with their flashing gold rings. I could only mumble again, "My God…"

"Michael, I really didn't mean to cause any harm. I only—"

"I can't! Not right now!" I couldn't look at him. I barreled toward the door, feeling his fingers on my elbow, trying to halt me. "Put your hand on me and I'll break it!" I ground out, jerking my arm away and twisting the door-handle.

"Michael, come on!" I heard him call, almost pleading. "Don't run away! Please!"

But I was speeding through the hallway toward the "artistes' entrance". I had eavesdropped on Nick's conversation with Jackie Skarupa here—his apology—what felt like æons ago. I shoved at the door, even as I heard the sound of his footsteps coming after. I burst into the sunlight and pounded across the little courtyard, needing to get away. I needed to be quiet for a second, to think, to figure out if I wanted to cry or batter at the theatre's walls with my fists.

Behind me, he cried, "Michael, will you stop! Let me explain! Talk to me! Just don't run away!"

I didn't want to punch walls—I wanted to punch *him*! I rounded on him and he froze, quailing before the rage in my eyes.

"You're a fucking *liar*, Nick!" I shouted. "A liar! You've been lying to me all this time! I thought you were different! I was starting to trust you!"

"You can," he tried to say. I saw his eyes begin to fill with tears. I found a savage, ugly *glee* in the sight.

"You've been living in my house!" I cried. "Sweet talking my parents, my siblings, getting all chummy with my friends! And you've been lying for months!"

"I haven't." His voice broke.

"You *have*, you asshole! It's the same shit it's always been! Another way to fuck with your old faggot friend, right?"

Then he was speaking quickly, as though he wanted to keep me from interrupting. "No, Michael! I wanted to make it better with you but I didn't know how. I didn't know I would go so far after leaving that first note. I just wanted to talk to you. I wanted to find a way to make up for the awful way I treated you. I knew you'd never give me the time of day. Then somehow I was in the middle of it. I kept thinking I should stop texting you, knowing you'd react like this if you ever found out. But I *couldn't*. Talking to you like that felt too much like the way it was *before*. I didn't want to let go of that. Because I…"

I glared. "Because you what?"

His breath hitched. "Because I missed you. I missed my friend."

My rage abated a little—only a little—replaced by numb tiredness. "You screwed with me, Nick. All those conversations I had with—with *you*—and you were, what? Telling me things I wanted to hear? Telling me things that would trick me into trusting you?"

"Never. I never told a lie. I never bent the truth."

"Really?" I gave him a disgusted look. "*Not* a straight man? Some poor closeted kid afraid to come out?"

His breath hitched again. A fat tear slipped from his eye, coursing down his cheek. He struggled not to let his face crumple.

Then I knew. As though under a blast of cold air, the skin all over my body seemed to tighten, keeping me from moving. I was a moron. Now it all made sense. And it all made such *perfect* sense I was an even bigger moron for not seeing it. It was a twenty-foot billboard. The conversation I had overheard between him and my mom, his getting so friendly with Brent and Calista and Liam, the way the secret admirer text message conversations had slowed once he was living in my house. Hell, even the *dancing*!

The strength threatened to leave my legs again.

"Oh Jesus…" I almost moaned it.

"My dad found out," he said, sniffing, trying to speak around the sobs catching in his throat. "That's why he told me to leave. I didn't want you to know. About me. I'm horrible, I get that. I was terrible to you, and all along I was just like you. I knew you'd hate me for it. I don't want you to hate me, Michael. Please, don't hate me. Not now."

I was silent, digesting this. I listened to his sniffles, his struggles not to cry uncontrollably, not knowing how to react.

"You're…gay?" I muttered.

Another sniff. Another shuddering breath. "Yes."

"How long have you known?"

"Since that day." His eyes were everywhere but on me, darting like wasps. "When we were in middle school. At my house."

"How… Why…" My brain felt sluggish as mud. "Why did you do all those things? After that?"

"I was scared. Of my dad. Of myself. Of what it all meant. I tried to deny it for a long time. But I knew, always, deep down, what I was."

"And the secret admirer bullshit? What was that for?"

"I don't know. I didn't know anything about you anymore, and as I started finding out stuff, I just kept thinking what a dumbass I had been. You were amazing, and my best friend, and I had been awful to you. I had all this stuff going on inside, I was going through so many things, and you were everything I wished I could be—that I wished I could have the *courage* to be. I knew you hated me, but I wanted you back in some way. I know I did it wrong. And I'm so sorry. I didn't mean to—to deceive you.

But I didn't lie. I always told you the truth."

"Who else knows?" My tone was icy. "You said there were two other people who knew about you."

"Calista."

I stared. "Calista?"

"She was the first one I told."

"You even had my friends in on it?"

"It wasn't like that. She knows I've been your secret admirer, yes. But not for long."

I gritted my teeth. Now I knew why she had been telling me not to crush on my mystery gift-giver. *It's always the last person you want it to be*, she had said.

And boy was she right!

I had been…what? Falling for him? For Nick Walsh?

"Who's the other one?" I asked. "Don't tell me it's Brent."

"Liam. I asked him to deliver your present and he sort of guessed."

"Why would he guess that?"

Nick bit his lip, looking agonized. He still wouldn't lift his eyes. "He said that me giving you a birthday present in secret was—was like me having a crush on you." He sucked in his breath, like he wanted to bite back his words.

Once more I stared at him. "Just goes to show how clueless he is about the ins and outs of our, quote-unquote, *friendship*."

Nick's face did crumple now, the tears running faster. I looked at him and saw myself the night he had appeared on my doorstep. Only he had reacted compassionately. I couldn't.

In a broken voice, cracking from his sobs, he said, "It's not a crush now, Michael."

"Not a…what?"

He shook his head. "Forget it."

"No. Rewind. It's not a crush…*now*?" I was spitting the words, feeling insane. "You had a crush on me?" When he didn't seem like he would answer, I almost shouted, "Nick!"

"Forget it, Michael, just…" His face was wet, breaths hitching around his words. He turned away. "I'm sorry. I'll go. I'll leave you alone."

He began to walk, almost running, back toward the courtyard. My eyes were locked on his retreating shoulders, seeing the damp patches where his sweat had marked his shirt.

"No. Nick!" I cried, coming after him. "Donick! You don't get to run away!"

I grabbed at his arm, turning him to face me. His tears had slowed, but the marks were on his cheeks. His eyes were red—red and wet and still unwilling to meet mine.

"Answer the question," I said.

He licked his lips, then said hoarsely, "I have feelings for you, Michael. Not just a crush. Not anymore."

"Feelings… What…"

"The last couple of weeks, spending time with you…it's more now." He sniffed. "Not a *crush*."

My grip slackened. I could feel the slide of the coarse hairs of his forearm under my fingertips as my hand slipped.

An awkward laugh, from shock maybe, gusted in my chest. "Gimme a break. You sound like you're in love with me or something."

Another sniff. Another shudder of breath. Another nod. Then his strained, tortured voice. "I think I am."

I blinked at him. I must have looked horrified, like some B-movie scream queen. I couldn't tell if my feet were rooted to the ground, or untethered and I was falling through the air. I said, "You are not."

Again, he nodded.

"You love me? Since *when*?"

"Since always, I think. Everything I've been doing, trying to make up for the shitty stuff I've done…it's really been for you. I wanted to be a better person, for you. Even if you never knew, never felt like I do, I wanted to be better. When we were kids…I'm not some stupid-ass, even if I've acted like it. I knew what I was doing. That day. I *wanted* to kiss you. Not because of some experiment, but because it was *you*."

I backed away from him. Now it was my turn to let my eyes flee everywhere but to his face. He took a step toward me and my hands shot out in a warding-off gesture.

"Don't," I barked. "Just…don't."

"I'm sorry, Michael. It all became a huge mess. I didn't want it to get this far. I didn't want to feel this way. It just happened. I wish I could make it all go away. I tried to make it better and only made it worse. I should never have auditioned for the Revue. I wish I could go back and not do any of it."

Somehow, amidst all the confusion and bewilderment and *hurt*, hearing him say *that* confused and bewildered and hurt me most of all.

I lifted my gaze. I must have looked hateful. He flinched and recoiled.

"You need to stay away from me," I said dully. "I don't even want to look at you."

"Michael—"

"You *are* an asshole. You're the same asshole you've always been. And I could throat-punch myself for falling for your bullshit, even a little."

I heard another sob leave him, but the sound only flared anger in me. I turned away, needing to be far from the theatre and everyone in it. He didn't try to follow. A small part of me wondered what he looked like, standing there alone with the tears running down his face. Did he watch me leave? Did he hang his head in the shame I hoped he felt a dozen times over? I couldn't even say whether I would feel pleased to see him in so much misery. I only knew that my belly had become a lava-pit—festering turmoil that threatened to burn me from the inside out.

DONICK

"I never knew that fear and hate could be so strong…"

IT'S TRUE, YOU know. I'm in love with Michael.

Two weeks of living in his house, watching movies together, playing with his siblings, falling asleep only feet from him after comfortable conversations in the dimness of his bedroom…it's proven to me, once and for all, that I'm not just crushing on Michael. I'm head over heels, crazy in love with him.

I've known he'll never reciprocate my feelings, yet having Michael in my life in some way has been enough. But he knows everything now. And if he told me once that he never really hated me, he'll never say that again.

As I stumble back into the theatre, feeling as though I'm attempting to stand atop a hill of marbles, I'm smearing tears into the sleeves of my shirt with my arms. I can't stop remembering Michael's words: "You need to stay away from me. I don't even want to look at you." Thank God no one passed us outside, and thank God I don't run into anyone now. I'm back in the dressing-room, gathering my bag, shoving the fucking *hateful* green Razr into it, though I would like to chuck it into the garbage now. Then I'm dashing through the theatre and out the front doors, almost running across the parking-lot to get to the street.

I have to get to Michael's house. I have to gather my stuff and be *gone*. I can't stay there now. I can't continue infringing on his family's kindness when whatever ground I've gained with him is now irrevocably lost. I wish I could vanish into some dark chasm and never see anyone at school ever again.

I rage inside at the bitter perfection of not being able to disappear and lick my own self-inflicted wounds. I have to be at the theatre for the show in a couple of hours— so many people are counting on me—still, the idea of performing for an audience, of being in the midst of my fellow cast-members when I feel like my chest has been flayed open, makes me nauseous.

The Penroses gave me a house-key, and I let myself in. I'm grateful no one's home. I dash into Michael's room, gathering my things, not yet even thinking that I have nowhere to go. I only hear a drumbeat between my ears telling me I need to be gone. Sleeping under a bridge will be preferable to facing Michael again. Though I won't be able to escape him at the theatre or at school, I can at least be far away from where he lives.

But I'm fighting tears once more. This is like getting kicked out all over again.

I fold up the bedding I've used and stack it at the foot of Michael's bed, then I let the air out of the mattress and roll it. Finally, I scrawl a note for Mr. and Mrs. Penrose. *Thank you so much for everything you've done for me, and for welcoming me in your house,* I write; it's hard to see through my swimming eyes. *Please forgive me for having to leave so suddenly and without saying goodbye.* I place the note in their bedroom where I know they'll see it, sling my bags over my shoulders and leave the house. I hadn't expected I would ever enter it again, yet having done so makes leaving all the harder. I've come to love it here. I could relax here, in a way, and feel wanted. This is where Michael is, of course. This is *his* place. And I love him.

I don't know how I get through the rest of the night, but I do. I return to the school—tired, sweaty, running late. I scurry through the door and into a bustle of busy students and the noise of the musicians tuning their instruments on stage. My passing cast-mates are in varying degrees of readiness—makeup half done, some in costume. I see expressions of relief as they catch sight of me, saying things like, "Where have you been?" Or, "You missed warmups! We were getting worried!" I ditch my bags in the hallway and hurry to the tech-booth to get my mic.

I haven't seen Michael yet, nor his Muskequeers, and I'm thankful; but entering the dressing-room, knowing he's in there, is my next challenge. It's more difficult than swan diving into a portal to another dimension. Yet somehow, I do it.

I have little time to pause and really notice how I feel like I've been sent through a washing-machine's spin-cycle. I have too much to do between makeup, double-checking my costumes and props, placing costume pieces and dance shoes backstage where I'll need them for quick changes. The dressing-room is all noise and activity, and with all my might I keep my eyes averted from Michael's direction. Yet sitting at my station, my bags shoved beneath the counter, I can feel him at my back like static in my hair.

It makes it difficult to focus on the makeup I'm trying to apply, hoping the greasy foundation hides the evidence of my tears. But I get it done. Then I'm attempting to dress and not feel self-conscious, trying to be friendly to the guys around me and not let on that my heart feels shattered. After all, I just confessed my love to a boy, and received his disgust in return—me: whom everyone views as some sort of bigoted homophobe.

Brent pops in to call, "House is open!" ("Thank you, house!" comes the room's reply.) Then again to say, "Fifteen minutes 'til curtain!" Then, "Five minutes!" Then there's nothing left for him to call but "Places!" and we're darting out, everyone grinning and bouncing up and down and whispering to each other. Even as my nerves fire into overdrive and my belly lurches to my chest, I'm scrambling to make sure my hair is held back from my forehead with enough hairspray, my mic is secure against my cheek, my character shoes are laced. I'm the last in the dressing-room when Liam pokes his head back in. He bops over and pauses behind my chair, leaning to throw his arms around my shoulders.

"Have the best show ever!" he exclaims. "Break all your legs off!"

I muster a smile for him in the mirror, a little mystified by the pink on my cheeks, the dark liner around my eyes. "You too," I say, and suddenly I'm overwhelmed with gratitude for his simple liking, when I don't know how anyone could feel anything for me but hate. Because I have nothing to hide from him, I reach up and touch his cheek with my fingers, careful not to smudge his makeup. "I'm glad you're in my life, you know," I say. "I'm lucky to have a friend like you."

He looks taken aback, but smiles broadly. "Me too." His fingers ruffle the hair at the base of my skull and he half-kisses my cheek to keep from smearing whatever color he's put on his mouth. I don't blush. I don't feel embarrassed. I just feel glad he did it—that it's okay for him to do it. "Love ya," he adds, then butterflies out of the dressing-room.

No one has said they love me in a long time. I can't remember when those words last left Pop's mouth. I must have been a little boy.

Out in the hall, I'm stopped by Jackie who throws her arms around me, then I'm stopped by Calista who tells me to break a leg and actually hugs me herself (so Michael either told her what happened and she's still my friend, or he's kept it to himself), and any number of others—both girls and boys—all grinning and excited, smiling at me, hugging me. I should feel happy, elated, pleased by their acceptance—I've worked hard for it, after all—but it's impossible. I press through the bodies in the wings, trying to get to the place where I'll be entering. The murmurs of the audience through the lowered curtain sound hollow and big, and somehow judgmental. I'm thankful for the dark so my face can stop aching with its false smiles. Still, a palpable energy sparks through the theatre, infusing everything with something electric. I've never felt anything like it before; it's heady, a thing you could get drunk on.

Yet I'm wondering…if the last couple of hours hadn't happened, would Michael, knowing what this moment is like for me—waiting for the curtain to rise and the band to launch into "Let Me Be Your Star", scared to death of failing—would he have paused to reassure me, maybe even put his arms around me and hugged me for the first time ever? It's a discouraging thought.

THAT ELECTRICITY, THAT magic vitality I felt as I waited for showtime, somehow takes over, gets inside me. The curtain rises and the lights come up, the orchestra plays, the audience's voice is like a roar. I'm nervous, but it's a strange nervousness. I'm not afraid. I know every note, every step. We've rehearsed and rehearsed (I've rehearsed and rehearsed on my own, hiding in my room with my earbuds in) and somehow I've never felt more prepared for anything. Even years of football games never felt like this.

I sing, I dance, I sweat, I smile, I race against time to change costumes in the cramped wings, dozens of other kids all around me doing the same. The audience reacts to me, to us; I'm like a glass filling with their energy, blotting worry and anxiety from my mind. For two hours I'm in a different world—one where there's no gay or straight, one where people don't hurt each other; there's only love, acceptance, kindness. In that world, music brings peace and joy; it feels like heaven to move my body to its rhythm; opening my mouth to sing feels like praying. I'm not me for a short, glorious time—I don't even feel like myself when it's time for Michael and I to sing to each other—a song infinitely more relevant *now* than ever before. What he may be feeling or thinking, I can't care. I know I will later—all of it will come crashing over me, burying me later—but for now, I feel like I can walk on water.

When the show is over, when we've taken bows as the audience, on their feet, roars their approval, the curtain slides down and there comes the mass exodus for the lobby. I've known this was coming. The cast wants to see their family and friends, be given flowers and cards. For a week, I've known Michael's mom and dad will be here, but I can't face them. And besides, aside from them, who else would be here for me?

I relish the quiet of the empty dressing-room, pausing in the bathroom to scrub the makeup from my face (a hefty job—it doesn't seem to want to come off). It's an odd feeling—this after-show ebb. It's as though the glass I imagined myself to be, brimming with the theatre's vitality, has drained and I'm empty all over again. It's hard not to be, with so much on my mind. I hang my costumes to air out and dry on a rack—I've never sweated so much, even in football practices. I can hear footsteps in the hallway as people come back, get ready to go out and party.

And where am I supposed to go?

I'm ready to leave before Michael returns, thank goodness. I say goodnight to the guys who have come back, then exit the dressing-room. I'm heading for the side-door when Liam and Brent appear. They pause in whatever they're laughing about and give me a look.

"You're not leaving?" Brent sounds affronted.

"Yeah." I try to sound casual. "Very long day. We gotta do it twice tomorrow after all."

"We're all going to Dorah Fine's Café," Liam says. "You gotta come with!"

I shake my head, faking a regretful look.

"Come on!" says Brent. "You ever been?"

"My dad likes that place," I say. "Digs the pastrami. We used to go sometimes. I'm just…not down tonight. No-fun-Nick. That's me."

"Stupid Nick, that's you," Brent says. "You don't have

a choice anyway. We're all driving together and Michael's mom and dad are coming too. What else will you do?"

So Michael hasn't *said anything*, I think. I wonder why…

"Really," I say, and can hear the little bit of waver in my voice as I might start to cry again. "I'm fine. I need to go though. I'm sorry. Thanks for inviting me."

Brent just looks confused, but Liam is studying me even as I turn toward the door. I'm barely outside when Liam's there, without Brent.

"What happened? Don't say nothing. Because it's something."

It's dark, I can barely see him, and because I know he can't see my face, I say, "Michael knows. About everything. And he's not happy."

Liam's tone is sad. "Did you tell him?"

"He just found out…then I supplied the rest."

"Even about—"

"Liking him? Yeah."

"Dang. So…what's up? You're staying at his house, right?"

"Not anymore."

"What do you mean? Where will you go? Back home?"

I scoff. "I can't go there."

"Michael wouldn't tell you to leave," he says, as though trying to convince himself that that's true. "Not when you have nowhere to go."

"He didn't exactly. Think of it as voluntary. Come on, Li, how can I stay there now?"

"I see your point." He sighs. "Where *are* you going then?"

"I figure I'll just start walking."

"'Stupid Nick' is right! I'll ask my mom if you can crash at our apartment. I'll call her right now. She just left because I was going to ride in Calista's car, but she'll come back. She raved about you anyway, so she'll feel like she's got a star over or something."

"I can't ask you to do that."

"Shut it. I'm going back in for my phone. Wait here."

Now it's my turn to sigh. Then I say, "All right."

I catch his smile as he opens the door, light falling across his face. Again that rush of affection for him sweeps me. I think what a pity it is I couldn't have fallen for him instead of Michael. Of course, there's the Gil complication; and Liam's not my type. Still, it just goes to show that we always want what's wrong for us.

LIAM LIVES WITH his mom in a tiny two-bedroom apartment about two miles from school. He's never talked much about her and meeting her is an experience. She seems more like a fun aunt than a mother. She's a tiny woman—small, like Liam—though she carries a lot of weight on her, mostly in the hips. Her makeup is a bit thick, her hair a frizzy cloud, yet she's kind and warm. It's hard not to like her, despite the fact that she's so excited to have me over it borders on weird.

There's a bit of desperation there—from both Liam and his mom. They're two people who have relied on each other for so long, they don't know how to rely on anyone else. Any outsider, like me, is an event. I can't be the first friend Liam has had over. Or maybe his mom thinks there's more between her son and I than mere friendship. She's so pushy, actually, that she's offering to make snacks, to order pizza; we tell her no so many times Liam begins to look embarrassed.

He must have told her a good deal about me already. It's strange to have this woman I've only just met asking me if I have a secret boyfriend (I wonder if she's aware of her son's "secret boyfriend"), and what it's like being gay and playing sports—as though that never happens.

Later, Liam tells me this:

"My mom can't help being how she is. She's kinda nervous all the time, worried about making an impression or how things look. I think it's because of my dad. He used to beat on her a lot—sounds OCD to me, actually, the reasons why. When she got pregnant with me, she told him if he touched her again, she would leave him. And he beat the shit out of her. She almost lost me. And enough was enough. I still don't know how she left and kept him from ever coming back, but he never has. Could you imagine how a dad like that would've reacted to having a sissy for a son?"

"Don't call yourself that," I say, then lay there on the floor of his room feeling like a fool for thinking my life is so rough when others had (and have) it so much worse.

I stay with Liam for the rest of the weekend until I feel how intrusive I must be and look for another option. After all, Liam wants to hang with the cast after the shows, and it's the last thing *I* want. I feel guilty, keeping him from eating at Dorah Fine's, hanging with everyone—he's looked forward to that since the first day of auditions.

Saturday's shows pass much the same way as Friday's. I'm a little low-energy for the matinée, which I don't understand, but I guess after such a high as opening night, that's inevitable. Being around the rest of the cast is no problem, and I can find it in me to enjoy it, but nothing changes with Michael. I don't look at him, and if he steals a glance toward me, I can't say. I feel, of course, like a complete and utter dipshit—humiliation has set in, remembering how I cried in front of him, laid everything open. My feelings smart like a burn.

What has he told his parents? Did he tell them how I feel about him? Why do they think I left? Perhaps they don't care; perhaps they're just glad I'm gone.

Calista stops me on Saturday and says, "Michael's parents said you were amazing last night. They were sorry they missed you."

I'm gratified by this. But because she doesn't say anything else, I suspect she knows what's going on. Do I see pity in her eyes? Maybe it's her version of an I-told-you-so. Could be both—and she was right. My decisions blew up in my face, just as she had warned.

I have a conversation with Mrs. Peebles between Saturday's performances that brings a little focus back.

"How has it been?" she asks. "Is performing still terrifying?"

I grin. "No, not at all. I'm actually surprised how much I've enjoyed myself. It's fun to be out there. It makes me wish I had joined theatre earlier. Graduation is in, what, like, six weeks? I've learned all this new stuff right at the end when I could've had these experiences years ago."

"That doesn't mean it's over for you. What are your plans after high school?"

I shrug. From this vantage, I don't see how I have any other option except to look for a job with a little more substance than being a dance teacher. *If I even make it that far...* I think. Without Pop's support, I'm getting worried. I can't couch-surf forever.

But I say, "It used to be football. Not that I cared about that. I'm happy I don't have to pretend anymore. But I haven't given it much thought. I never took the SATs and my grades aren't the best. A university wouldn't want me. I guess…community college?"

"No shame in that. There are a few nearby and they all have performing-arts programs. If you have any seriousness about being on stage, take theatre, sing more, keep dancing. I mean, you'd make a fantastic choreographer."

I mutter to myself, "Not too much of a cliché." At her puzzled look, I just shake my head. "I guess I'll have to see."

"When the show is over, after next weekend, I mean," Mrs. P. says, "come see me some lunchtime, or after school. Let's talk a little bit about the future. I have some suggestions, and if you have any questions for me I'd be happy to answer them."

"Sounds good," I say—and it does, even if it's only a pipe-dream: doing something with my dancing, or any of the things I've learned while working on the Revue. I mean, if Michael didn't get in anywhere, how the hell would I?

Mrs. P. takes my hand, clasping it in both of hers. "I'm really proud of you, Nick. You've been through some stuff during this show…and you've stayed strong. I think of the young man who looked so terrified of auditioning, and I sit in the audience and watch you now. You glow when you're on that stage. That's a gift a lot of artists wish they had, and simply don't. Our show wouldn't be the same without you. I hope you're proud of yourself. I hope you're as happy you came to auditions as I am."

My smile is tight. I can't think of anything but how

miserable the last twenty-four hours have been. But I say, not with complete untruth, "Yes, I am."

Her expression gets a little serious. "At auditions," she says, "I knew you by reputation only. I told you I worried about…certain behaviors, you remember? Sorry, I don't mean to embarrass you, it's only, now, you're almost a different person. Much more…I don't know how to explain it…maybe…relaxed? Whatever it is, you've really risen above your past. A lot of people had faith in you these last couple of months and you didn't let us down. Mrs. Moes hoped to see you last night to tell you. You've got a lot of people rooting for you, Nick. You're a delight to everyone who knows you, including me."

An odd phrase for her to use. *You're a delight to everyone who knows you.* I've only ever felt like I brought hurt to people, or wasted their time. As much as I appreciate Mrs. P.'s words, they're hard to believe.

Surprising ME A little, come Monday morning, there are a few friends I've made in the Revue who offer to let me stay with them for a day or two, Brent included. "My *obaa-san*," he says, "doesn't know what the hell is going on most of the time, so she won't mind." Because I don't want to take advantage of Liam and his mom, I take Brent up on his offer. He tells me Calista told him what had gone down between Michael and me—at least as far as the secret admirer thing (Brent's eyes get wide and bright as he asks me unwelcome questions about how I carried on being Michael's secret admirer without giving myself away); however, there's no mention of my feelings for Michael, despite Calista knowing. If Brent knew he would *for sure* want to talk about it. Either way, Brent wants me to know he's there if I need to talk. I *don't* want to talk, not yet anyway, but I still appreciate his concern.

His *obaa-san* is a nice lady—very short, yet broad, with gray-threaded black hair cut very like Calista's Scooby-Doo Velma style. Because it's novel, I take it on myself to call her Nanahara-*san*. She smiles a lot and her speech is heavily accented. She acts bewildered a great deal of the time and I wonder, as she gets sicker, what may happen with her care. Will Brent's father and mother one day find themselves having to come back from Japan permanently, or will they bring her back there to live with them? Then what would happen with Brent? But I like Brent, and I like his *obaa-san*, so I'm grateful to be able to sleep on their couch for a couple of nights.

This unsettled thing I've got going on…I can't do it forever. But what should I do? I've never, in my life, felt every one of my almost eighteen years and had the sense that I was no more than the age of Cady and Topher Penrose.

I concentrate on schoolwork and keep my head low, minding my own business as much as I can. But Michael is constantly sneaking into my thoughts. Lunchtime is terrible without our text messaging, my evenings long and static. No rehearsal now, and certainly no Michael to watch movies with. And like the beating of my own heart, the eternal ache of the place inside that loves him…the place that crushed, but which has now been crushed.

On Wednesday, Thursday, and Friday, Mrs. P. and the other arts teachers arrange a kind of preview for the school at lunchtime. In place of any lame karaoke set-up, they have one number from the Revue performed per day as something of an advertisement. I'm happy none of them are numbers I'm in, but Thursday it's "Cover Girl" and it's announced that I choreographed it. It's enough to make me want to run and hide, but I stay on the edge of the quad and watch the gathered students, watch my cast-mates sing and dance my choreography, watch Michael glow under the sun, reflecting its light onto the faces of the cheering crowd.

Then I feel so depressed I turn away, hurting and mortified.

The final weekend of the Revue closes in and I both relish and dread it. I dread it, because an enormous part of me doesn't want it to end. It's been an emotional battle, but it's also been the most fun I've ever had in my life. It also feels like I'm locked in a dream. This theatrical world isn't real. It's a small postage-stamp of frozen time and has to end. I feel the need for getting back to the normal routine of life. Growing attached to the picture in time we've made with the show feels dangerous. After all, if my friendships with some of the people in the Revue aren't destined to go on after that last curtain, I would rather get that hurt done and over with sooner rather than later.

Still, I'm happy to be with everyone on Friday night. We all act as though we haven't seen each other in months. That's theatre-love, I guess. I'm happy to laugh and joke with the guys in the dressing-room, happy pressing makeup into my pores (my skin doesn't like it—I haven't had zits like this since I was in ninth grade…ugh!), happy to groan with some of the cast over the rancid smell of our costumes. I feel a measure of joy at warming-up with the dancers, singing scales with the singers.

Biggest of all, I feel a new sort of…I don't know…comfort

in my own skin. Maybe it's that I have no one important to hide from anymore, but I let myself hug Liam when I see him, or stand with him and Brent and put my arms around them. Once, Liam even pauses in the dressing-room and sits on my knee. I feel my face get warm, but I slip my arms around his waist and sort of snuggle my cheek into his shoulder. Maybe it's a way of broadcasting (there are some looks—*knowing* looks, I might add, especially from Brent). Maybe it's that I'm truly beginning to not care what people think. Maybe it's because Michael will see and a gross part inside of me wants him to be troubled by it. Maybe it's just that I love Liam and want people to know how much his friendship means to me.

Michael, of course, says nothing.

But once the music starts and the theatre fills with applause, there isn't anything that can take away my grin.

FRIDAY'S SHOW IS great! Afterwards, I'm finally cajoled into going out with the cast. Being at Dorah Fine's Café is strange because I've only ever been with Pop, but time spent there with my new friends is more than enough to drive *him* out of my thoughts. We sit in a huge bunch at an enormous length of table as several harassed servers do their best to take orders and bring buckets of ranch dressing, not to mention constantly refilling the ramekins of carrots and dill-pickle chips. The Muskequeers sit at one end, and Liam, thankfully, drags me to the opposite end where Jackie and some other dancers cluster. I try not to look toward Michael, but it's difficult. He must resent my presence, because I'm surprised at the occasional turn of his eyes. We both look away though. He must hate that I'm here.

Saturday's shows are more high-energy than last week because we know the Revue is almost over. The audiences have gotten bigger as our very short run progresses, and the matinée is almost sold out, the evening show completely ("Standing room only, guys and gals!" Chalice says, glowing). So we do it all again with increasing bittersweet sadness, the cast's loving on each other getting progressively more intense. I wonder how people who want to do this for a living can stand this constant routine of new friends and close relationships, all formed and ended in the space of a few brief months.

That evening, as we stand whispering in the wings, waiting for the show to begin for the final time, Jackie says, "Everything we do now is the last time we do it. No more chances to get it right. Every note, every step, is going to vanish like it's never been there…gone as soon as we finish it."

"That's not depressing or anything," Liam says.

She shrugs, smiling, and I realize I don't even notice her strange eyes anymore. "Look at it this way, Li," she says. "It leaves you open for the next performing experience. An artist doesn't want to always do the same thing over and over. That's crazy-making. Old stuff ends so new stuff can take its place."

Then it's final showtime. I think about what Jackie said and try to lock every moment of the performance in my memory. From the wings I observe as much as I can (torturing myself by watching Michael sing "Popular" to Calista and Brent, knowing he and I will have no more excuses to be in the same room after this night, blaming myself for having driven him away, *again*!) I'm sad to get to the end of the masquerade portion of the show, because the David Bowie and Madonna songs have been my favorite dance numbers. As my solo approaches, I'm determined to give it everything and make it into a memory I can hold onto, especially for the times when things get hard.

Michael doesn't leave the wings once "Cover Girl" and "Girl For All Seasons" have ended. He pauses in the shadows to watch. He's never done that before, but I won't be intimidated. I cross the stage into my light and get lost in the song, in the choreography.

I can feel how buoyant I am. I can sense the audience's energy rising to meet mine. It also seems as though there's only the music and myself, no one else. When I reach the song's end and hit my last pose, the roar from the seats is deafening. I'm panting, grinning, holding for a few seconds as Chalice and Mrs. P. instructed.

And if I hadn't, if I had gone off right away, I might not have heard the shout.

"Fag! *Cocksucker! QUEER!*"

I don't need to wonder who's said it. I know Josue's voice. It echoes from the walls.

There are gasps. I can make out craning heads. Chatter ripples—uncomfortable laughter; angry, offended murmurs. I wish I could look unruffled and impassive, but my smile falters. If a person could die of shame, I would expire right there. The light-cue changes and the next song begins as I hurry off. I had felt like a light-bulb—now I feel like a dead battery. I approach the door in the wings leading to the backstage hallway, passing Michael as I go. I hear him mutter my name, but I say, "Don't!" and keep going.

It isn't that the names hurt (they do—of course they do), and it's not that at the core of the shouts, they're true. It's that it's exactly something *I* would've done not so long ago.

I have five minutes to change costumes for my number with Michael, and as that song "Without Love" from *Hairspray* pipes through the monitors, I can feel my hands, my knees, quaking, making me clumsy. Only a handful of the cast heard the shouts, but soon everyone will know. I think: *This is it! This is the humiliation I gave to so many people. It's not the immediate hurt. It's the knowledge that others witness it— other people see the moments of indignity and disrespect.*

I dash back into the wings in my black slacks, white dress-shirt, and vest for "If I Never Knew You". (Michael and I wear the same thing—his vest is the color of his eyes, mine is the color of a bruise.) As he has every show, he's waiting just within the sight-lines of the curtain, only now he's gazing at me, watching my face. I don't have the room in my brain to think about the difference from the cold ignoring I've received since last Friday. I only want him to look away. His lips move, and I can only imagine him saying, "Are you okay?" Or even, "What goes around comes around." I just shake my head, my eyes lowered, and manage to mutter, "Don't say anything. Please."

Then we're on stage; the orchestra is playing the song; I'm singing, he's singing. I feel nothing but a sense of degradation. I've just been called a faggot in front of 600 people. Now I'm singing a love song to another guy—a guy I love, who despises me.

My enjoyment of the show is gone now. I'm relieved there are only a couple more numbers before the final curtain. I can barely concentrate and I'm certain the audience can sense the vanishing of whatever light Mrs. Peebles claims I bring to the stage.

Just let the show end! I think. *Let it end so I can take five minutes for myself in the dressing-room to fight back the emotions crawling through me like parasites.*

Mrs. P. is at the door.

"Oh Nick," she sighs. "I'm sorry."

I try to smile. "I've had it coming."

"No, no one deserves to be humiliated."

"Believe me, I know."

She pauses. "The person who shouted—"

"Josue Jimenez."

"Yes, well, he picked a bad time to pull a stunt like that. There were two vice-principals in the audience to witness it. I'm fairly certain Mr. Jimenez is looking at suspension, if not worse."

"That won't stop anything. An asshole is an asshole."

Again, she pauses. "I know," she says at last. "People like that…mean-spirited people, they never change. That boy will always be that way, I'm sure. I know as a teacher I shouldn't disparage another student, but I'm pretty pissed off right now. If the administrators even *think* of going light on him, I'll raise a fuss. That's what theatre is for—finding acceptance when it doesn't seem like it can be found anywhere else. That stunt flies in the face of everything I want for my students." Then she adds in a rush, "Not that I'm saying there's any truth to what was shouted, I only meant that—"

"There is though," I say, and I sound listless. "I *am* gay. I've wrestled with it long enough, but there's no one to hide from anymore."

"Oh." Mrs. P. blinks. She must see the emotion on my face because she suddenly draws me into a hug. "Even more of a reason this needs to be a safe place. I'm sorry it turned out not to be for you."

"Someone's always going to hate me just for being me," I say. "I need to get used to it."

She pulls away. "I wish that weren't true. But I won't mince words and say it's not."

I'm just opening my mouth to say something I don't quite feel—something like, "I'll be all right," or "Everything will be okay," when the dressing-room door bursts open and one of the dancers pokes in her head.

"If anyone's naked, hide those dinks!" she exclaims, grinning, then looks mortified to see Mrs. P. "Oh!" Her voice is faint now. "Sorry…"

Mrs. P. says, "I'll pretend I didn't hear that," then leaves, touching my shoulder one last time.

I offer the girl in the doorway a false smile. She says, "You need to come to the lobby. Like, now!"

"Why? More insults waiting for me?"

She scowls. "Yeah, that *was* gross, but no. Someone wants to see you."

I frown. "Who?"

"Your dad."

MY LEGS NO longer seem to bend at the knee as I make my way to the lobby. Whatever I was feeling before is obliterated by fear.

Why is Pop here? Did he actually watch the show? And, oh God! He heard Josue's nasty name-calling!

For the first time, at the last time, I'm in the lobby after the show. It's humming with theatre-patrons—parents, grandparents, aunts, uncles, siblings, teachers, students—all milling about, clustered around members of the cast. I spot Michael and Calista standing with a couple who must be

Calista's parents, and Brent is with them, his grandmother clinging to his arm. For a fraction of a second, Michael's eyes find mine. But I can't be troubled by that right now. Standing alone in a corner, looking supremely uncomfortable and out of place, is my father. He's wearing a suit and tie.

His lips twitch into almost a smile when he catches sight of me. I'm too hesitant to look anything but wary. I pause a few feet away.

"Hi Nicky," he says awkwardly. "Wow, those ABBA songs…that was really something. I hadn't heard them in years. "Take a Chance on Me" and "Dancing Queen"… Just, wow. Your momma and I used to listen to them before you were born. She had her ma's old records. I've still got 'em somewhere. I should pull 'em out."

The words come quick and scattered—he's almost babbling. Yet this is information I've never known. ABBA doesn't seem like it would be Pop's thing, yet he and my mother listened to them when they were young? But mentioning my mother, after the last time he brought her up, plunges me into bitterness.

I can only say, "What are you doing here?"

His eyes are partially hidden behind his glasses, yet I still see them skipping away, like mine.

"I came to see you."

"Why?"

His lips tighten, beard twitching. He lets out a breath.

"I'm not gonna lie," he says. "It was Nadia Penrose who convinced me."

"Michael's mom?"

Pop nods. His gaze turns toward Michael. Mine follows. Again I almost catch Michael looking in my direction. He knows the sight of my father, of course. This must look like stellar gossip, Pop and me talking here in the lobby of the theatre after everything that's happened.

"That boy has quite the voice on him."

I stare at my dad, hardly blinking.

"His mother stopped by. To tell me where you were. I'm glad she did. I was worried."

"*You* told me to leave."

"I didn't tell you to leave, Nicky. At least, not to move out like you did. I needed you to stay out of my way for a bit was all."

"Same thing."

"No. Look, you just dropped something giant on me. I didn't know how to handle it. I'm still not sure how to handle it. Talking with your friend's mom was helpful though. I was glad to know where you were—"

"You could have called or texted me yourself, at any time." My anger and hurt are simmering very close to the surface.

"I could have. But I wasn't ready."

"Now you are?"

My voice has risen. Pop glances around. He lowers his voice, like a cue for me to follow.

"Nicky, you dumped a lot on me all at once. I never been great with emotion, I know that. Maybe, yes, some of that has to do with your momma's passing. I thought a lot about what you said to me. I realized I said some pretty rough things, reacted badly. But like I said, it was a lot to take in. I thought I'd known you for eighteen years…and it turned out I didn't. That…hurt, I guess."

"Like I could ever have talked to you about any of this."

"That's fair." He glances toward the chocked-open doors

to the house. I'm surprised to see something stir in his eyes, something almost vulnerable. "Nicky," he says at last, his eyes finding mine, and maybe for the first time ever, really *seeing* me. "I had no idea you could *do* anything like that."

I say nothing.

"I mean, I didn't know you could sing. And I mean *really* sing! And your dancing…" There are actually tears in his eyes. I've never seen him show so much emotion before. "You been going to that studio all these years, and I didn't know you could dance like that. You were wonderful."

I can only blink for a second or two, nearly appalled. I mumble, "Thanks."

"I saw in the program that you choreographed too." Pop swallows. "There's been all this stuff inside you, and I never let you show it to me." A breath hitches, sighs out, as though he's working himself up to what he says next. "I'm proud of you."

I find myself distrustful, however floored I am to hear those words.

"You're proud of me?" I repeat. "Your faggot son?"

His eyes drop. "I'm sorry, Nicky. Things a person don't understand can be scary. What you been going through… it's foreign to me, even now. I've thought, and spoken, in the same way my own pop did. He was very old-fashioned and lived in a time and place when…well, words like that were normal."

I frown. "Michael was twelve, Pop," I say, incredulous, trying to keep my voice low. "You called him awful names and ordered him out of our house. I lost my best friend because of it. Because I thought I had to think like you."

He looks wounded. "I reacted badly."

"Understatement."

"I know. I didn't know how to deal with…what I saw back then, any more'n I've known how to deal with all these new things about you. I just don't understand. But I'm trying, Nicky. At least, I want to begin to try."

He's trying… I'm trying… Everybody tries to be different, and do we ever succeed, I wonder?

"I can see now," he goes on, "that you've been unhappy. I see why you felt you had to be secretive. You were right. Your momma *would* be ashamed of me. I just don't know what to think about all this new stuff about you."

"It's not so new."

He nods, says he knows that. "I saw Josue in the audience. Heard what he shouted."

I could cry as I mumble, "*Everyone* heard."

"It was ugly. I don't want that for you, Nicky. People treating you that way just because you're—you know… like that."

"Gay, Pop. Get comfortable saying it. It doesn't go away."

"It was cruel. I hate the idea of you being treated like that. I'm afraid people will hate you 'cause of it."

I remember what I had just said to Mrs. Peebles. "People will hate me anyway," I say. "They would've hated me if I was successful at football and had married a supermodel, Pop. People hate, they do awful things—and there's never a good reason for it."

He says, "But you're happier, right? I mean, not feeling like you have to hide?"

I think of Michael, how wonderful he is, like a fire on a cold night, and how he's not for me to get close to.

"Not particularly," I say. "But I could be. I just don't want to be hated by the people who should love me the most."

"I don't hate you, son," he says. "I have a lot to get used to. But I can't begin to learn how to get used to it, to accept it, if you're not at home."

"You want me to come back?" My voice is full of disbelief.

"Of course. You belong at home. I didn't want you gone like that. Maybe we both just needed time away from each other."

"That's what Mrs. Penrose said…"

"She told me you left their house last weekend and she didn't know where you went."

"I've been couch-surfing."

"I'm sorry."

"Weird," I say, "hearing those words from you. And you've said them a few times now."

"I can't change my way of thinking without your help, Nicky. I know that sounds like some bad TV dialogue or something, but it's true. *Will* you come home?"

I'm exhausted from going from one place to another, sleeping in unfamiliar rooms, imposing on strangers for food, showers, a place to wash my clothes. Going home would be nice. I miss my room, I miss the comfort of familiar things and ways to do stuff. But it's hard to forget the look on my dad's face when he confronted me in his office.

"What'll happen now?" I ask.

He doesn't hug me—he's too macho for that or whatever. But he does give me a playful knuckle to the chin.

"We'll try to start over," he says.

So NOW THE Senior Showcase Revue is done, and it was one of the best experiences of my life. Pop isn't perfect, but I feel like he's come to understand me, at least a little. I have new friends, and know so much more about myself and the people around me. There's no one left to hide from because the people who matter most know all my secrets. I might have fallen in love for the first time, and lost that amazing boy in the process, but if it means finding me, then I can be okay with it.

Because now I have the hardest amends to make, and though it might wreck me, I can handle it. Because I know who I am, and it's not that little tenth grader who hurt Dinah MacFarland so badly.

MICHAEL

"**M**ORNING, SLEEPYHEAD," MOM said. "We figured you'd sleep in after the cast-party last night. We all waited for breakfast so you could eat with us."

"It's basically breakfast and lunch combined," said Georgie; and then, pointedly, "you know, since it's pretty much lunchtime."

Dad said to her, "That's brunch, and put your phone away." Then to me, "How was the party?"

"Fine. Much tiredness after the show, but we had fun. Lots of food, lots of drinks—*soda*, we were at school in the theatre. Come on! Music, lots of noise. Good times."

"Micuh, why you wearing jammies?" Topher asked.

"Because I'm lazy. I didn't even brush my teeth yet. Come here, let me breath on you."

"Topher! Cady! Please!" cried Mom. "Enough screeching! Anyway, are you relieved the show's over, Honey? Or sad?"

"It was my last Revue. So, yeah, sad. But also sorta glad. A lot went on these last few months."

"You'll be on to bigger and better things now," Dad said. "College theatre and whatnot. I bet graduation feels closer than ever, huh? And prom is in a couple of weeks."

"Damn, I dropped an egg," Mom grumbled. "Cady, no! Don't say that word. Momma shouldn't have said it either. And keep away! You'll get your feet in it. Love, keep her over there, will you?"

"Cady Rose, stay at the table, please! Speaking of colleges," Dad went on, "we're still waiting to hear from your last two, aren't we, Ninja? It's taking a long time." He paused when he saw my face. "You haven't heard anything, have you?"

"Well..." I released a breath. "Yeah, I did. Hard no. From both."

"Oh Sweetheart," Mom said. "Why didn't you say anything? When did the letters come?"

"A few weeks ago."

"You kept quiet all this time?" Dad sounded perplexed.

"It was the night Nick showed up."

Georgie muttered, "He's so hot."

Dad said, "You're twelve, Georgia Rose. The only thing you should think is hot is the bacon."

"I'm almost thirteen."

"Ninja? Why didn't you tell us?"

"I dunno. I was upset. Then Nick was here. And *he* was upset. And...I guess...his problems seemed bigger than mine. We were all sorta upheaved, you know? With him staying in the house."

"Nick, Nick, Nick!" Cady chirped.

"Where's Nick?" Topher joined in. "I miss Nick! I want Nick to play wiff us again!"

"I want Nick to read me the book about the birdie

looking for his momma!"

"Yeah! We love Nick!"

"Keep it down, you two," said Mom.

Georgie, watching me, said, "Is that just left over pillow creases? Why's your face red?"

"Get outta here!" I cried.

"Georgia Rose, just look at your phone. And you two! Pipe down!" Dad turned back to me. "You must have been so disappointed. All your schools…I'm sorry, son. I wish you had talked to us. You shouldn't have had to carry that all on your own."

"I didn't exactly," I said after a beat. "Nick saw I was upset. I didn't hide the letters from him. I talked to him about it. A little."

"Good," said Mom. "You like to internalize stuff, Sweetheart, I know. But with how happy you were with your auditions, the campus tours… I'm glad you didn't bury it all."

"Talking to Nick helped," I said, reluctant to admit it. Then I stared at the table for a second or two. With equal reluctance, I added, "Actually, he was sort of a distraction. I couldn't think about colleges much with him around."

"He seemed like he tried to keep out of everyone's way. He slept in your room, but you seemed okay with it. He would have taken the living-room, you know."

"I don't mean that. He…well, I guess he was…easy to talk to. We watched movies a lot and talked about anime and stuff."

"I'm glad Nick's not gay," said Georgie, looking up from her phone, "because he's *so* hot! But seriously, if he were gay, he would be perfect for you, Michael. He likes all the same dork-stuff you do and he doesn't think you're annoying."

I glanced around. "You don't need to look at Dad like that, Mom. It's not a secret anymore. I know. Nick *is* gay."

Georgie cried, "What?"

"Did he tell you?" Mom asked.

"Basically." I stared at the table again.

"Nick is gay?" Georgie exclaimed.

I took a breath. "Remember the notes that were left in my locker? And the phone case I got for my birthday? Well—"

"That was Nick?" Dad's eyes brightened.

"Oh come on!" came Georgie again. "Another gay guy? Really? Do you know *anyone* straight, Michael? You *turned* Nick I bet, having him sleeping in your bedroom. You were watching *Sailor Moon* once. I could hear. That'll do it."

Both Mom and Dad said, "Georgia!" At last she fell silent.

Dad only watched me, but Mom said, "I knew. His father told me when I stopped to tell him where Donick was. Seemed to think I would already know. I talked with Donick about it too. He seemed worried about your reaction if you found out, Honey. He was afraid of offending you."

"Well yeah!" I said.

"Is that why he left?" When I dropped by eyes and said nothing, Mom pressed, "Sweetheart, I'm not in the mood for pulling teeth here. Please tell me you didn't make him feel like he needed to leave."

I bit my lip. "I might have."

"Oh Michael…" Dad sighed out.

"He said he loved me, I—"

"He said he *loved* you?" Georgie set her phone aside for good. "Love? Like, the way you love a friend? Or, like, *in love*?"

I replied, slowly, "He said he was *in love* with me." Silence fell. Again I glanced around. "Don't everyone talk at once."

"I love Nick!" Cady exclaimed. "I miss him! I want him to live here again!"

"Me too! Me too! I love Nick too!" Topher added.

"Look," I said, unsettled. "I didn't exactly tell him to go. I just didn't know how to react. He was living here, sleeping in my room. I had no idea he was text messaging me every day from some secret phone, leaving me notes and presents."

"You were texting every day?" Georgie asked.

"I didn't know it was him."

"But still..."

Mom said, "You really have been playing it close to home. I had no idea about any of this. Where did Donick go?"

"I heard he stayed at Liam's for a while, then at Brent's. He's home now, I guess."

"Oh?"

"Yeah. His dad was at the show last night. Nick didn't stay for the cast-party. Liam said it was because his dad asked him to come home and they had a lot to talk about or something."

"Thank goodness," Dad said. "Good news."

Mom agreed. "Michael, Sweetheart," she then said. "I can't say I'm surprised by this. I told you already I always wondered about him. I wasn't shocked when his father told me. And I'm not shocked to hear he has feelings for you."

"Not just feelings!" quipped Georgie. "Love! Nick is *in love* with Michael!" Then, catching my stare, "Dang, if looks could kill..."

Mom went on, "That boy has always worshipped you."

"Huh?"

"Don't act dim, Michael. He has. When you were kids

I always saw it. And all these years later, where did he go when he had a crisis? Right here. To you."

"He lied to me!"

"How?"

"He pretended to be someone he wasn't!"

"Again, how?"

"He could've told me he was gay a while ago instead of getting all secretive." I paused. "Which I guess he pretty much did. But I didn't know I was talking to Nick. I spent all that time texting someone I was beginning to think was like a best friend, and it turned out to be him."

Dad said, "Nick. Who used to *be* your best friend, you mean?"

"We haven't been friends in years."

"He lived here for two weeks, and pretty much spent all his time with you. Come on, Ninja. We could hear the two of you up late talking when you should have been asleep. It was like elementary school all over again—you two watching movies, your cartoons and stuff. Your secret admirer was right under your nose. Maybe you're more frustrated you didn't see it."

I glanced at Mom. "What are you smiling about? Why are you laughing?"

"Nothing, nothing." Another big grin. "It's just—well, someone is in love with my son. Someone sees that you're wonderful, Sweetheart."

"Oh man, are you getting emotional?"

"No! Okay, maybe a little. It's just...a parent thinks their child is wonderful and hopes other people will too. I think Donick is wonderful. And he loves you. Someone wonderful loves my wonderful child."

"Gross. You act like he and I are gonna start dating or something."

"He's *so* hot!" Georgie said. "What a loss to the girls of the world. If you, like, *don't* go out with him, Michael, you're a derp."

"Why in hell would I go out with him?"

"Why in hell!"

"Cady!" Dad gave her a warning look.

I said, "Seriously, why? Just because someone has feelings for me doesn't mean I have feelings in return. And it's Nick! That's terrible!"

"You *are* a derp," Georgie said. "I might only be *twelve*, and the idea of Nick being gay is, like, *such* a disappointment, but even *I* can tell he's perfect for you. He thinks you're great, obviously cares about you, has *everything* in common with you, and, oh yeah! He's in *love* with you!"

Topher piped in. "Nick loves Micuh?"

Georgie said to him, "That's right, Toph. Nick loves Michael. Don't we want Nick to come back and see us?"

"Micuh! Bring Nick back! We love Nick too!"

"Keep it down!" Mom said. "Here, you two. Your eggs are ready. Georgia, Michael? Over easy?"

"Me too," said Dad. Then, "Ninja? Do you really dislike Nick that much? Don't just shrug. Come on. You enjoyed having him around the house, admit it. We can all agree, I think, that we liked having him here. The twins obviously dig him. So? What's changed?"

"I don't know. I feel like...I had started to get to know him again, then suddenly he pulls the rug out from under me, just when I was trusting him, and changed the game. Again. Minus the face bashed into the locker, it felt too similar to what he did to me six years ago."

Everybody just stared at me.

"Last night, at the show," I added, "some jerkoff in the audience shouted stuff at him at the end of his number."

Mom frowned. "Shouted stuff?"

"Called him names. You know."

"That's terrible," said Dad. "Like what?"

"The usual disgusting stuff you call a gay person." I sighed. "Right there, no music, applause dying down. The whole theatre heard it. The look on his face…"

"So more people know about him than just a couple of his friends then?" Mom asked.

"I don't think so. The person who did it is a friend of his, or *was*. Definitely not someone he would have trusted. I think it might have just been names to call. The jerk could have been suspicious, I guess, but I really don't know."

"Poor Donick…" Mom stared hard at the stovetop.

Georgie asked, "Was he okay?"

"Shaken, I guess. He seemed checked out the rest of the show."

"Did you at least say something to him?"

"I tried. He didn't want to hear it."

"Well, duh! You told him to leave our house and haven't been talking to him! You're a *total* moron, Michael. I wouldn't be surprised if he's, like, working on getting over you right this minute! You deserve it!"

"Georgie, shut it! You don't know what you're talking about!"

"Yeah I do. Joel and Dillon were shady. You were too good for them. Nick is perfect for you, and I'm starting to think *you're* not good enough for *him*."

"Gee, thanks. The only reason you think that is because *you've* got a big ol' crush on him."

"He's hot! Look me in the eye and tell me you *don't* think he's hot!"

A pause. She stared at me. Dad stared at me. Mom stared at me.

"What?" I cried. "*Everyone* thinks Nick is good-looking!"

"But do *you*?" Georgie asked.

Another pause. She stared at me. Dad stared at me. Mom stared at me.

"I *said* everyone, right? Stands to reason I make one of every." I huffed out a breath. "Look, I feel guilty, okay? For making him think he had to leave. He only went out after the shows one time, and I'm sure he didn't hang with everyone because I was there. He wasn't at the cast-party and…I guess…I wanted him there…for some reason. Even if it was just to check if he was okay. I can admit, I miss him, yes. But it's the *idea* of him. The guy I was getting close to. But it's confusing because I don't really know if I'm missing *him*, or if I'm missing my secret admirer."

"Same thing," Georgie said.

"I kind of agree," put in Mom. "The secret admirer stuff was just Donick's way of showing you that you matter to him. Especially when he knew it wasn't possible to show that himself. Not when you've been so angry."

"I guess I know that," I muttered. "The couple of weeks he was here, I could have been feeling really crappy about schools, and my complete failure to actually get into one… but I didn't. I liked having him around. It *did* feel like it used to be sometimes. But also not. Also, completely different. New, I guess. Look, I know I basically reacted to the gay-thing and his feelings for me the same way his dad did. I just…don't know what to think about anything where he's concerned."

"Well," said Dad, "you might want to figure that out, son. No one's saying you need to date the guy—"

"Um, yes, some of us sort of are!" Georgie interrupted. She and Mom exchanged a look.

"—but Nick obviously could use your friendship. He's going through something right now that you've already been through. You could…hold his hand through it, so to speak." Dad couldn't even make it through that last part without snorting with laughter.

"You're loving this, aren't you?" I said.

"Whether he's a *boyfriend*," Dad went on, more serious, "or just a friend, you shouldn't let someone who cares about you that much get away. Then you really *would* be a…a derp."

"Nick is Micuh's boyfriend?" Cady asked in an absent sort of way, pushing her eggs around her plate with her blunt little *Moana* fork.

"Bring Nick back, Micuh!" Topher cried.

"Can we not talk about this anymore?" I ground out. "I'm sorry I ever brought it up. I need to eat the whole pound of bacon now. Mom? The eggs ready?"

DONICK

"I'll just have to forget the hurt that came before,
Forget what used to be.
The past is on the cutting-room floor.
The future is here with me.
Choose me…"

DINAH MACFARLAND:

I know Dinah from middle school; we're the same age, and once we were in the same grade. Then high school happened, and coming back for sophomore year after summer vacation, Dinah had to repeat ninth grade. Why? She missed half the school year because she was pregnant.

She's this very petite girl. Back then she had long straight hair the color of honey. She came back to school after having the baby with her hair chopped very short and dyed a shade of red like a toy fire-engine. In middle school she was the first person I ever knew to start "dating" someone; some douche-bag with the actual name of Dwayne Johnson—no joke. From there it was a new boy every couple of months… until high school and the baby. As far as I've ever seen, her serial dating days ended with her becoming a mom.

But who was the father?

For a long time she guarded the father's identity like Smaug guarding the Arkenstone. After all, she and the guy were no longer together at that point. I only found out who he was from that aforementioned gem of a human being, Eliel Lantz. The father was Eliel's best friend—a baseball player named Bobby Gallagher. He was in eleventh grade when he knocked Dinah up.

He was the sort of guy who never stopped goofing off; whether in class or on the baseball field. He didn't seem to have a care in the world, as though it didn't matter he was going to be a dad at sixteen. I hated him for it, even as I found that knowing he was for sure doing *it*—like, for real, and not just whacking off—was kind of sexy. Go figure. I was a confused, self-loathing high school freshman.

Dinah vanished before Christmas and wouldn't be seen again until the next school year. Word spread about how she was doing—she had had a little girl—and how her parents were handling things; did she plan to come back; what kind of mother she was. As far as I observed, nothing seemed to trouble Bobby Gallagher.

Probably over some stupid guy-shit, Eliel and Bobby had a falling out the following year—the year of the back-to-school night locker messages. In a bid to somehow get back at Bobby for being a "bitch-ass schizo" as Eliel called him, he, Eliel, decided he wanted to target Dinah as a way of indirectly targeting Bobby. More explicitly, he wanted to target Dinah's and Bobby's newborn. So what happened was thought out and crafted by Eliel...but carried out by me. Why me? Because I was new on the varsity team and felt desperate for acceptance.

Still, I made myself sick going along with Eliel's bullshit.

But hasn't that always been my MO? One would think I was born unable to think for myself, always adopting the thoughts and behaviors of those around me: Eliel, Josue, Ryan, my own father. Even now, looking at what I did in the harsh light of day, I don't think any amount of pressing that reset-button will ever erase what I did to Dinah MacFarland. Like in *Macbeth*, some stains will never come out.

Picture this: a small baby-doll in a pair of footie-pajamas (of the sort I watched Cady and Topher Penrose wear every night I lived in their house)—the kind of doll with puckered lips for a plastic pacifier and saucer eyes that roll open and shut beneath wiry eyelashes. Next, imagine a length of twine looped and knotted into an approximation of a miniature noose. And in place of a gibbet, imagine this noose strung from the metal fastening of a girl's locker. Put these pieces together and I can paint a clear picture of the disgusting prank Eliel Lantz talked me into—talked me into with shameful ease.

Those first couple of days after Pop asks me to come home, I think about Dinah a lot. I wonder if in confessing to her parents that she was pregnant she had faced the sort of fallout I had in confessing my secret to Pop. A lot of areas of my life have suddenly been rubbed into a sort of smoothness, and I'm thankful, yet Dinah has come to stick in my brain like a splinter under a fingernail. I think more about her, and her daughter, than I think about the awkwardness between myself and Pop. There's no point anymore in putting off confessing to Dinah that the joke had been my doing. She's the last person haunting me, so to speak, and why put off the inevitable? I dread my talk with her in every atom of my being, but I have to do it.

I didn't witness her reaction to the doll, but I saw her tears, the look of stunned hurt on her face, just the same. Another guy on the football team actually filmed it on his phone, sending the clip to Eliel who then showed it to the rest of us. I saw Dinah later in the day though, and her eyes were red-rimmed, face swollen from crying.

Dinah will be easy to find. She is, after all, in my English 11 class.

Despite my resolve, Monday passes without me having the courage to stop her once the bell rings for dismissal. But on Tuesday I can't bear the torture of waiting any longer. With my lungs feeling caught in a steel trap, I dart out the door after her and call her name, stopping her in the hall. She pauses and turns; we might be a pair of rocks washed by the river of students flowing around us.

"Can we talk for a minute?" I ask. "I don't want to keep you if you have to be somewhere though."

"Hey Nick," she says, looking at me innocently enough, but then her features darken. Her face frosts a little and I think, *Oh God, she knows already.* The frost laces her voice as she asks, "What do you want?"

"Just to talk." I hope my expression looks neutral. "Someplace quiet?"

"I have to go to my locker. It's on the second floor at the back of the library. You can come with me."

I fall into step beside her, hooking my thumbs into my backpack straps. We're silent for a bit, the only sound coming from the squeak-squish of the rubber soles of her combat boots. She used to dress very girlie too, until the baby. Now she's all leggings and flannel shirts, shit-kicking boots and studded chokers.

"How're things?" I ask.

"Okay, I guess. Trying not to fail English. American lit is boring as hell. I'm sick of everyone trying to be offended over *Huckleberry Finn* and looking for lame symbolism in *The Catcher in the Rye*. Like, just read the goddam book." She pauses. "I'm also thinking a lot about getting held back. I should be graduating. It's a drag having to be stuck here another year."

"I feel you. But I'm sure it'll fly by. Junior year is tough but twelfth grade is a cake walk. Well, for most seniors. Not for me. I've had too much to make up."

"Oh yeah, your shoulder. How long were you out of school?"

"Three months. I got way behind and barely scraped by. Well, I crashed and burned in English. But I didn't have to make up the whole year, so you still win in the bad luck department." We're silent again, passing students and teachers, making our way up the stairs in front of the library.

At last I ask, "How's your daughter?"

She shoots me a look and says, "She's fine."

"How old is she now?"

"She turned three in February."

"That's great. What's her name?"

Another strange look. When Dinah answers, it's with suspicion. "Katherine. It's my mom's name. I call her Katie."

I ask how she spells it, and when she tells me I add, "Michael Penrose has a little sister with the same name, only they spell it C-A-D-Y. That's funny."

"Nick, just stop, will you?"

"What?"

Dinah halts, looking impatient. Her brusqueness

alarms me.

"A lot of people are talking about you, you know. About whatever this thing is that you're doing, apologizing for being a total knob. That's noble or whatever, but it leads me to believe you've got some confession to make to me, and I don't know if I want to hear it. The last few years have sucked. You'd be shocked at the garbage I've had to listen to from everyone around here. A lot of hurtful things are said all the time. Though," she adds, still derisive, "no one ever asks how Katie is doing, so that's new."

"I just…need to tell you—"

"But maybe I just need you not to. I don't know what you'll be expecting. Forgiveness?"

"No, not if you can't give it. It's not about forgiveness. It's about owning up to my mistakes."

She scoffs. "What is it then? Did you call me a whore behind my back? Did you tell a bunch of your wiener buddies that you screwed me? I'm such an easy slut, right?"

"Of course not."

The horrified way I say it galvanizes me with what a hypocrite I am. Simply talking badly about her behind her back would have been nothing compared to what I actually did.

She looks impatient. "What then?"

I feel my chest get tight once more. If only a big earthquake would strike right now and toss me into the jagged ruins of the building.

I blurt it out. "It was the doll."

I think she maybe didn't hear. She might be a doll herself, staring blankly and fixedly into my face. But I wait. Her nostrils twitch a little, her lips pinch.

"I wasn't the one who made it," I start to say, "but I put—"

"I hate you."

Her voice is a feelingless whisper. Her expression hasn't changed, but her eyes are filled with a combination of fury and horror and detestation. And she *should* detest me. She should rail and scream, just like that girl did outside the band-room. We should be in a public place where she can cause a scene. We should be in the office so the administrators can expel me from school.

"Dinah," I say, "I'm sorry. I've felt—"

"Stop talking." Tears are standing in her eyes. I stop speaking at once. My own eyes prickle in guilt and sympathy. "You don't get to say that. You don't get to tell me you're sorry." Her voice cracks and fat tears slide down her cheeks. "I have had enough on my plate trying to be a good mom, and not rely on my parents to care for my daughter all the time. Sure, it's all my fault, I know. I made some stupid decisions. But I love Katie more than anything. And when I came back to school after having her, all I heard about was what a mistake I made; what a whore I was. Bobby didn't defend me, didn't stand by me. Your jock friends were always telling me I would never be able to raise her right, that I should have given her up…or *aborted* her. Anything to keep her from having a mother like me. Then finding that…that *thing* hanging from my locker— No! *Don't* say anything! I don't care who made it, or if some asshole somewhere put you up to it! You still *did* it!"

"I know. I'm not trying to diminish that, I only—"

She cuts me off with the motion of her hand, tugging her flannel sleeve up to her elbow. For a second I think she means to hit me. But she's unsnapping the black leather cuff around her wrist and holding her palm out toward me. At first I'm staring at her fingers, confused. Then I see the scars atop the blue tracery of veins in her wrist. Facing me like this, they look like an inverted cross; an evil, evil thing.

"I went home that day," she says, her voice trembling, "and I did this. It felt like the last straw. I tried to end my life because everyone seemed to be telling me the world would be better without me in it. That Katie's life would be better without me in it. Can you even imagine how hard this has been?"

I can, yes. But I won't tell her. This isn't about my struggle. It's about hers. She sniffs, re-snapping the cuff about her wrist. I move to help but she jerks back and hisses at me not to touch her. She tugs down her sleeve and crosses her arms.

I think I must be trembling all over. I had no idea. None. She tried to kill herself…because of something I did to her. How my eyes burn. I can feel the tears wanting to fall, but somehow I sense that if they do, if I cry for her, it will make it worse.

"So I hate you, Nick," she says flatly. "I hate everyone who made these last few years hell for me. You don't *get* to say you're sorry. You don't get a show of trying to make amends. I almost died. And if it wasn't for Katie, I would have tried it again. I would have tried again because of people like you. I don't know why assholes do the things they do. But you leave wreckage in people's lives, then never think about them again."

What good will it do to say that that isn't true? *My* conscience may be reminding me of all the rotten things I've done over the years, but plenty of people are exactly how she says: unremorseful. They do whatever they want to the people around them and never hold themselves accountable.

"Do not speak to me again, Nick. Ever. Got it?"

I nod meekly.

"I don't even want to look at you."

The tears want badly to fall, hearing the last thing Michael said to me spilling from her mouth.

I stand, shamed, a lump in my throat, and see her turn away, walking off with her head high, some sort of dignity coming from her, even when I know she's been humiliated more than a few times.

I would like to tell her it's okay to be mad. I would like to tell her she doesn't have to forgive me. I would like to tell her I hope one day she'll be able to let go of her anger and find a way to be happy—to always, always think of her daughter. But I stay silent. After all, she told me never to talk to her again. And as dissatisfying as it is, knowing I'll have to carry this with me, maybe forever, it's a fitting penance, isn't it? Because of something I did—forget whether it was directly or indirectly—a girl almost killed herself, almost depriving a little child of its mother. I know how that feels too.

WEDNESDAY, WITH DINAH still weighing on me, making me feel rotten, I decide I'm tried of eating lunch alone in the library. I won't go to the drama-room, of course—like I would be welcome there. I go to the dance-studio instead and surprise Liam and Jackie. Their welcoming grins and responses of, "What's taken you so long?" eases my mind. I'm grateful that someone somewhere accepts me as I am. They tell me I should eat with them every day, and I say I will.

I'm not sure where it came from, but at least with the students who were in the Senior Revue, the information about me coming out has started to spread. If anything, it seems to make the girls want to be my friend even more, and the other gay guys in the arts-department more interested in being around me—however uncomfortable that feels at the moment. Even Gil runs into me and slaps me on the back, saying he's happy for me. (I'm sure he heard about it from Liam—though I think the two of them are still keeping things on the down low; I never see them around campus together.)

After a three day suspension (and a ban from going to prom this and next year), Josue is back in school and giving me looks to kill. He never approaches me, never says another word to or about me as far as I hear. I think after his cat-calls at the show, he knows he's being closely watched. Ryan mostly avoids me too, but I get the impression sometimes he would like to talk—maybe just to ask what's going on with me so he can have the truth. Either way, he doesn't look quite as hateful as the other guys I used to hang with.

But I don't care. I see them around campus and feel how removed I am from them—how static they are, how unchanging. I wake up in the morning, look in the mirror, and sometimes don't recognize myself. It's a good feeling. I've done what I wanted to do: made peace with my darkest moments. It's not so black and white as thinking I've truly started over, but I no longer feel like that asshole bringing wreckage into people's lives. For now, that's more than enough for me.

I became so used to being at rehearsals every day that suddenly being free after school takes some adjustment. Pop gave the car back and I sometimes drive around listening to playlists I made on my iPod of music from the Revue, and songs my new friends exposed me to. That "Gold In Them Hills" song Michael sang at his birthday party breaks my heart and gives me hope all at once; I play it often. The same with "Defying Gravity". I was especially struck by Calista listening to Florence + the Machine and find myself playing "Shake It Out" a lot. I feel as though I had lived much too long with a graceless heart, and cutting it out in order to restart was the best thing I could ever have done.

At home, Pop often doesn't know what to say to me. He wears a shamed look and I wish I could take it from him, even as I think he needs to go through some restarting himself. His work hours are the same and he comes home late a lot. Still, we both seem to be making the effort to spend time together, even if it's just sitting and watching TV, or making dinner for each other.

Once, he asks, "Is there…someone…in your life, Nicky? Someone you haven't told me about?"

And though I think, *What if I actually had to now tell him that, yes, Michael—or someone—was my boyfriend!* I can safely shake my head and tell him, "No. No one."

"Anyone you have…interest in?"

I wonder, why these questions? Across the dinner table, his expression is pained, but curious. He's making some sort of effort to be open-minded.

"There *was* someone," I say. I have to work the words out of my mouth. Talking like this with Pop is like undressing in a doctor's office—necessary, yet awful. "But it's nothing."

"You're a handsome kid," he says, snatching food off his fork. "What's the problem?"

I swallow. "The insides are important too. My insides

weren't his thing, I guess."

He mulls this over, chewing slowly. Then he says, "Well, if ever there is anyone…you know, someone you're… interested in, who likes your insides or whatever…" God, how miserable he looks, like passing a thumbtack instead of a kidney stone, "…I hope you'll tell me. I mean, I hope you won't be afraid to…introduce me."

I try to smile and not look awkward, but I'm not sure I succeed. "I don't see any bridges in my future, Pop," I say, "but when that one comes, I'll cross it."

Though he's staring very hard at the Saraswood Dance Centre logo on my T-shirt, he is nodding. Suddenly he gets to his feet. "By the way," he says, "I pulled out some of your momma's old albums. I was looking for her ABBA records and I found the one with her favorite song. I'll put it on while we eat."

A minute later, from his old stereo in the living-room, scratchy clicks and pops signal the needle sliding into vinyl grooves. Piano and guitar come to me and Pop is back in the kitchen.

"'Andante, Andante'," he says. "Your momma played this one over and over. Used to sing it to you when you were a baby. Too bad you guys didn't have it in your play."

We go on eating, and the moment is surreal, listening to music with Pop I wouldn't have banked on him listening to in a thousand years. And my mom used to sing to me? I didn't know. Pop hums occasionally, even as he chews, and I'm further taken aback to hear he carries a nice tune. Maybe, just maybe, behind his glasses, his eyes are a little wet. We finish the meal mostly in silence, him and me— and like a third, the sweet strains of a cherished song.

O N FRIDAY, LIAM arrives in the dance-studio very late for lunch. I saw big sloppy signs throughout the week advertising another karaoke-thing for Friday's lunchtime. I can hear the music all the way across campus. I assumed he might have wanted to watch some of the singers. Yet suddenly he's in our midst.

"Nick," he cries, "come with me! So many bad singers! It's great!"

I grimace. "I wouldn't be caught dead."

"*You* should sing something," Jackie puts in.

"Why do you hate me?" I ask.

Liam tugs on my arm, whining, "Come on! Lunch is almost over, and it's nice out. It smells like feet in here."

"Doesn't usually bother you," Jackie says. "What's your deal?"

"Fine!" he says, throwing up his hands. "I guess I'll just watch the *American Idol* rejects alone!"

"Or," I say, "you could stay here and finish my chili-cheese Fritos."

"Figures you would say something sexy like that. But no! Be boring!"

Then he turns and stomps out.

"Too much Starbucks?" I mutter, gazing around at Jackie and the other dancers.

A few minutes later, my phone buzzes. "He's not gonna give up," I laugh, and swipe the screen.

The text message says, *I didn't think Liam would fail so spectacularly. I'm not sure if my Secret Admirer still carries his secret phone. I guess I'll have to ask you to let my Secret Admirer know he should come out to the quad. There's something he needs to see. And hurry!!*

I can't register what I'm reading. It's hard to fathom that it's Michael's name printed over the text message, let alone what it says. I actually stare at his name hard, sure I'm mistaken. But I'm not. So, what does this mean? Has he forgiven me? I mean, if he hated me, why would he be asking me to come to the quad? I don't fear some trick; I know that's not in Michael's nature. But I shouldn't get my hopes up. One of his Muskequeers is probably going to sing and asked him to get me out there to watch.

Jackie leans over my shoulder and reads the text.

"I'll come with you," she says.

One or two of the others pack up and we troop out in a little group. My nerves have fired into overdrive. Maybe no relationship with Michael whatsoever is preferable to this shaky sensation.

The final beats of some rap song fade out, followed by the sound of polite clapping. Whoever had been attempting to rap probably wasn't very good.

I don't know the girl who speaks into the microphone now, but she sounds like Kristin Chenoweth. She says, "A round of applause for Maximus DeBoe! Wasn't he great? Quit the day job, friend! All right, we've got time for just one more song, yo! Up next we've got a group of dudes from the Kliewer High choir department! Give 'em a hand!"

So Michael's going to sing. Why didn't Liam just tell me that? And why does Michael want me there? If I can't see his name without remembering our last conversation, he surely can't either.

His voice echoes around the quad. There's a surprising amount of cheering for him.

"Yo yo, peeps," he says. Somehow that doesn't sound

stupid coming from him, talking to an audience like that. "I'm Michael Penrose, if you don't know me, and these three are…"

Other amplified voices bounce in: "I'm Iken O'Rourke!" and "I'm Bronx Warren!" and "Sup guys, I'm Taysom Puck!"

Michael chuckles. "Yes, those are their real names." Laughter from the crowd. "We're gonna preview a song we've been working on for our last choir concert, coming up in a couple weeks. This'll be a little different than the usual karaoke. That might be a good thing though." More laughter. "So, true story. I've had this secret admirer for a couple months."

I almost trip. My breaths are nothing more than quick little gasps of air. What in hell is he doing? I'm half across the quad and I can see where people have gathered around the raised concrete platform painted purple and gold: the school colors. The figures of Michael and the other singers are just visible over the heads of the crowd. Big black speakers on poles take up space behind them.

"I only recently found out who it was," Michael goes on, "and it…well, really shocked me, to say the least. So, this is an old Billy Joel song called "The Longest Time". I want to dedicate it to my secret admirer. I hope you're here, listening somewhere." His voice has gotten louder, as though he's trying to make it reach me. When he speaks again, my steps slow almost to a halt; it's as though the air has grown thick, like taffy. "Because…well, Secret Admirer," he says. "I want you to go to the prom with me."

There are cheers at this. Michael turns to the choir-guys, blows a note on a tuning-harmonica, counts them in, and they begin to sing.

Did I just hallucinate? Did Michael really ask me to go to the prom with him? He wants…to go to prom with *me*?

I don't know if Jackie and the others are still following me. My eyes are fastened on the platform as Michael's voice blends with those of the other guys, filling the quad, echoing across campus. I near the edge of the crowd and pause there, completely and utterly floored.

I catch the words, "*What else could I do? I'm so inspired by you… That hasn't happened for the longest time…*"

I'm what brain-dead looks like, I'm positive. I twist my head from one side to the other, making sure I'm not the only one seeing this; that I haven't fallen into some fantasy where Michael…what? Wants to be my friend again? Wants to go to prom together? Two dudes going to the high school party to end all high school parties…as friends? Or…as what?

What the hell is going on?

I spot Liam in the crowd, grinning, periodically peering about. Brent and Calista are with him, Calista holding up her phone, either recording or taking pictures. I spot other faces too—people from the Revue, a few of the kids I've apologized to; Roddy, Kristina…even Gabby is there, who planted the whole idea in my head in the first place about trying to make amends to the people I've wronged. I wonder what brought her out of the library. Of course, I had told her all about being Michael's secret admirer. She knows exactly who he's talking about, and I wonder if she's shocked. She catches my eye, smiles and waves. I'm sure the wave I give back looks like I'm mostly asleep.

As the song continues, "*Who knows how much further we'll go on…Maybe I'll be sorry when you're gone…I'll take my chances…I forgot how nice romance is…*" I begin pressing my way through the crowd. Somehow I break out toward the front just as Michael sings, "*I don't care what consequence it brings…I have been a fool for lesser things…I want you so bad…I think you ought to know that I intend to hold you for the longest time…*"

I can't remember when last I took a breath. As they break into the "*Whoa…whoa whoa whoa*"s, Michael catches sight of me. If I thought him smiling before, it's nothing to the grin that lights up his face. Now he's singing right to me. I feel his gaze like a weight, not unpleasant, yet also disarming, seeming to see right through to my bones. Trickles of hot and cold alternately run over my skin, the hair standing on my arms.

There are raucous cheers and applause as the four guys finish. I hear, "I wonder who his secret admirer is?" and "Is his secret admirer gonna say yes, you think?" Michael has gone on smiling, watching me, and though I can't take my eyes from him, I'm too stunned to look anything but blind-sided.

And *I* wonder too. Will his secret admirer say yes?

The girl playing MC gets on the mic again, saying something about how amazing the choir-boys are. I lose track of it as the crowd starts to disperse. The boys who sang backup for Michael leave the platform. I can only stand there and stare up at him. He takes a tentative step, then pauses himself, as though he's afraid to come nearer. No one else approaches—Liam, Calista, Brent, all of them must know to stay away. Again I think I might be in the middle of a hallucination.

"Hey," he says.

"Hey," I manage.

His cheeks are flushed. "Did you hear the whole thing?"

I nod. Why can't I smile? Or even look neutral? Why do I keep looking vacant like Emmy Rossum in *The Phantom of the Opera*?

He gives an awkward laugh. "Well?"

I say in a faint voice, "Will I...go to prom with you?"

His smile is little, and crooked, and sweet. Like it used to be. "Yeah, ya doof."

"You mean that?"

He nods.

"Like, really? You want to go to prom? With me?"

Another little laugh. "Yes, Donick Walsh, I, Michael Penrose, want to go to prom with you. But the question is, will *you* go with *me*? I'm sort of a jerk."

A little focus returns and I shrug. "So am I. What about Calista? You two were going together."

"She keeps turning me down. I decided to take the hint. So I guess you have to make a decision. Can you see yourself going to prom with an overly tall gay kid, who isn't very nice sometimes, and gets turned down for dates with lesbians?"

Now I do smile, and laugh. Michael's smile gets little and crooked and sweet again, seemingly just at the sight of mine.

"If you're kidding, Michael," I murmur, "I'll fall apart right here. You know that, right?"

"I'm not kidding." He shrugs. "And if you fall apart anyway, I promise I'll try and put you back together."

I want suddenly to reach out and touch him. But I'm so afraid.

"Now will you give me an answer already?"

"You and me, at the prom?"

"You and me," he repeats, "at the prom."

"Yes," I say, nodding. "Yes..."

His grin gets huge. He steps toward me—but the bell for class goes off, jolting us both.

"I have so many things I want to talk to you about," he says.

"Let's leave then. We'll skip."

"You can't. You have English. You can't risk falling behind again."

I sigh. "I know."

"After school?" he says. "I'll meet you at your car."

"It's in the corner of the lot," I reply. "Under the pine tree."

"I know," he says. He steps a little closer. The nearness of him steals my breath. I feel his palm slide over the back of my hand. He murmurs, "After school," and then he's gone.

I HAVE TWO TEDIOUS and interminable classes to sit through—classes I can't pay any attention in at all—because I'm thinking, replaying, and picking apart every bit of how lunch ended. It occurs to me that Michael never said *why* he wants to go to prom with me. I can't reason with the way he smiled at me when he sang, the faint blush in his cheeks, the brush of his hand across mine.

Michael was happy to go to prom with Calista, so maybe that's what this is about. He wants to go to prom with a friend. After all, when a person falls apart, friends put you back together, right? I can live with that—I have to. As I've been saying, I would rather have Michael any way I can get him than not at all. Still, I don't want him under any sort of delusion as to how I feel about him. Going to prom together might not mean all that much to him, but it means everything to me.

Once the final bell rings, I charge out of class and hurry to my locker, eyes peeled for any sign of him. I don't see him, so I head toward the student-lot, nervous and shaking all over. Just like when I talked with Dinah MacFarland, I'm almost wishing for an earthquake so that everything will be shaken up and he and I will have an excuse not to face each other so soon.

I get to the car and halt in the shade of a crooked pine, its resinous scent spicing the warm air. I throw my backpack inside, then perch on the hood, peering across the lot toward the gates, searching for any tall, dark-haired figure. At last, I spy him walking with Brent and Calista. My palms start sweating, everything about me feeling awkward. He separates from them, they all laugh and shout things at each other, things I can't quite make out, then his Muskequeers are moving toward Calista's Hyundai (and do they dart looks toward the corner of the lot, toward the crooked pine tree?). Michael is walking almost leisurely in my direction.

When he's near enough to hear me, I bounce off the car's hood, face him, and say in a rush, "Look, I know you said you want to go to prom and that's great. I'm totally down. But the thing is, I don't know *why* you want to go to prom with me. I'm a total asshole and I've done horrible things to you. I kept secrets from you. I was completely dishonest. And my feelings aren't any different than they were before. I'm still in love with you. I can deal with that. But you need to know the truth about my feelings if we're going to be friends again or whatever."

God, that little, crooked, sweet smile. He says, "I know all that."

"And you're okay with it? I mean, I don't know if these feelings will ever go away."

"I hope they won't."

"Why?"

He shrugs. "Because. What would I do about mine?"

"You're what?"

He chuckles. "My feelings for *you*, ya chode."

I blink stupidly. "Your feelings for…"

"Yeah. You."

"You don't have feelings for me." I say it as a statement of irrefutable fact.

As though it's the most natural thing in the word, he replies, "Yeah, I sorta do."

I stutter once or twice and manage to get out, "Since when?"

His shrugs his shoulders, says, "Since always, I guess," and comes to lean against the car. I stare at him, speechless for a moment, then move to lean against the car too. Our elbows are brushing, and I notice it—I notice everything about him.

I shake my head. "You're screwing with me."

He laughs. "I promise you I'm not."

"If that's true…what changed?"

"You. And me. I'm sorry about how I reacted the day you told me. And about the whole secret admirer thing. It sucked extra hard because I was beginning to fall for that mystery person, just like I had fallen for you when we were in middle school. It felt just like that, all over again. It wasn't about my face in the locker, or the scar." I dart my eyes at him, and there it is, a little squiggle beneath his right eyebrow, hanging like an apostrophe over his bottle-green eye. "It was because I loved you, and couldn't have you. I wanted my secret admirer, and suddenly couldn't have *him*. It took a while to put all that emotion together and realize that I *could* have him. If I wanted him. Because he was you. And you told me that you loved me." He grins. His cheeks get very pink. "You said it again, just now."

"It's the truth."

"I know. And the way *I* just said it? That's the truth too."

I'm too taken aback, too nervous, too overwhelmed to say anything. I simply lean against the car, staring off across the parking-lot as I feel Michael slide a little toward me. His shoulder, his hip, his thigh settle against mine. How many minutes spin out in silence—not exactly comfortable—I can't tell, but it seems a small eternity.

Michael says, "So I've been wondering. Are you circumcised?"

My face could fry an egg in two seconds flat. I almost choke. My horrified expression makes him laugh. He bumps my shoulder with his own.

"I'm kidding. It was so quiet I was beginning to be afraid you'd never talk again."

I bark out a nervous laugh and sputter unintelligible things.

"What?" he asks. "Nobody ever asked you that?"

"No!"

"Not even Brent?"

"No!"

"Surprising. He collects that information like I collect anime."

"He does?"

"Oh yeah. He'll ask any guy just because he wants to know. It's been happening for years. Hence Calista calling it the Penis Floorshow. If he can talk about it, he will."

"And he just…asks guys about something like that?"

Michael shrugs. "It's nothing big, right? No pun

intended."

"Well, yeah! That's sorta personal!"

Again, Michael shrugs. "I know about him, he knows about me. We know about Liam. We know about most of the guys in the theatre department. It's interesting."

I blink at him and sputter a little more. Again he bumps my shoulder with his own.

He says, "I would tell you. If you wanted to know."

If Michael's aim was to get me talking again, he picked the wrong subject, because suddenly there are *things* going through my head—not just the idea of admiring him from afar, or wondering what it would be like to kiss him, *now*, not just as foolish boys—suddenly there's the reality of the press of his shoulder, his leg against mine, the remembered pull of his shirt across the muscles of his back, and all that skin beneath his clothes—hairy, pale, hidden.

I swallow and say, "I would tell *you*. If you *really* wanted to know."

He bites his lip, almost as though to suppress how big his smile could get. He drops his eyes. He clears his throat. "I would rather know about this boy you kissed once."

"He was my best friend," I say, playing along. "And I had realized I wanted to kiss him for a while. Somehow I got him to agree to try it."

"He must have wanted to kiss you too."

"You think?"

"Oh yeah." He pauses. "I think…I think if it had been easy back then, if we had felt like we could let ourselves feel that way, nothing would have come of it. Think how awkward it could have been. I mean, best friends don't become more than that usually, right? It gets weird."

"That's true."

"Not having you around for all that time," he goes on, catching my eye, and it's so hard to hold his stare because the way he looks at me is nearly paralyzing, "it made me realize how much I wanted you around when you came back. Only I sent you away again."

"Was that all that changed your mind?"

"No. It was mostly my family. Actually it was mostly the twins."

"Cady and Topher?"

"Yup. They kept saying, 'Go get Nick, Michael! We love Nick! Nick needs to come back!' And after telling myself over and over that would never happen, it was inevitable I realized they were basically reading my mind." He chuckles. "They all saw it, really…Mom, Dad, even Georgie. Speaking of dads, how are things with yours? You guys okay?"

"Mostly. We're both still sort of on best behavior."

"You got your car back."

"He's acting like the last month never happened."

"But how's he dealing with, you know…*you*?"

"He says things sometimes, things I would never have imagined coming out of his mouth—you know, like, really supportive stuff. Then I wonder if he's still kinda dazed by it all. Like, one day it'll sink in and he'll be grossed out again."

"I doubt knowing about you and me is going to make him happy."

"I dunno. He talked about you after seeing the show. He thinks you're an amazing singer. He feels really bad about how he treated you when we were kids. He actually said if I ever date anyone, he wants to meet him. So—"

"We'll just raincheck that as long as we can, how 'bout?"

"Sounds fair. I'm not quite ready for my new life to be *that* in Pop's face yet."

Michael gets quiet. Then he asks, "What about everyone else's faces? If we're seen at prom together, especially after my little announcement at lunch, there won't be anymore hiding. Are you okay with that?"

"Well, Josue, Scott, and Ryan are probably already trashing me to anyone who will listen. All of my new friends know already. Who's left to hide from?"

"You sure?"

"Positive."

"Like, if I walked across campus with you, and I wanted to hold your hand, in front of everyone, you'd be fine?"

I lift my hand and hold it toward him. He eyes it, moves his arm, and then his fingers are sliding against mine until our hands are like a knot. Holy smokes, it feels amazing! He's here, with me, and he's said he loves me! It's as though all the happiness in the world is focused into the single simple action of one hand curling around another.

He looks into my eyes. I have to glance up slightly because, yes, he's just the tiniest bit taller than me. When he talks, his voice is low, almost a whisper because we're so close.

"And what if I wanted to kiss you?" he asks. "What would happen then?"

Amazing myself with my own boldness, to say nothing of his, I reply, "I guess you'll have to try it and see."

Now *my* smile is little and crooked, and heaven help me, how sweet it feels to have it on my face.

January 26th, 2018—July 23rd, 2018

ACKNOWLEDGMENTS

There are many people I wish to acknowledge in the various capacities in which they influenced this novel—whether as an ear listening to descriptions of the plot before I had written a word, or the watchful eyes of editors/proofers, or those involved in the audiobook production. I would, in particular, like to thank all the early "beta" readers who took the journey through the book's original run on the Kindle Vella platform. I'm grateful for your reviews, weekly favorite votes, and thumbs-up. I must also express gratitude to all the NetGalley reviewers, librarians, and booksellers who read and reviewed ARC copies. I'm appreciative of everyone who had a hand in shaping this novel. I must list as many of you as I can remember. Here you are in no particular order...except alphabetical order. Haha! Susan Bautista, Jack Brinson, Adam Conner, Mikhaila Dattoli, Whitney DeBoe, Deyan Audio, Kenneth Fernandez, Loran Frazier, Elizabeth Jones, Lepton Productions, Alex & Leah Kleynhans, Oh Lenic, Joel Leslie, Bryan Lincoln, P.J. Ochlan, Ana Osorio, Rob Peters, Qamber Designs & Media W.L.L., Deepa Samuel, Simplify Productions, Mr. & Mrs. Sinatra (Sin & Sass), Will Stanton, Amy Shira Teitel, Kenneth Thomas, Arlene Torst, Susie Umphers, Eden Winters, Ashley Woods, Jordan Woods.

SENIOR SHOWCASE REVUE
SET-LIST

Music plays an enormous part in "Donick Walsh and the Reset-Button". When I began to formulate the story in my head, I knew I would need to know exactly what this fictional Senior Showcase Revue would look like. The format is based off of very real musical revues I participated in while in college (realistically, this is not the sort of show that could easily be produced in a high school setting, I know). These productions were always marketed as "donation-events" and not traditional "ticketed-events" due to the extensive use of copyrighted music. However they might have been viewed, they were some of the best theatre experiences of my life. Having gone on to direct and choreograph later in my professional life, I also looked forward to the task of picking music and songs that would compliment the story I would be telling. The Revue's set-list went through about as many revisions as the text of the book itself. The song-list as you see it here eventually struck me as perfectly fitting the story, while also satisfying the very real production I began to direct and choreograph in my head. The earlier drafts of the novel touched much more heavily on these numbers and how they were staged, not to mention some of the students participating in them. Since many details are now on my own personal cutting-room floor, I thought it might be interesting for readers to see how the show plays out, with a few notes as to each song's origin. Let it also be noted that the quotes throughout the book are taken directly from either the songs on this list, or any music mentioned throughout the text. Here it is: the Senior Showcase Revue—"Born To Make History".

ACT ONE

"Let Me Be Your Star"—Emmy and Grammy nominated song from the short lived TV show *Smash*. I adored this show while it aired. Plus, I'm a big fan of Megan Hilty.

"Get The Party Started"—Pink's song, yes, but I used the version recorded by the great Shirley Bassey. The strings in the intro are epic!

"Dream A Little Dream Of Me"—a standard from the 1930s. I used Michael Bublé's version in my playlist. I envisioned a student who could accompany himself on his own guitar.

"Lida Rose/Will I Ever Tell You?"—from *The Music Man*. The first of three songs to showcase the quartet of barbershop-boys detailed in the novel.

"Any Dream Will Do"—from *Joseph and the Amazing Technicolor Dreamcoat*. I imagined the barbershop-boys continuing in the role of the children's chorus.

"Another Suitcase In Another Hall"—from *Evita*. The barbershop-boys would be the answer to the soloist's "So what happens now?" in each chorus.

"Always Look On The Bright Side Of Life"—from *SPAMalot*. Originally I had chosen a completely different song to be the Revue's tap-number. This was always the audition song from the start of the book though. Somehow, I couldn't get my original pick to work with the flow of the show (again, I was practically directing this thing in my own head) and when I decided in one of my final drafts to change the song to this one, it all seemed to work.

"Popular"—from *Wicked*. What can I say that Michael

hasn't already said? It's overdone, but I got a kick out of imagining the sort of number he, Calista, and Brent would create out of it. Also, a little connection here: Megan Hilty, mentioned above, was playing Galinda the very first time I saw Wicked in Los Angeles. She performs the very best rendition of "Popular" in my opinion. Find it on YouTube. She's brilliant!

"Drive My Car"—one of my favorite songs recorded by The Beatles. I envisioned this as an opportunity for a group of students who had formed their own band to perform the song, and then segue as the band playing the music for the following medley of songs from *Mamma Mia!* A lot of that detail ended up cut.

"*Mamma Mia!* Medley"—This would close out act one. The songs I envisioned included were "Super Trouper", "Gimme! Gimme! Gimme! (A Man After Midnight)", "Mamma Mia", and "Dancing Queen".

ACT TWO

"Cut, Print…Moving On"—another song from *Smash*. This isn't as well known, but I love it. I also thought it a perfect act two opener, not to mention great at fitting with the theme of the book as a whole, as many of the songs do.

"As The World Falls Down"—from the film *Labyrinth*. I envisioned this as beginning a lengthy masquerade-ball themed section of the show that would continue through the next four songs, culminating in "Vogue". Which is fitting since Madonna always said David Bowie was one of her biggest influences.

"Diamonds Are A Girl's Best Friend"—Iconic Marilyn Monroe from the film *Gentlemen Prefer Blondes*. I used the *Moulin Rouge* version for my Revue play-list however. I love the percussion in that arrangement, plus, a little Madonna sampling of "Material Girl". Can't complain!

"The Mirror-Blue Night"—from *Spring Awakening*. This is such a random pick from this show, but I love the arrangement of this song, and I thought the lyrics fit Nick's journey.

"Defying Gravity"—another one from *Wicked*. However, I used Idina Menzel's pop-version. I picked this one solely because of how perfectly the message set itself against the theme of the novel.

"Vogue"—Madonna is my diva! I can't say anything except of course I would have this song in the show. It's my number one favorite song of all time!

"Cover Girl"—literally my favorite New Kids on the Block song. I listened to it obsessively when I was a little kid in the 80s. Then, coincidentally, after I had completed the first draft of the book, the song popped up in *IT: Chapter Two*, listened to by Ben "Haystack" Hanscom right before a pretty terrifying scene that Michael would have loved!

"Girl For All Seasons"—from *Grease 2*. Can't say much more than I've already said in the book. In my opinion, this film is underrated. My feeling is that it's better than the original *Grease*. I know, blasphemy! But fight me on it.

"I Can't Do It Alone"—from *Chicago*. I know it's not a well-liked song, but I actually enjoy it a lot. I picked it specifically so Nick's dance-skills could be showcased in the Revue.

"Without Love"—from *Hairspray*. This is another song I had to cut most mentions of as they appeared in the original draft of the book. I like its message and I find it a very feel-good song. It seems to fit well in the Revue, and in this spot within the show.

"If I Never Knew You"—the end credits song from the film *Pocahontas*. It's always been one of my favorites and it randomly popped up when I shuffled the music on my iPod one day right before I started writing. I ended up listening to the song quite a lot. For me, it encompassed Nick's and Michael's relationship perfectly. I knew it had to be featured—and I should torture them both with it.

"History Maker"—the opening credits song from the anime *Yuri!!! on Ice*. Brilliant song! Great lyrics! Plus, I'm a sucker for a three-quarter time-signature! As a big fan of Japanese media, this was an anime series that really struck me when I watched it. I enjoyed its almost ambiguous take on the relationship between Yuri and Victor. It felt to me like the sort of LGBT depiction that someone skittish, like Nick, would be able to appreciate.

ABOUT THE AUTHOR

Nathaniel Shea is the pen name of award winning audiobook narrator, Shea Taylor. With a background in musical theatre and English literature, Shea's first love has always been the written word. He has moonlighted as a high school librarian, a copy editor, and a theatre director/choreographer. "Donick Walsh and the Reset-Button" is his first published novel. He lives near Los Angeles with his family and eight chattering budgies.

CONNECT WITH NATHANIEL!

 @NateSheaAuthor